PsyChic in Seattle

A NOVEL

MIMZI SCHRADI

Mimzi Schradi

Eagle Feather Press

ISBN: 0615649572
ISBN-13: 9780615649573

The lunatic, the lover, and the poet,
Are of imagination all compact;
One sees more devils than vast hell can hold,
That is, the madman, the lover, all as frantic,
Sees Helen's beauty in a brow of Egypt;
The poet's eye, in a fine frenzy rolling,
Doth glance from heaven to earth, from earth to heaven;
And, as imagination bodies forth
The forms of things unknown, the poet's pen
Turns them to shapes, and gives to airy nothing
A local habitation and a name.
Such tricks hath strong imagination,
That, if it would but apprehend some joy,
It comprehends some bringer of that joy;
Or in the night, imagining some fear,
How easy is a bush suppos'd a bear!

William Shakespeare
A Midsummer-Night's Dream, V, I, 7

Acknowledgements

To dreamers everywhere...and writers who dare to dream...

To Jon P. Fine, who introduced me to Amazon and his world of publishing...and showed me how to achieve my dream...

To James Strauss, author and friend, whose quoted words never leave my mind, even in the dark moments..."Never, ever, ever give up." (Winston Churchill)...

To David Morrell, author and master teacher, whose lessons on inspiration and editing set my course to completion...

To my colleagues—the Sno-Island Writers—whose constant encouragement led me from the beginning to the final stages of this book...

To my East Coast connections—my good buddies...(especially GMBRS) and my family...for their belief in me when I didn't always believe in myself...

To my West Coast family and friends...especially, my son, Sean, his wife, Tany and my daughter, Dara, her husband, Karl, and Brett and Jared, who lend me their ears and give me unconditional love and support...

And...to the persistence of the hummingbird in flight—flapping its wings at an inconceivable rate—and Robert H. Schuller's unforgettable quote, "*What would you do if you knew you could not fail?*"

The answer is this book.

Chapter One

Tangie...You know how sometimes you wish for one kind of life and you get another?

That's me...*Tangie*—with a name I think is perfectly beautiful—*Angelina*—but nobody considers my baptismal name as my true identity—They just call me *Tangie.*

Blame Bryan, my baby brother. He couldn't say Angelina...so my parents went along with his idiosyncratic pronunciation—even encouraging him as he grew older... I can still hear my mom saying, "Oh Bryan, you are so cute"...

So here I am—*Tangie*— known by some as *Tangerine.*

Thanks, Bryan, for giving me a fruity life.

Not that I'm a *fruitcake* or anything—just a little *odd* you might say—But you have to be a little crazy to do what I do.

Really, all I ever wanted—growing up—was to be myself—*Angelina Seraphina*—college graduate, wife, stay-at-home mom and occasional community librarian for a few hours when the kids were in school.

What did I get?

Single. No prospects for a husband.

No kids—except when my brother's twins come over for the weekends in the summer and during vacations from their preschool.

I did graduate college—but not as a librarian. Nowadays I work on trying to figure out...how not to spill the beans...that I have this crazy gift.

There I said it. It's crazy, I admit it but what can I do?

After graduating from *Seattle University* with a Liberal Arts degree, I enrolled in a master's program in Musical Therapy at the *University of Washington*. So naturally, I dabbled in counseling—yeah, me...as the counselor. A well-known private practice, known as *The Place*, picked me up as an intern. My internship didn't work out. Seems I knew way too much about my clients after just two introductory sessions and of course, that creeped me out...even the clients that didn't talk or give me eye contact seemed transparent to me. Too much information—I overloaded my circuits and almost had a nervous breakdown myself—I gave my notice and hightailed it out the door.

While strolling down the *University of Washington* campus, contemplating my failed future in counseling, I thought, I could always teach. I do have a double major degree from *Seattle U*. That should count for something. Wrong. *Teaching*—Language Arts and American History to teenagers at *Roosevelt High* is a great job—for the right person. As it turns out, I happened to be the least capable person to be a high school mentor. I looked right, I sounded terrific to my students and fellow teachers, but inside I exploded in silence. Dealing with my students and their problems, tormented me at night—The teaching part invigorated me during the day, but once asleep in my cozy little bedroom, after correcting a gazillion papers, I'd wake up to nightmares—The kids' poor choices—the wrong paths they chose—terrorized me...I'd wake up in a cold sweat each night—I couldn't help it—Seeing their pain and self-destruction consumed me. I couldn't take it...and I never slept. I could see their life histories and their potential prospects—some fantastic, but some depressing as hell. I didn't like being an eavesdropper. Young people need to have their own lives...I found myself advising them way too much about their opportunities and their pitfalls—I began to panic—my burnout zoomed to warp speed. Some teachers last thirty years. I lasted three months—not even one semester. I remember my departure from academia--December First...the beginning of second quarter. I got out of bed, after another sleepless night, and almost passed out in my kitchen, after one hour of sleep and the sound of school bells ringing in my ears. As I brewed my double espresso with half-closed eyes and burned my hand foaming the milk for my morning cappuccino—that beverage being the only thing that got me going in the morning—I said to myself, *"Tangie...you can't do this anymore—what's the shame in admitting defeat?"*

So, the next morning at seven a.m. sharp, armed with determination and the will to survive, I prepared myself to face the firing squad—Mr. Lapine, my supervising principal. Come to think of it, this last morning became the first morning I'd been on time since the school year began. I should note that each school day, before the kids filtered into his cubicle to receive discipline for their discrepancies, Buzz Lapine delighted in hanging out in the administration office lobby and displaying these *Popeye* muscles. He would nod to me with his droopy chin—as if to say, *"Late again, eh, Ms. Seraphina."*

The students standing nearby would snicker at the lecher, calling him *La Pain* behind his back, which fit him to a *T.* I always smiled at the little cherubs when they did that. Just couldn't help myself.

This particular morning, I stared at *Buzz La Pain* as he lurked in the doorway, and, with a somber smile on my face, handed him my resignation. He flexed his muscles, glanced at my notice with his beady eyes and grilled me...with a gruff, almost hoarse voice, saying, "No one quits *Roosevelt* before the end of the term—What have we done to deserve this? We thought you liked it here..."

I felt a whiff of cigarette smoke streaming from his wool sports jacket and choked, gasping for breath. *What a twist of fate!* My eyes lit up. I had the answer right before me. I began coughing. Then I pulled myself together and lied without blinking, saying, "I love my job, *Mr. La Pain*, err...Mr. Lapine, but...I've contracted a contagious disease—and the doctor ordered me to bed rest—indefinitely." *Coward. No backbone. Now what do I do? No job...No income—A washout at twenty-two.*

At home that night, I thought, *Tangie...try to find a job with less emotional involvement. Yeah...like that's gonna happen.* I read the want ads until my eye sockets began to droop...every employer I contacted assured me my people skills would be my greatest asset. How could anyone fathom how painful it is for me to deal with people and their problems—considering my majors in college? I struggled with my internal demons and my personal contradictions until my latest brainstorm: *"Why not create my own business?"* I could be my own boss, keep a safe emotional distance from my clients, and not have to explain anything to anyone. Yes...I hit pay dirt with this one. I could conceal my gift—without detection...The perfect solution: *Missing Persons Detective Agency*...The consummate fit. And my motto: *When life gives you lemons, try Tangerine...The Angel Scent Detective.*

So now, I work for myself—I love it—and I make a living. My clients like my style and my work ethic. They think I do tons of research, which I sometimes do, to be honest...but what really ices the cake is my gift...and I swirl this into the research. At present and for the past five years, my gift helps to provide me personal satisfaction, food, shelter and clothing—you see, I have a weakness for fine garments—I salivate at the Nordstrom's sales.

About my gift—I just know stuff. How I perceive the essence of circumstance is a mystery to me—one that remains unsolved. So for now, I call this mystery my gift, because that's how my mom tags my talent for perception. She's one of the two people privy to what makes me tick. The second is my buddy, Don—from my college days—I used to have a major crush on him—Well, it turned into something more serious than a crush...but he went into the priesthood...and I went psychic.

Okay, so today's January First and it's snowing in Seattle. Snowing in Seattle! Now this is a rarity for our Pacific Northwest city of seven steep hills, all of which sit in a bowl between two mountain ranges—The Cascades and The Olympics. Usually the mountains get all the snow—lots of it, and we get the rain—tons of it.

Another rarity—for me—is having a boyfriend. You got it. No *Mister Right*. No babies. No prospects. Dating isn't even fun anymore. Over dinner and a movie, I picture spending the rest of my life with my *date* and I get sick to my stomach. I've learned to rely on my instincts. One guy I met in a club, and dated for a while, really turned me on... Strong, handsome, witty. Great athlete. He attended *Notre Dame*. So why did I drop him? In one of my horrible dreams, I saw him beating a guy to a pulp in a bar, after being insulted—his short fuse and a need to fight, guaranteed him a trip to prison. Yep. My nightmare came true.

Suzy saw his name and the crime in the paper: *Involuntary manslaughter.* That turn of events scared me into celibacy. I decided, what works for my clients, works for me. I listen to my hunches. Downside—I miss out on a lot of fun—Can't even go bowling for kicks. I used to get smashed, so I could blot out my premonitions and just kick back—but hangovers are murder—I hate puking and killing brain cells. So I stay sober—and single.

New Year's Eve—Party time for most people...but party time does not include me. I did my usual *Herald in the New Year with Style.* Brother Bryan and his childhood sweetheart, Andee, now his wife—*they married young...at eighteen*—went out on the town. I stayed home and babysat for their sons, my four-year-old nephews—Jeffrey and Jason—*The Twin Terrors.* I let them wreck my house—It's always a mess anyway. They reveled in blowing horns and beating drums—well, my pots and pans—and ejecting silly confetti all over my living room floor. Easy to clean up—except for the pieces that got into my hair and what they sprayed all over Pebbles. Pebbles lost his confetti in his bath...I'm still pulling that dang-fangled stuff out of my scalp.

Yes, I'm single...and I have a house. *Surprised? Gotta satisfy those nesting urges one way or the other.* I prefer having my own little cottage, rather than a condo. Except, I hate to cut the grass. Love the yard, love the garden; hate the grass. Probably because it's mostly weeds. Maybe when my business is back in *The Black*, I'll hire a lawn man—*A tall, tan hunk of a guy with sinuous muscles popping out of his tee shirt...*

How desperate can I be? I live in a fairy tale world of my own making. It abets my desire to create excitement...to capture passion in my life...

Anyway, my craftsman—or *craftswoman* as I like to call it—house is *me.* Small, cluttered...in need of improvement. Situated in Ballard, just shy north of the main business section of Seattle, it sits atop a small hill in the old Scandinavian town, that is home to fishermen, young families, retired baby boomers, yuppies...and plain ol' working folk like me. In my modest abode, the spare bedroom, next to the kitchen, serves as my office. The master bedroom, in the loft upstairs, provides comfort for me—and for any romantic guest I may entice over—*so far none.* On the main floor—as soon as you walk in the door—a small living room grabs your attention with its gigantic fireplace, which seems out of place in the diminutive space. I love my *parlour*, as I refer to my entertainment area—*I'm somewhat old-fashioned*—It is here that I showcase my art treasures from my few travels abroad, and continually add new family photos to the gallery on the mantle. Running out of space there. Maybe I'll get one of those digital picture frames that stores thousands of photos and changes every three seconds or so. I bet the thing would hypnotize me and I wouldn't get any work done...Just sit there and stare at a picture frame. I know my limitations.

The one unfortunate situation about this room is *Pebbles*—my West Highland White Terrier. In his puppy days, he staked his claim on my *parlour*—He decided it makes the perfect kennel. All his toys, bones, socks... and my stolen underwear—are arrayed on the top cushion of my only couch, his chosen bed, where he relishes peering out the window—when I'm gone—watching for intruders...protecting his domain.

Most of the time I take my pooch with me. In Seattle, there are many dog-friendly restaurants so Pebbles gets to join me for breakfast, lunch and dinner when I'm on the road. One of my favorite places to eat lunch and meet clients is *The Dawg House—no kiddin'* in the University District—better known as the *U. District*...and definitely *Husky* territory. When I attended the *U. Dub* as a grad student, I spent most of my study hours in the library or in this humble establishment—and some habits are hard to break. *The Dawg House* serves up giant shakes, great burgers...jumbo hot dogs on rye bread... *Hum...I'm getting hungry...Wonder if they're open on holidays? I could go for a Chili Dawg.*

Anyway, being as I'm my own boss, and talk to myself a lot, Pebbles is my confidant—and right-hand canine on many cases. He's also the ultimate guard dog—all twenty pounds of him.

Don gave Pebbles to me a few years ago—Actually seven years ago today. Back then, I loved being twenty, going on twenty-one—I loved life...right before *Reality* hit me in the face with a capital *R* and I figured out *Life* doesn't always love you back. Today is the anniversary of my break up with Don—when my first—*and only*—boyfriend told me of his decision to enter the priesthood. Since then I've had seven years bad luck with men...I blame Don. He started it all. I remember the heartache like it happened yesterday...*One never forgets misery...*

Strolling through the campus of Seattle University, Don and I amble down the path to the library to study for finals…or so I think. While walking past the student union, Don, like a magician with a black hat, extracts a white furry bundle out of his jacket.

Mesmerized… I say, "Oh Don, you bought us a dog—A Westie! How did you know I love Westies?"

I pick the little pooch up and start nuzzling him. Love at first sight.

"You've only told me like 100 times…every time we pass Mac Dougall's Westie Farm…up in Arlington."

"Ah…yes…on the way to your parents' home…Funny…Hint, hint…I never thought you paid attention to my reveries..."

"I always listen to you…and Tangie...this is your dog."

"We should name him Pebbles…because we love to walk the beach..."

"Tangie, call him whatever you wish—He's yours. He'll watch out for you."

"Oh, Don! Dogs are for fun...I have you to protect me..."

"I won't always be here."

"What? Do you have a fatal disease?"

I place my hand on his heart and brush his lips with mine.

"You can't do that anymore," Don says with more emphasis, and pivots his body away from my caress.

"What? Touch your heart?"

"No...Kiss me...On the lips."

"Oh—Now it's mouth cancer. You don't even smoke. Don, you're perfectly healthy!"

"Yes, I am…Tangie—That's not the point. Listen to me…you know I attend Mass every day."

"I love that you've got religion. Maybe after we get married, you can study to be a deacon."

"Tangie...Angelina...I can't marry you."

"Oh Don...Cold feet, huh? That's okay. I'll wait. I love you enough...and I know you love me."

"I do love you...Tangie...Angelina...but...look into my eyes..."

"No." My eyes begin to tear up. "Whatever it is...I don't want to know."

"Angelina..."

"I love it when you call me that. No one else does."

"You know, you're an angel."

"No, I'm not. I'm a hot-blooded woman...who loves her man...and this enchanting little bundle of fur he gave me."

I start shaking and could feel tears running down my cheeks as I whisper, "Please, Don...don't say anymore."

"Angelina...I hate shattering your dreams..."

I pet the pooch for comfort. He licks my hand and the tears start falling. "My dreams? What about our dreams?"

"The last thing in the world I want to do is hurt you."

"What are you saying, Don?" I begin to plead with him...I hate the choking sobs that rise to my throat. I anticipate that with his next sentence...the axe will fall...my dreams will become dust...and my worst fear will become reality.

"I'm leaving you, Tangie."

"Leaving?" I scream silently, trying to block out his entire message to me. Like a drowning victim, I petition him..."Are you going on a trip?"

"No. It's permanent. I can't be with you anymore."

I collapse like a discarded rag doll on a stone bench alongside our path and embrace the fur piece cradled in my arms—my security blanket. The puppy kisses my cheek, as the branch of a weeping birch brushes me on my eyebrows. I glance at the threatening tree for a minute, welcoming the distraction, however painful. It rests within a cluster of brother and sister birches. I remember sitting on this bench before, under these deciduous trees...in autumn...when these very same weeping trees danced...costumed in gold leaves kissed by the last sunbeams of summer. Now, in winter, sorrow consumes them...they hang limp...no dancing, no happiness, no warmth...stark naked amid the grey of the day. Mad at me, no doubt for disturbing their solstice slumber...No doubt when the wind picks up, they'll whip me with their branches, urging me to move on...and so it goes... No help from Mother Nature...I look up at Don and begin to groan, pleading, "What do you mean, Don...That you can't be with me anymore? Am I poison or something?"

"No...of course not, Angelina. You're wonderful...I love you...But, I'm relinquishing my hold on you...I'm moving out of town. I'm...I'm entering the priesthood."

"The priesthood! You've got to be kidding."

"I'm not," Don says, as he positions himself on the icy bench, alongside me—and Fur Ball. He encircles my frozen body in his arms and hands me a handkerchief.

I blow my nose and say, " I thought we would be together…for our last year… Seniors at Seattle University—Then…in the summer…after we graduate…there would be a wedding—our wedding…How could I not see this coming? Sweet Jesus! I see everything else."

Don attempts to soothe me…He lowers his voice, grasping the icicles that used to be my hands, as he explains, "You see that I love you…and I do...but this is my ministry…I cannot refuse it...It's a vocation…Honestly, please believe me when I say, I tried to give it up…my call to service…but it's overpowering…"

Don gently squeezes my hands and forces me to look at him.

"Tangie, It's definite…I'm entering Holy Angels Seminary on Monday."

The wind starts blowing, brushing my hair across my face like a whip. The trees bend towards me…ready to strike. My eyes sting…I close them—blocking out my pain, my awareness, as I feel the warmth of Don's hands thawing out my icy blood. God, how I love his hands…

With as much force as I can muster, I will myself to disregard what he is telling me…I put his right hand on my cheek and pray for a miracle…Then I slip into a world of my own making…but it only lasts for a fleeting minute. I open my eyes and know I have no choice. I must kindle the dying fire inside me and live, or nourish my dreaming—fading away…to nothingness. My pride keeps me going…calling me back from my despair. My body stiffens and I force myself to resist Don's touch…Pushing him away, I stand up, abandoning him…allowing him his solo position… with the hovering branches—which now hurl their threats upon him. I start shouting, "Do you even have a clue to what you are doing, Don? Do you know what you are giving up? Holy Angels? You're leaving me on Monday? That's two days away! What are you thinking?"

I can't stand it. I bury my head in the puppy and start wailing—loud sobs whose treble pitches carry across the campus and rise above the wind like banshees.

Three students, dressed in ski gear, come frolicking along the path, stop in their tracks and stare at me like I'm a sideshow. Who cares? Let the world know—Love is a four-letter word. I dab at my eyes and wipe my nose with my wrist.

Don notices the onlookers, but with a flicker of his eyelashes, dismisses them and continues his litany. He is unflappable. His words come across clipped and distant. I don't recognize my lover any more.

"Tangie," the future priest chants, "I won't be taking many belongings. I want you to have my guitar, my books, and my mother's homemade quilts that you like so much. Where I am going, there's no room for them. They're yours, if you want them. I've arranged with the seminary to start next week, so we could spend my last two days...together. Peacefully. Unstressed."

I stare at Don and bite my lower lip until I taste blood. I snarl at him, no longer in control of anything I say. "Peacefully? Unstressed? Great! You really are something, Don...I can't fathom you...and you don't even get it—you'll never know how I feel. This is your ridiculous idea of fair play? What a bargain! You get God... and I get this crummy dog."

The crummy dog starts licking the tears streaming down my cheek and he doesn't stop until I sit down again. Don then takes over, enfolding me, for the last time, in his huge arms...as the sobs consume me. Grief devours my heart and soul...My mind flashes back to my dad dying...abandoning me as a child...The same empty feeling...Me having no say in my despair. Don brushes his hand on my chin and his eyes stare into mine...as he swears to me, "I will always love you, Tangie...Never doubt that I love you. I promise I will be there for you...if you ever need me...Even though I can never marry you, I will keep you forever in my heart...I will be your life-long friend."

I think to myself...Two years together...and now this...

Yes...Two years ago, on Christmas Eve, Don gave me an engagement ring. I study the ring now as it shines at me through my blurry vision. I can barely see through my tears, which by now are flowing like Snoqualmie Falls. Snoqualmie Falls—used to be our favorite romantic weekend destination...we escaped there whenever we got a chance. How can I forget? It's the place where Don proposed to me...after we hiked around the falls and devoured a seven-course dinner at the lodge. I cherish the memory of us...strolling outside to look at the mammoth falls all lit up...under the winter stars... and then...I remember Don asking me to be his...forever. That life-changing event seems like so long ago...and me—being a sucker for romance—I take him at his word—Forever! What a fool! —A forever fool in love.

I inch the ring off my finger, looking at it's precious gleaming for the last time. With my eyes, I kiss it goodbye, open Don's hand, and return it to him. As I close his fist, with my still freezing fingers, I whisper, "I release you from your promise to me. Have a holy life." I pick up the scruffy little puppy and snarl, "Don't worry about me. I don't need a friend. I have a dog."

I turn my back on him and start walking away, at a brisk pace, willing my legs to move. My heroics don't last long...a voice whispering in my ear urges me to make peace with him...and it is this voice that eventually wins out—you see...I still love him. I cease sprinting my way to the dorm and stop in my tracks. I shake my head, pet the puppy, turn around and begin moving like a snail with a heavy shell in the snow, inching my way back to Don. I observe him sitting like a frozen statue on the stone bench. As I draw near his presence, I notice his large, gentle hands in his long blond hair, his shoulders shaking. From my vantage point, I can hear him sobbing...Perhaps his heart is broken... like mine. I take a deep breath, tiptoe towards him and tap him on the shoulder. Don looks up and stares at me with red swollen eyes, a look of wonder crossing his face as he attempts a smile. I notice tears staining his rugged face. He opens his mouth to speak, but nothing comes out...He has no more words.

I hear myself announcing to him, "You'd better be an absolutely stupendous priest...because if you aren't, I'll storm into that seminary like a swarm of avenging angels ...and before everyone, snatch you back!"

At that moment, I wanted to hate him...I really wanted to hate him...It would be so much easier to forget our love—If I despised him. But he is my first love, and so far, he's my only love.

I wonder if it's appropriate to ask a priest, your former fiancé, to pray for you to find a new boyfriend...I've been on my own a long time. I'm getting desperate.

"Somehow I don't think it works that way," a little voice whispered in my ear.

Chapter Two

Well, another *Auld Lang Syne* has flown in and out like the winds of time. Today, back to *The World of Work*. Consequently, I sit in my office...having sipped the last of my three cappuccinos, trying to motivate myself.

Maybe I'll make out a list of goals for the New Year. That'll get me going... I'll formulate categories: *Work...Home...Personal*. *Work* should be easy so I'll do that first...

My Goals for Work...

One: Get to work on time.

Well, since I sleep in *The Building*—having a home office—that should be easy. I might even make it to work *early* a few days this year.

Two: Dress up for work.

Okay...If I have to take my calls and plan my schedule in anything other than my pajamas, then I'll be late for work and negate Number One. Maybe I could compromise...I'll dress up when I meet clients—for the first time only.

Gotta make a good first impression. After that, they're stuck with me—and vis-à-vis.

Three: Finish my cases in a timely manner.

Now that would be easy—if I were doing one case at a time, but I'm always juggling...Maybe I could prioritize. Let's see. What's more important? Missing child? Missing wife? Missing husband? Definitely put the husband last...Child first...Wife in the middle. Women are always in the middle of things.

Four: Get in *The Black*.

When I check my bank balance, I see police blinkers coming at me. Maybe I need an accountant. I'd have to pay. If he'd be cute, it'll be worth it...*But what if he's a she?* Then I do my own books. Maybe I can check the *U-Dub* for a starving M.B.A. student. Check the *Will Work for Food* bulletin board. I'm a pretty good cook. *Yeah! That's the ticket.*

Five: Don't get personally involved in my cases.

Yeah, like that's gonna happen. But this year, I'm really gonna try on this one. Okay...Enough of work...on to the home front...

My Goals for the Home...

One: Clean daily...weekly...monthly...

Think I will circle monthly. That way I'd probably wind up cleaning before each holiday—that's almost every month.

Two: Bake more.

Gotta have those chocolate chip cookies for Jason and Jeffrey...and macaroons for me...and peanut butter snacks for Pebbles—and old Mr. Jarrick's cat—who is forever haunting my back doorstep, looking for handouts. What he doesn't eat, the crows do. Gotta watch out for my furry and feathered friends.

Three: Empty out the garage so I can protect my car in the winter.

No can do. Have five years of files I cannot throw out. Car will just have to become a rust bucket. Plus, I gotta keep my bike that I never ride, dry.

Four: Put curtains on the windows.

Really, Tangerine...It's been five years. No way. I'd spoil my view of my friendly—deadpan neighbor—Mr. Jarrick...trimming his dead hedge on the side of my house. Plus..I'd miss my partial peek of Mount Rainier from my *parlour* window.

Five: Get a new couch with no chew holes and no dog hair.

What for? Pebbles wouldn't know what to do with a new couch... And I'd be yelling at him all the time to get off it. No...The old one stays. Maybe I'll make a couch cover. *Right...You never sew, Tangie...Get real!* Enough of the house...Until I can afford a housekeeper, I'll stay away from home projects.

Now to the hard ones...*My Personal Goals...*

One: Get a man.

Okay. So I've got a one-track mind. At least I'm consistent. I put this one first every year. A lot of good it does me.

Two: Don't be so sensitive.

Yeah, right. Sensitivity is my main thing. Attached to *the gift*, it's my double-edged sword. Come to think of it, I could have PTSD—Post-Traumatic Stress Disorder—brought on by being abandoned by my dad at an early age and my boyfriend at twenty. Okay, so Dad didn't abandon me. He died young—But sometimes I wonder when I'll recover from that trauma. It was not his fault he was in a car accident...Nor was it my fault for dreaming about it...and not telling my mother—before it happened...I didn't know then...I was only seven.

And...as for Don...Well, I wrote that story yesterday. Yes, I'm sensitive...and I blame you, Don. So on to Number Three. Two's a dead-end.

Three: Try to have fun with my friends and not worry about the future.

Now for an ordinary person, that would be a no-brainer. But I'm not your average citizen. I work at it. God knows I try. Some day I'm gonna do it. I'm gonna confide in one of my Seattle good buddies. Besides Don...and Marianna—my mother—no one is privy to the real me. How's that for trust?

There must be one other person I can trust. God knows I need someone to talk to—face to face...my own age—once in a while. I can't keep clinging to Don...He's in Chile...A good safe distance from me. I can't do the face-to-face thing with him. And I perceive that stressed-out expression on Mom's face every time I confide in her. It starts out all innocent, with her raised eyebrow—Her left one—Then she gallivants over to her piano and starts playing *Hungarian Rhapsody No. 2.* If she's not near a piano, she simply starts humming it. When I hear that piece, I know for sure she's worried. She tries to mask her fear from me, but I notice it—I *hear* it. Kinda hard to tune a rhapsody out.

So...Yes. I've made a decision. *Priority Number One*: Select a friend. Unbosom myself to the lucky winner.

Chapter Three

What a bust yesterday turned out to be. No one went to work, but they forgot to tell me. Everyone was either:

A. Still hung over from New Year's Eve or...
B. Still partying or...
C. On vacation.

Get real! *The Huskies—The University of Washington Football Team—* have not won the *Rose Bowl* since the Eighties...but fanatic fans still book flights in August to go to Pasadena at the end of December--just *hoping* this year will be different...and the whole darn city of Seattle closes down. Citizens...Wake up! *The Huskies* have not had a winning season—What you are thinking happened light years ago. The entire state is in this *just in case* mentality—Gotta close the schools, the banks...the credit union. Why, I ask? I need my friends...I need my clients...I need my money!

As you guessed, none of the people I called answered their phones. No clients, no witnesses, no friends. Even my mom—Marianna—unavailable...She was out on another *hot* date with *her Charles*—whom she met on *e-Bay*—while selling some of her old books. Mom has like a trillion books and they're taking over her household. Every room—books. You have to move them off the toilet when you use the facilities. I'm glad she recognizes the fact that hoarding can become a disease...and that she's doing something about it. Aside from the bathroom thing, I love going to her home. She has all her books categorized and all books in one field hang out together in one room.

In the kitchen her cookbooks rule—naturally—all 300 of them, including her garden books. Marianna put in a greenhouse window over her sink, for her herbs. That's how she justifies the living quarters of *Gardening with Ciscoe, Sunset Guide to Gardening with Flair* and assorted books on landscape architecture.

In my old bedroom, all her mystery, suspense, true crime and thrillers hang out. Wonder *why? She has floor to ceiling shelves of them...from Another Day in Paradise to The Missing Matador*...to *Zooey Doesn't Live Here Anymore.* Many of her favorite *local* mysteries are signed—my mother goes to lots of writers' conferences—she's now an *aspiring* author. I tell her, "Write about anything you want, but leave me out. I've got enough trouble keeping things undercover."

Mom converted my brother's bedroom into her study. In this place her true adventure and non-fiction books dot the four corners and drape over all level surfaces except the windowsills...My mother has a thing about not blocking nature from coming into the room...No blinds or curtains in her house...Just books. Scattered in categories all around her writer's den include self-help, advice, how-to-do anything, biographies and autobiographies. Collected photos of her favorite historical authors adorn the walls. Albert Einstein, Franklin D. Roosevelt, John F. Kennedy, Mark Twain, and her favorite classic rock stars have replaced Bryan's posters of the *Huskies Football Team* and the *Seahawks*... and his 101 pictures of Andee. Bryan brought all his memorabilia with him when he moved out after high school, and my mom took over. My mother—Marianna—does have one signed photo of her favorite singer...with his band. She enshrines this on her desk, next to the wedding picture of my dad and her. My mother and father look so young in that picture...I'm sure they met at a concert...I can see the tickets in the lower right hand corner of the picture. It must be hard, remembering the good times...She's gotten by on memories until Charles—who hangs out at her house non-stop... and escorts her on a regular basis to *Benaroya Hall*, the *Seattle Repertory Theatre* and *McCaw Hall*. Mom seems to like him...and he adores her.

Mom reserves her bedroom for poetry and music books. Marianna quotes Shakespeare endlessly and she loves music—all kinds. She always tries to play *Name that Tune* with me—I always win—even if I don't know the song.

Her music books spill out into the living room—where her baby grand piano takes center stage. She's not an accomplished pianist, but she can sure sing. At Christmas, she plays carols and makes Bryan and I join in the music making…and now, Andee, Jason and Jeffrey sing along with us. Christmas Eve is always filled with music at her home, where we all gather around the piano. I play the flute…I think I took up that instrument in grade school, because of my brother. In the fifth grade, it was easier to play the flute than to sing alongside my brother. He always drowned me out as he harmonized—slightly off key. Mom would say, "Oh, isn't he cute?"

Groan.

Well, let's see...Life should begin happening again in *The Emerald City*. I can call my buddies and invite them all over for dinner and size them up...Play a sort of *Whom Do I Trust* game without them catching on. I know it's devious but what can I do? I need a confidant!

Yes, my phone is ringing—finally! *I bet it's my new client.* Yep, it's Clancy Hendricksen, all right. I'm sure he wants to set up a meeting. After I talk with Clancy, I'm gonna e-mail my Seattle friends—Jean, Suzy…Walter…and…may the luck of the Irish show up for my dinner party.

Chapter Four

Got up early today. Took Pebbles for his morning stroll to the park and around the neighborhood. The stroll turned into a five-mile hike. I have a non-stop terrier. Loves to mark his territory. When my pooch finished watering all the plants in Ballard, he dragged me home. At ten a.m. I changed from my morning sweats into my work clothes—suede black boots, ebony jeans, and black cashmere turtleneck that my mom gave me for Christmas. I topped my outfit off with a fleece-lined chocolate-colored quilted velour vest with a matching hand-knit scarf wrapped around my neck.

I assembled Pebbles' going-to-town tartan doggie vest on him—No easy task—wrestling a feisty Westie—but I prevailed...after an hour of chasing him around the house, and picking up the potted plants he knocked over.

Bad doggie!

I was so mad at him, I almost left him home...but he looked so cute in his vest, I succumbed to his charms. Together we stomped out the door, down my porch steps, which were in need of shoveling. I'd shovel the snow, but I don't have a shovel. Put that one on my list. I may need one if it snows again...It could. One could hope. Pebbles leaped in my yellow *Escape* and while he slobbered on the windows barking at anything that moved outside, I inched my way on the blanket of white, virgin streets—unplowed and unspoiled by human interaction and automobiles—to the *Dawg House*—my selected meeting place on the *University of Washington* campus—to discover the plight of Clancy Hendricksen, my first client of the new year.

Yum, yum! Finally…I got to eat my *Chili Cheez Dawg*...before noon, no less. I washed it down with a chocolate shake to get dairy in my diet. Pebbles chomped on two plain *Kiddie Burgers* and lapped up two bowls of milk.

Sitting at a window booth with my new client, Clancy Hendricksen, I watched *U-Dub* students stroll down *The Ave*—the traditional moniker given to the main drag by long-gone students—and listened to Clancy's tale of woe. Clancy sipped his third cup of coffee, finished off three *Deluxe Hamburgers* with no cheese and bared his soul to me. I snuck some of his *Sweet Potato Fries*. He didn't seem to notice. I never order fries, but I love sneaking them from others.

Turns out, Clancy's mother disappeared when he was four and Clancy blanked out on any memories of his father. His mom dropped him off at an unfamiliar building with a note pinned to his jacket. She abandoned him—leaving him to fend for himself at the doorstep of a church. Clancy remembered the name—*Our Lady of Peace*—and found out the location: Edmonds, Washington.

*I wonder what kind of mother would desert her own child? I guess in time I will find out…*Right now, Clancy, sixteen years later, is a student at the *U-Dub*—that's short for *University of Washington*…in Seattle. He confided in me that, ever since that last day with his mother, at *Our Lady of Peace*, he longs to rediscover her. He yearns to understand why she left him. He told me that thoughts of her frequent his dreams…and keep him from moving on…into his manhood.

To start the search, Clancy gave me a picture of himself at four, wearing the same dark blue wool suit he had on when his mother abandoned him…I noticed in his arms he held a light blue tattered blanket—A treasured blanket, he informed me…His *Doona*—The last relic of his mother…which comforted him at night…until it became threadbare… and his adoptive parents threw it away.

Not much to begin the hunt, but I told Clancy I'd give it a shot. I looked into his green eyes for a clue, but saw nothing there except bewilderment and sadness—like an unclosed door with a storm raging outside.

I took out my camera. "Do you mind if I take a photo of you? It might help for research purposes."

"Not at all." Clancy smiled, revealing even white teeth. He sat up straight and put his hands on the table, revealing callused, sunburned fingers. I noticed he kept his auburn hair cut short on the sides, but curls still formed on his forehead, giving him a cherubic look.

I snapped the picture and Clancy's smile disappeared.

"How do you get along with your adoptive parents?" I asked.

"Oh, Alice and Tom are caring and supportive—always have been. They never spoke ill of my mother...and they didn't force me to forget her. However, they held high expectations for me—They leaned on me a lot—to do the right thing at the right moment. Sometimes I would get exhausted, trying to please them. Sometimes, I just wanted to be me. But, Tangie...I don't know myself...who I am..."

I nodded. " I understand, Clancy. Could you tell me what *right things* your adoptive parents expected you to do?"

"Oh...they encouraged me to play sports—and...wanting to please them, I first played soccer, then football and wrestled for a few years. In college, I switched to rowing...that takes up a lot of my time...but I love being on the water. I row a single shell...which suits me fine.

"That's cool—competing...and rowing on Lake Washington, Lake Union and around Puget Sound."

"Yes...I do it for fun and relaxation, but I'm still competitive..."

"Good for you. What else did your adoptive parents consider *the right thing at the right moment?*"

"They insisted I be successful in school. Hence, I studied hard, got straight A's...most of the time. I still do—Not an easy task at the *University of Washington.* It's a lot tougher than high school—and I'm not playing contact sports...I devote many late evenings to my studies...I don't go out drinking with my frat brothers...They head to the bar and I head to the library..."

"I remember those days, Clancy...Hard to say *no* to your friends. About your adoptive parents...they are both still living, are they not?"

"Yes. Both are professionals and still working. Tom is getting close to retirement age, but he loves his work. Not particularly warm and fuzzy, but affectionate enough..."

Clancy looked out the window for a moment and then at me. I could see tears forming in his eyes. "I don't know if they really love me—I never hear them say the words...not big on hugging and all that...Seems like they're always busy with their professions..."

I touched Clancy's hand for a moment. "For some people it's hard to be demonstrative...that doesn't mean they don't love you..."

"I know, I know...but just once in a while, I'd like to hear the words... and feel their love."

"Do they know you are searching for your mother?"

"Yes..."

"And?"

"Now...they are neutral on that subject. Tom said, *Clancy, my boy, it's up to you if you want to research your heritage—Your mother and I won't get in your way.* Alice added to his acquiescence, but I noticed some hesitancy in her voice..."

"How is that?"

"She said, *Clancy, you are old enough to find out why your birth mother left you...I know you want to find out the truth...but I hope you can handle it...*

So I guess they don't mind me searching."

I nodded. "They sound supportive...and caring."

"Yes...they are...and I've considered that...and you know, Tangie... this is a big compromise for them. Anytime I brought up looking for my mother—in grade school and later in high school—they totally skirted the issue..."

"Do you have any siblings, Clancy?"

"No. Just me. I grew up alone...in a household of adults...doing the *only-child* bit—trying to fit in...A part of me always missed my mother—my birth mother—especially during the holidays...Like... someone was missing. Now I find parties...gatherings are easier...more comfortable—I've got some good friends here at the *U*—My frat brothers are great, even if they razz me about studying."

"Girlfriend?"

"Yes...*Jessica*."

The way Clancy said her name—low, soft, whispery...I knew he wanted to be serious about her...and that she possessed a strong hold on his heart—a heart that is still breaking from his childhood trauma.

He continued. "I want to commit to Jessica…have a life with her in the future…but I'm frozen in my past. She's the reason I want to find my mother...and any other family I might have...so I can move on and concentrate on my life...present and future. I need to come to terms with my past. Jessica's been very understanding, but I find myself pulling away from her…and I don't want to lose her, like I lost my mother…It's like I'm afraid to love her…Afraid she might leave me and I'll be alone…"

"You think finding your mother will cement your relationship with Jessica?"

"Don't you?"

I looked into Clancy's eyes and saw hope and anguish mixed up together, like a salad needing a better dressing. "I hope so, Clancy. I'll do my best for you."

Clancy arose and shook my hand, thanking me. I took his strong, firm grip and through the hard calluses formed on his palms from months of rowing, I felt warmth and honestly rolled up together in his grasp. Jessica would be a lucky girl.

I wrapped my scarf around my neck, leaned up and gave Clancy a hug, something I don't do as a rule with clients…but he looked so needy. I promised to get back to him as soon as possible…and we parted ways. As I walked outside the *Dawg House*, I took one last glimpse at Clancy seated by the window…staring into his empty coffee mug…I noticed tears streaming down his cheeks. He put his head down on the table… and I saw his shoulders shake. He's probably lost in those sad, lingering memories…memories which for him, are always just below the surface.

The wind kicked up and I could feel it coursing through my hair… the wind…urging me on…motivating me to begin this new journey of discovery. Avowing a simple oath…I acquiesced…*I'll do anything to encourage love—especially the love of two young college students…I remember those days…if I could help the little lost boy that lingers inside the soul of Clancy…there'd be no end to the satisfaction I'd get...from solving this case…and reuniting Clancy with his mother.*

I trudged back to my *Escape* with Pebbles at my side. The snow, which first appeared on New Year's Day, began to melt. *Rats. I love the snow. It never sticks around long enough for me.* I jumped over a slushy puddle and hopped into my *Sport SUV*, putting Pebbles next to me on the passenger side, in his doggie seat. With the sun at my back, I cruised over to my other hangout...*Starbucks* on Fremont. I ordered a tall, non-fat cappuccino to take away the heartburn from the chili dawg, and a biscuit for Pebbles. I found an empty table near the wall and plugged in my laptop. Don't have an *iPhone* yet...Maybe with my next windfall client. I'm still in the Nineties, pay-wise. I gotta get with the Twenty-First Century...and I gotta check my e-mail...have to plan my day. Stomach pains interrupted me before I checked my twenty-five waiting messages. Not the hunger kind. Not the coffee. Too much caffeine, not enough foam. I went to the counter to beg for some more cream.

What's the matter with me? I used to have a cast-iron stomach. I could eat anything. Now look at me. I've gained ten pounds since Don left seven years ago and today I swear I pulled a grey hair out of my head. So what if I used to be skinny. Now I'm twenty-seven and over the hill.

I looked at my biscotti and gave it to my furry companion who gratefully gobbled it up. "You're gonna get fat, Pebbles...that's your last treat today."

"Ruff," was all I got in return. *Like he cares...Pebbles reminds me of that old song, I Wish I Were a Dog.* Judy Hansen sang it to me when I was six—she wrote her own words to an old tune. Hum...Judy Hansen—she used to hang out with my mom and dad...before Dad...I think she moved to Nashville...But...yes—doggone it–she really captured Pebbles' spirit in that song...Dogs live in the present—they don't worry about anything. *Lucky beasts.*

My *MacBook* buzzed, "You've got mail."

Finally! I deleted all the junk mail—that is all those weird *forwarded items* that come into my box *ad nauseam*. Then I checked with anticipation the replies to my inquiries—to see if there were any takers for dinner tonight—Two *No's*...one *Yes*. Turns out, Jean and Suzy were still cavorting in Pasadena...No joke...They went to the *Rose Bowl Parade* but didn't go to the game because the *Huskies* weren't playing—*duh!* They'd be back in a few days. Depends on the shopping. Suzy loves to shop.

Jean just tags along to keep her company. They enunciated the weather is warm and sunny in California...So much for my snowbird friends. Walter, on the other hand, answered me with a *Positively yes!* Told me he loves my cooking and he'd bring my favorite wine. Now that is thoughtful of him...

Gee—I don't think Walter and I ever ate together—alone—just the two of us. Our gatherings usually included Jean, Suzy, Walter and me.

Walter used to date Suzy, but that fizzled after Walter took Suzy on *The Camping Trip*. To hear Suzy talk, Walter dragged her to Timbuktu. Suzy doesn't do nature. She does *Nordstrom's*. She and Walter are still friends, like Don and me, so she and I have one thing in common—being friends with our ex's.

And Jean...well, she's my rugged, individualist buddy. She pilots a floatplane for a living. She flies her *Otte*r out of Lake Union—making excursions to the San Juan Islands and Victoria, British Columbia. That's Jean, my daredevil friend. In her spare time, she sky dives. She's also my neighbor—lives across the street. Sometimes I feed her cat for her when she's out of town. *Oops!* Just remembered...Spunky needs some nourishment...Must stop there on my way home...

Anyway, Jean owns her own *Otter* and works pretty steady, except in the winter months. Like me, she's without a steady man in her life. Unlike me, I think she likes it. Right now, she doesn't want to be bound to any one guy. Jean relishes life and guards her freedom—pretty much like the eagles she keeps company with in the sky.

Suzy is my dingbat friend. I love her, but she drives me nuts. She flits from one guy to another and then complains she doesn't have a real boyfriend. She's my age and has had about twenty more *relationships* than me. I think Walter placed at Number Fifteen. Poor Walter. He didn't have a chance. Suzy's gorgeous, but fickle.

Walter...Dinner for two. What will we talk about?

Chapter Five

Walter. I think I'm seeing Walter in a new light. He arrived all dressed up in clean jeans and an ironed shirt. All right, he wore a flannel shirt over a tee shirt with *School Rocks* scripted on the front...but he looked cute...and this time, I could feel his muscles through his shirt when he hugged me...after he sailed through my front door like a breath of fresh air. My heart kind of jumped a beat. That never happened before. I hugged him back and I felt an arm around my waist...strong...secure... I liked it. Plus, his hair looked and smelled fresh...and styled—not all scruffy, like the last time I saw him. I appreciate good grooming in a guy. I grinned at him, placed my hand in his and led him into the kitchen, where I had the table all set for our dinner together.

Walter's a junior high school teacher...teaches social studies and language arts to eighth graders. The kids love him...probably 'cause he dresses like them most of the time. Like my mother, he writes...on the side. Unlike my mom, he's had a few pieces published...mostly sci-fi short stories in some *Trekkie* magazine, and a literary piece about jazz in some obscure publication—but hey, it's recognition, right? Tonight he captured my attention when he presented me with a bottle of *Pinot Gris* and a bouquet of yellow roses—*a favorite wine...a favorite flower—how did he know?*

"Hey Tangie...sorry you couldn't be at the *Rose Bowl*, with Jean and Suzy. I thought I'd bring you some roses to cheer you up."

I looked at Walter who had my dog Pebbles mesmerized...Pebbles just sat at attention, waiting to be petted by my guest, who promptly complied with Pebbles' wishes, while providing him with a treat from his pocket. "Good dog," he said, then petted my polite pooch. *Weird. Pebbles is never well behaved around visitors...usually he annoys them to death... but it appears to me that Walter holds a secret charm.*

I grinned at my dinner guest. "Thanks for the beautiful bouquet." I hugged the flowers, smelling the delicious odor that only yellow roses possess...and blushed, for some unknown reason.

"I just know how much you'd like to be in California right now." Walter chuckled, as he struck a match and lit the candles I positioned in the center of the table.

"Yeah, right. That's right up there with paying my taxes. You're sweet, Walter." I reached into the cupboard of my kitchen and pulled out a chipped antique vase and placed the flowers inside it along with some water from the tap. "How'd you know I love yellow roses?"

"Let's say, I had a clue." He took the vase from my hands and placed it in the center of the kitchen table, next to the candles. "Just because you're the detective doesn't mean you know everything." He smiled at me and dimmed the overhead light in the kitchen, leaving us in candlelight.

"Is that so?" I gave him one huge smile. I couldn't help myself. He caught me off guard. I didn't expect *charming* to be one of his character traits. But there it appeared...and me, so ready for *Prince Charming*...I could feel my breath coming and going in short, hard to catch, spaces.

"Yes, Tangie. I'm on to you. So what's for dinner?"

"Chicken Paprikas..."

"My favorite."

"Have you ever eaten it?"

"No, but I just know it's my favorite."

Great. Another psychic. "Okay, Walter. Why are you here?"

"You invited me."

"Yes, but..."

"But, what?"

Despite my quivering knees, I decided to make him squirm—*a wicked sense of humor overpowers me sometimes.* "Why the flowers? Why the wine?"

"You're my friend. Friends bring friends wine. Friends bring friends flowers."

I held up the bottle of wine. "This is an expensive *Pinot—Zenato Pinot Grigio delle Venezie*...and roses aren't cheap, especially in winter. You're a struggling teacher."

"So I splurged. I'm a teacher, but I'm not cheap. Plus, it's close to New Year's."

"That was almost a week ago."

"Close enough." Walter took the wine from me and uncorked it. He poured the wine into the waiting glasses on the table and handed me one to taste.

I placed the wine by my nose and swirled the glass around as I breathed in the aroma. Intoxicating. "To whom shall we toast?"

"How about us?"

I smiled, clinked his glass and took a sip.

Walter smiled back and chugged his wine. *Seems he's thirsty.*

"Say, Walter...look into my eyes."

"Sure, Tangie. Are you going to tell me a secret?"

"Something like that..."

"Ah, I always knew there was a *method to your madness*."

"More than you know." I winked at my guest, gave him my most endearing smile, and finished off my glass of wine. *I can play coy on the proper occasion.*

I looked into Walter's eyes. I saw warmth, understanding...and fear—fear of what I couldn't fathom—yet...but the thought of finding out intrigued me. The next moment, I didn't feel like being funny anymore. A strong, primeval need took over my body. I reached over to the stove and turned off the Chicken Paprikas.

"Hey, Walter..." I murmured...taking a few steps closer to my guest...and placing my arms around his shoulder. "Would you do something for me?"

"Anything, Tangie." Walter reached around my waist, untied my apron and let it drop to the floor. I could not breathe. Walter extinguished the candles with two quick breaths, as I regained mine.

"Please...call me *Angelina*."

Chapter Six

Don't know how it happened...but I've been kind of tied up the past three days and two nights. No, no one kidnapped me...but I think I finally, with finesse, seduced a guy...or was it the other way around? Doesn't matter. After seven years of near-celibacy, it's an achievement for me—finding someone to trust...and as a bonus...discovering passionate nights filled with pure pleasure...I am the cat that ate the canary. So naughty...and Walter is so delicious. I have a little guilt...especially since Suzy dropped in this morning, unannounced and found Walter in my kitchen...in his underwear. Mine were on the couch with Pebbles. I swear that dog has a panties fetish. I spend more money in the lingerie department at Nordstrom's than I can afford—Yes; I'm fussy about my underwear. Just gotta remember to keep my unmentionables out of Pebbles' reach. But the last two days, I've been kinda lax—You see... Walter never left. I think his puppy dog eyes got to me...or maybe the champagne we drank after the *Pinot Gris*...or our dancing to my CD of favorite romantic ballads...or my practically dragging him up to my loft...Or did he drag me? *Rhett Butler and Scarlet O'Hara*...Either way...I felt so enchanted about everything...*everything*...until Suzy walked in and burst my balloon.

Caught in the act—*Cheating*...with Suzy's boyfriend...All right—Her *ex-boyfriend*...but I still feel bad. Chicks don't take their friends' boyfriends, even their ex's. But really, Walter placed as Suzy's Number Fifteen...How could she miss him? She's moved on...She already has

Number Twenty-One…all picked out. But that doesn't matter to her. I know she's miffed at me. I'm miffed at me. I offered her a latte…

"Suzy…Let me make you a Hazelnut…After I put on my bathrobe…"

She declined…overly polite. "I have to go to work."

Now I know for a fact, Suzy never refuses one of my lattes and she doesn't even have a job...She has a trust fund. I tried again..."Stay, Suzy... it will only take a minute for me to find the coffee; it's around here somewhere..."—*It's been two days since I cleaned up the kitchen...*

Suzy just fluttered her fake eyelashes at me and quivered…like my grandmother's cat…that lost the quail she'd been hunting. *I remember that quiver.* Suzy then turned her body away from me and strutted out to my back porch, the same pathway of her entrance, her streaked blond hair bouncing as she slammed the door.

I heard a "woof, woof," from Pebbles as Suzy stormed out.

I petted my pooch as tears started forming in my eyes. I said to myself, *"Okay, Suzy…you win. I will start locking my doors…save myself a lot of grief."*

But…this time, grief won. I felt myself losing control and started to tear up. I went into the *parlour* and plopped down on the sunken couch and started sobbing. Pebbles jumped up next to me and licked my cheeks, but I pushed him away. Walter—who after Suzy's arrival, slipped into his jeans for the first time in two days—came over and sat down between Pebbles and me. The couch sunk so low the three of us perched practically on the floor.

My newfound love-interest took me in his arms. "It'll be okay, Angelina."

"I think you better call me *Tangie.*"

"Uh oh...what's wrong?"

"I just lost a friend."

"*Suzy*? Have no fear…She'll get over it. I give her a week. Then she'll be calling you like nothing happened."

"But something did happen...between us."

"I know." Walter started kissing me on my neck. "Isn't it wonderful?"

I wanted to agree. I wanted to say that he was the best thing to come into my life…ever…that he had this Grecian body that I lusted after… *My Adonis*...and that I loved the way his midnight black hair curled on his forehead...and covered his right eye. His eyes—those steely blue pools—drove me crazy last night...as he embraced me in the moonlight. I wanted to stay in his arms...forever...and I wanted...I wanted...to...

Instead, I pulled away from him. "Walter...I will never forget these last two nights, but...I'm *Tangie...*you know...crazy, unbalanced Tangie. I'm not the *Angelina of the Evening*. She's just a dream."

"I like dreams, Angelina."

"Walter...I'm just not ready for this...It's too intense."

"I thought you like *intense*."

"I do. I did...I don't know. I'm confused. I need some time to think...I need some clothes on...I need some..."

"Breakfast?"

"Yes. I'm starved!"

"It's almost done. I did the short order thing while you napped in the loft...before you chatted with Suzy..."

"Well, I wouldn't exactly call that chatting...more like cat fighting...and besides...a girl's gotta sleep."

"A girl's gotta eat. Come on. Have some of my thin pancakes. I prepared *Crepes Fantastique*...just for you." Walter led me into the kitchen, picked up a cover and displayed a platter of mouth-watering heavenly crepes and strawberries, topped with whipped cream.

Now where did he get the whipped cream?

"You're full of surprises," I murmured.

"More than you know."

"Oh, I know a lot."

"You don't know how to make crepes."

"Well, I'll just eat them then. They happen to be my favorite."

"I know."

My contribution to the breakfast consisted of *Cappuccino for Two*... Walter knows I am the barista...but he is the cook.

I chomped the crepes. "Fantastique." I sighed and closed my eyes. *Walter is true to his word.* Melt in your mouth good...*How does he know these things? He knows my likes, my needs…my desires. Jean and Suzy talk... They talk all the time about "poor Tangie...no man in her life"...I'm sure of it. The connivers. Walter got wind of it, I'm sure. This will teach Suzy to gossip about me—the motor mouth—Poetic justice—Now I don't feel so rotten… Walter's available…and…I have to think about that situation.*

After breakfast, Walter helped me clean up the kitchen. Good thing. My chef used the last clean frying pan to make the crepes. And I located the missing coffee, before we sat down to eat.

As we sat smiling at each other, sipping our second cappuccino, I got this really weird feeling about Walter. He didn't plan on leaving…even if I tried to throw him out—*which I don't want to do. I suspect he enjoys playing mind games with me…and that is beginning to freak me out.*

So...I decided to have *The Talk* with him. I was just about to open my mouth, when Walter came up behind me and started massaging my neck and shoulders. Another bit of heaven. I relaxed a wee bit. I sighed, involuntarily.

"Ah…a little to the left…and now the lower back…ah…just right…"

"You seem a little tense, Angelina."

"I am. That feels so good…now the shoulder blades...Ah...Thank you…Walter." I felt myself beginning to melt...then, I mustered all the resistance I could, before my resolve totally slipped away. I propped myself up, facing him.

"Walter…you and I—we have to talk."

"I love to talk with you..."

"Walter, why did you come over here?"

"You invited me."

"Yes. But why did you accept my invitation? Was it out of pity?"

"Angelina...*Tangie*...I don't operate that way. I came over because you're my friend and I hope more than that…*now*..."

"Walter." *I could see this talk was going nowhere...*

"Angelina."

"Call me Tangie."

"You were *Angelina* last night."

"I know. But it's back to reality this morning. I'm Tangie. You're Walter."

"Me Tarzan. You Jane."

"Cut that out! I'm trying to be serious."

Walter smiled at me and picked up a fork. "There's one last lonely piece of crepe left." He plopped the morsel in my mouth.

"Mm...Yum." I closed my eyes and then opened them to reality. "Stop that, Walter...You're confusing me."

"Jane?"

"I'm not your *Jane*!"

"Okay...I'll be good. I promise. Just say what you want to say—I'm all ears." Walter put down his fork and crossed his arms and nodded, like Stan Hardy of *Laurel and Hardy* fame.

I let out an audible sigh. "I think we need to slow things down." Then...my mind went to his mention of ears—which triggered a memory of him kissing mine...and my mind went blank again.

"Get to know one another better?" Walter asked.

I recovered my senses, breathed in...and nodded.

"I agree...Angelina." Walter smiled that *Cheshire Cat* grin I've come to love. He placed a kitchen chair next to mine and sat down.

I looked in his eyes...searching for something. "You do?"

"Yes."

"Okay. So what's next?"

Well, Angel...*Tangie*...Listen to me." He leaned forward as I leaned back. "We can be platonic lovers."

I couldn't help but smile. "I already have one of those. Remember *Don*?"

"Oh yes. I remember you talking about him. Well, his heart's in the right place, but he's not meant for you."

"Tell me about it." I felt a chill, remembering my last love, leaving me.

Walter took my hands and massaged them gently with his. "How about I tell you something else? I think you need a roommate. You've been alone too long."

I pulled away my hands. "I've got Pebbles. He's a great listener." I leaned over and petted my furry friend, who remained snuggling up to Walter.

Walter scratched Pebbles behind his ears. "Angel...*Tangie*...he's a *dog*...you need a human sounding board...and that's where I come in."

Pebbles placed his head in Walter's lap, begging him to continue. Walter complied and patted my pooch's head.

I stood up. "You, Walter? No way. How can I get to know you if all I do is sleep with you?"

Walter pulled me back down and put his arm around me and looked into my eyes. "Don't you see, Tangie? That's the key. We'll live together as *platonic* roommates. We'll get to know more about each other. We already know that the sex is magnifique. So...if we become close friends—best buddies—we can have another hot date...when we both agree it's *time.*"

I smiled, thinking good thoughts...remembering last night. "You'd do that, Walter? Wait?"

"I've got lots of time. I'm only twenty-five."

"You're younger than me? Oh no! I'm robbing the cradle!"

"I'll be twenty-six next month. I'm exactly fifteen months younger than you...but I haven't been hiding out like you."

"Yes you have. You teach junior high. You hide out from the real world there."

Well, technically I teach...until finals are over next week. Then I'm taking a sabbatical...I need some time to write...and...Anyway, I have some ideas...I want to get down on paper...before they're gone...somehow...I can't see myself supervising the lunch room and breaking up teenage fights the rest of my life..."

"How will you support yourself?"

"Oh, I've got some savings tucked away. My plan is to take a year off and...pursue my dreams—If it works out—great. If not, back to the nine-to-five rat race."

"Teachers don't work nine-to-five. They work all the time." *I can still picture the stacks of papers cluttering my desk, chair, table and bed from my brief stint teaching high school. No rest for the weary in that profession.*

Walter smoothed his curly locks back over his head in a determined manner. "Exactly...and Tangie...that's precisely why I've got to give my muse a shot."

"So...Walter...where do you begin...and how?"

"Well, I thought maybe I'd move in here, with you. I could sleep on the couch...keep my clothes, keyboard and books in your garage basement...and maybe share your office. I just need a corner for my laptop and..."

I opened my mouth to say something, but nothing came out. I must have looked like a duck without a quack. Walter smiled at me and continued his plan.

"Tangie, I have a new sofa...I could donate it to your living room. Blue...My couch would match your décor...Plus it's a *Lazy Boy*...makes into a comfy bed...Just think, Sweetheart...I could help you out...be your go-for, your chauffeur...your short-order cook—I'm good."

My mouth closed. What could I say? *I love breakfast...and I need a new couch.*

Chapter Seven

Okay. So now I have a roommate. Looking back at my *Personal Goals*, I did want a man in my life—and Walter's definitely a man...in all the right places—*Places I remember so well...*

I just didn't expect things to turn out this way. So far, he hasn't driven me crazy with small talk. He's neat. He is a great short-order cook. I don't think I ever ate from the four food groups at breakfast before he arrived...And, so far, he does not interfere in my business. I like that.

Tonight I'm meeting another new client at *Ivar's Seafood Restaurant* on Seattle's waterfront. The guy must be rich—or he's made his mark on this world. Asked me to meet him in the inside dining room, so we could talk in private. *Ivar's* is two restaurants in one. One is high class—which includes an expansive dining room with view seating. The other is outside...Open all year—rain or shine, snow or sun—This is the one I usually frequent. It also has a waterfront view, but mostly of seagulls stealing your food. Along with me, teenagers on cheap dates, working class people with kids, and tourists dine alfresco. You place your order at the seafood bar and take your food to nearby picnic tables. In the winter they place glowing heaters on the deck. All kids—young and old—thrive on feeding the seagulls. The younger kids never eat—Too many distractions. They delight in driving their parents—and everyone else—crazy. The scene always ends the same way—with the seagulls harassing everyone for food. All it takes is one French fry. Vicious panhandlers.

The inside dining room has none of these problems; people get dressed up in their fancy duds and pay a lot more money for basically the same food. Better service, room with the same view, but higher up. Outside you get no service and you have to wait in an enormous line, which if you can believe, races to the finish line...unless of course, you don't know what you want. You better figure it out before you get to the counter or else there's mutiny in the ranks. You could be tossed in the drink.

After introducing himself on the phone, my new client told me a friend of his recommended me—as a detective that gets the job done. The client also said he'd pay me whatever I thought necessary to complete the assignment. *I like that. It's nice to know I've got clout. Maybe I'll be in The Black soon...Maybe even take that Alaskan Cruise for which I've been saving and putting coins in the kitty bank—for the past five years. This'll be the ticket—Gotta remember to put "North to Alaska" on my list of goals.*

The whole time I'm hunting for Clancy Hendricksen's mother, I'm kinda thinking Clancy's not rolling in dough. He's a college student. His adoptive parents are probably professors. We all know how well education pays...Clancy's case is just gonna pay the electric bill...But every little bit helps—and as the ol' saying goes, it is better to light one candle than curse the darkness..."

I closed my laptop, stood up and contemplated heading out the door to my appointment, when Walter strolled in from walking Pebbles...

Walter flashed his adorable smile. Strong white teeth...And those dimples. I'd be squeezing his cheeks all the time, if I weren't the mistress of self-control.

Walter leaned down and unleashed Pebbles—who dashed into the kitchen to lap up some water. Then he hung up his plaid jacket with fleece lining on the clothes tree near the door. "Hey Tangie...Did you know Pebbles is a great *Frisbee* player? He catches the disk in mid-air. Not easy with his short legs. He just loves to fetch. Unusual for a terrier."

"Well, no. That's news to me...but, you know, Walter, there is no end to Pebbles' talents."

"He is quite the hit with the neighbors down at the park. They all love him—especially the kids. He just rolls on his back for them to pet his belly."

"What can I say, he's irresistible...Kinda like..."

"*Me?*"

I ignored his bid for attention and his fishing for a compliment... although his question rang true in my ears... *Walter can be irresistible... and I really wouldn't mind petting his belly.* I smiled as I made a request. "Say Walter...I've got to meet a client at *Ivar's*... at the indoor dining room... I usually take Pebbles with me, but I'm thinking I should leave him here. Is that okay with you? I don't think *Ivar's Indoors* allows dogs."

"*Ivar's*, huh—The indoor dining room?" Walter elevated his natural perfectly sculptured eyebrows. I sensed a bit of interest... or something else...

Yes...Dead giveaway—Walter... displaying a touch of jealousy—but... geez Louise, how I love his dark eyebrows... expressive, questioning... thick, soft to the touch.

Walter came over to me and took my hands in his. "Be careful,"

"What's to be careful?" I caressed his irresistible eyebrows with my lips, leaning into him as I did so. "It's just a dinner meeting, Walter." I kissed him on the cheek. "My guess is Mr. Santigo doesn't want his wife to know what he's doing. Why the concern?"

Walter brushed his lips with mine... but I could feel a deep longing under the casual kiss. He looked at me with what I perceived as sad eyes... hypnotizing eyes... He took me into his arms and hugged me in a crushing embrace... like a soldier does his sweetheart before going off to war. He kissed me again... hard on the lips...not platonic at all... and gave me the answer to my question.

"I care about you... that's all."

He released my body, but my head continued to reel around like on a merry-go-round, dizzy from his embrace. After I got done hyperventilating, I caved.

"Okay. I'll take my cell phone with me. I'll call you in about an hour, to let you know all is fine. Don't worry."

"Good. Thanks...But I'll still be pacing the floor."

"Walter...You're my knight in shining armor when you worry...but don't be. I'm a big girl. I can take care of myself."

"I know you're a big girl—especially here." He caressed my buns and grinned.

Maybe I don't need to lose ten pounds after all...

I put on my coat, picked up my purse and gave him a short hug goodbye as I reminded him of our agreement. "*Platonic*, remember?"

"Oh, that kiss is just a foreshadowing of our future together."

"Walter, sometimes I think you're as crazy as I am."

"That's why you like me."

"That's why I'm going. I won't be late getting home."

"Call me."

"I won't forget."

Well, I did forget. Walter phoned me—just as Mr. Frederick Santigo poured me a second glass of *St. Michelle's Johannesburg Riesling*. Good thing. I almost forgot one glass is my limit while conducting business.

"Excuse me, Mr. Santigo. "I've got to take this call…It's important. I'll be right back."

I left Mr. Santigo…glaring at me behind his *Foster Grants*…seems he doesn't like being upstaged by a cell phone. *Tough*. Walter would be calling all night if I didn't take pick up. I parked myself in front of the *Ladies Room* and listened to Walter's tirade.

"Hey Tangie. It's been over an hour."

"Sorry. I got tied up."

"He's not pouring alcohol into you, is he?"

"I'm all right, Walter. I know my limits."

"How does he look?"

"How does who look?"

"Your client."

"Mr. Santigo?"

"Who else?"

"Well, so far, rich...but normal, except for the shades. Tells me he hates bright lights."

"Maybe he's a rock star."

"He's a little jittery, I noticed...like he's being watched."

"He might be. Be careful."

"Yes, Walter...Please...don't be so suspicious...I'm okay. Gotta go...I'll be home soon." A warm feeling possessed me and I smiled... *Walter seems close...near by.* I shrugged my shoulders, closed my cell, turned around and gasped.

Fred Santigo—stood before me...eyeballing me as he touched my hand with his cold fingers.

Santigo extended his arm to me. "Is everything all right?" I could sense him turning on the charm. "You look concerned, Ms. Seraphina..."

Fred Santigo is appealing, if you like that type. Short, dark and handsome. Wealthy. He ruffled my feathers a bit—in all the wrong places. *I don't like hovering.*

"I'm fine...Just a family matter. How about if we finish dinner? I'm starved."

I placed my cell phone in my little black purse, took Santigo's arm and followed him to our booth—situated beyond the tables, past the eye-catching display of lobster, shrimp and oysters behind glass. As I sauntered along, beside my future client, I caught a glimpse of a young man with bright red hair, somewhat like Clancy's, but more of a dye job. Weird—The dude resembled Walter, except for the horn-rimmed glasses and classy pinstriped suit. *I wonder if Walter has a rich twin hidden somewhere.* The carrot top dude sat alone at the bar, sipping a glass of red wine and staring at the ferries winking at him, as they crossed back and forth from Bremerton to Seattle. He looked kinda lonely. *If it weren't for Santigo, I probably would go up to him and ask him a few questions. He looks interesting—probably because he resembles Walter's long-lost twin brother, except for the red hair and glasses. He even has dimples.*

Santigo stopped in his path, wondering why I slowed down...I smiled at him in response and we continued to our raised perch overlooking the waterfront.

I never get tired of the breathtaking views that constitute the signature of the Pacific Northwest. Here in the early evening, with twinkling lights and shimmering vessels traveling around the Puget Sound, Seattle becomes a fairyland. Gathering my thoughts, I force myself to pry away from the intoxicating view and get down to business. "So, what is it, exactly, that you want me to do for you, Mr. Santigo?"

"Please...call me Fred."

"*Fred* it is."

"I want you to find my wife."

"Oh, so there's a Mrs. Santigo...and she's missing."

"Yes."

"How long?"

"Three weeks."

"Three weeks?" Have you contacted the police?"

"No...you see...I thought she was visiting her sister near Kodiak, Alaska. Her sister resides on a remote island...in the Strawberry Islands area—Akhiok. She teaches school there. Reaching her by phone, without a satellite connection, is difficult."

"So your wife didn't call you."

"No. I said goodbye to her in the morning...at our home. There was no way I could take time off work that day...I had a meeting with a customer. I watched her get into a limo that I reserved for her...to transport her to the airport. I assumed she caught the flight on time... and visited her sister as planned—But—she didn't call or write to me... and she didn't come back... I don't know what to do...If anything has happened to her..."

Fred started to get choked up. He stopped talking and wiped his eyes and forehead with a white silk handkerchief engraved with an *S*.

"I still don't understand why you didn't contact the police."

"The past few weeks, the whole time...I thought she stayed with her sister...but she didn't...she must be somewhere else...But where?"

"I really think the police could help you."

"I don't want them involved. Look. She's probably out of the state. They'd just nod their heads and ask me to fill out papers. You...you... would look for her."

"What about the F.B.I.?"

" I can't do that...if I contact them, they'll send me back to Chile. I came here as a youth, but my parents...mi padre...mi madre...they were not...you know...*legal*."

Great. So now I'm helping an illegal immigrant.

"Ms. Seraphina...Please...I cannot leave the country...That would serve no purpose in finding my wife. Help me. She means the world to me. I love her more than I've ever loved anyone—more than life itself."

"What's her name?"

"*Terese.*"

Well, I got the skinny on *Terese*...Younger by sixteen years than her husband. Beautiful. Slender...Petite with dark hair...almost black, like Walter's. As I looked at the picture Santigo gave me, Terese's sad, hypnotic eyes, iridescent green and gorgeous, stared at me. They reminded me of the eyes on the Art Deco cover of *The Great Gatsby*—They dominated the photograph...like the focal point in Cugat's painting. I told Mr. Santigo—*Fred*, that I'd begin looking for Terese at *Sea-Tac Airport*... that I would check *Alaska Airlines* to see if she ever got on the flight... and then branch out. I thanked him for dinner and took his pre-payment envelope. Before we parted, I shook his hand, getting a strange shiver that started in my hand and crept down my spine. Fear, sadness and longing, all rolled up together like a carpet tightening its grip around my body, surrounded me. I released myself from his grasp and reached for my coat. Santigo got to it first and with his cold hands, placed it on my shoulders.

"I will make it worth your while when you find her," he whispered.

He smelled of breath mints and he smiled at me with a perfect set of dental work—Too perfect. Something about him didn't ring true.

I looked in the pocket of my coat, produced my business card and placed it in Santigo's right hand, which was adorned with an expensive diamond and ruby ring on the fourth finger. *Yep...The guy's rich all right. Terese probably married him for his money and then got second thoughts. Cold fish is not on her menu. Better to wise up after the wedding than not at all.*

Santigo took my hand once more as he said his goodbye. "Thank you, Ms. Seraphina. You are most kind."

Kind, I thought...*Not kind—Curious. More is going on here...than just a missing wife. Unfortunately, I'm hooked...But not by the grieving husband bit. Fred's just too slick for me. Even with those shades on, I can see through him. He's not what he appears to be—Urban successful businessman. Bet he's into something not so business-like. I may have to do some checking up on him… in my own discreet way of course…Investigation is my middle name. Maybe I'll throw Walter a bone…give him an assignment…He wants to help…he offered to be there if I needed him…I think this case merits help…Not one I want to tackle alone…This is gonna be a big one.*

Chapter Eight

The next morning, I planned to drive up north, just a hop, skip and a jump from Seattle, to *Our Lady of Peace* to see if anyone there remembered Clancy. I scheduled an appointment with the parish secretary, Mrs. Adrianne Cooper. I decided to put off opening *Pandora's Box*—the Santigo case, a few days. I needed think time. Clancy would be a good diversion. Plus I needed to accomplish some tasks to justify my paycheck—My conscience cycling—full speed ahead.

Before I opened the front door to leave, I glanced at Walter asleep on his bed—the pulled-out couch...with Pebbles spread out next to him, leaning against his feet—which stuck out of his down comforter. *Funny, he still has his socks on*. As I recall from our few nights together, Walter becomes his own electric blanket when he sleeps. Good in the winter... Very good. The temptation to snuggle up with him almost overwhelmed me...He would be oh so willing...and oh so soothing—Good thing I maintain a strong work ethic.

Last night I returned to Ballard, after my meeting with Santigo and found no sign of Walter and Pebbles. Out jogging I presumed. I had just put my final foot into my jammies when I heard the door open and Walter whispering to Pebbles, "Good dog." I breathed a sigh of relief. *It's amazing how Walter's presence affects me—now look who's doing the worrying.*

Right now, I lingered on their peaceful figures before I closed the front door. Hum... *Walter has his jogging clothes on...from last night...over some other garments. Maybe he got cold last night...Maybe he just gets hot when I'm around. Usually he doesn't wear a whole lot of clothing when he goes to bed or when he runs. Maybe Pebbles makes him slow down—that darn pooch is always marking his territory...and Walter cools off from all the stops. It seems to me Pebbles is getting really attached to Walter. Traitor. Seven years of meals and he passes me up for a jogger. He used to sleep on my feet. Now he doesn't leave Walter's couch at night. Maybe Pebbles is trying to tell me something. No. The platonic thing with Walter still stands...I have my own way with Pebbles. I'll entice my pooch back to me...with bacon. Yes. He's a pork junkie. That's the trick.*

Going against the traffic, I cruised like a yellow hawk, flying the speed limit, and well, maybe a little over it on I-5 North. Got to Edmonds in record time. My car clock read seven-thirty a.m. and I craved caffeine. I spotted *Genevieve's Pastry Shop* and pulled into a waiting parking spot right in front. I had time for an espresso and some nourishment.

A perky waitress—Becky—greeted me as I walked into the morning rush hour and led me to a tiny booth by the window, so I could watch the comings and goings on the street. Photographs of old Edmonds adorned the walls. Must say, part of this town still looks the same—*Old Milltown*, they call it. I told Becky that cappuccino, smoked salmon with cream cheese on a toasted bagel did it for me...and then asked her with a smile, to throw in a side of fresh fruit. *Walter spoils me. I eat healthy in the morning because of him. This breakfast will keep me going for hours.* I heard my favorite pop musician singing *O Holy Night* somewhere. Oh...My cell phone. *It's after Christmas. Gotta change that ring tone.* I scanned my cell for the caller—Walter. *I'll return his call later. I hate it when people talk on their cell phones in restaurants. Like I wanna hear strangers' personal stuff. Gag me with a spoon. That air of self-importance some people exhibit when conversing in a public place drives me nuts.*

I relaxed while eating my breakfast, looking at the local paper and studying the folks passing by...imagining myself living here. This place struck me as serene and folksy...After birth, people stayed here, went to school and raised their families...and the cycle went on...just like *Grover's Corner* in *Our Town...I remember trying out for the part of Emily in high school. I got it and relished acting. Learning the lines came easy, but I hated kissing George...He always did more than the script allowed and I didn't appreciate his roving hands...Plus, I only like to kiss guys I'm attracted to big time. But at least I can say I "did the dance"—I acted...even if it turned out to be a one-time deal.*

Becky came over and offered me another espresso. I declined, saying I'd be leaving to take a stroll around town. As she picked up my cup, her hand brushed mine and I could visualize her struggle to make ends meet. I left her a hefty tip under my plate. I used to be in the trade myself, during my college days. *Thankless job. I sense this waitress works long hours—A single mom with three kids to support. I know how tough life is for her...yet she doesn't complain...just comes into work everyday with a smile on her face.*

As I opened the door to leave, she caught me. "Thank you so much... Have a fantastic day."

I smiled. "You too, Becky."

As I walked down the sidewalk to scan the streets of downtown Edmonds, I could see the antique shops showing signs of life—merchants arranging their display windows and turning on their *Open* signs. I strolled down the hill towards the waterfront—so peaceful this clear, crisp morning...Ah...the Olympic Mountains standing at attention in the west... right below the sunshine. Darn. I missed the sunrise today. I forgot to look east when I got up...and check out the Cascade Mountains—to catch a glimpse of Mount Rainer from my loft. Sometimes I'm too wound up in thought.

A sure sign of good weather in the Seattle area is when the Olympics make their appearance. If you can see this mountain range, you can see anything...The Cascades, Mount Rainier, Mount Baker... everything in full splendor. Nature's beauty always cheers me up. I can be in the worst possible mood...and if I walk outside, breathe the fresh air and admire the view, I'm good for the next few hours. Works like a charm.

I studied the ferries crisscrossing the Puget Sound from the Edmonds Ferry Dock to Bainbridge Island. When Don and I attended college together, we used to walk on the ferry and ride back and forth for hours. How I loved those cheap dates. We'd sit outside on the open air decks, eating clam chowder and drinking coffee...Catching glimpses of eagles soaring overhead and occasionally a whale surfacing while making its way home to the San Juan Islands...Not much has changed on the ferry runs over the years...same scenery...maybe a few more pleasure crafts in the water...maybe a few more patrol boats...Lately, I just take the ferry if I'm working a case. Pity. I'm missing out on one of life's simple pleasures. I glanced at my watch and it matched my prediction. Eight-forty. Time to walk to *Our Lady of Peace*. No need to re-park my car...No meters in Edmonds.

Adrianne Cooper couldn't be more helpful. She knew everyone and everything about the parish, including Clancy. She told me she started working at *Our Lady of Peace* when she turned thirty-three years old—Just about the same time Clancy appeared on the doorstep. Now, pushing fifty, she *remembers everything like it happened yesterday*. She remembered who found the lost boy—Veronica Burroughs, the cook and cleaning lady for the pastor. Unfortunately, Veronica passed away last year and would not be of much help.

She told me the pastor at the time, Father Michael Finnegan or *Father Finn*, as everyone called him, left *Our Lady of Peace*...but he could be found in a parish further north...in downtown Everett, Snohomish County. Snohomish County is just above King County. Although Edmonds is a short distance from Seattle and King County, it resides in Snohomish County. Father Finn, Ms. Cooper informed me, is the pastor of *Saint Anthony's Parish*. I wrote that down, along with the address. As I did, I remembered a connection to it...I knew that parish.

Ms. Cooper continued. "Selene Russo, who came to pick up Clancy sixteen years ago, still works at *Social Services* in Snohomish County and... she is a member of *Our Lady of Peace*."

I grinned. "That's super. Mrs. Cooper, you are an answer to my prayers."

"Call me Adrianne." She revealed a warm, cheerful smile that echoed, *"I'm here to help. That's my job."*

I nodded. "Thank you."

Adrianne tilted her head. "How is Clancy? I'd love to see him."

"He's doing great. He's a student at the *U Dub*." I reached in my purse and pulled out the photo I took. "Here's a picture of him, all grown up."

Adrianne looked at the photo a bit and smiled...and then studied it some more. . . tapping her pencil as she did so.

"He's a handsome lad, Tangie. . ."

"Yes, he is. Anything else on your mind?"

She closed her eyes as if trying to find a memory.

"I can't help thinking. . . there's something vaguely familiar about his face...like it's a face out of the past..."

My heart started to beat faster. "Do you recognize him?"

She opened her eyes. "Well, it seems to me. . . that he looks like someone—someone I used to know...or met at one time, but I can't quite recall. I meet a lot of people."

I gave Adrianne my card. "Adrianne...if you think of anything or anyone at all...give me a call. It would mean a lot to Clancy."

"Certainly, dear."

I shook her hand and smiled. Thanks. . . I'll be in touch."

As I exited the church building and walked down the manicured path to the sidewalk, I paused, turned around and studied the tall structure. I tried to picture Clancy as a little boy propped up against the door—an upsetting picture. Yet, at the same time, I unconsciously admired the elaborate stained glass windows adorning the walls of the church. *You don't see stained glass as much in churches these days, as in days of old—too expensive. But Edmonds is upscale. Nothing here is done cheap, and that includes the churches. I wonder how the stained glass windows greeted Clancy when his mother dropped him off...*

I heard that smooth, tender voice. . . *singing Holy Night*, again. Rifling through my purse I pressed *answer* just in time. Walter calling. Again. I pressed the middle button and voila—a voice of panic.

"Tangie...I've been trying to reach you. This creep, Santigo, keeps calling here—every half-hour. . . asking for you."

"Why don't you just let voicemail take it? It's my business phone. You don't have to play secretary."

"I thought it was you."

"Why would I call myself? If I wanted you, I'd call your cell."

"I guess I am just worried about you. You've got a point. Anyway, I told the dude I am your secretary."

"You did what?"

"Tangie, just listen..."

"I'm all ears."

"There are some bad dudes out there. All your clients aren't the needy, squeaky-clean college guys."

"I know that." I used my calm voice, disguising the fact that in two seconds I'd be totally freaked out. I didn't want to think about the criminals that roamed the streets of Seattle. *I roam the streets of Seattle...and I don't want to mingle with them—ever.*

"Well, Tangie...I thought...me, being your *secretary*, could also be interpreted as your bodyguard."

"Great. Now all I need is someone to scare away my clients."

"Not scare. Just keep you on equal footing with them. No one will mess with you. They'll know you have back up."

"Okay, Walter. Point well taken. Actually, I was going to ask you to help me out with Santigo."

"The creep."

"Don't let him hear you call him that."

"Sorry. I don't like the guy."

"You don't even know him."

"True. Okay, Tangie. You win...I can be the modicum of charm for you. I can play your secretary—straight, gay or in-between."

"Walter! No acting...please...just be yourself. I love you that way."

"You do?"

"Yes. You're my new best friend."

"That's it?"

"For now. Remember our agreement?"

"How can I forget? You remind me every day. Tangie...I love you."

"Ditto, Walter. You really are my best friend. I'll be home for supper. Wait a minute...Do you want to take Pebbles and me for a ferry ride? We can walk on at Seattle near *Pike Place* and eat dinner on Bainbridge Island. There's a winery near the ferry dock there...I think it's called something original...like the *Bainbridge Winery*...and there's a restaurant attached."

"It's a date!"

"Walter...calm down. It's dinner. I'm not ready for our *hot* date yet."

"How about a first date?"

"We did that already...Remember the roses...the wine...our first days and nights together?"

"How can I forget...I think of our love affair everyday."

"How about a friendly, second date. *Semi-platonic*...one or two kisses goodnight date?"

"I suppose I could handle that," Walter said, compromising with me. I could swear I heard him panting on the other end of the phone.

"See you around five or six...okay?"

"It's a date. Pebbles and I will be waiting with our tongues hanging out. Drive safely—obey the speed limits."

"Don't I always?" I thought of the image of his tongue hanging out and sighed. *Walter—Why do I sense there's more to him than he is willing to tell me? And why does he invigorate me? Could it be his...pizzazz—his joie de vivre? Could be...and why is he is settling in like a comfortable shoe? Yes, he's acting like a regular gumshoe, all right. I know I'm single...and not accustomed to co-habitation...and I don't remember everything about my parents' marriage... But...that's exactly what it feels like—comfortable...good...I'm thinking maybe too good. Weird. Walter didn't even ask me where I'm headed. He seems to know my business without me telling him. Maybe I talk in my sleep. No. The fact is there—staring me in the face—There's more to Walter Cunningham than meets the eye. But, hold on...I'm a private eye, and for sure, I'm gonna find out. Walter has secrets—but, not for long. I'm on to him.*

I tucked my cell phone in my purse, breathed in the fresh air and smiled...humming to myself...*The day is young and traffic is light...for a change*...I jogged to my *Tweetie Bird*, hopped in and cruised up to the freeway, deciding to head north to *Saint Anthony's* in Everett and visit Father Michael Finnegan—*Father Finn*.

I recalled that *Saint Anthony's Church* is famous for it's annual *Sausage Festival*...Don used to drag me up there every year—when we were together—to support their school fund. He attended *Saint Anthony's Catholic Grammar School* and assured me that Catholic schools have the best fundraisers—At his insistence, we frequented a lot of charity functions. An easy mark for good causes, Don never refused an opportunity to help—either with his hands or his wallet—A benevolent soul…one of the things I loved about him…and still do.

*Weird…*I didn't see that his interest in fundraisers extended beyond his involvement in charity...He felt the call to the priesthood long before he realized it himself. He didn't see it. I didn't see it. *It's true—Love is blind. I know that now. Sometimes you only see what you want to see—That always invites trouble. Most of the time I cause my own angst.*

I breezed through South Everett, even with the road repairs...got off on Broadway, turned onto Everett Avenue, turned once more and parked in front of the historic church.

Saint Anthony's Church always struck me as quaint. Constructed of brownstone with an inviting cobblestone path, it reminded me of small village churches in merry ol' England, that I visited during my college trip to the British Isles. As I ambled down the meandering path to the entrance, boxwood shrubs surrounded me, greeting me with their lasting presence. I marveled at the manicured lawn—lush green...unusual for the end of winter. Not a brown blade in sight. No dead leaves or branches lying on the walkway, as in my neck of the woods. A meticulous gardener loves his labor. I moved around the curved path, towards the front of the church, and felt an urge to hop up the steps like I did as a young girl…but resisted the urge…I steadied my gait and walked respectfully up to the landing and pulled on the heavy wooden double doors leading into the church. Neither door budged. Locked. *Gee, I could remember when churches remained open twenty-four/seven.* I shrugged my shoulders, turned to head back down and plowed into a stately gentleman, almost knocking him off his feet. As my mouth opened to apologize, I noticed his tan fisherman's sweater, blue Dockers and Nike running shoes. His crop of white hair caught my attention and his presence reminded me of a *Cary Grant* picture my mom has hanging in Bryan's bedroom, along with her other movie memorabilia.

I pleaded in embarrassment. "I beg your pardon, sir. I didn't see you."

After the gentleman steadied himself, he relaxed his grip on the top of the handrail, ignored my feeble attempts at an act of contrition and smiled at me. "Were you wanting into the church, miss?"

"Well, actually, I'm looking for the pastor."

"Oh, there's been a death in the family?"

"Oh, no. Nothing like that."

"Would you be wanting to hear confession, then?"

"No, I'm just looking for Father Michael Finnegan."

"Oh...Then perhaps I could help you."

"Do you know him?"

"Very well, indeed." he grinned, playing with my embarrassment. "As much as I know myself. But the pastor goes by *Father Finn*."

"So, I've been told. In that case, perhaps you could tell me where I could find *Father Finn*. My name is Angelina Seraphina and I would like to speak with him."

"Ah, *the fiery angel*."

"That's me."

"And this is about—?"

"Well, it's sort of private."

"Ah, then I will just have to introduce myself."

"*Father Finn?*"

"That's me."

"Oh, my goodness...Without your collar on, I didn't recognize you as the priest."

"Yes, well, when I'm out for my daily constitutional, I wear civvies."

Ill at ease, I started to stutter..."I...I...I..."

"Would you like to come sit in my office? I'll have my secretary brew us up a pot of good Irish tea. You can warm up and we could chat."

"That would be w...wonderful. Thank you, Father Finn." *Thank God, I found my voice.*

So I sat in Father *Cary Grant's* office and grilled him on Clancy.

"Father Michael...er...Father Finn...You used to be pastor at *Our Lady of Peace?*"

"Ah, 'tis a long time ago...and my service lasted a mere two years... The former pastor took a missionary post and I replaced him for a wee bit."

"Do you remember Clancy?"

"Clancy?"

"The little boy left on the doorstep…at *Our Lady of Peace Church.*"

"Oh...Clancy...Why yes…I could not forget Clancy…poor lad..."

I saw the wheels spinning...

Father Finn continued, "What a pity...We tried to do the best we could for the wee lad."

"I understand…you did…but could you tell me what happened… after you found him?"

"Well, after we gave the little one a cup of cream and some biscuits... the housekeeper—Veronica—she was besides herself with tears…I think she wanted to take the poor lad home with her…But my heavens… The poor woman was getting up there in years…She couldn't care for a wee one…No doubt the whole situation broke her generous heart, but I called Selene Russo...I knew her to be a social worker...as well as an active parishioner…during my stay at *Our Lady of Peace...*"

"She still is..."

"That's commendable. Well, Selene found Clancy a suitable home. We never located his birth parents, you know. God knows we tried. Clancy stayed in foster care until Selene discovered acceptable adoptive parents, through the *Catholic Community Services*—The Hendricksens, I believe. They applied to be the adoptive parents and seemed to be the best fit for the child. They wanted to have a child of their own for years… but the Good Lord never granted them one…until Clancy…They passed heavy scrutiny…for sure...I suppose Clancy's life is stable now."

"Yes."

"Do you know Clancy?"

"Yes, I do, Father…but not very well…I just met him. He's my client. He's asked me to help him locate his birth parents, specifically, his mother."

"Well, I hope Saint Anthony is gracious to you. He's the saint who helps you find what you are looking for…people, belongings, anything that seems to be a lost cause…You could try praying to St. Jude, also."

"I will take all the help I can get," I grinned.

"Well, Angelina, at the time…when the lad lost his mother, we searched for his family…but nothing we did seemed to help…no one turned up...We sent out flyers, put a story on the television news...and in all the newspapers from Seattle to Bellingham...Not a smidgen of luck."

"Father Finn, if I show you this picture...Do you think it would help you remember anything? It's Clancy as he looks today. He's twenty and a student at the *University of Washington*."

Father Finn glanced at the photo I handed him and then, like Sherlock Holmes with his trademark magnifying glass, he put on a pair of reading glasses and scrutinized the person staring at him.

"Red hair, hum...Looks like an Irishman...and there's something vaguely familiar about the face...about the older Clancy...not the little boy. I cannot put my finger on it...Do you mind if I photocopy this?"

"No, not at all," I said.

"Maybe something will trigger my memory...It's not as sharp as it used to be."

"Do you remember Adrianne Cooper?"

"Of course I do. I hired her."

"Well, Adrianne's still the secretary at *Our Lady of Peace*...and she said the exact same thing about the picture...That this photo of Clancy reminded her of someone but she can't say who."

"'Tis a bit of a mystery, wouldn't you say, Angelina?"

"A wee bit, I'd say, Father Finn."

I left Father Michael Finnegan after thanking him for the tea, which I found to be delicious. The Irish know how to make tea. Plus the crumpets his secretary served along with the strong Irish brew would keep me going a little longer. "I'll be back for the *Sausage Festival*," I promised. *I owe him, big time.*

Checking the sun, then my watch—both signaling noon—an easy time on the highway—I headed south on the freeway. Smooth sailing on

I-5—*just enough time to get to the airport before rush hour. I could do this. I love to multi-task. For my sense of duty, I have to complete at least one task for Santigo before the day is done, so I can give him a report. Plus, I can deliberate Clancy's case on the way to Alaskan Airlines.*

Clancy resembles his father, or a male relative who is in some way connected to Our Lady of Peace. What way…is up to me to find out. I am sure that both Adrianne and Father Finn knew or met this person—sixteen or seventeen years ago...maybe someone just passing through…or someone directly involved in the parish. But who could that be? I guess I'll need to be patient—not one of my strong points—and wait for their memories to jar loose.

Listening to my favorite jazz station—I cruised south…thinking, *absolutely a ten-star travel day. No traffic. Clear skies. All the mountains are out.* I could see the North Cascades Mountain Range when I was heading north to Everett. Now that I'm traveling south, I looked east and my eyes feasted on Mount Rainier, the crown jewel of the Cascades—I didn't miss *The Mountain* after all! And…to complete the perfect picture—when I glanced west, I could see the entire Olympic Mountain Range coming out to greet me. Enthralled, I opened the sunroof on my *Ford Escape Hybrid* to breathe in the fresh air...*Ah...Doesn't get any better than this.*

Mount Rainier, first named Mount Tahoma by Native Americans, looks like a giant ice cream cone against a sea of blue when there are no clouds…*Today is one of those days…Even though the Pacific Northwest is my only home…and has been for twenty-seven years, I'm always a kid again…when I catch Mount Rainier gazing at me. I change the radio station to 98.1—King FM. The Mountain deserves Classical Music. Vivaldi. Four Seasons. Fitting. Life is good. Heading south, I'll be against the traffic that would form coming out of the city.* I smiled, gunned my *Tweedy Bird* and flew to the airport... not slowing down until I came within spitting distance of the parking garage.

Chapter Nine

Arriving at *Sea-Tac Airport*, I grabbed my ticket at the entrance to the parking garage, accelerated up the circular ramp and snatched one of the few remaining spots...on the roof. *Oh well. Can't have everything.* I tramped over to the elevator so I could descend to the sky bridge and get across to the terminal and head to the counter at *Alaska Airlines*. When I got in the elevator, it was empty, but just after I pushed the button to descend...two families with six small children between them rushed in, followed by a rather strange-looking couple. These two travelers ambled into the confined space, nearly crushing me with their carts and suitcases. As a *Good Samaritan*, I held the door open for the last of the lot. I winced as the disheveled older man wearing oversized leather gloves while pushing his walker, practically ran into me as he scooted into the elevator. He stared at me with dark, piercing eyes as if to say, "about time." His female companion slammed into my body with her elbow. Apparently my act of kindness went unnoticed and I started gasping for air.

Next, claustrophobia settled into my being—*Trapped—Now I remember why I hate elevators. Rapid breathing consumes my body—Anxiety captures me as the elevator stops at every floor on the way down. Rats. I'll never survive. I inhale and exhale slowly, remembering my decompression exercises and try to calm myself down. Well at least these travelers aren't psychotic. Don't know about the kids though.* One of the little boys kept sticking his tongue at me. I smiled at him...but lost my footing and accidently stepped on his toe when the elevator stopped suddenly halfway to the second floor. The little boy started wailing at the top of his lungs, despite my profuse apology. No way did he believe it was an accident. *Add migraine to the list of elevator side effects.*

When the elevator finally reached the second floor, where travelers could use the sky bridge to their get to their airlines, the two families scrambled off, with one of the mothers sighing loudly and dragging the screamer by the hand, as the other pushed a baby stroller, complaining about the bumpy ride to her husband.

Next to exit...the pair of unfriendly weirdos. The older skinny guy wore a frayed Greek fisherman's cap that shaded his face—and as he pushed his walker and stepped gingerly—like he walked on hot coals, he revealed a hunchback. I shuddered as he walked by, brushing up against my hand as he did so. *Not a good sign.* I started to sweat. *Probably beats his wife in private. Not a nice man.* The woman seemed very energetic... She pushed the cart full of luggage— and carried a cane, which seemed out of place for her...*Maybe it's her companion's*...I noticed she wore a wig and I could smell strong, expensive perfume. Her cheap wig...obvious... to anyone...and her thick, wire-rimmed glasses did nothing to enhance her appearance, although her figure seemed fit and trim...*Weird—nothing seemed right about these two.* The woman grunted at me as they left the elevator...*I guess I would grunt if I were pushing that airport cart of luggage. Heavy stuff.* I noticed neither one of them wore Velcro shoes, but rather stylish designer leather boots...my eyes followed them as they departed and disappeared out of my sight.

I exhaled—finding myself left alone in the corner of the elevator like a smashed bug. I pried myself off the wall and raced through the automatic elevator door before it pinched me as it closed...but I was too late. It captured my pinkie finger—practically crushing it, before reopening and releasing its grasp upon me. I wailed like the little boy, whose toe I stepped on, and shook my hand, trying to make the pain go away. Travelers with rolling suitcases rushed by, walking around me, staring at me like I impeded their progress. *God, I hate airports—So impersonal—Tons of people. Not much social interaction... Positive, that is.*

After crossing over the sky bridge, and entering the main terminal, I decided to get a latte to revive my sinking spirits. I spotted the *Alaska Airlines* ticket counter and a sign for *Starbucks* at the same time. *Starbucks* won. *Alaska* could wait...*plus something drew me to Starbucks...just a feeling—and not the pain in my hand...something more than a hunch...*

I ordered a double-tall hazelnut with whipped cream and a cup of ice for my finger. I asked the barista, "Get many folks in here from *Alaska Airlines?*"

"Yeah, all the time. Most of our customers fly *Alaska*. I like it when the pilots come in. They're good tippers."

I handed her an extra five. "Hey, if I show you a picture, do you think you would remember the person?"

"Probably not."

"Humor me."

The young woman took the bill. "Hell, why not? Never busy this time of day anyway. It's the afternoon lull."

I scrambled through my purse, grabbed *Terese* out of the envelope I kept in a side pocket, and handed the picture to the barista. The barista in exchange handed me my hazelnut, along with a cup of ice. I sighed as I took a sip to revive me and placed my injured pinkie in the cup of ice.

Kim –as I noticed on her nametag—replied, "Oh, this one."

"Do you know her?"

"I remember her...I actually remember this one—Really big tipper."

"You do? Great! She's a friend of mine and I missed meeting her here...three weeks ago. I think we got our signals crossed. Our friendship goes way back, but we haven't seen each other since we moved to different towns."

"When I saw her, she looked like she needed a friend."

"Now I feel really bad...What did she do? Did she say anything to you?"

"Not much. Just ordered a tall skinny mocha and sat down at that table over there."

Kim pointed to a table with a peak-a-boo view of the Olympic Mountains.

"She sat there for quite a while, the whole time, glancing around her...as if waiting for someone to appear." She gave me the biggest tip I received since I started working here. That's why I remember all this stuff. Anyway...after about forty-five minutes, I went over and asked if she wanted a refill...on the house. She just said, *No, thank you...you've been very kind*...real classy-like. Then she looked at me with those sad eyes. One of them looked a little bruised...like she had just fallen or..."

"Hey Kim...Did she say anything else?"

"No. She just sat there for about twenty more minutes looking out the window. Then she took her stuff and headed to the ladies' room."

"Did you see her come out?"

"I did. She tried to hide her identity, but I recognized her fancy walk...like a model's...and the fancy luggage...and the bruise. But you know the most interesting thing? She went in the ladies' room with black hair and came out a blond."

My eyes widened and my throat became parched as I got the words out, "What about the walk?"

"Well, she was trying to do the fancy model walk, but she was limping at the same time...like she had a sprained ankle or knee or something. I felt sorry for her."

"Me too. Say, here's my phone number. If you can think of anything else, call me. I gave Kim another five and asked her, "Hey Kim, could you do me a favor? If anyone else asks about her, don't say anything...Call me first. Those bruises may not be from an accident."

"Don't worry. I get the picture...I've been there myself." I noticed her closing her eyes for a moment and taking a deep breath.

"Thanks, Kim. I appreciate your help. More than you know."

She resumed normal breathing...back to business mode. "No problemo. Hope you find your friend." She smiled at me. I noticed a piercing in her tongue as she thanked me. "Best tip I've had all week..."

The afternoon lull ended and customers began filling the café. I picked up my latte, dropped my ice cup in the trash, as my pinkie stopped throbbing, and wandered around the coffee shop...checking out the cookies, the teddy bears and souvenir mugs. I sequestered myself at the table that Terese camped at three weeks ago, hoping to get some sense of what she feared so much...I started musing...*Okay...Santigo may be beating on his wife. But why wouldn't she go to Alaska? She'd get away from him. Maybe he sent someone to go with her. He could have some goon working for him. Maybe she caught on and snuck off just in time...Maybe there is something else that I'm missing here...* I looked out into the corridor and watched the people walking to their destinations...hoping for a clue to pop in my head. . . I closed my eyes and visualized. . . a plane ascending and disappearing into a cloud formation...just as Terese vanished...out of sight. Like that plane in my imagination, she's out there somewhere. . . I just can't see her. *"Terese,"* I pleaded in silence, *"Where are you?"*

No one would help me at *Alaska Airlines. "You're not a relative of Terese Santigo, therefore we are unable to divulge any information. . ."* –The pat phrase. Heck, I thought, worth a try. I turned around, walked away from the information desk and spotted a lone porter pushing an empty cart. . . on his way back to the outside check-in area. *Porters are like secretaries—They know everything.* I followed him out the automatic doors onto the sidewalk area near the drop off point for cars. He appeared to be older than my mother by about ten years, neatly dressed, with a kind face. Also a speedy porter—I ran like a jackrabbit to catch up with him and I had no cart to push. He sensed me on his trail, because he whirled around and faced me. "Any luggage to check, Miss?"

"Uh, no," I mumbled...Then my brain ignited. I squeezed a ten-dollar bill out of my purse and pleaded in my best forlorn voice, "I can give you a tip for your time, if you'd just look at this picture. It's my sister and I can't find her."

"She doesn't look anything like you."

"I'm adopted."

"Well, I can help you out a little."

I gave him another ten. He began his recollection.

"This pretty *sister* of yours comes over to me with this large gentleman...but he's no kind of a gentleman, if you ask me. He keeps glarin' at her, like he's mad at her or somethin'. She has these two bags with her an' jus' wants to check in one. . . an' keep the other one on the plane. So the big dude gets all huffy like. . . you know what I mean?"

I nodded and he continued.

"Well, then he starts gettin' in her face, like up close. . . real mean-like."

"Yes, I can imagine...Go on..."

"Well, Miss, the young lady—your *sister*—jus' keeps holdin' onto the carry-on and will not let go. Weird. This king-size *mother*...well... you know what I mean...this bully...an' this skinny little thing seem all wrong together..."

"That's an understatement..."

"Well, Miss, I think she embarrassed him...she gave me a really big gratuity and said, *Thanks, Sir.* You know, I don't get called *Sir* much anymore. Anyway, she's a looker, your sister...like a movie star. Maybe that chunky honky's her bodyguard. Those bodyguards talk rough sometimes and don't mean it."

"Oh, I think he meant it—And he's no bodyguard—My sister doesn't have one. Does he have a name? Did my sister call him anything?"

"I heard her say somethin' to him...*Stop it Horse!* No...come to think of it, it was more like, *Stop it Horst!* That's it...It just sounded like Horse. That's why I remember it."

"Did you see her later?"

"Yes, indeed, as a matter of fact. Yeah...I saw her racing out of *Alaska Airlines*, like she was going to the *Kentucky Derby* or something...This was...um...right before the plane took off...I saw her headin' down that hallway." The porter pointed in the direction of *Starbucks*.

"Did she notice you? Did she say anything?"

"Just, *Thank you, Sir*, and handed me another fifty. This second time, I noticed a bruise on her face and a bit of limpin' on her part...and she wore a blond wig...probably so that dude wouldn't find her...Poor kid. I thought about asking her if she needed any help, but she waved me off and disappeared down the corridor...into the crowd. That's it."

"Thank you, uh..." I glanced at his identification badge. "Mr. Benson...Thanks so much for your help...and could I please ask one more favor?"

"Sure, Miss."

"Could you please keep this conversation between you and me?"

I parted with another twenty...*not as rich as Terese.* "My sister is in peril...this Horst guy must be the menace...the menace...she told me threatened her...uh...last year."

"Yes, Ma'am," James Benson agreed, and pocketed my last twenty.

I shook his hand and looked into his deep chocolate eyes below his thick dark eyebrows, sprinkled with silver. *I saw kindness and caring—Also...bedroom eyes. In his day, Benson entertained a huge following of ladies... A natural charmer...but I also know he's the kind of man that remains true to the love of his life—his wife—This is a guy who understands honor. He'll keep his word.*

I sat down in front of a deli stand and took a deep breath...letting the air out slowly...I closed my eyes and relaxed...freeing my mind to wander. *Terese never left the Seattle area...she never went to Alaska. She didn't disappear into the sky on that plane...she hopped on an airporter or a metro bus for parts unknown. Smart girl.*

Tomorrow, I'll present Terese's photo to Walter. He will know what to do next...I'm sure...and I bet a dinner on the town that Walter...or someone he knows...can doctor up Terese's picture...using computer graphics...and make her a blond. Walter's a computer geek...he knows a lot about that stuff. Then, I'll contact all the buses and airporters that leave Sea-Tac and see what their destinations are...Maybe even check the cab companies. Someone should remember her...I might have to come back to Sea-Tac. Ugh...Not a pleasant thought. Another not so pleasant thought. Have to contact Santigo. Will do that at home. Don't want him getting my cell phone on his Caller ID—he'd be bugging me all the time...

Okay...When I get home...gotta call Santigo...Only then can Walter and I relax...take that ferry to Bainbridge Island for a nice romantic dinner...Just the two of us. Hum...and what about Pebbles? Not to worry...I can find a sitter for him. Funny how things work out sometime...Anyway I just want to forget life's woes for one night.

Starvation took over my body. I got up and perused the deli...deciding to grab a B.L.T. from the case...I'd have to drink the bottle of water I kept in my car—no more spare change. I gave the girl at the counter my last ten-dollar bill and told her to keep the change. I took the bacon out of the sandwich, wrapped it in a napkin, and put it in my pocket. *Pebbles will be glad to see me...most definitely.* I smiled and chomped on the lettuce and tomato sandwich. *Who needs meat? I need to lose five pounds anyway.*

Chapter Ten

I don't know who won the prize for happiest to see me...Pebbles or Walter. Pebbles 'cause he smelled the bacon and started licking me to death...Walter because he took me in his arms and kissed me gently on the lips...reminding me of what awaits in our future...*Yum. Thoughts of passion and lust swirl around in my head...*until I am dizzy...and Pebbles interrupts our interlude, first by barking like an insane coyote and then by nearly choking to death on his bacon.

Walter picks my pooch up and shakes his little body, dislodging the bacon, which Pebbles promptly attacks as soon as he is placed back on the floor...and he chews it again, but more slowly this time. My body starts shaking with laughter...all warm and fuzzy inside...and the afternoon at the airport becomes a distant memory.

Walter took me into his arms again and I melted, almost giving into my need for reckless abandonment. Then I remembered our agreement.

"Walter...You are supposed to wait until tonight...after our second date...for our good night kiss."

"I know, but I couldn't help myself. You look delicious. And you smell like bacon...Angelina...I've missed you—you've been on the road a long time...my radar surfaced and I got in worry mode."

"How much trouble could I get in between two churches and an airport?"

"You'd be surprised."

"Did Santigo call again?"

"Not after I told him you'd call him back before five p.m."

"Yikes...It's ten to five. I've got ten minutes. I'll make this a short call. Then we can catch the next ferry."

"Hey, Tangie...Guess what? Jean offered to watch Pebbles. She's home tonight and she misses her favorite pooch."

"How convenient...a dog sitter...Gotta hand it to you, Walter...You work wonders." I smiled and twirled off my scarf.

"I try..."

"I'll go call Santigo—*the creep*—and freshen up. I'll be speedy...I promise."

"I'll be waiting."

Walter gave me his special endearing grin that turns my will power to mush. Then he plopped himself down on our new couch, burying his head in *The Seattle Times*, with Pebbles at his feet. *Walter's cover—He'll be all ears to my conversation with Santigo. I know these things.*

I went into my office and left the door ajar, deciding not to have secrets from Walter. *He seems to be finding stuff out anyway about Santigo, so I'll keep him posted. Save him the trouble. Gotta trust somebody, sometime.* I went to my office closet and took out the red dress that I bought for New Year's Eve—two years ago...hoping for a hot date...but never had an opportunity to wear it. I would squeeze into it tonight. *So what if it rides up to my...*

Tonight I am the "fiery angel", as Father Finn would say. Little does the Irish priest know...well, maybe he does...he listens to a lot of confessions...the padre's on to me. I smile. Tonight will be special.

I disrobed and tossed my work duds onto my closet floor, next to the overflowing hamper, while pushing the buttons to get Santigo's business office.

"*Numero Uno Bath Boutique*," a woman's voice answered with more than a hint of a German accent.

"Gutig abend. This is Angelina Seraphina. Is Fred Santigo in? I'm returning his call."

"Yes. Von moment please, if you don't mind vaiting."

Fred's secretary decided to put me on hold for ten minutes. *Fine way to treat me after I attempt to use my German. So my accent lacks finesse. It's been ten years. Maybe the secretary's just adhering to orders...I'm sure Santigo is miffed with me. Payback. That's how he operates. That's okay—I have time to get dressed. I store all my dress-up clothes in my office. Convenient. Like I said before, I like to multi-task.* I sucked in my stomach and donned my silk sheath, then slipped into my red satin sling back pumps.

As I twirl around enjoying myself—playing dress-up...Tonight I will be the "Lady in Red"...My dangling pearl earrings with matching pearl and ruby necklace grab a hold of me—beckoning me to put them on. I shake my head up and down—Why not do the glamour thing? Yes. This time, I'll go all out—The finishing touch on the seduction theme. Guys love pearls. I apply my makeup in front of the mirror hanging behind my door and put my strawberry blond hair up in a French twist, with a pearl and diamond fastener—well, fake diamond, but it looks good. Actually, tonight my hair looks a little tangerine. My name is taking over my body!

I finished my ritual of getting ready for my special date...and...to stop the butterflies in my stomach, I occupied myself by opening the bills mounting on my desk. I started by throwing the used envelopes in the trash. A recent business letter caught my eye...I.R.S. glaring at me through a cellophane window...*Uh oh...Panic demands I open it*...just as Santigo's voice trumpeted on the line, his voice all sugary and slimy at the same time.

"Angelina, so good to hear from you."

"Yes, Fred...Thanks for picking up. My secretary told me you called."

"Your secretary is not helpful..."

"Well, he works cheap."

I heard Walter snickering in the living room. I smiled. I could picture his face as he glued himself to the conversation...

"Angelina..." Santigo sighed, continuing his inquisition. I could hear him tapping his pencil on his desk. "I am expecting a progress report. What have you discovered?"

"Not as much as I would like." *Liar, liar pants on fire.* "I went to the airport today." *True...no lie told here.*

"*Alaska Airlines* would not tell me anything as I am not a relative." *Also true.* "Perhaps you could call them."

"I did. I also went in person. That led me nowhere. I thought you... with your charm...you'd have more luck."

Now look who's lying.

"Well, charm doesn't work on those guys." I twirled my hair and got out my lipstick. "I think maybe flying up to Alaska to see Terese's sister might help. Do you have her address and telephone number?"

Santigo began to clip his words...Not a happy camper. "I can get her address for you. She has no phone. I already told you that."

"Well...I thought if I spoke to Terese's sister...sort of woman to woman, she'd open up...perhaps give me some clues...or a starting point. I think it's worth a try."

"I suppose you'll want me to foot the bill?"

"For me and my secretary."

"For you, *yes*. Your worthless secretary, *no*."

Okay, it was worth a try, wasn't it?

"That would be fine, Mr. Santigo."

"Angelina..."

"Yes, Mr. Santigo?"

"Remember, call me *Fred*."

"Gotcha."

"I'm counting on you to turn something up."

"I'm on it. I'll be in touch."

I hung up the phone and frowned. *Santigo is a downer. Don't know why I took his case. Must be Terese's eyes. Calling out to me—"Help me, please..."*

The eyes have it—But I'll think about this case tomorrow. I unscrewed my lipstick, looked in the mirror over my side bookcase and finished applying my makeup. *Tonight is for lovers.* I sucked in my stomach for the last time and smoothed out my skin-tight dress, dabbed my favorite French perfume behind my ears...picked up my beaded evening bag, pushed the shut-off button on my *MacBook*, grabbed my red and black silk scarf, draped and waiting for me on the desk chair, and like a maiden in Greek mythology, sailed out the door to my waiting *Adonis*.

Chapter Eleven

Ah...Nothing is better than a moonlight ride in a boat—even if it's on a ferry. Once we arrived at the south end of the waterfront in downtown Seattle, Walter and I found a parking spot heading up a hill, but near the terminal. We took a short jog—*not an easy thing for me in my satin pumps*—and embarked on the *Chinook* leaving for Bainbridge. We strolled around the vessel—Going from deck to deck, going inside and outside to the viewing area...Watching the lights of Seattle fade in the moonlight—like we both did when we were teenagers—before we became working stiffs. Walter told me he used to take his favorite dates ferry hopping—like Don and me—but he assured me that this date happened to be his very favorite because I'm with him.

Walter is turning out to be a smoothie. Not that I'm complaining. I kind of like it—even if Walter has ulterior motives. Maybe I do too. I'm tired of being a one-some. Yes, I do have Pebbles...but a dog is a dog...and Walter...Well, Walter has potential. I like that about him. He cleans up good—like tonight. He looks so cool in his black jeans, blue shirt, leather vest and hiking boots. Eddie Bauer meets Microsoft...An outdoorsy-computer geek. I know I am falling for him... especially when he leads me off the ferry at Bainbridge Island—arm around my waist, like I am his girl...and when he smiles directly into my eyes when I say, "Let's walk to the winery...it's just down the road...a couple of blocks." He pays attention to me. I like that.

The Bainbridge Winery invited us in with its charm—beckoning us with soft lights and soothing landscaping. Intimate. The owner, Sal Palante, greeted us the moment we opened the door and showered us with samples of every wine on the shelf. Tuesday night—We had the place to ourselves. We tasted all the wines—red, white, dry, sweet. When my feet started to slide and my heels turned sideways, Walter took my arm and led me to the nearby dining room, deserted except for one party of two white-haired couples enjoying a late dinner in the corner. Walter pulled out a chair for me at a table by the window and I fell into the seat like *Betty Boop*. "Oops," I said. "Better eat some food!"

One of the white-haired gentlemen at the corner gave me a wink and I smiled at him. No one in his party laughed or raised their eyebrows at me. *Who knows, maybe they remember themselves thirty years ago. Maybe Walter and I will be sitting at that corner table, years from now, checking out the young folks. Seems like time goes by so fast. Like the last seven years...I just sort of fretted them away. Not gonna do that anymore. And I don't have to...I've got Walter. I've got my man. No more lonesome nights...No more pouring my heart out to Pebbles...No more...*

We sampled the char-grilled halibut with a delicious crispy soft Parmesan topping, string beans with slivered almonds and pine nuts... and the most delicious salad I've ever sunk my chops into—Cilantro shrimp with lime juice, baby bud lettuce and paper-thin homemade tortilla chips. I ate my salad and half of Walter's—*Ravenous—that's me. Walter has that effect on me. Or maybe it's the wine. The way the evening is going, I'll be lucky to keep my dress on till we get home.* My desire matched my appetite...Call me, *Psyched on Romance.*

Walter sat across the table from me, studying me, sipping his espresso. "Dessert?"

"Maybe later...At home."

"I like the way you say that."

"I'm sorry I ate your salad."

Walter took my hand and put it to his lips. "You can eat my salad anytime."

"You're very generous, Walter."

"I am, Angelina...with certain people—People...I care about..."

"That's one of the reasons I..."

Suddenly I could not hold my head up. It kept flopping down.

"Angelina...Are you all right?" Walter got up and came over to me, putting his arm around my shoulder and feeling my face.

"The room is spinning..."

"Too much wine."

"Too much shrimp..."

"No, I think the wine..."

"I love the wine...I love the shrimp...I love..."

"Me?"

"Yes...You too. Walter, I think I'm gonna have trouble walking home."

"It's okay, Angelina...Put your arm around my neck. We'll walk out like lovers."

I did. We did. Walter paid the bill and then, I don't remember much. I remember our ferry ride home...Walter sat me on the benches on the outer deck, trying to sober me up. Did not work. I do remember looking at the stars. Don't remember the car ride home. I slept through that...I do recall Walter lying me on my bed and kissing me goodnight... Then the sweet darkness as he shut the door softly...so as not to disturb me.

Too tired to feel guilty, I dwelt on being grateful. I lay on the bed unable to move...arranged there, like a dressed-up doll, in my semi-passed-out state—alone...*Poor Walter...Poor me—All my hormones foiled by the evils of alcohol. Maybe I should join A.A.—Don't wanna mess up my next chance for a really good....*

I made a vow. "I promise, Walter...next time...I'll stay sober—only one glass of wine." This being my last thought before I sunk into the welcoming Land of Nod. *But ah...what delightful visions...Walter and me...and me and Walter...and...well, a girl can dream, can't she?*

Chapter Twelve

"Ring, ring, ring..." Somewhere in the recesses of my mind a phone is singing, loudly, like an off-key soprano. I cannot raise my head from the pillow. "Walter," I whisper, "Can you get that? My head is spinning." No Walter... no Pebbles...just me—and my splitting headache. Rats. Okay...I think I can function...until I sit up. Then the room starts spinning again. Uh oh...I'm gonna be sick...

After I shower and doctor myself—with two extra-strength aspirin and a double-shot espresso, I feel almost alive. I go into my office, put my latte mug on a coaster in the corner of my desk and listen to my messages. The voices coming at me sound like jackals barking. I skip over Santigo...more of the same Blah...Blah... Blah there. *The last message catches my attention—I know that voice—The secretary at Our Lady of Peace...Uh, have to look up her name...my brain is not working...can't think...Can't drink...anymore. Period. Anyway, she wants me to stop by and chat about Clancy. She has an idea. Well at least somebody does this morning. I give up and concentrate on sipping my Grande espresso as the phone deafens me with its howling. "Please...not Santigo. Can't take him this early."*

I looked at the clock next to my computer. Eleven-thirty. Almost noon. No wonder Walter skipped out—Romping around at the park, with Pebbles, no doubt. I stood up and went to the front picture window and glanced outside. I did a double take and opened my eyes, wide. Snow! Snowing in Seattle! Two times in one year! A record. Where'd this white blanket come from? Last night the stars shone in all their brilliance. The night air caressed us with its warmth...Well maybe that was the wine...Maybe I was just seeing stars...

The phone started growling again. This time I picked it up. "Hello, Mother." I answered with a sweet tone...grateful for her voice not being that of Santigo. Before caller ID, I always knew the person on the line... before the phone rang...still do.

"Tangerine. Thank goodness you're home. I was afraid you'd be out driving in this weather."

"Mom, it's just a little snow. It's beautiful. Plus, I've got four-wheel drive."

"So do I. A lot of good it does me. My hill is closed. Blocked off. At least the neighborhood kids can have fun sledding."

Walter, the crumb...went sledding without me; I'm sure of it. He's such a kid.

"Hey Mom, can I ask you a question?"

"Of course, dear...Go for it..."

Sometimes my mom likes to sound like a teenager...Maybe she's practicing her dialogue for a new story—She really gets into her writing.

"If I went to Alaska, do you think you could watch Pebbles for a few days? I might need to take Walter with me..."

"Walter?"

"Yes, Mom...Walter's my new secretary."

"Hum...Of course, dear...Yes...I'll watch Pebbles—I love him as much as you do, you know that. But why go to Alaska in such bad weather? Why not wait until summer...or at least spring? You could take a cruise."

"Love to, Mom...but this is business."

"Oh well, go...if you must...but promise me you'll wait until the snow stops. I'm sure the airport is closed."

"Oh, I'm not flying out right away...I need to get a few things settled here first."

"Good...Later is better than sooner. Say, Angelina, could you please help me pick out an outfit—When the weather clears? I'm having my picture taken."

"Oh, one of those glamour photos?"

"No silly—The parish directory. Come to think of it, *Glamour Shots* would not be such a bad idea...Charles would..."

"Sure, Mom. I'll be in touch before I leave for Alaska. I'll call you tonight..."

"You'll come over when the snow's plowed?"

"I promise—But you know, Mom, they never plow the snow. They just wait for it to melt. Just let me know when they open your road and I'll be there."

"You're such a good daughter."

"I know." I smiled...picturing Marianna in the purple satin dress that I will pick out for her. Charles may have a heart attack. I'd better be careful.

After my mother disconnected, I traded my robe for snow clothes—long underwear, wool pants, turtleneck shirt and fleece vest. Just as I put on my black suede boots and got ready to hunt for Walter and Pebbles, the idea hit me over the head like a lead paperweight...*"Parish directory! That's it! Clancy's uncle...Uncle Joe...I bet he's in the parish directory!"*

My hand began to shake—as I searched for my cell—either from excitement or D.T.'s from drinking. *Glad I'm sober now...I'm thinking clearer...*I recovered my lifeline, punched the number for *Our Lady of Peace* and asked for Adrianne Cooper. *Yes! I remember her name! My head may be throbbing but my mind is back.*

Adrianne answered on the first ring and informed me she could squeeze me in this afternoon...She could use the company...

She said, "Things are slow around here due to the snow...plus, Selene Russo may be dropping by today...Remember me mentioning her? She's the social worker who helped Clancy."

I hit the jackpot. I blocked out how miserable driving anywhere around Seattle in a snowstorm can be...and...that I'd be heading north... right into the convergent zone—and more snow. I jumped up and did a little tap dance around my desk and into the hallway—Nothing could stop me.

Adrianne interrupted my jazz number. "Ms. Seraphina...Tangie...you don't mind coming up here in a blizzard, do you?"

"Heck no, I've got four-wheel drive."

I put my phone down, just as Walter entered the front door and shook the snow off his jacket. Next to him, under his arm, a bundle of white—*Pebbles*. I couldn't tell where the snow ended and the fur began. My pooch wore his fleece doggie jacket but even that blended into the whiteout.

"You two look like the abominable snowman and his dog."

"We missed you."

"I missed you two, too!" I ambled over to Walter and Pebbles and gave each of them a hug. They felt freezing cold, but their affection warmed me up. I love the closeness of company first thing in the morning.

Walter took off his gloves and placed his freezing hands in mine. "Warm me up." He brushed my lips. I responded—ready to cave, when my work ethic kicked in. I felt myself pulling away from him, as Pebbles did his dance routine while shaking snow off himself. Good thing all my furniture is second hand—Well except for Walter's couch. That one looks designer-made, compared to my thrift store finds.

I looked up at my indoor snowman and heaved a sigh of disappointment. "Walter...I'm sorry...I have to go to work. I have a lead."

"What's the rush? It's snowing out! I thought maybe we could have brunch followed by a romp in our winter paradise—make a snowman, snow-woman and snow dog...one happy snow family."

"I want to...I really do...but I need to do this."

Walter frowned for a moment and then perked up, saying, "Need help?"

"No. This one I can handle."

Those puppy dog eyes again. I threw him a bone. "Say Walter, I have to go to Alaska for Santigo. Would you like to come with me?"

"Now?"

"In a few days."

"Sure...but only if you let me pay my way."

"You're the struggling writer...Remember?"

"I've got money put aside...for travel expenses. I could write it off on my taxes."

"I don't want you going in debt for me."

"I go only if I pay. Male pride and all that."

"Done." I shook his hand, which had warmed up considerably...I could feel the heat—the electricity between us—as I touched him.

Walter's smile re-emerged and I smiled back, relieved. I didn't have the money, but I knew I needed him—*that I am sure of...Call it intuition...whatever...I've become dependent upon him—his strength...his closeness...his trustworthiness...How did I function before—without him?*

Walter took off his jacket and hat and hung them near the fireplace to dry. "Hey Tangie...At least eat brunch with me before you head out into this storm. I don't want you braving the cold on an empty stomach. I'm a fast short-order cook." He patted my rear end and turned to head for the kitchen.

I laughed. "It's a deal, Chef Cunningham. I cannot refuse a man in an apron. I'll check the news and snow update while you whip me up some waffles."

"How do you know I'm going to make waffles?"

"Oh just a hunch." I smiled and plopped on our new comfortable couch that didn't sink to the floor, but hugged my body. I leaned against a plush throw pillow, grabbed the remote and turned on the news. Pebbles came over to me and I took off his snowy vest, wrapped a shawl around him and put him on the couch, next to me.

The weather forecast depressed me. Lots of streets closed. *I'm glad I live near Highway 99—So far, still passable. After that, I take a short sled ride over to the freeway...If I'm lucky, I'll find a connecting road to I-5 that's been plowed by the time I get there...or I could just stay on 99...all the way to Edmonds...Traffic lights there, but it could be an alternative snow route...*

As I mentally planned my morning journey, a *KOMO* news bulletin grabbed my full attention and sent a sinking shiver way down to my tootsies. My teeth started to chatter and I got up, paced around the room, put the doggie vest by the fireplace, next to Walter's coat and set the remote to high volume.

"Police are looking for a suspect in the murder of a young woman, age eighteen to twenty years of age...found between *Pier 70* and *Ivar's Seafood Restaurant*. Anyone who has any information on this crime, please contact Seat*tle Police Department*. All details will be kept confidential."

"Rats. I dined with Santigo...near that crime scene. The poor girl... how horrible..."

Walter walked in the room as I muttered to myself. He wore his red chef apron embroidered with the words, *I Love to Cook*. He scanned the news broadcast then cast his eyes on me. "I could check out the murder victim while you work on your other case. I could pay the police a visit... for you. Just give me Terese's picture."

"You don't think it could be Terese, do you? I'm getting freaked out."

Walter came over and hugged me. "No...but it wouldn't hurt to check...I could do that..."

I nodded. "Okay, Walter. That is a good idea...just to make sure. You don't mind doing that for me?" *I hate police stations. I always get tongue-tied when I talk to the cops. Probably all those speeding tickets in my teens...I turn into idiot girl when they question me—I always feel guilty.* I took his hand. "There may be a connection somewhere."

"I will talk to the police, Tangie." Walter squeezed my hand and put his other arm around my waist. Ah...wonderful to *feel the warmth of his body—Too bad Bacchus and his brew overpowered me last night.*

I leaned into him and brushed his cheek with my lips. "Thank you, Walter...in advance."

"No problemo—I have a buddy that works at the *Seattle Police Department*...I've been meaning to pay him a friendly visit anyway."

I touched my *secretary's* lips with mine. "Walter...I'm giving you a raise!"

Walter sighed and held me tighter in his arms. "How about a prolonged, passionate kiss?"

"Now...that's one thing I can afford..."

After *the kiss*—a kiss definitely on the hot and heavy side—I hugged my secretary with the longing of a mermaid wanting to sail away with her sea captain...not wanting to jump back into the cold water, ever. I caressed his arms and his chest and unconsciously started unbuttoning his shirt…Walter took the plunge…and jumped ship. Physical hunger got the best of him.

Men…what is it with them? They need their food…kind of like bears—Feed them and they're happy…but in this case, Walter is the one who nourishes. He led me to the kitchen table where we devoured his breakfast of blueberry waffles topped off with whipped cream, with bacon and orange juice on the side.

"I will never fire you, Walter. You are invaluable." I finished off the last of my Belgian waffle and chugged my second glass of fresh-squeezed orange juice. "I feel much better—glad to be here…ready to face the world."

"Me too…plus I like to watch you eat."

"I'm sorry…I didn't even think to make more espresso…Do you want one?"

"No…I picked up a latte at the store, during my walk with Pebbles."

I heard a low growl and then a bark. *Pebbles.* After he sat up and begged, crossing his front paws, I placed a small piece of bacon in his mouth.

"Oops…I already gave him two pieces, Tangie."

"He never has enough of his favorite things…Kind of like you…"

Walter grinned at me, leaned over the table and tasted my lips. "Yum."

I groaned. "Um…thanks, Walter…I loved breakfast…and…I'm sorry…about our snow people. Can we create them when I get back? And afterwards…take a walk…in the moonlight and just fool around—like kids again...You will be here, won't you? You'll wait for me?"

"Of course I will, but the snow might be gone."

"Pray…"

"I will...that you don't get in a wreck. It's nasty out there."

"How are you going to get to downtown Seattle—to the police station?"

"Oh, I'll get there fine. There should be one or two buses running. Don't you start worrying about me."

I forced myself up out of my wobbly kitchen chair, not wanting to leave. I kissed him on his cheek—not trusting myself to seek his lips. "Thanks for last night."

"My pleasure."

"Next time, I promise I will not get plastered."

"I know." He smiled. "I love that promise. I'll hold you to it."

Walter squeezed my waist and I found my desire to work fade. His eyes danced and I starting inhaling like a drowning swimmer on her last breath...Oh how I craved his lips...his touch drove me crazy. The room started to spin—but not from wine this time.

"I'll see you tonight," Walter whispered in my ear as he kissed it and then pulled away from me. "It's time we went to work."

"Curses," I muttered under my breath. *Walter, it appears, has a stronger work ethic than me. The one time mine doesn't kick in, his does. We'll never get together at this rate.*

Chapter Thirteen

It appears Walter, my right-hand man, shoveled the driveway before I got up, so I could drive my *Escape* up and away from my house with no problem. The street turned out to be a different story...Ice chunks everywhere. My car clock read half-past noon. No problem. I could get to Edmonds by two. One and one half hours to do a twenty-five minute ride should do it. *Wrong. That's snow in Seattle for you.* At least I didn't get into that ten-car pile-up on the freeway or slide off the road heading down the ski slope hill in Edmonds on route to Main Street. The guy in front of me didn't fare so well. I called *911* on my cell to inform the police. That poor dude could be there in the ditch for days if someone didn't pull him out. I would have stopped but my SUV wouldn't. No brakes on the ice. Snow and gravity took over until I reached the bottom of the steep incline. San Francisco has nothing on Seattle when it snows here. Maybe they'll de-ice the road before I head back up the slope. One could hope. *Don't wanna sleep in Edmonds tonight. I have other plans...*

I approached *Our Lady of Peace Parish Center*—Empty—except for the presence of two sturdy snow vehicles in the unplowed lot—one a *Ford Ranger* and the other a *RAV-4*. We could be at Stevens Pass, from the looks of things...Edmonds looked like a ski resort—Deep snow—about a foot on the road. The adjacent play area for children looked like a frozen graveyard. Not a good day to swing. Heck...you could barely see the swings—Just snow-covered benches and climbing tires that looked like headstones. I did hear laughter from afar. Children around the corner—sledding down a steep hill closed to traffic. No cars on the road equaled heaven to little ones. I remember those days. *Some of my fondest childhood memories are snow days. They are rare gifts around here...Like precious jewels—diamond crystals falling from the sky... and they are free.*

I entered the parish office and before I extended my greetings to the Adrianne Cooper, I noticed packed shelves above the church secretary's desk. I looked to the side and next to her work area, in the corner, stood a floor-to-ceiling bookcase. Lots of parish directories—especially on the top shelves—*The Mother Lode.*

I sighed like a kid in a candy store.

Adrianne got up from her desk and shook my hand. Then she turned and introduced me to Selene Russo. Turns out they just finished eating lunch together. I could smell the remnants of *Jersey Mike's Subs. Wonder if Mike delivers? I start salivating—hungry all over again. Good thing I ate Walter's scrumptious breakfast or I wouldn't be able to control my urges. Mike's Subs* do something to me...and I get hungry just smelling the oil and vinegar.

"We were just about to have some coffee," Adrianne said. "Care to join us?"

I nodded. "That would taste good after my trip through winter wonderland."

"We were just talking about your case...Please, sit down." A warm, easy-going sound resonated from Adrianne's throat. *Comforting.* She motioned to a nearby chair and left to get a pot of coffee.

Selene studied me. "So you know Clancy...Ms. Seraphina."

"Yes...well, I just met him. Please...call me Tangie. Everyone does."

"Sure...*Tangie.* Adrianne tells me you are looking for Clancy's mother."

Adrianne placed a warm cup in my hand and motioned to the cream and sugar on the desk. I nodded. "Thanks, Adrianne."

I turned to Selene. "Yes...at Clancy's request, I am searching for his birth mother. Clancy's at that age—you know—where his roots are important to him. He'd like to put some pieces of himself together before he moves on."

"He must be about twenty, now, is that right?"

"Correct."

I studied Selene, noticing fine lines beginning to form around her eyes, but she appeared fit and trim, possessing the body of an athlete. She probably still played soccer or skied...probably both. She looked ready for the slopes in a dark blue Norwegian wool sweater with snowflakes woven into it. She completed her outfit with *Gloria Vanderbilt* jeans and *Timberland* hiking boots.

"Ms. Russo," I began...

"Call me Selene."

"Of course...*Selene*...Would you mind telling me...about your visits with Clancy after Father Finn and Veronica Burroughs found him at *Our Lady of Peace?*"

Selene took a sip from her coffee cup and studied me carefully. Then she put the cup down and put her hand on her cheek and lifted her left eyebrow, as if in deep thought... She closed her eyes and didn't say anything for about two minutes...after which her face relaxed, her eyes met mine and she obliged me. "I interviewed Clancy before we placed him with the Hendricksens."

"And?"

"You can't imagine how sad it is to talk to a lost child...especially one whose mother abandoned him."

"Do you remember what Clancy called his mother? That might help."

"*Mommy*. Only it sounded like Mummy. Sometimes he called her 'Mommy Tear'. I think he meant Mommy dear, or maybe they played a game together and she was Mommy Bear and he was Baby Bear."

"Go on." I sat on the edge of my seat, encouraging her.

"I remember my sessions with Clancy...They broke my heart. He cried for his mother all the time. He kept saying his Mommy Tear told him...that she'd come back for him...that she'd come back for him...but she never did—The poor child—Inconsolable. Nothing anyone did or said made a difference to him...He remained totally focused on his missing mother."

"Do you remember anything else that Clancy said?"

"Yes." Selene closed her eyes, remembering. Then she opened her eyes and stared at me. "Can you imagine my distress?"

I nodded.

"I mean...the poor little boy...he told me about the people in his life...I became distraught myself...He spoke in such a soft voice, trying to hold back tears..." Selene closed her eyes once more. "He just about broke my heart when he said:

Rick hit me...hit Mommy. Not nice man. Mean man. Bad man. Mommy cried...we left. We took a long ride. We rode around and around in the snow. Then Mommy left me in front of the big house with the big roof...with the star on top. She told me to wait. I cried. I told her I'm cold. She told me to go inside and wait for Uncle Joey...She told me she'd be right back. I did what she told me...but she never came back. She never came back and not Uncle Joey either...

Those are his exact words—They are imprinted in my memory. I think he mistook the cross on the steeple for a star...He was only around four years old. Such a beautiful little boy...So sad...So hopeful...until the end—when I had to tell him his mother would not be coming back to him...That day...I hated my job."

An overwhelming sadness crept into my psyche...Sadness for Clancy...sadness for Selene, sadness for the mother. "I can understand how you felt...to be the messenger of such unsettling news to a child."

"Yes...I felt awful...I remember the freckles on his cheeks...his red hair...his sparkling green eyes. Loving, caring...sensitive...He thought his mommy was hurt and that she needed him...He just thought of her—Such compassion for someone so small. How could a mother abandon such a beautiful little boy? As I told him the news, I could see him shrink into a place that filled his heart with loneliness and grief...and he withdrew from my attempted hug. I know I am trained to deal with these circumstances, but it still hurts. I never get used to it..."

I shook my head. "Maybe the mother didn't have a choice. Maybe she tried to protect him. Clancy doesn't have any bad memories of his mother. Just Rick. His mother didn't hurt him."

"No. She just abandoned him." Selene glared at me momentarily, before regaining her composure.

I crossed my legs and took a deep breath. I started to get anxious myself, finding myself biting my lips and sweating under my warm clothing. I felt the room closing in on me...stifling. I took another deep breath, and then sipped my coffee before I continued questioning her. "Did Clancy have any possessions on him?"

"Not really. Just his clothes and a blue tattered blanket, which he kept with him until the Hendricksens adopted him."

"And which his adoptive parents threw away..."

"It's been sixteen years..." Selene reminded me.

"But not for Clancy—He is still living in the past...I'm sorry, Selene...I feel bad too...and I thank you a lot. I know talking about this is upsetting to you."

"You're right." Selene raised her head and sat up straight, brushing some stray hair out her face with her manicured hand. "But thanks to you, I know Clancy's doing well...that he's appreciated the opportunities in his life. As social workers, we don't always know how our cases wind up...We just hope..."

"Yes...one can always hope." My eyes wandered over to Adrianne Cooper, who perched on her swivel chair in silence, listening as Selene and I chatted. "Um...Adrianne...I wonder... May I take a look at the parish directories? Perhaps one of the faces would look familiar..."

She remained silent for a moment, tapping her fingers and then nodded. "I think that would be all right...but keep this between us...the directories have to stay in this office. Selene and I will help you."

I smiled in appreciation.

Adrianne remained solemn. "Today's kind of a free day for the two of us. But if any of us discover anything new, I am sure you will be discreet with the information?"

"I can assure you, *discreet* is my middle name."

Chapter Fourteen

The last book claimed victory. Adrianne told me not to bother with it... as Father Finn wasn't even in the parish yet, but I persevered.

"It's the last one..." I pleaded.

"Have a go at it then."

I opened the directory to the inside front page and stared at a picture of Joseph Caine. Father Joseph Caine—former pastor of *Our Lady of Peace.* I felt my stomach get a little queasy. Not from hunger. Not from anxiety. I saw the eyes of Clancy's long lost relative...*Uncle Joey*...staring at me...inviting me into his life.

I closed my eyes as I handed the telltale directory to Adrianne—which I kept opened to the first page. I opened my eyes to see Adrianne turning green. Not from indigestion. She handed the book to Selene with shaking fingers. Selene examined the photo of the priest on page one and compared it with the photo lying on Adrianne's desk—the recent photo of Clancy, as a young man.

"Uncle Joey..." was all she could say.

I left Adrianne and Selene in semi-shock, myself feeling like a crumb. I am sure I spoiled their afternoon. I promised I would keep the information to myself and only contact people who would help Clancy. No sensationalism. I told them I would keep them informed about my progress.

"There's probably a perfectly good explanation to all of this," I assured them...but I don't think they believed me.

I decided to drive up to Everett. The sun hadn't set yet, and I yearned to speak to Father Finn—in person. He could help me. I knew I could not discuss this one over the phone. Before I left *Our Lady of Peace,* I thanked Adrianne—as she snapped out of shock long enough to ring Father Finn for me...and inform him of my pending visit. Selene sat like a mute bird perched on the wooden chair...drinking her third cup of coffee...lost in the past...grasping at the "*what if's*"...in her mind.

Heading north on I-5, a good portion of the freeway belonged to me alone, except for the cars piled up on the side of the road. No doubt their drivers listened to the news of gloom and doom, abandoned their vehicles, hitched rides or walked home while the snowstorm rumbled through Western Washington. All the drivers, that is, but me.

As the freeway remained deserted in the center lane, I encountered no trouble reaching Everett and as *Saint Anthony's* bordered a street near the freeway exit, I didn't get stuck—not even once on the steep incline. Good thing. I didn't want to ruin my suede boots sloshing through snow. On other cases, I've had to desert my car and hike...with cold hands... Freezing feet...Wet body...No fun at all. My luck prevailed this time.

Father Finn greeted me with a warm smile and led me to his sitting room, where on the table by the window, sat a steaming pot of Irish Breakfast, with two cups, side by side, waiting my arrival. The twinkle in Father Finn's eyes, which I cherished during our first meeting, turned to disbelief and concern when I displayed Clancy's picture next to Father Caine's picture from the old parish directory, side by side.

"There's got to be some explanation for this," the Irish priest exclaimed. "I know Father Caine—He would not be party to the desertion of a child."

"Maybe he didn't know."

"Ah, Lassie...That's the ticket."

"Do you have any idea where he is now?"

"Yes, as a matter of fact, my dear, I do. I write to him every now and then—we manage to keep in touch. He's up in Alaska...In our Outreach Missionary Program. He is the pastor of a small mission parish in Kodiak."

I could hardly contain myself. "I am going to Kodiak, Alaska...on business...in a few days. I could arrange to meet him at his mission. Would it be an imposition for you to call or write him? Could you tell him I'm heading to Kodiak and would like to speak with him?"

"Well, Father Caine has a satellite phone he uses for emergencies. I think this would be classified as one, don't you think?"

I nodded and smiled with some hesitation. "Thank you, Father. This will help relieve some of Clancy's anxiety. I don't imagine he will be at peace...until he knows why his mother abandoned him."

"I am more than glad to help you, Angelina...I have but one question for you. Why, for Saint Peter's sake, are you going up north in the winter? Cannot you wait until spring? It's much safer to travel then..."

"Well, 'tis a mystery, Father Finn...and I've just got to get to the bottom of this one, you see."

"Well then...you be careful, Angelina...Watch out for those Kodiak Bears."

"Now you know they only come out in springtime."

"Perhaps it is safer in the snow, then."

"Perhaps...but don't count on it. Wish me luck."

"I will pray for you...for Clancy...and for Father Caine."

Somehow I think we needed all the prayers we could get.

Chapter Fifteen

The ride home grabbed me like a bear coming out of hibernation. *No pun intended.* Darkness enveloped the highway and I opened my eyes wide to imagine the lanes—as the dividing lines were invisible—compacted with snow. Fortunately, most businesses were closed and the trucks and busses I passed on the roads totaled about ten. The number of cars on the side of the road amounted to many more. If you didn't have four-wheel drive or chains, you were destined to wind up as curb bait. It took me forever to get to my little house in Ballard. I white-knuckled the climb up the final hill, curved the roundabout next to my neighborhood, and parked down the street from my warm and toasty abode. I figured, that if I needed to go out again, I could get traction better at the bottom of the street, if the snow continued to pound us. *Getting stuck in my driveway is my least favorite thing. Plus, the steep incline nosedives into the garage. I'd be stranded there for days.*

When I stepped out of my igloo on wheels, my arms shook and my feet wobbled—the same kind of feeling you get when you take your ice skates off after skating for hours on end, in the bitter cold. I started my deep breathing exercises, and hiked up the steep mountain of snowdrifts to my front steps. Walter, sweet soul, shoveled the walk all around my craftsman home. Trouble is, ice formed and I felt my feet slipping under me. I only fell through the air twice. I wised up and walked on the grassy part, or what used to be the grassy part. It evolved into one huge snowpack. Better than ice. Wonder where Walter got a shovel? I never owned one but knowing my secretary—the master of discovery—one would appear. Sure enough, I noticed a spanking new deluxe snow shovel on the top of the porch, next to the front door. I inched up the slippery steps and when I got to the top of the landing, I turned around and stared at the still-falling snowflakes. Huge. I could make out their crystal shapes. Wish I had a microscope. I remembered the moonlight walk we planned in the snow…and sighed—Right now that would be about the greatest thing to do…I couldn't stop smiling...until I turned and scooted over to the front door.

"Yeow!" I shrieked.

There lay a severed head. *Yes, I know it's little. I know it's probably just a rat's head or the remnants of a small bunny...but it's not a good omen. I hate dead things…Especially at the entrance to my sanctuary.*

I heard footsteps inside. Walter tramping down the stairs from the bedroom loft. The door opened and my secretary peeked out.

"Angelina! You scared me."

"I scared myself. Look..."

Walter smiled. "Someone left you a present, Tangie...or a peace offering. Have any cat admirers?"

I thought of Spike—Mr. Jarrick's cat. The beast.

"My neighbor's cat. He's vicious. He catches mice and torments them before he devours them. This is the first time he left me their remains."

"Maybe he likes you."

"Well I don't like him. He's nasty." I thought of the gaunt, mangy cat that prowled around my house at night until Pebbles went nuts and started barking like a ferocious animal.

"Maybe he's hungry. I could put some food outside for him. He's probably lonely and in need of a good meal. Have you ever seen your neighbor feed the poor thing?"

"Come to think of it, no. I do hear Mr. Jarrick yelling at Spike a lot. Spike's a really disgusting cat."

"Maybe if someone fed him regularly, and petted him once in awhile…"

"Oh no, you're not doing that number on me, Walter..."

"I'll pay for the food. We can't let him starve…it's winter…and cold out here."

"Who says he's starving? Plus, you don't understand. He'll be here all the time. Begging for food. We'll never get rid of him."

"No, he'll be grateful…come for the food and leave. Then he'll do the same thing the next day...Trust me. It's the only solution. He's picked you as his caretaker."

"Great."

"Tangie, you know, cats are more like humans than we realize. They depend upon food and companionship just like we do...without it, they become wild and detached...no conscience."

"Walter, you're baiting me."

"Look at it this way, you'll be gaining an attack kitty."

Well, we squeezed in our moonlight stroll in the snow, but it consisted of a hike up the neighborhood hill…to the grocery store to get cat food, treats, a water bowl, food dispenser and cat toys. I have to admit—I enjoyed playing with all the cool stuff they have for felines.

"Maybe Spike and Pebbles will be friends." Walter grinned as he picked up a wand with a feather at the end of it.

"Don't push your luck." I nudged him and laughed, feeling giddy. "Pebbles lives to bark at that cat. Now he'll be chasing the poor devil all around the front yard."

Walter smiled at me as he paid for the treasures for Spike, our new freeloader. Then my hiking companion stuffed all the kitty supplies in his backpack, and reached for my hand and led me out the door into our winter wonderland. We ambled down the hill in silence…walking at a slow pace, enjoying the stars, the moon and the diamonds on the ground, glistening along our pathway. *I love these peaceful moments in time—If only they'd freeze like the ice—stay with us longer. When I look back…I realize life is made up of small things…that grow and become a larger part of who we are… they shape our personalities…our wants, our desires…Right now I desire closure.* I started to skip along up the hill…in the snowdrifts, breathing in the fresh icy cold air. When Walter caught up to me, I told him all about Clancy, his mother and Uncle Joey.

"When are you going to call Clancy?" Walter asked. "He has a right to know about his family...Poor kid...I empathize with him."

I looked at Walter...Trying to understand the depths of his concern. "Yes...I'll give him a progress report tomorrow. I don't have the stomach to do it tonight...I'll wind up with heartburn and won't be able to sleep."

We approached my little craftsman house, which could pass for a gingerbread house in the snow, with the leftover Christmas lights shining in the snow. When we got to the top step of the porch, I sat down and surveyed the neighborhood. Calm. Peaceful. I hated to discuss business while enjoying my respite from angst, but I felt compelled to ask Walter about his afternoon.

"How did your visit with the police go?"

"Productive. You can rule out Terese as the victim. The dead girl had brown eyes and dark brown hair. Dark complexion. Terese has green-blue eyes and black hair and no doubt is Western European ancestry—French or Irish. The victim is of Hispanic descent. Probably not born in the U.S.A. Seems like the evidence points to South America."

"You know, Walter, I've had this creepy feeling in the pit of my stomach ever since I heard *KOMO News* announce that her body was discovered near *Ivar's Restaurant*. You know I ate there with Santigo...and Fred Santigo's from South America—from Chile."

"Tangie, the victim wore a hand-crafted bead bracelet... The police told me the jewelry came from Chile...They traced its origin. I also spotted a tattoo on her arm, but it was more like someone branded her...Like in the concentration camps...in *Nazi* Germany."

"Now that is creepy. Do the police know how she died?"

"*Steve*—my buddy—told me they think...maybe a drug overdose... for now, they are treating it as a homicide. He said if we discover anything to let them know."

"Did you tell him about *me...or Terese?*"

"Of course not. You asked me not to. I told Steve a *friend of mine* did a disappearing act a few days ago without telling me or any of her friends or family...I explained that all of us are concerned."

I sighed. "Well, who knows, maybe Terese will be a friend of ours someday."

"A distinct possibility. Especially if we find her."

"Yeah, Walter, but a remote possiblilty. A known fact...people who run away, don't want to be found."

Walter nodded in agreement, got up off the porch steps, pulled me up to him, and caressed me. "I'm sorry, Tangie...I know these things are tough for you..."

I nodded. "Thanks for going Walter. I really appreciate it. Did your friend believe you, Walter?"

"Well he didn't ask me to take a lie detector test. He did ask for a picture. I put him off—Told him I'd try to contact her family, but that they live in Canada."

"Now you're scaring me. I don't want you to get in trouble on my account."

"Don't worry, Tang. I 'm okay. You see...*Steve*—my good buddy in the department—trusts me. He and I go way back."

"Don't tell me you two went to school together?"

"Hey, cops have college degrees, you know. Especially detectives."

"Well, I'm glad you didn't have any trouble. You really are my best friend...my partner in detective work...my *secretary*..."

Walter grinned at me and opened the front door. "Let's go inside, Tangie. It's getting cold out here. I'll make you a fire."

I sighed, took his arm and followed him into my minuscule foyer where we kicked off our boots on the lonely frayed braided rug hugging the aged wood floor. Walter dropped the cat supplies in the corner and went over to the hearth and lit a match. Turns out before our walk, he assembled all the building blocks for a fire. *What a guy. But you know...it's easy for Walter. He has no angst. I'm the opposite type— Frantic...Worried...Uneasy.* I plopped myself down on the couch and leaned against Pebbles' pillow. *Wet dog smell.* Walter came over, sat down next to me and placed a fresh scented pillow under my neck. Ah...I began to relax—Warm, safe, in Walter's strong arms. I drifted off to sleep. I felt myself being carried into my bed and the covers being placed over me—A soft kiss on my lips and then I heard the sound of a light switch...sweet darkness...calm. Still, all through the night, I couldn't sleep. I kept waking up...scared and alone—I started having dreams about Spike killing mice and Pebbles running in circles trying to tear the darn cat to pieces. Then these really scary dudes pounded on my door, broke in and forced me to go with them. That's when I screamed. Loud. Walter came running from his sofa bed and climbed the stairs to my loft...He climbed into my bed and shook me until I heard his voice.

"Angelina...wake up. You're having a nightmare."

"I can't go back to sleep, Walter, I'll have another nightmare..." I cried as I crushed him with my hug. I couldn't help myself...I found myself clawing his arms...holding on for dear life. "Horrible dream—They're after me—Don't want to go back there!"

"Who's after you?"

"I don't know...but they're horrible..."

"You're all right, now...I'm with you."

I sat there for about twenty minutes clinging to Walter. I sighed. "Thank you, Walter."

Walter whispered, "Come with me, Angelina..."

He led me downstairs to the foyer and handed me my boots, gloves and my winter parka, ordering me to put them on. Then he steered my limp body outside into our winter wonderland. More snow falling—a blizzard in the making, but not scary...just exciting...like a breath of fresh air after being cooped up in a stuffy room.

"We never made our snow people." Walter reminded me. "I think now is a good time. We can add a dog and a cat. They will protect you from the bad guys."

I smiled, bent down and made a snowball and threw it at him. "You're crazy...you know that?"

"I know. That's why you like me."

"No argument there...Let's *do the dance,* Walter—There are snow creatures waiting to be made."

First we perfected our snow couple. I gave the girl my green wool scarf, and Walter gave his guy his blue *Seahawks* hat. Then we tackled the pets—beginning with the pooch and ending with the puss. As I carved the finishing touches on the snow dog's ear, Pebbles appeared at the window and started his *"Ruff...ruff...ruff." Psychic dog.* Walter ran up the stairs and let him out. No danger of him running in the road and being hit by a car tonight. No cars, no people—Just the *Man in the Moon*—Tonight spelled Freedom with a capital *F*. Pebbles raced in circles around us and jumped on his snow likeness. Then he tried to eat the snow that fell on his head...as Walter and I tumbled around laughing and started making snow angels on what used to be the front lawn. Walter rose up and put a toy mouse in our snow kitty's mouth. As he did so, I lay silent on the snow...grinning at his genius...I heard a movement by the lamppost. A feline shadow peered out from under a snow-covered rhododendron—Spike—admiring the snow sculpture.

Sometimes the good outweighs the bad. And tonight turned out to be good—Very good, indeed. On a scale of one to ten, I'd give the end of this evening—and Walter—a twelve.

Chapter Sixteen

I crammed my schedule for the next three days preparing for our trip. Walter made things easy because he is organized...He handled many of the details of traveling...securing our reservations for our planes and hotel... Well...the inn. No hotels on Kodiak. I made a hasty call to Clancy and related my progress on his case. He seemed hopeful. I didn't tell him the whole story. I related how I tracked down a possible relative living in Alaska and I would fly there to find out for sure. He didn't ask a lot of questions, but he offered to pay my airfare in advance. I assured him I could handle it. He promised me that the next time we met, he would reimburse me; he told me to keep track of all expenses I incurred in Alaska.

I liked Clancy from the beginning, but so far, he's exceeded my expectations of him. Unlike Santigo—who gives me nothing but a headache... and whom I place in the category of worm—Don't know what Terese saw in him. Her Fred might possess redeeming qualities, but so far I haven't latched on to a single one.

Right before Walter and I left for Alaska, the temperature warmed up, our snow family melted... and by the time our departure time arrived, our temporary escape from life's heartaches faded into a distant memory— but *a memory I will embrace always.*

Because the rains came and washed our magical kingdom away, I looked forward to traveling up north. *Compact snow and ice are now my friends. Snow inspires creation. What does rain inspire? More rain—Wet, cold hands and feet—No creatures to form, no balls to throw...Well, there are puddles to jump...and flowers to grow..."*

Walter and I dropped Pebbles off early at my mom's so I could spend a little time helping her get ready for her photo op. I could see her gratitude in the tears forming in her eyes. She looked awesome—A vision of elegance…dressed in her plum satin dress and shimmering necklace of pearls, with diamond and pearl earrings to match. Dad gave her that set for their tenth anniversary—Mom treasured them…I always tear up when I see her wearing them. As she posed for Walter and me, I clapped my hands and Walter gave her an appreciative stare that signaled, "Wonderful."

"Do you think Charles will like it, Angelina?" My mother fluffed her platinum hair.

"He'd have to be dead not to think you're a knock-out, Mom."

"Oh you're just saying that because I'm your mother."

"Well, you're not my mother and I think you are positively stunning," Walter chirped.

"Why, thank you, Walter." Mom smiled…and winked at me. "You keep this secretary, Angelina. He's a charmer."

Don't worry, Mom. He's a keeper. His charm is one of the reasons I hired him." I smirked. Couldn't help myself.

"Okay, Tangie...Time to hit the road." Walter squirmed, then got up and put my coat around my shoulder as I slipped my arms inside. *Seems being the center of attention makes him ill at ease.* Up until now, I viewed him as *Mr. Cool.*

I squeezed his cheeks. "I love it when you take control."

"Watch it, Angelina...You might get more than you bargain for..."

"I can't wait."

My mother listened to our banter and grinned. "Goodbye you two. Have fun. Be careful…"

I hugged her once more, careful not to mess up her makeup. Walter shook her hand and then took it and raised it to his lips. "Thank you, for the pleasure of your company, Mrs. Seraphina…I am enchanted to meet you at last."

"The pleasure's all mine, Walter. Call me Marianna."

Now, My mother never told any of my dates to call her Marianna… not even Don…until we were engaged. *Walter is such a smoothie. What technique. Probably takes pointers from Eddie Haskell in those classic comedy reruns on late-night television. I love him anyway.*

"Pebbles...where are you?" *Now where is that rascal?* "Oh, Pebbles..."

Nothing. Not a sound. *Darn. I wanted to say goodbye to my pooch. No furry feet running anxiously to find me. He always deserts me when I bring him to Mom's. Probably eating leftovers in Marianna's kitchen. She always leaves special treats for him in his grand-puppy dish.*

"Oh Angelina..." My mother answered my concern. "Don't worry about Pebbles. He'll be fine."

"I'm sure he will, Mom. Thank you...I know he's in good hands. Walter and I have to be on our way or we'll miss our flight..."

"Call me when you get there, dear..."

"I promise. Don't worry." I kissed her goodbye and smiled at her as I watched her deep blue eyes fill with tears—like they did whenever I left good ol' Washington State. I knew she'd be a nervous wreck until I telephoned her from Alaska. *Mothers are like that.*

I grabbed Walter's hand as the two of us tramped down the sidewalk to the *Escape*. "Next stop...*North to Alaska...*"

Chapter Seventeen

Okay, so here I sit next to Walter in our *Boeing 757 Jet*—bound for Anchorage. After this flight, we take a commuter jet to Kodiak. It's gonna be a long day. We settle in our seats and the plane takes off pronto. Walter proceeds to doze the moment we hit the clouds. I must admit, he did get up before dawn and get everything in its place before we left. Left lots of food and water out for Spike in those automatic feeders and he picked up the house so it wouldn't be a disaster when we returned. I can't complain. What a guy. I look at his sleeping face, smile to myself and kiss his cheek. He smiles back at me in his sleep. I sigh and almost wake him up…I want to hug him at that moment, but I resist the urge, lean back in my seat and try to relax.

My thoughts twirl around in my head and then drift back to my mother's concern over my latest caper…*Marianna…so ecstatic we paid her a visit even if it was six in the morning…appreciative that I helped her get all dressed up for her glamour shot. Who knows? She might need a sexy photo for her book jacket, if she ever gets published…or if she ever finishes her manuscript. I hugged her especially tight when I greeted her at the crack of dawn. She noticed. She notices everything. She whispered in my ear, "Is everything all right?"*

I lied. "Of course, Mom."

I told her nothing of the knot I've had in my stomach for three days. I know things are gonna get bad. I just don't know how rotten. So, I reassured her. "Mom…I'll only be gone four or five days and Walter will be with me."

She perked up. "I am glad of that…It's not good for you to be alone all the time."

"He's good company."

"So I've noticed." She smiled at me and gave me another hug. "I will have to have you and Walter over for dinner when you get back."

"That will be great." I smiled back at her. Mom rarely cooks anymore...But she does great take-out...

So here I sit...trying to keep her love and concern...and her smile in my mind. Somehow it soothes me. I close my eyes.

The plane jerked and descended rapidly for a few minutes but it seemed to last for hours. It bounced and bumped and I felt my stomach rise to my throat. Walter woke up and grabbed my hand. "Turbulence," he whispered. "Don't worry, Tangie...it'll stop soon."

I looked at him. *How does he stay so calm? I am ready to throw up.*

"Put your head down, Tangie. You'll feel better."

I did as he suggested. It helped.

"Take two long breaths and breathe out slowly."

Walter—The Psychologist.

The aircraft continued to do the bump and grind for about twenty more minutes. When it stopped, I could speak again. "I'm glad I didn't eat much for breakfast. I didn't lose it." I smiled in triumph.

"I'm glad." He grinned back at me, and put his arm around my shoulder. I leaned against him, feeling myself melt into the warm muscles that filled his shoulder and arm—a cozy pillow under my head. *I just love his tenderness.* This time I did fall asleep, not waking up until we landed in Anchorage.

When the captain gave the all-clear sign, Walter and I followed the throng out the plane and into the terminal. We had about fifteen minutes to catch our connection to Kodiak. We booked down the corridors with our carry-on luggage and reached the gate one minute before the steward shut the door.

Walter showed the steward our boarding passes. "Thank you, Sir."

We climbed the steps into our second aircraft, which made our first—the *Boeing 757*—seem like a luxury cruise ship. Good thing I got used to bumping and grinding. The only positive thing that I can say about this flight was that it didn't last long. One hour, fifteen minutes. I timed it. If I had to do this flight on a daily basis, I'd get used to it, but I know I wouldn't like it. Not ever. I can see why Father Finn encouraged me to wait until spring to travel. Winter weather is scary up here...Even if Kodiak is milder than most of Alaska, you have to go through the worst parts to get there.

Before our commuter jet landed on Kodiak Island, it descended curiously close to Barometer Mountain...like a hawk checking out its den. I watched as the plane landed with a few bumps, braked and came to rest right at the foot of it. I felt my stomach doing the ol' twist and turn.

Walter took my hand and smiled at me. "I admire your calm."

"Calm?" *I think horror would be more my state of mind.*

We ambled off our final transport into a rugged kingdom of white and freezing cold. Bone-chilling cold. Even with my lined boots and gloves on, I lost feeling in my feet and hands...*I wonder how cold you have to be to get frostbite*...So much for the warmer islands of Alaska. Walter hugged me, and took my arm, leading me forward. "Let's move quickly to keep warm."

Darkness began to descend on Kodiak, even though the clock said afternoon. We hailed a Kodiak cab that was parked by the side of the snow-covered road...the road that led away from the small airport. The *Chevy Suburban* with chains on its tires and a welcoming heater greeted us. We crawled inside with our luggage and asked the driver to take us to the *Bear Pause Inn*—our destination for the evening. *Hopefully they got our reservations. If not, we're screwed.*

Our cabbie grunted and gunned his vehicle. Walter and I jerked forward without any will of our own and then we couldn't help but smile at one another. This is Alaska—rough and rugged. Not for wuzzies. I rubbed the door window with my gloved hand, so I could see and peered outside. Even in the approaching twilight, I could see the February paradise that is Kodiak. Raw, unspoiled...magnificent. Everything white,

white, white...with giant trees that dwarfed anything in the Seattle area... Along the road, near the brush, I looked for a glimpse of wildlife, but I looked in vain. No bears—in hibernation for sure. No cougars—hiding from humans…no doubt...Not even a deer in sight. I did get all excited when I saw a lone eagle soar in the moonlight, flying home to roost in the trees. I looked at Walter, who like me, never traveled to Alaska before today. He peered out the window and let out a deep breath. He turned to me. "Hey Tangie…Let's go for a walk as soon as we drop off our bags."

"Yeah, a walk to a restaurant. I'm starved."

The driver spoke. "Hey you kids want a good place to eat?"

"Sure."

"*Salty Jack's* the place. Best place on the island. If you want…drop off your bags…I'll wait for you. The restaurant's not too far from the *Bear Pause*…And I can pick you up when you're done...or show you the way to walk home."

I looked at Walter and he nodded. "That would be great. Thanks."

We deposited our luggage in our rooms at the *Bear Pause Inn*. I expected a grungy fishing resort. Wrong. The place echoed clean and well kept. Each of our spacious suites featured a hand-stitched quilt on a downy soft bed and an elegant stone fireplace with lots of wood stacked nearby. The owner greeted us and showed us around the inn, with a wink and a smile. He told us to let him know if we needed anything. We thanked him and told him of our quest for food and said we'd be back later and chat with him.

Our driver stood against his rig, gazing at the moon like a lone wolf. I thought any moment he would let out a howl. Instead, he reached out his hand to Walter, and then me. "Hi, I'm Gus…and I've decided to be your tour guide for this evening."

We didn't argue with him. He seemed like a solid guy to have around. I surmised Gus couldn't be as old as he looked—too much spunk. From his conversation and interests, I placed him at fifty but he looked about two decades older. Hard livin' and hard drinkin' takes its toll. Judging by the number of bars we passed since our arrival in Alaska, I can understand how easy it is to get caught up in that lifestyle. Liquor flows easy around here.

I leaned forward as we chugged along in his truck. "Hey Gus... What did you do before your taxi service?"

"Well, mostly I drank...and fished. Well, I still fish...but not for a livin' anymore. Everyone fishes around here. Most people drink. A few sober up...like me.

"Good for you, Gus." I reached up to the front seat and patted the top of his shoulder. "That's a hard thing to do—How'd you accomplish it?"

"Well, I wouldn't exactly call it an accomplishment...You see, I grew up here. My ol' man and the entire family fished for salmon, halibut and anything else they could catch. Me...I practically was born on my father's boat. I went out to sea with him, year round—until I lost my leg up near Nome one winter. I ventured into panhandlin' for gold—Big mistake on my part. Got frostbite." He tapped his calf. "Now you wanna talk about cold. That's the place for cold. I was out drinkin' as usual one night and got lost walking back to the camp. I passed out in the open—worst thing to do in Nome. My body temperature placed below ninety degrees when they found me...At least they could save my hands and the other leg. Almost lost my nose too—But I still got the honker." Gus tapped his nose. "Now I drive my cab and make sure the heater works."

"Gee, Gus, I'm sorry."

"Don't be. I'm better off now. Only problem is sometimes I have to stop the rig for the bears. They sometimes hog the road and no way I'm gonna get out and argue with them."

"They're all in hibernation, right now though, aren't they?" I could feel my body tense up. I needed reassurance.

He didn't give it to me. Instead, he whispered, "Well, sometimes you'll spot a rogue that hangs out longer than he should...looking for food, instead of hibernating...Those ones can get mean. I leave them alone."

"Smart move." Walter joined in the conversation, and changed the subject—to my relief. "Say, Gus...What's good to eat at *Salty Jack's?*"

"Bear."

I grimaced. Gus wouldn't give it up.

"Just joshin' you. Try the King Crab or the White King Salmon. Best in Alaska...or anywhere—*Specialties of the House*, of course. Want me to pick you up, after? Here's my card. Call me if you need me."

I thought of rogue Kodiak bears, not in hibernation…on the prowl. Suddenly a stroll by moonlight lost its appeal. "Yes, Gus." I took his card. "We'll give you a ring, for sure…when we're done."

Walter smiled and whispered in my ear, "Seriously, Angelina, you know all the bears in Kodiak are hibernating—all the bears except me..." Then he swung the door and hopped out, extending the door open for me and clasping my gloved hand. He shoved Gus a fifty and thanked him for his service. Gus smiled and as he did, I noticed a twinkle in his eyes and a grin that would have been grand except for a couple of missing teeth. I bet he could tell a doozey of a tale about that mishap. I'll be polite and not ask him.

I shivered uncontrollably—What a dramatic change in temperature from the warmth of the *Suburban*. It is still daytime in Seattle, but here…in Alaska, evening comes a few hours earlier. Plus, they're an hour ahead of us here. *I think the clock ticks faster. Fewer hours of daylight in the winter months, make for more time in the hay. Now, that's not such a bad thought. Hum…*

Walter, as if reading my thoughts, put his arm around me and led me past carved fishes along the boardwalk path leading to the restaurant. We walked up the stairs and came face to face with a life-size cedar stature of Salty Jack, whose glass eyes stared right through me.

I shuddered. "He knows we don't live here."

"Angelina, he has a wooden head. Come on, it's not tourist season. We're eating with the locals. We'll blend."

And blend we did…or so I thought. I like dining with Walter—A man at ease in four-star restaurants—And *Salty Jack's* is definitely four stars. Despite it's remote location, *Salty Jack's* defines a gourmet restaurant in spades: Wine steward…Two servers per table…Great food to rival anything in Seattle—fresh…fruits and vegetables—flown in daily. . .and their seafood—local and indescribable. *Copper River Salmon* is usually my favorite, but this *White King Salmon*—on this night—caressed my pallet—The ultimate seafood. None compared.

"Hey Walter..." I suggested, as my secretary finished the last of his King Crab and licked his lips like a cat wanting to hold onto every morsel. . ."Why don't we come here again, sometime when we're not working? You know. . .just for fun?"

"Angelina, what are you suggesting?"

I took a sip of my third glass of *Pinot Gris* and answered, "I could get used to this...and remember I'm not gonna get inebriated tonight." I held up my wine glass and tipped Walter's. "This here is the last of the *Pinot*."

"I'll drink to that." Walter enveloped my arm and finished his wine.

I put my glass down and smiled. "We are having entirely too much fun to be working."

"Wait until tomorrow. We have to hop on a floatplane."

"Out of the frying pan..."

"Don't worry about it. Finish your wine. Let's enjoy tonight."

"Oui, mon cher."

This time, Walter clinked my glass. "To us."

"To us...tonight..."

"Tonight..." Walter leaned over and brushed my lips with his and looked into my eyes. His tenderness disarmed me. I felt the heat rising. *Who needs warm clothes? I have Walter.*

So simple. . .and sweet—like precious Hungarian keflis—cookies my mother would bake for me once a year at Christmas time and the whole house would smell heavenly. . .Oh God, I am falling for this guy and nothing can stop me. I return his gaze and see his desire mixed with concern and caring—The perfect cocktail. I'm sure he knows I feel the same. . .Hooked. . .No getting away. . .and not wanting to get away—just wanting to grab each other and get closer and closer. . .body against body. . .flesh against flesh. . .I begin undressing him with my eyes. . .I can see Walter doing the same to me. . .The restaurant. . .losing its charm. . .Our suite at the inn. . .beckoning. . .And neither one of us noticing a large hulking figure studying us from across the dining room. I would come to see his face—later—in nightmares and flashbacks, but not right now. The beginning of surveillance on us—the beginning of us being in harm's way and did I have a clue? Not one.

Here I sit with Walter…Gazing into his eyes. Me—Without a care in the world at this moment—Clairvoyant—Not seeing the danger around me—Blocking out everything in sight but Walter. Sometimes hunger comes first. Even psychics have their priorities.

Chapter Eighteen

Well, another romantic evening bites the dust. In the restaurant, things begin to heat up—Our passion grows to a boiling point...Walter and I can hardly keep our hands off one another...Gus picks us up as requested and we neck in the backseat of his Chevy, like teenagers. Our driver smiles as he takes the bills from Walter...after dropping us off at the inn...and drives off like an apparition into the darkness.

Although only seven p.m. it's dark as midnight, so Walter and I agree to hit the sack early. I can hardly wait—even though we rose at dawn this morning...and we have separate rooms *for business appearances*, nothing will stifle our passion. Besides, it's time we spice up our relationship—this location...being perfect for romance.

I invite Walter into my boudoir for a nightcap. A bottle of champagne sits on my bedside table—compliments of the management—*How do they know these things?* Walter willingly cooperates and uncorks our evening elixir. I put on some dance tunes—the radio works—and I lounge on the queen-size bed. Walter comes over and pulls me to my feet, tilts my back and kisses me hard on the mouth as we begin a mock tango. Neither one of us is *a* professional dancer...but who cares...We've got rhythm...and we move well together...*like the flamenco dancers I saw in Spain...a long time ago*—I sigh and say to my dance partner, "I need a rose to clench between my teeth..."

"Flowers, *Senorita*, are in the hall," Walter replies and disappears out the door...no doubt to pick up a rose from the arrangement adorning the foyer table we passed on our way in…leaving me standing with one leg in the air.

I go over to the radio, select some gypsy music on the classical station, and practice sliding up and down the bedpost while arranging my hair to one side of my face, like a Spanish dancer. I freeze in place with my left leg up in the air…positioning myself for Walter's entrance when the door creaks. I am ready for the fruit of my passion to appear...I raise my arms to welcome my love and…in comes...

"Horst!" I scream—"No!"

I whisper in my head, *the tormentor from the airport! Terese's tormentor…*

I yell again…and again. "Walter, Walter! Help!"

Walter doesn't hear me—No one hears me…Before I can get another sound out of my mouth, Horst has me pinned on the bed…with my hands behind my back…and he starts squeezing my legs. I bite his arm. I kick him. He doesn't release his grip. Next he has his hands around my waist and then my breasts. I start hyperventilating and bite him again…hard. That's when he puts his hands on my throat and I can't breath anymore.

Voices in the distance…I hear voices…I try to yell…"Help…"

But nothing comes out—no sound, no breath and I begin to fade... My vision becomes blurry. My world is fog and pain. I try frantically to keep my eyes open...encouraged by the sound of voices coming closer, but my eyelids are so heavy…Frantically, with one last burst of energy, I kick Horst one last time…where I know he will feel it, and we both fall off the bed onto the carpet. He releases his grip on me and I can breathe again. I start gasping and I force open my eyes…they begin to focus ...I see a blurry distorted Horst flicking my rescuers away like flies on paper. He hops up, turns, gives me a menacing glare. He cracks open the shutters of the window and leaps out the second story, like a demented, twisted version of a favorite super hero—only no cape.

I close my eyes, wanting to block his crazy grimace out of my senses. It doesn't work. His face will not go away. "Walter..." I whisper. "Walter…"

I hear myself screaming, silently, out of control…then coughing, gasping for air. "Where's Walter?"

A low-pitched voice answers me. "He's all right, Miss…the doctor's with him now."

"Doctor?" Panic consumes me. "What happened? Where is Walter?"

"Next door, in his room. The gentleman staying across the hall—thank goodness—is a physician—Dr. Conway. He's attending to him now. If you want, he can take a look at you when he is done..."

"I must go to Walter...I have to see him..."

"Sure, Miss—but...you look a little shaken."

I look up into the kind eyes of the owner—Nathan Sheldon. "Thank you... for helping me...I think I'm okay now..." I look around at two other people staring at me...a youth in a serving apron and an attractive woman with flaming red hair. The youth is rolling his shoulders around as if they hurt him and the woman is bending down and straightening out her dress.

"Thank you... all of you...for coming to my defense," I whisper, as I rub my neck and feel ridges where smooth skin used to be. "Thank you so much...but I need to see Walter..."

Nathan Sheldon grasps my hand and guides me to a standing position. I walk somewhat unbalanced out the doorway, holding onto the wall in the hallway. Walter's door is ajar and I peak in the opening.

I see Walter lying on his bed...blood is dripping out of his nose... one eye looks puffy and red...the other one is closed. He looks like a chap in a boxing match...where no prize is given. Just pain. A woman with long black raven hair stands at his side like a sentinel...dressed in khaki pants, hiking boots and a white blouse which has black embroidery on the left side—the name, *Bear Pause Inn*—with a paw print underneath. The guardian is holding an ice bag on my beloved's forehead.

"Oh Walter." I start to sob, burying my head on his chest. I feel his chest rise and hear a large sigh of relief.

One eye opens.

"It's okay, Tangie," Walter whispers. "Nothing's broken—except maybe my pride. That guy caught me by surprise, but I landed a few punches before he KO'd me.

I speak through my tears. "Me too. No punches, but I kicked him where it hurts...and I bit him."

"Good girl." Walter sighs..."You okay, Angelina?"

"I think so." I lean into him, put my hands on his shoulders and kiss his cheek. "After he pounded on you, he came into my room...I didn't hear anything at first...I was dancing and waiting for you...I looked up and there he stood—like a Colossus...he scared me to death. He grabbed my neck and started choking me...I couldn't breathe...I felt myself fading fast...Then Mr. Sheldon...and the others showed up...They scared him off me—he jumped out the window...after he thrashed them around a bit..."

I look around the room...Seems the party moved into Walter's room. "Thank you," I say to the spectators who join me at the bedside. "Thank God you came..."

"I'm sorry, folks." Walter gestures with his right arm to the *Bear Pause* staff...and *on-call* doctor. "No help from me. I blacked out...if it weren't for this angel of mercy, I don't know where we'd be...She saw the jerk pounding on me and shouted for help."

I look at the woman holding the ice on Walter's head. She glances at me with piercing violet eyes. I guess her age to be around forty. She looks younger, but possesses an air of maturity...like she's packed a lot of living into her years. Her snug hiking style uniform enhanced her sturdy build. *She's a tough cookie*, I think. Yet, I see kindness flowing from the budding smile she gave, as she asks, "Are you okay, Miss?"

"Yes, thank you. I will be. You helped Walter...I am so grateful."

"Well, I only called for assistance—The others got knocked down. I didn't do much."

"What is your name?"

"Ceira."

I take her hands and their warmth soothed my trembling limbs and I stopped shaking. "You are a blessing, Ceira—You deserve more than our thanks. We'd be toast if you didn't sound the alarm."

"I thank God I didn't go home early this evening. I almost did."

Nathan Sheldon, *the boss*, comes closer to Walter's bedside, takes Ceira's hand and shakes it. "Don't you worry, Ms. Seraphina. Tonight Ceira gets a promotion...Plus, I am giving her some extra vacation time next week."

"Well, she deserves it."

Ceira's face brightens. "Thank you, Mr. Sheldon. My family will be happy to have me home. If it's okay with you, sir, I will be leaving now. My George will be worryin' about me. The little ones are probably starving by now."

"Go home..." Nathan Sheldon smiles at her. "Take care of your brood...but before you do..." He pulls out some coupons out of his shirt pocket..."Here—These are for you and your family...some vouchers for dinner at your favorite restaurant. Take George and the kids. Give yourself a night out."

"Many thanks. You are very kind."

I mimic Nathan's smile as Ceira makes her exit.

Mr. Sheldon turns to me. "Miss...the staff...all of us at the *Bear Pause*, are sorry for all your trouble—and for Mr. Cunningham's injuries. I'm on my way to talk to the sheriff about the intruder. Later on, I'm sure he'll want to question you and your... ah..."

"Secretary. Walter's my *secretary*."

"I see...Hum...of course...Well, um...If you two need anything here at the *Bear Pause*, just give us a shout."

"I already did that."

"Well, you know what I mean...There's the phone...Call room service...anything you need. It's on the house. Just call."

I nod, overwhelmed by his generosity..."Thank you."

After our exchange, Nathan, along with the remaining house staff—consisting of the red-haired thirty-something lady, who is probably his wife or his main squeeze—I didn't get to chat with her yet—and the doctor—who happens to be the guest across the hall—and the youth—a young man around eighteen who stands there tapping his foot the whole time, who probably acts as a porter or short-order cook and who probably is family...leave us alone in the room.

I sigh. "Walter...I know this inn does breakfast but I'm not sure about other meals...and I don't think they have room service."

"They do now. See what we started?"

We chuckle. I sit down on the bed, hug Walter, put my feet up and snuggle up close to him. "My hero..." Walter leans up and tries to kiss me as his eyes began to close. "Hey Walter," I whisper, kissing his lips in return. "You know that brute that attacked us? I'm convinced he's the guy who stalked Terese—I'm sure of it. He looks just like a description

Mr. Benson—the porter at the airport—gave me…Mr. Benson described him to a T."

Walter yawns. "You sure, Tangie?"

"Yes. I'm positive our attacker is Horst—the beast that terrified Terese."

"It figures. Now he's coming after us." Walter speaks in a whisper… as if his mouth is parchment. I leaned over to the bedside table, pour a glass of water and hand it to him.

"You know what, Walter? He probably thinks we'll lead him to Terese...or that Terese told me something."

"Fat chance of that happening…we don't know anything…and he doesn't know who he's dealing with…" Walter starts slurring his words…*He didn't have too much to drink this evening…Maybe he's just tired…*

"Hey Walter...Do you mind if I use your shower? I feel dirty and slimy after having that psycho's hands on me…and I don't want to go back to my room tonight. No wonder Terese took off. If I spent one more minute in his company I'd be ready for the funny farm…or dead."

"Lock the door."

"I intend to...I don't want Horst coming back."

"No, I mean the bathroom door...Otherwise, I won't have will power to leave you alone…and I'm pretty banged up, Sweetie…"

"Oh Walter, you're a mess. Maybe you need a shower more than me."

"No, you go first," my would-be lover yawns. "Leave me some hot water…I'll keep watch for you…we don't want any more surprises tonight."

I kiss his forehead. He felt a little clammy. "Thanks, Walter…you're sweet, but I have a feeling you are headed to dreamland."

I open the door to the knotty pine bathroom, step into the shower and turn on the water as hot as I can stand, washing away the touch of *Horst the Mad Man.* My neck feels tender to the touch when I put the wash-cloth to it. "Ouch." I try to shut out Horst's face—beet red and explosive…his massive hairy neck—looking like that of a blond buffalo and his eyes all puffy—bulging out of his face like a man possessed. *Either he takes drugs or pumps himself up on steroids or maybe he's one of those crazy fanatics—That's it...He programs himself to violence, and likes it.* Despite the heat of the shower, I shiver—reliving my close call. I close my eyes and will myself to see other things, other people. *"Walter,"* I murmur to myself. I start picturing myself with my beat-up *Adonis* and all the tension disappears. I stay under the shower for a few more minutes, enjoying the warmth...feeling my body temperature rising...then I shut the water off and dry myself with the warm luxurious spa towel resting on the spacious heat rack. A surge of excitement rushes through me. I can't wait another minute. I drape the towel around me, open the door and tiptoe over to Walter's bedside.

He lay peacefully on the right side of his four-poster bed...but this time under the down comforter. Someone cleaned him up, bandaged his face and dressed him in pajamas while I showered...I didn't even know he owned pajamas. Never saw them before. The doctor must have come in and washed his wounds. Walter—sleeping like a newborn baby, looking like he didn't have a care in the world—smiling...with his eyes fluttering...in REM sleep. Peaceful. I bet the doctor gave him some heavy-duty pain pills. I study the door. Just the thought of venturing out into the hall alone and returning to my room gives me the willies. So I light the ready-to-go fire in the hearth, lock the door, dim the lights and for tonight, close down my flashbacks of Horst. I climb into the bed next to Walter, placing my head on his chest. He moves slightly, enough to place his arm protectively over my head and neck, and sighs. I snuggle closer to him and close my eyes, wearing nothing but a towel...but by morning that too is fled from sight, leaving me vulnerable to my sleeping prince.

Chapter Nineteen

I awoke to heavy pounding on Walter's door. *"Oh no! Horst!"* I sat upright in a panic—wide-awake now...shivering in bed, despite its warmth. I wrapped the covers around me...not having a clue what else to do. I looked at Walter—still sound asleep. He could snooze through a hurricane. Then I heard a deep voice, booming...but not Horst's voice—This one reeked of authority...strong, but not frightening like Horst's voice. Despite my shaking uncontrollably, I let out a sigh of relief—This person would not harm us.

"Open up, please. It's the sheriff. Sheriff Tokala. I'd like to ask you a few questions. The lady next door is not answering."

The sheriff on the other side of the door probably thought that would get Walter up. Wrong. Walter kept right on sleeping through all the pounding and yelling. *"What did that doctor give him?"* I got up and went into the bathroom and found a bathrobe on the heated rod and put it on. I looked like *Sweet Pea* in the *Popeye* cartoons. But at least it covered more than the missing towel did. I went to the door, unlocked it and peeked out.

"I'm the lady next door. I was afraid to go to my room last night."

"May I come in?"

"Let me wake Walter up first. The doctor gave him something to help him sleep and he's all drowsy...What time is it?"

"Eight-thirty."

"A.M. or P.M.?"

I know the sheriff thought I'm losing my marbles...but wrong...I am being serious.

"A.M."

"Well at least we got some sleep."

"Looks that way."

"I'll just be a minute."

I closed the door and ran to put my day-old clothes on. Didn't want to be questioned in a bathrobe ten sizes too big for me. I shook Walter and handed him the bathrobe.

He smelled it and opened his eyes. "Yum. You smell good."

"Walter, get up. Please—The sheriff's here. What did that doctor give you?"

"Something to help me sleep. I think it worked."

I pulled Walter up and helped him put on the robe. He lay down again. I pulled him up. This time I propped his head against the headboard. "Now stay there and look awake."

"I'll try. Maybe some coffee would help."

"Room Service! I'll call Room Service."

"You do that, Sweetie."

Walter sounded drunk. Not a good way to sound when meeting the Fuzz. Oh well, at least he's sitting up.

I picked up the phone, called the front desk and asked that the kitchen deliver a pot of coffee and anything else they had for breakfast... up to Walter's room, as he wasn't feeling so hot. I think Sheldon's main squeeze answered. She has a low husky, sultry sounding voice—just the kind of voice that could carry Nathan Sheldon to places he wanted to go. She assured me she'd put a rush on my request. I thanked her and went to the door to fetch the sheriff.

Sheriff James Tokala entered. All six foot six of him—A lean yet muscular Native American whose eyes buzzed like those of an eagle—they enveloped my personage, the room...and Walter in one fell swoop. Tokala pounced on me first. "Sorry to disturb you at this hour, but I know you have to catch a flight...so I came early. I didn't want to miss you."

The police always know everything...especially this guy. He's da Man. Something tells me I better be on my toes.

A knock on the door—*Saved. Breakfast...Thank you, Room Service.*

"Come in," I said...and Ceira strolled in, carrying our feast. She must multi-task. *The Holiday Inn*, this is not. I thanked her more than once, trying to get her to stay. She took one look at Sheriff Tokala, handed me the tray and without a word, made a hasty retreat. He had the same effect on her. Panic. I pretended to be nonchalant and brought the tray over to Walter's bedside table and set it down. I poured him a cup of coffee, with two sugars added. *He likes his coffee sweet, like me.*

I offered some to the sheriff who declined...so I poured some for myself. Then I pulled a chair up, next to Walter's bed, sat down and faced Sheriff Tokala. "What would you like to know?"

"Well, Nathan...that is, Mr. Sheldon...tells me the two of you were attacked by some thug last night."

"That's right...Walter out in the hall...and me in my room...the room next door."

Tokala stared at Walter who was making a feeble attempt to drink his coffee. Walter looked like a chimpanzee that had just undergone brain surgery. I got up and felt his head. Still clammy...I began to worry.

Walter finished the cup and sighed. "That helped, Sweetheart. Could you pour me another, please?"

I scrambled to do as he requested and he drank the second cup with another sigh of relief. I sighed along with him. I could feel Tokala's eyes buzzing in our direction.

Walter lifted the covers, pulled his legs out one by one and struggled out of his bed. I tried to take his hand, but he waved me away and walked with a limp to the bathroom. "I'm sorry, but I have to take a shower."

I stuttered as I explained to Tokala, "The doctor gave...the doctor gave Walter something to...something to help him sleep...He never takes anything...nothing—not even aspirin. I think whatever...whatever the doctor administered really threw Walter for a loop."

"So I see."

"Thank you...Thank you for being so...so...patient. Do you mind if I eat something? I'm starved."

"No, go right ahead."

I'm not really hungry. I'm stalling. There's no way on this earth I want to talk to this guy alone. I think he knows that...He likes to see me squirm...and so he's content to wait for Walter.

Ten minutes later, after I ate two scones, two slices of thick sliced bacon, a bowl of strawberries mixed with bananas, and drank two cups of coffee, Walter emerged from the bathroom a new man—dressed in clean jeans, a turtleneck, brown plaid shirt and hiking boots, groomed and ready for action. Only the patch over his right eyebrow and a swollen left eye gave him away as the victim of a beating. *Sunglasses would fix that.*

He put out his right hand to Tokala. "Pleased to meet you, Sheriff..."

"Tokala."

"Walter Cunningham. And I'm sure you've met my boss, Angelina Seraphina."

I stood up and focused on Tokala's eyes. "Call me Tangie."

"All right. Thank you for meeting with me." He looked down at his notes. His eyes crept to Walter. "It appears that you and Ms. Seraphina... *Tangie*... are victims of an assault."

Walter looked up. "Yes. I stepped into the hall...to borrow a rose out of a basket... when this goon comes out of nowhere and attacks me. Why would he punch me for taking a rose? But what really gets me is, after he knocked me out cold, he went after Tangie...ah...Ms. Seraphina."

"That's me—The other victim." I started to squirm and my knees started to shake.

"Well, Ms. Seraphina...err...Tangie...Do you know the assailant?"

"I never saw him before."

"Do you have any idea why this man would attack you...and Mr. Cunningham?"

"Maybe he likes flowers. Maybe you should ask the goon."

"Easy, Ms. Seraphina."

"Please, call me Tangie."

"All right, Tangie."

Sheriff Tokala could see this was going nowhere.

"Look, Miss...I'm just trying to piece things together."

Walter spoke up. "Sheriff, as you can see, Tangie is not herself this morning. This whole incident spooked her out. She couldn't return to her room last night because she's terrified. Perhaps you could ease up on her a bit."

"I have no intention of upsetting Ms. Seraphina. These are just routine questions. Could either of you give me a description of the perpetrator?"

"Big," I said. *Huge contribution.*

"About six-foot five," embellished Walter.

I sat down. "Surly...scary."

"Large hairy neck...blond, almost white hair...Deep-set eyes, somewhat vacant," continued Walter.

The sheriff nodded. "Any unusual features?"

I piped in. "He likes to strangle girls."

Walter interrupted me. "Strong as an ox. Probably takes steroids or works out a lot. Muscular. He wore a dark green windbreaker over a fleece jacket and white turtleneck underneath. He had on nylon pants over jeans with brown work boots."

"He has a scar." *Finally I'm contributing something worthwhile.* "No... maybe it's a tattoo...Yes...it's a tattoo."

"Where?"

"On his right hand...no...his arm...I noticed it when I was biting him."

"Describe the tattoo, please."

I looked at Tokala. His deep-set eyes...now focused on me. Not a man to fool with...I sat down on the bedside chair. "The tattoo is black...with a bunch of numbers...and letters in a row, followed by a broken cross...No...a Swastika."

"*Terrific.* All we need around here are some Neo-Nazis."

I groaned. "God, I hate those guys. Maybe it's a prison tattoo."

"Maybe it is. I'm glad you noticed that. It will help identify him when we catch the perp."

"Good. I don't like the idea of him running around here loose."

"I assure you, Ms. Seraphina, we don't either. We'll do our best to get him. People here watch out for things out of the ordinary. Strangers stick out on Kodiak Island...I have lots of eyes working for me. On the other hand, there are a lot of places to hide—if you aren't afraid of the wilderness.

I tried to keep a straight face and pay attention to Tokala without panicking. *Not an easy task.* I glanced at Walter—cool as a cucumber… *how does he do it?*

Tokala stared at me. "Would it be possible for the two of you to come down to the police station and look at some mug shots?"

"Well, Walter and I have this floatplane to catch, but we'll be back on Kodiak tonight. We could come see you then…" I crossed my fingers… "Or tomorrow..."

"Tomorrow then."

I let out an involuntary sigh. The sheriff noticed.

Walter put his hand on my shoulder. "Where's the police station?"

"I'll send a driver to pick you up."

I got up. "Then, it's all settled." I sighed again, hoping Sheriff Tokala would leave. My palms started to sweat...a sure sign of my anxiety kicking in to full gear... *I felt the need to escape. I'd make a really bad criminal. Couldn't do the time.*

The sheriff's eyes began searching mine. *He knows I am holding out on him.* "Thank you, Ms. Seraphina." Then he turned to Walter. "Thank you, Mr. Cunningham...Sorry for your injuries…and sorry the weather is so severe. Our climate in Kodiak is usually mild. Here on the Emerald Isle, we get less snow than the rest of Alaska."

"You could have fooled me." I succumbed to dry humor...my mode of self-defense.

"The wind is supposed to pick up tonight. Get back early."

I took a deep breath and let it out slowly as Sheriff Tokala closed the door. I leaned against it and glanced at Walter.

He shot me a deadpan look. "That was fun."

"Yeah, right up on my list of favorite things to do in the morning. We get attacked and the sheriff talks about the weather. You know… Horst is from—God knows where—but not from here. He'll never be in any of their mug shots."

"So level with Tokala…Tell him what you know."

"I don't know if I'm ready to do that." *And this I don't say to Walter— "Who trusts psychics, anyway?"*

"Tangie…One of these days, you must learn to trust people."

Walter—the Mind Reader…

"Walter, I trust people. I trust you."

"Maybe it's time to branch out."

"Yeah...Maybe Tokala will pull in a sketch artist and we could get a drawing of Horst."

"In Kodiak?" Walter laughed. "Dream on."

"Not the booming metropolis...but they probably have a sketch artist."

"Wanna bet on it?"

Walter, feeling better, couldn't resist teasing me...Sometimes he likes to play the cad.

"What do you want to bet?"

"What do *you* want to bet?"

He's such a parrot. "Okay, lover boy...Dinner,"

Walter raised his eyebrows, mimicking Groucho Marx. "That's it?"

"I'm not ready to play *Strip Poker*...and neither are you. Have you seen your face?"

Walter pouted. "I thought you liked my face."

I smiled at him and handed him a pair of sunglasses. "Come on, *Mr. Bodyguard*, we have a plane to catch."

"Uh, Tangie...I didn't want to say anything in front of Tokala, but your clothes are a mess...You'd better change."

"What?"...*I must be losing it...No...I just didn't look in the mirror...I just threw my old outfit on when the sheriff came*...I looked down at my outfit..."Oh, Walter...I'm a mess." I raced into the bathroom, stared at my reflection in the mirror and let out a shriek. Then I waltzed past Walter's bedroom and opened the door leading into the hall. "Give me ten minutes," I yelled, as I strode toward my room. "That beast...He ruined a perfectly good Nordstrom's blouse!"

Chapter Twenty

When I emerged from my den twenty minutes later, I found Walter waiting outside my door...with Gus—all ready to head over to the local marina. Last night, before our dinner and Horst diversion, I scheduled us a flight leaving at 10:30 a.m. for Akhiok—which is an island accessible by floatplane or boat—where Simone lives and teaches school. We'd return 3:30 p.m. according to the flight schedule. As I calculated, we should be back by five p.m.—just in time for a visit to Father Joseph Caine.

The *Beaver* lifted from St. Paul Harbor on schedule. The sky burned bright blue diamonds as we soared over the landscape like a master eagle in flight. Much more thrilling than our commercial jaunt and our roller coaster puddle jumper—I actually enjoyed this flight, feeling in synch with the aircraft—connected to the flying. All this high-tension energy fed my mind and the wheels in my brain started humming. I contemplated how I would confront Simone—What tactics I would use to question her.

Walter dragged out his digital camera and snapped away...pretending to be an aerial photographer—for all I knew it was another one of his hidden talents—*Walter Cunningham—Professional Photographer.*

I resumed my pondering. *"What would be the right thing to say to Terese's sister? What if she won't talk to me?"*

Being a true ruby in the rough, Gus arranged for our pilot, Captain Turner, to wait for us on Akhiok, and Gus also secured a local who would drive us around Akhiok—Michel le Bec. Gus informed us Michel knew everyone on Akhiok...so we were all set. Good thing Santigo gave me a sizable advance. No way could I fund all this travel up front. *Maybe Santigo really does care about Terese. Maybe Horst isn't Santigo's goon. Maybe there is more to this whole mess than the obvious jealous, abusive husband scenario...If Santigo is not abusive, what then?* Maybe Simone could shed some light on the whole mess.

Akhiok Touring Cab—That's what the sign read on the door of the four-passenger Dodge Dakota waiting for us when we docked near the shore. A young man with black hair and a short beard, wearing a flannel fleece-lined jacket with a hood and a windbreaker over it, leaned against the passenger door and gave us a slight wave of his hand. Captain Mike Turner, issued us a warning as we deplaned at Akhiok Harbor. "I fly between weather systems, and one hellava wind storm is due tonight. I'll wait on the dock till 3:35. After that, I'm leaving—with or without you two."

"Aye, aye, Captain. We'll be here." I assured him with a salute.

Walter shook his hand. "No problem, Captain Turner."

As we walked away from the dock and crawled into the Dodge Dakota, I murmured to Walter, "The captain must get his weather reports from the sheriff."

Michel Le Bec, our tour driver, shut my door and climbed into the driver's seat. He looked at Walter and then me. I noticed his warm grayish blue eyes sparkle when he spoke. "Where to, folks?"

"How many schools do you have on the island?" I questioned in return.

"Just the one...Akhiok School."

Okay, so if Simone is here we'll find her. "Would you please take us to the school? We'd like to meet one of the teachers there."

"There's only one."

I recovered my business sense in a hurry. "Oh, that's right...only one...Simone."

"You know her?" Le Bec asked.

"No...but I know her sister." *Well, I know about her sister...not really a lie.*

The tour truck lurched forward with Walter in the front with his long legs and the driver, and me with the short legs crunched up in the boot seat behind them. We bumped and chiseled our way down a windy, rocky and snow-packed road alongside the sound until we reached a white clapboard building.

"This here's the school." Michel Le Bec pointed to a small stone and wood building, surrounded by a huge yard, with a path leading down to the beach. "Over there..." He gestured to three small cabins, all painted a light shade of gray...with faded blue trim on the windowsills and aged cedar shake roofs. "Those cabins are the living quarters for the teacher—*Simone*—and rest of the staff." Smoke rose up from each of the three chimneys on the stark dwellings, giving them a lived-in inviting appearance. "I think school's out early today. Presidents' Holiday, perhaps...or maybe it's the weather. It's not always this wicked out here. No kids on the playground. Guess they all stayed home today."

If a playground existed in the yard, I couldn't see it. Just ice and snow. I could see an obvious clearing though...no trees visible this close to the shoreline. The sun peaked out of the clouds and brightened our surroundings for a little while...turning the sky from gray to blue.

"Could you drop us here, Mister...le Bec? We don't expect to be long."

"Michel...Please...Call me Michel."

"Sure. Thank you, Michel." I shook his hand...*Strong, rugged handshake. Good soul.* "Call me Tangie...This is Walter."

Walter extended his hand. "Thanks, Michel. You don't mind waiting for us? We should be about an hour."

"Got no place to go in this weather...Think I'll take a hike down to the water and watch the waterfowl, but I'll keep a watch out for you two."

"Thanks, Michel." I pulled my wool hat over my hair as I felt a sudden breeze. "That's very thoughtful of you."

"Pleased to meet you both. I'll leave the rig unlocked in case you get back before me...It's a mother out here when the wind picks up." Michel smiled, then picked up a pair of binoculars and trudged off to the rocks by the shore.

Walter hopped out of the cab and extended his arm to me as I crawled out the back seat. "We better get a move on, Tangie."

He sensed my hesitancy. *I'm glad he came. Indispensable—Walter's new name. He knows he's got me hooked.*

Walter grinned, crunched my hat over my ears and grabbed my hand to guide me along the snowy path to the cabins.

We trampled through the snow up to the small buildings that were connected with a single porch. A single cedar bench sat in front of each cabin. I went up to the first door and knocked. No answer.

Second door. Two knocks. One answer. No Simone, but a gentleman who looked to be about seventy-seven squinted, as if bothered by the sudden burst of sunshine and our questions. He pointed next door. "Simone lives there."

I thanked him and moved ten steps to the right. I reflected on the gentleman. *He has a kind voice, but I think we woke him up from a nap.* I could smell Listerine and Alcohol odors battling around his head and oozing from his mouth. The gentleman closed his door just in time—*That combo of odors creates a gag reflex in me.* I noticed Walter smirking at me. If I didn't feel so woozy, I would have punched my secretary in the gut. *The cad. He takes pleasure in my misery.*

"Door Number Three," I announced, noticing a welcome sign made out of driftwood and shells, nailed to the plank next to the door. Besides the allotted bench, a wooden swing hung from the ceiling of the porch. I would have sat down on it but it was covered with a snowdrift. I motioned for Walter to knock on the door. He got the prize. Simone in person…but I was the first to speak.

"Hi…" I spoke with a confidence I did not feel. "I'm Tangie…and I'm not selling anything. Are you Simone Royale?"

"Do I know you?"

"Well, no. My full name is Angelina Seraphina...and this is my secretary, Walter Cunningham."

"And?"

"I'm a private detective from Seattle. I deal with missing persons… and I've been hired to find your sister. She went missing the day she left *Sea-Tac Airport*—on route to see you."

"That's strange. I just heard from her last week. Got a letter...No phone here, you know..."

"Yes...I know. That's why we're here in person…you say you got a letter?"

Simone continued to stare at me and nodded slowly…not yet willing to trust me.

Walter spoke up. "We've got about an hour...Then we have to catch the floatplane back to Kodiak...before the weather turns."

"Yes." Simone nodded. "You know, there really isn't any place to stay overnight here...unless you know someone. It's a small island...not geared to tourists...We just have a few hikers now and then. You don't want to miss your plane." She looked us both over and seeming satisfied with our appearance, continued. "It's cold out here on the porch; why don't you come in?"

Simone led us into her cabin and shut the heavy plank door. She motioned to the wood stove in the corner...where we could warm up after standing outside in the freezing cold. She continued to stare at me. "How can I help you?"

I took off my gloves and warmed my hands near the blower on the stove, and looked around the room. Small...like an efficiency apartment in Seattle...living room/bedroom combination...one closet... small kitchen in the corner with a hand-carved picnic table with matching benches underneath...for dining purposes. The table was adorned with a red cloth and a vase and dried flowers sat in the middle of it... an attempt on Simone's part to cheer the place up a bit. Utilitarian wooden shelves fastened to the wall to hold dishes and pots and pans, and a small pantry appeared built into the wall. I noticed a bulletin board on the wall above the picnic table with pictures of children, presumably Simone's students, and various children's artwork fastened above and below the photos.

I smiled at Simone. "You must like your job here."

"I do." She smiled and showed a beautiful set of perfect teeth.

"It's always good to like what you do. Tell me, when Terese wrote you, did she say if she was in any trouble?"

"No, not at all...Terese just said visiting me didn't fit into her plans at the moment."

"Maybe she didn't want to involve you. There's this creepy guy following her. I think she's on the run to get away from him."

Simone raised her left eyebrow. The other, with the earring pierced on it, stayed intact. "Terese loved her husband—Fred. He worshipped her and she loved his attention and his money."

"You never saw any signs of discord?" I asked.

"No, they were always lovey-dovey…but what do I know? I'm just the Plain Jane school teacher sister."

Simone didn't look Plain Jane to me. Her natural blond straight hair hung even around her shoulders and her blue eyes sparkled as she spoke. Her slim, tall build probably turned heads, even if she didn't notice. Shy people are like that. They don't realize their true potential. Even in her argyle wool socks and worn-out ski sweater, which hung loosely over tight jeans, she radiated that fresh glow models envy. *If she thinks she's plain, Terese must be a knockout.*

"Simone, why did you come to Akhiok?" I asked, trying to understand.

"Oh, adventure...the challenge...Plus, the teaching job. It's hard to become a full-time teacher in Seattle—unless you want to substitute. Here I have my own school...I love the students...The pay's good...free room and board...well, lunch with the kids...I cook my own dinner…but the school district helps me with the groceries…and I'm getting really good experience. I can always return to Seattle if I want to...but now I'm not so sure...This place grows on you...You should come here in the spring…it's so beautiful then..."

"So I've been told." I thought of Father Finn's words.

Walter decided to enter the conversation, after being quiet for an unusual amount of time. "I used to teach...I'm taking a break for awhile."

"Where?"

Averting his eyes from mine, Walter coughed. "*Lakeside School.*"

This time I raised my eyebrow.

Simone responded immediately to Walter. "Bill Gates' old alma mater? No shit! Congrats landing that one…but why would you leave?"

"Same reason you're here...for the challenge." He spoke to Simone, but he winked at me.

My turn to be perplexed… Walter never told me he taught at *Lakeside.* I thought he taught delinquents at a crummy junior high. *What's Walter cooking up now? Ah, yes...Building confidence, camaraderie with the witness... Good cop, bad cop. I get it—Thanks, Pal. Now…for the hard stuff—Gotta grill the sister.*

"Hey Simone…I hate to ask you, but could you show me any recent letters or gifts Terese sent to you?" *I mean let me touch them so I can get a vibe from them…*

"I could do that." She went over to a small oak desk, which perched under the front window and overflowed with stacks of papers and books. A stapler and tumbler of pens and pencils kept the stacks company—Standard faire for teachers. Simone opened the top drawer and pulled out an envelope. "This is the letter that came last week." She walked over to the corner of the room by the door, took a scarf off a hook and handed it to me like she was giving me part of her sister. "Terese knitted this herself and sent it to me for Christmas..."

"Terese knits?"

"Yeah...We're both kind of crafty. Our mom was the hippy type."

"I know what you mean...My mom used to make a lot of my clothes for me when I attended elementary school...Do you mind if I sit down for a bit?"

"Take the day bed. It's the most comfortable."

Walter leaned against the wall and Simone sat down on the only chair...a straight ladder-back chair, near the desk. With the three of us crowding the place, the room warmed up a bit—It invited us to relax. I sat down on the day bed. A handmade quilt adorned the sleeping quarters...Peering from the center of the quilt, an eagle leaped at me...as it soared into the sunset with peaked mountains and purple sunsets. The object d'art out shown everything else in the room, adding an artistic flair to the otherwise shabby-chic interior, giving the cabin added class. *Simone does quilting to pass the long winter nights.* I focused first on the letter that Terese sent to Simone. I examined the envelope—Bonney Lake postmark. *That's important. I must remember that.* I took the letter out. I read it silently—Usual sisterly stuff. One line got to me...

"Know that I love you, know that I care...No matter what anyone says, I'll always be with you. Don't know when I'll see you again. Love, Terese."

I put the letter to my face and felt love and sadness... and hopelessness. *Terese is running out of options...and time.* I handed the letter back to Simone. "Terese is in danger. That guy I told you about...He may come out here...to your island...looking for her. Walter will write out a description of him for you...I'll inform the authorities in Kodiak—to keep an eye on you, just in case. Keep the letter, but burn the envelope. I won't divulge any information that you give me."

Simone's face turned white—almost corpse-like. She got up off the chair, took the envelope from me, opened the door to the woodstove and tossed it in... watching it catch fire and burn. She turned to me, just catching on to the gravity of the situation. "So this is serious... Terese is in danger... I am in danger... and there's no one here to protect me... except Pete... He's next door... the caretaker... and he's seventy-five."

Well, I was off his age by two years. Not bad. "Does he have a gun?" *Silly question. Everyone in Alaska has a gun.*

"Yes."

"Good. Tell him to keep it loaded and keep watch... I'll tell Michel to keep a lookout. He seems dependable."

Simone nodded. "He's not here all the time, but he's attentive to me when he's around... Sometime he helps me with the children during recess... and during lunch..."

I detected a bit of longing in her voice. *I bet she's shy around men... unlike her sister.*

"Say, Simone," I asked. "What did Terese do before she met Santigo?"

"She used to waitress... at a high-class fancy restaurant in downtown Seattle... That's where she met Fred... at *The Thirteen Coins*... Do you know the place?"

"Yeah. Never been there, though."

Walter probably has... Probably went there with Bill Gates... What a player... He had me fooled... But we will have the talk... Tonight...

Simone started twirling her straight hair, twisting it in circles as she continued her story. "Well, Terese never had any interest in school—the studying part, that is—Just the social life. She loves clothes, television, cars... her cell phone... All that chick stuff. And she loves guys with money... and they love her. Santigo happened to have the most, so she married him."

I looked down at the cashmere scarf on my lap and ran my fingers through it... Long, wide, camel-colored... ultra-soft... folded with loving hands as it was placed in a box by a sister who did not understand her sibling. "Terese loves you very much, Simone. She wanted to come see you, but she was frightened... she had to get away..."

"Fred?"

"No. Someone else. At first, I thought it might be him, but now… no. He knows the goon that's following Terese, though. I'm sure of that...but I don't think Fred put him up to frightening her...Someone else did—someone we don't know."

Walter handed me the description he wrote down. I looked at it and gave it to Simone. "Take this."

I got a business card out of my pocket and placed it in her hand. "Write me...or call me if you can get to a phone...any time. I promise I'll help you."

"My supervisor has a satellite phone that I can use for emergencies. She visits the school every other week."

"If Terese contacts you, tell her she has nothing to fear from me...or Walter..."

"How can I be sure?"

I rose from the day bed, went over to Walter and took off his sunglasses. "Look at Walter's face. He…and I…are being targeted...just like your sister."

I unwrapped my scarf and displayed the marks on my neck—remnants of Horst.

Simone stared at us with the frightened eyes of a caged animal.

"Please, Simone…for your safety...Don't tell anyone what we talked about...Someone's searching for Terese and he doesn't play nice."

Simone's cat eyes started to tear up. "My sister is all that I have in the world... After Mom died, it's just been the two of us...We haven't always gotten along, but I love Terese...I want her to be safe…I want her to be happy."

"We are going to do our best to find her...but please...even if Santigo writes to you or tries to reach you in any way...Tell him nothing...You can say we talked but don't give out any information except she never showed up. He's liable to screw things up. He's not the brightest guy. Tell him you are simply disappointed Terese didn't visit. That's all. Be convincing."

"I can do that."

"Give me your address...and your emergency phone…I'll keep you posted. If I find her soon, I'll send you a postcard saying: S*pring is here in Seattle*. I won't go into detail until I'm sure she's safe."

"Thank you…I'll look forward to hearing from you…hopefully with good news."

"Good luck with your students. I hope the weather clears soon."

"I'm grateful for my students—they keep me busy…and my mind off my problems. They're my second family, you know. If you find Terese, tell her I love her and I forgive her for everything—Tell her to come to Akhiok…Tell her how beautiful it is here…She could be safe with me…I wish I could say these things to her in person..."

"Me too…If I find her, I will share your sentiments…Think good thoughts. "I shook her hand. Steady, firm handshake. *Simone may be shy, but she's not a pushover.*

"Thank you." She hugged me in appreciation.

I looked in her eyes and saw worry and pain, college loans and rotten old boyfriends, unresolved conflicts with her sister and no parents. *No wonder she's on this desolate island. It's a good fit.*

Simone picked up the letter and scarf, brought them to the desk and laid them down like they were her only treasures in the world. She opened a carved wooden box and pulled out a business card with the Akhiok School emblem on it—a totem of salmon, eagle and raven. "Send me mail at this address. I'll get it. You can also call me at the number listed, in case of emergency. Someone will contact me personally or forward a message to me."

I nodded and smiled at her. "Will do. Trust us…Walter and I will do our utmost to find her."

Before we said a final good bye, Simone offered to make some tea before we went out in the cold…apologizing for not asking sooner.

I shook my head. "No…maybe next time, Simone. We can't miss the plane's takeoff…we'll be stranded here…and we have a meeting with the sheriff…"

Simone's eyes widened. "I understand."

Resigning herself to being alone, she looked like she could use a close friend to lean on…She stood propped up in the doorway, waving to us as we walked down the path to Michel's truck. I felt bad leaving her. She reminded me of a little worn-out teddy bear I had once, long ago... ready to fall over at any minute. *She's controlling her tears—but they'll begin to flow the moment we're out of sight.*

We climbed into our waiting cab. Before Michel shut the door for us, he turned, smiled and waved to Simone. Then he went over to the driver's side and climbed in his rig. We sped off towards the dock, hoping to arrive on time. Michel got us there with three minutes to spare. Walter handed him a tip and I made a request. "Keep an eye on Simone for us, will you, Michel? She could use your friendship and watching over right now. She's going through a tough time."

Michel looked at me and I saw understanding in his eyes...and something else. *Dang! The guy's in love with her and she doesn't even know. Maybe she'll drop her guard and let him into her heart. I hope so. Nothing like a crisis to bring people together...I'm a sucker for true love.*

Michel nodded at me.

Walter shook his hand. "Thanks for your help, Michel."

Michel nodded again. *Man of few words—The dependable type. No hype. No show. He's there if you need him...A good friend to have. Simone will be in good hands.* We left Michel le Bec standing alone, alongside his cab, staring out into the horizon like a lonesome dove. We hopped into the *Beaver*—just as Captain Mike fastened his seat belt and revved up the engine.

Chapter Twenty-One

The flight on the *Beaver* turned out to be short and uneventful, which was not to say it was not beautiful. We watched the sunset and the clouds roll in gently like cotton candy. Too bad other things crept into my mind. I took three deep breaths...letting them out slowly...forcing myself to relax...*Heaven knows when I'll be in a floatplane again.* Might as well enjoy the moment. The tailwind carried us towards our destination and the darkening skies began to lull me to sleep. I heard in the recesses of my mind Walter chatting comfortably with the pilot and my body rested like the baby in the old lullaby, *"Rock a bye baby in the tree top..."*—only I dozed in a noisy plane, whose engine produced a calming effect on me. *Weird. Maybe I'm just exhausted.* I nodded off to sleep. Then, in what seemed to be no time at all, *"Down will come baby, cradle and all."*

I awoke with a start. We landed...on choppy waters—still in one piece. I took a deep breath and let it out slowly. Grateful. We taxied over to the part of Kodiak Marina reserved for aircraft and pulled alongside the same dock we departed from—Number One. *Easy to remember... like Santigo's plumbing supply business...Numero Uno...*

Walter thanked Captain Turner, who shook his head in agreement, as Walter gave him two Ulysses S. Grants.I wondered about this, but being near comatose from sleeping so soundly, I didn't react. Walter got out of the *Beaver* and I followed. He helped me crawl out without falling over. I felt like I just took off my ice skates after skating for two hours. A minute after my foot left the door, I heard the engine revive up...and the pilot and his floatplane disappeared. I surmised that Captain Turner has a private dock somewhere nearby...Lots of wilderness with secluded fishing cabins and log homes along the waterfront around here...I noticed a few earlier when we first took off on route to Akhiok—Lots of places for people to find solitude…or to hide out.

Walter and I tramped off the pier and headed back toward our pick-up point. Gus appeared out of nowhere…*Johnny on the Spot.*

"Hey, Gus," I said as we hopped in his toasty vehicle. "Do you know the pastor of the mission outside of town?"

"You mean Father Joe? Heck, everyone knows him. He's been m' savior since I lost m' leg, you know…He's okay, that padre. Hell, I wasn't even Catholic then…wasn't nothin'…and he took to helpin' me. First he helped me get around, driving me places and stuff...Then he started forcing me to walk again...But the most important... he believed in me...got me to quit the drinkin'...Around here, that's a miracle."

"Would you mind taking us to see this *Miracle Man*? You could you drop us off, and come back for us...or wait for us at the mission...I'd really like to speak with him. We won't be long. Walter will keep you company."

This time, Walter raised his eyebrows. I whispered in his ear, "Walter, I think I should talk to Father Joe alone. What I have to say, I don't think he'd appreciate the two of us being there...He's gonna have a tough time with this one."

"It's your call, Babe," he whispered back. "I'll be here if you need me." Then he squeezed me around the waist and kissed my ear. I melted. At this very moment, I wanted nothing more than to make out with Walter. I hear a tune in my head…"You are my life…you are my love… don't ever go, don't ever go…With you I hear music in my soul…don't let me go…don't let me go…" *Ah...Gus' radio...not my brain...but I can't deny it's a good thought…Love that tune…and I love…*

"Crunch." The *Chevy Suburban* ground to a halt.

"Here we are, folks. Mind if I snooze a bit?" Gus yawned. "I'll keep the heater running so as you won't get cold when you get back."

"Go right ahead." Walter answered our cabbie for the two of us. He took a flashlight out of his parka pocket and smirked…"I'll just sit back and read this here tourist guide. You go ahead, Tangie."

"Be good." I smiled at him and caressed his cheek with my gloved hand. Then I headed down the snow-covered wooded path to *the Mission of Saint Francis.*

The stately log mission church with a chimney and steeple of equal height shone against the snow background...illuminated with outdoor lighting. A tall stained glass window echoed the enchanting entrance. I gasped as I encompassed its beauty. The entire setting reminded me of a *Currier and Ives* print, Alaskan style. The mission could make money—selling postcards of its place of worship and its surroundings. As I got closer, I studied the detail of the artistic window greeting the parishioners—It embodied the wonder of Kodiak Island. I noticed the background setting—the forest, with the natural world in harmony—the Kodiak bear standing in harmony with the wolf and eagle, and beside them—the Christ figure in Native American clothing, surrounded by children of all races ...joining in a circle with the animals...with glacier peaks and the sea nearby. The message: All are welcome in this place of peace.

I tried the entrance...It was open...unlike the churches in the Seattle area that close their doors to strangers...except at peak periods...or business hours. I glanced at my watch. Five o'clock—Perhaps Father Joe was having his dinner. I looked around the foyer, which appeared empty except for a statue of Saint Francis, depicted holding a bird on his arm. I strolled into the stillness of the church and dipped my fingers into holy water and blessed myself as I had as a child. *It's been a long time.*

I looked up at the altar. Simple. A wooden crucifix hung on the wall above...and a light fixture hanging from the ceiling shone a soft light upon it. A few flowers decorated the lectern. On the right, candles sat like sentinels around the statue of Mary. One flickered, burning a soft light into the corner darkness. *"Better to light one candle...than to curse the darkness."* On the left side of the altar stood a lone piano and a stand-up microphone...and further down a safe distance from the music area, sat an oversized wood stove, which I assumed heated the sanctuary. A tall bin with enormous stacks of wood stood nearby. One person with his back to me was kneeling down, praying the rosary...He murmured softly...meditating on his beads, lost in prayer. I eased myself into a pew. *"What am I going to say to Father Joe?"*

I sat in silence for about five minutes and rested peacefully amidst the calm in the church, enjoying the quiet. A door creaked. I turned my head around and recognized a priest walking towards me…I guessed him to be around fifty-five—close to my mother's age. He came over and sat down next to me. He had a full head of hair, red with gray sprinkles in it and a matching beard, neatly trimmed. He appeared to be about as tall as Walter and judging by his gait as he walked into the church, physically fit. Alaska agreed with him. He looked younger than his years. Except for the white collar around his neck, you would not suspect him to be the priest. With his beard, he looked more like a logger or a trapper.

He took off his woolen gloves and reached out a hand to me. "Might you be Angelina?"

"Yes…and I am glad to finally meet you." I took his warm hand in mine. "How did you recognize me, Father Joe?

"Well, as I was coming back from my late afternoon hike, I saw Gus with his head hanging out of his truck. I went over to see if he needed my assistance. Turns out he was just napping. I guess I woke him up. There was another chap with him in the back seat, reading. He informed me you came inside…and wanted to see me…"

"Yes, thank you, Father Joe." I extended my hand. "My name is Angelina…"

"Ah, yes…Angelina." We have a beautiful church, don't you think?"

"Yes, Father. It's lovely."

"The people of Kodiak built it by hand. Every log, every stone...It took fifteen years to get it this wonderful. A local artist, Jim Trench, did the stained glass."

"It's beautiful…I admired the window on my way in…"

"It has a way of welcoming visitors…"

"Father Joe, did Father Finnegan tell you I'd be coming?"

"Yes, indeed."

"Can we talk here?"

"Business?"

"Personal."

"Well, if it's of a personal nature, perhaps we could go into the confessional." Father Joe gestured to a small wooden box big enough for two people to sit uncomfortably next to one another.

Claustrophobia set in...No way I was going in there.

"I didn't come all the way to Alaska to make a confession."

"What then?"

"It's about a baby."

"Okay, Miss, perhaps we could go into my office. It's small but it's private."

Father Joe led me to the back of the church and turned right. He took out a key and opened a door which had a soaring eagle carved onto the upper part of it. The bird looked like it was protecting the priest's private den. Father Joe motioned me to walk in. Neat. Tidy. Miniscule...But definitely larger than the confessional. I could handle the office. Father Joe pointed to a folding chair opened up alongside the desk. Another folding chair leaned against the wall. Perhaps three people, tops, could fit into this inner sanctum.

"This used to be a closet."

"I can see that."

"I told the parishioners I needed an office, so they cut a hole in the logs, put in a small window and carved me this door. It's a good place to meet with engaged couples and folks planning weddings and funerals and people like you...with personal problems. It's small, but private. Now what's this about a baby?"

"Well it's about Clancy."

"That's a name I haven't heard in a while."

"Well, Clancy...He's twenty now...was left on the doorstep of *Our Lady of Peace Church* shortly after you left."

"Ah...yes...I remember now...Father Finn was there at the time...He wrote me something about a child being abandoned at the church. He said they never found his parents. Poor lad."

"That's what Father Finn said."

"What?"

"*Poor lad.*"

"Yes...family's so important."

"Father Joe, I have something to show you."

I took out the two photos...one of Father Joe himself...from the parish directory...and the other, Clancy in a recent college photo. I presented them both to him. He laid them on his desk and studied them, like a scientist looking under a microscope. His hand started to shake.

"Who is this?" he muttered, pointing to Clancy.

"I thought you could help me out."

"How old is this lad?"

"I told you...Twenty. His name is Clancy. This is the child, now grown up...who was left at your church. The social worker, Selene Russo..."

"I remember Selene...she was also a parishioner..." Father Joe said.

"Well, Selene questioned the child, Clancy. He told Selene that his mother's name is *Tare* and that she left him there to wait for *Uncle Joey...* and that she left and never returned."

"*Uncle Joey...Uncle Joey...*" The mission priest repeated over and over. His eyes became wider as the photos seemed to take on a life of their own...grabbing him and shaking him with their power. He looked up at me with tears in his eyes.

"Angelina...Miss..."

"Seraphina."

"Ms. Seraphina...I have a sister, *Claire.* I haven't seen her since... since..."

"Since?"

"Since she ran away...She was seventeen at the time...My mother was very strict you see...and Claire didn't have much of a social life...Then this boy in my sister's class came calling on her...Well...Claire liked him—Rick...a lot. My mother hated him. She told Claire that Rick was just after one thing...and she forbade Claire to see him." Father Caine stopped talking for a minute and closed his eyes...He cleared his throat and stood up. "Tare...*Tare*...could be Claire..."

"Yes...*Tare* could be Claire...Clancy was only four when he was abandoned...He probably couldn't pronounce all his consonants..." I nodded my head in agreement.

"My mother wrote to me..." Father Caine brushed his hair with his hand and sat down. He opened his top desk drawer as if looking for something...and then closed it again. "She told me she was having troubles with Claire...and begged me to come home. But I didn't. I had just begun my vocation...as a new priest...I couldn't leave my parish so soon...I was thirty-two then. I want you to know, I've been celibate as long as I've been a priest. It took me a long time to take my vows, but I never broke them. But, it's uncanny...This young man looks so much like me...and my father...His grandfather...I am thinking...he must be my sister's child."

"Did you see your sister before or after she ran away?"

"Once. Before she ran away. I was able to go home for a short visit... to my childhood home in Portland, Oregon...That's where my mother and Claire lived... together. When Claire was a senior in high school, she began rebelling against my mother's rules. You see, my father died the year before and my sister had a really hard time dealing with his death... She and mother were constantly fighting—blaming each other for his death."

"Why is that?"

"My father was an alcoholic. My mother was the enabler; my sister, the forgotten child."

"How did you fit in?"

"The over-achiever. I tried to do everything right...the peacemaker. But I failed. I failed my sister. A week after I went back to my parish in Edmonds, she ran away with Rick...Left no forwarding address...I could help everyone else...but not my own sister..."

"Rick..." I said to myself. *"Clancy called Rick a bad man...Said he hit his mom...Hit him..."*

"I'm so sorry, Father Caine...Could you tell me about your mother?"

"After Claire left, Mother became very bitter. Blamed me. Blamed my father for dying and leaving her alone. Said everyone she loved left her. Then she got pancreatic cancer. She didn't tell anyone until it was too late to get any kind of help...It had progressed too far...and she was in so much pain..."

I looked into Father Joe's eyes and saw the affliction connected to his youth—growing up in an alcoholic family...and his inability to stop the destruction of his family.

"Please go on...I'm sorry...I know this is hard for you."

Father Caine clasped his hands as if in prayer, then looked up at a crucifix on the wall. He continued speaking in a somber, even voice... but it rose in pitch and stumbled as he went along. "Before my mother died, I went to see her on her deathbed. She started confiding in me about how cruel she was to Claire. You see…Claire had come home… once...after she left...and my mother threw her out, calling her a tramp. Told her not to come back. She probably used up the last of her energy to do that...To think her last act was one of anger and hurt. My mother was heavily medicated when she told me this...I don't think she even knew it was me..."

"At least she had you to talk to…even if…"

"Perhaps…but I know…in her mind, she unburdened herself to someone else...and it's so strange…she never once said anything about a baby...just pointed to her prayer book and cried out in agony...I don't know if it was from her illness or grief. Her unburdening to me was not a formal confession…she didn't even know me. If it were, I would not be discussing all this with you..."

"I understand, Father. I think it's important that we find Claire."

"How? I don't know where to look."

"I'm a detective. I can do these things."

"What things?"

"Searches. Uncovering clues. Do you have any photos, papers, any information that could help me?"

Father Caine stared at me for a moment, opened up his desk drawer and this time, pulled out a leather folder. He placed it in my hands.

I opened it. A photo of a young girl stared at me. I held it up. "Claire?"

"Yes…that is Claire's graduation picture...but as far as I know, she never graduated...my sister left school before she received her diploma..."

In a calm, deliberate manner, the priest opened the front drawer to his desk one last time, and pulled out a tattered manila envelope. "I saved a few of my mother's treasures...the prayer book she always read... and some other mementos...I could loan these to you if it would help..."

"It would help..."

Father Joe handed me the memorabilia as if he entrusted a relic to my care.

I stood up, shook his hand and thanked him. Then I looked into his eyes and saw warmth, understanding...and a little glimmer of hope. *He's a good priest. I think he'd be a good brother and uncle…given the chance.*

"I'll be back..."—All I could say at the moment, but I meant it.

I departed the office, and walked through the church towards the outside door. I paused in the foyer to peer once more at the stained glass window, searching within the picture for understanding and clarity. I stood there like a statue, meditating on the children holding hands with the creatures of the forest and the figure of Christ smiling down at them—and for a moment, I thought, me. My hand gripped the knob of the door, but I could not turn it and leave. I stood silent, frozen. I took a deep breath and summoned the will to open the door, but became distracted by the sound of Father Joseph Caine's footsteps...running after me.

"*Clancy*." The priest called, in a raspy voice. "*Clancy* was my father's name."

Father Caine came closer. The tone in his voice changed back to somber. "My sister's name is Mary Claire Caine. She's my baby sister—she's always been in my heart. If you find her, tell her I love her and that I'm sorry. I didn't know...I didn't know..."

I nodded and noticed tears flowing down his cheeks. Father Joe shook my hand once more—as if I were the only connection he had to his family. I could feel tears forming in my eyes. "Thank you, Angelina... for your help. Have a safe journey home." He opened the door for me to leave. A rush of wind and pounding snowflakes attacked me. I waved goodbye as I ran to my waiting vehicle. I jumped in next to Walter... and burst into tears. Walter hugged me, kissed my cheeks and I buried my face in his warm parka.

The promised storm began pounding on the three of us like a beast of prey, without let up...warning us to seek shelter from the havoc threatening to destroy us—and the ones we loved.

Chapter Twenty-Two

"I'd better get you two back to the lodge while I can still maneuver this rig. This here gale's a doozie. Strong winds...downed power lines—any minute now. We'll be lucky if a tree doesn't crash down on us." Gus gunned his four-wheeler and we bounced back in our seats.

"That's all reassuring." I grit my teeth and hung on to the armrest.

Walter smiled and patted my hand. "Just like November in Seattle."

"Yeah," Gus continued. "It'll come in mighty powerful and just as fast, disappear—out to sea. Good thing you two aren't flying tonight."

"Yeah, good thing..." I parroted. *Cold showers in the morning for sure. Brrr. Well at least we have a fireplace in our room. Room...Which one will we sleep in tonight? "His or Hers?" Tomorrow we have to talk to the sheriff. Bummer. Maybe I'll level with him. I've got to let him know about Horst. That's only right. So what if he thinks I'm a kook. I can live with that...I have all my life.*

About 10 p.m. the storm decided to torment us. Walter and I finished polishing off the last of our feast—compliments of room service. I lounged on the bed in my suite, looking at the photo of Claire enshrined in it's leather case and picked up the manila envelope Father Joe entrusted to me, deciding to search its contents. Just as I peaked inside, the lights flickered and died.

"Rats! I was gonna do some research."

"Come on Angelina. It's not so bad. We could get romantic."

I got up off my bed and went over to our makeshift dining table, put my arms against the vacant chair and leaned back over the roaring fire to get warm. Walter followed me. He put his arms around my shoulder and pressed into me. I wanted to stay like this forever—feeling his strength—but then I remembered his remarks to Simone…earlier today about *Lakeside School…He has been deceiving me…*Walter ruffled my feathers and I fumed—it's hard for me to turn off my anger like a faucet. *He's holding out on me…I cannot forget…*I forced myself to turn around and shake off the spell he so deftly cast upon me.

"What's this about *Bill Gates…*and *Lakeside School?*" I could feel the steam coming out of my ears and blowing my words into his face like bullets.

Walter put his hands up. "I only met him once...well maybe twice...I shook his hand. Hell, he visited his alma mater—my school…"

"Oh, so it's your school now. I bet you attended *Lakeside…*as a kid… before you became part of the staff."

"I cannot lie to you, Tangie." Walter broke eye contact with me as I fumed.

"But you misrepresented yourself to me. Why the poor teacher bit?"

He looked down at me and attempted a smile. "Endearing?"

"No. Phony. I hate liars." *Well I'm one myself, that doesn't count here.*

"I never lied to you. I just didn't embellish."

"Yeah, right."

"Angelina...I just wanted to be around you...You seemed to need my help."

"I do." *That is the truth.* "Just don't lie to me anymore."

"Fair enough." Walter held up his hand. "Boy Scout's Honor. Now... do you want to tell me about Father Joe…and why you became so upset after meeting with him?"

I nodded. "Actually it's about Clancy." I took Walter's hand and motioned him to follow me to the bed—which he did without any urging on my part…

To tell the truth, this suite's freezing—no power, and Walter's a good blanket. I snuggled up to him in the dark, and proceeded to tell him the entire story of Clancy, the abandoned child…only pausing now and then to sip a few glasses of wine with my *blanket*…Together we polished off an entire bottle of Chardonnay…falling asleep before I got to the manila envelope part…I remember thinking…*Well, that can wait, I'll read it later…when I can see.*

I drifted off to sleep in Walter's arms…*Dreaming about coming back to Kodiak in the springtime…and dogwood trees… with Clancy at my side…and then I was in the forest…and the bears came charging…out of hibernation…I saw one coming closer…after Horst…and then Gus appeared…telling me Kodiak bears don't usually attack people but they'd make an exception with Horst…The last part of my dream took a turn…I remember this the best…Walter and me, together…and then…I could see Terese's face…smiling at me…I could find her, I suppose…Perhaps this is not a dead end…Perhaps it's not a dream…*

Chapter Twenty-Three

Nine a.m. in the morning...Brrr—Why didn't I stay in bed? Getting up, dressed and packed...after cold showers—In Alaska, that's no easy task. The power comes back on just as I step out of the bathroom, soaking wet, frigid. Figures. Just like during the Seattle windstorms. No justice for freezing souls. Maybe it's nature's way of cooling our passion. Well, at least I could blow-dry my hair; it wouldn't freeze into icicles when I went outside. Seattle is looking very good to me as I pull on my one and only cashmere turtleneck. However, Kodiak is growing on me in a weird way...Like being held captive by a wild animal. Unspoiled beauty. Rugged, open spaces...No traffic gridlock. No I-5. I do miss my lattes however. No restaurant does espresso here. It seems like such a long time since I made a cappuccino...since Ballard...in our own Home Sweet Home... "Be it ever so humble..."

Let's see...we have a one p.m. departure time via the ol' puddle jumper jet to Anchorage and then back to Seattle via Alaska Airlines. I simply cannot wait... Maybe we'll be home for a late take-out dinner at Mom's and retrieve Pebbles the wonder dog. I forgot to warn her about my Westie's underwear fetish. She probably had to go shopping. Perhaps she'll switch from Fruit of the Loom to Victoria's Secret. It could happen...

Wish Walter and I could dine at Salty Jack's Restaurant once more before heading home...but that's put on a back burner...for another time...gotta face Sheriff Tokala... Walter signaled me with a hug and a whisper in my ear, interrupting my meditative state of mind...*reminding me...*of our escort... the police car...waiting for us like a somber beating drum. My good thoughts turned to gloom. *Time to face the music.*

Sheriff Tokala showed up five minutes after his uniformed policeman deposited the two of us in his office. I know because I stared at the old wooden clock on the wall, counting every minute. He strode in like a cougar, analyzed the visitors to his lair, nodded and led us to a stack of books. Mug shots.

Walter eyed me, eyebrows up. I caved.

"Sheriff...I don't think we'll find the assailant in those books. He's not local."

"Do you want to level with me?"

"Well, yes."

"Good."

"May I sit down?"

Tokala motioned to a straight back chair next to his desk. "Sit."

Walter smiled. *The cad. He has a perverted sense of humor. Enjoys seeing me squirm.*

So I sat and started pulling at my fingers. *Nasty habit. Dead give away when I'm nervous. Probably makes me look guilty, which of course I am. Withholding evidence...but now, I am like that little girl in the confessional... ready to bare all. I swear I hear Walter chuckling. He'll pay for this... He revels in my misery...*

"Well, Sheriff..." I began, stuttering as usual...in Tokala's presence. "The man who...who attacked Walter...and myself...meets the description of...of a thug...a creep from the Seattle area...The same creep who harassed a young woman—a young woman...by the name of...Terese Santigo at *Sea-Tac Airport*—right before...right before she was to board a flight out here...but she never made it...She's the wife of one of my clients, and she's g...g...gone missing—right after meeting up with this guy—the creep—I discovered his name...his name is *Horst*...That's all... That's all I knew about him, before our own encounter with him—and we told you about that. You see, I'm a private investigator...I specialize in missing persons...I flew out here...I flew out here with Walter—my secretary—to search for Terese."

I shut up and handed Tokala the photo of Terese...the one Santigo entrusted to me.

He took the professional photo from me and studied it for a long time. Then he leaned back in his desk chair and closed his eyes...thinking, I presume. *This sheriff makes me nervous. Especially when he doesn't talk. I look at Walter. Not a bead of sweat on his brow. No guilty conscience. How does he do it?*

I decided to speak up and break the silence. "Terese's sister, *Simone*, lives...and teaches on Akhiok Island. I came out here to interview her."

"Why didn't you tell me all this the other day?"

"Confused?"...*Correct—Not lying. Cannot lie to da' Man.*

"So why are you telling me all this now?"

"So you know. Maybe...maybe a police artist can draw a sketch of the thug who attacked us from our description."

Tokala laughed. "In Kodiak? We're not that well equipped here."

"Great." I thought. *"Now I owe Walter dinner. He's always right. And he knows it. I hate that about my fearless secretary."*

Tokala studied me for a while and then stood up. "This is a small force. Perhaps when you return to Seattle you could give the police your description and they could fax a sketch to us."

*Walter to the rescue again...*He stood up and faced Tokala. "We could do that for sure."

I gave my secretary my wide-eyed look.

Walter winked at me, and confided in Tokala, man to man. "I have friends at *Seattle P.D.*"

"Good." Our interrogator seemed impressed by my secretary. "Here's my business card...Phone number and fax included. Have your department contact me."

Oh, so now it's Walter's department. He's gonna have some explaining to do.

"Will do," answered Walter, with just the right amount of respect, and shook Tokala's hand like they were old friends. *How does he do it? What a technique...*

Sheriff James Tokala centered his eagle eyes on me one last time. *I feel like I've become Lucy on the I Love Lucy Show—Gotta admit I watch those reruns on the classic television channel. Trapped by my own wit. I'm always the one on the hot seat. Walter's always peachy keen. It's not fair.*

Regaining my composure, I pulled out my business card from my purse and chirped, "Here's where you can reach me if you are so inclined." I attempted a smile as I rose from the chair, holding onto the back of it, trying to hide my shaking knees.

Tokala took the card and returned my smile...the first smile from him since we met. I didn't know if he was mocking me or forgiving me. He looked me straight in the eyes. "Thank you for leveling with me, Ms. Seraphina. If you don't mind, I would like to make a copy of this photo of Terese. I'll keep it on file, and the department will keep a lookout for her—and let you know if she appears on Kodiak."

I nodded. "Sure. Thanks, Sheriff." Tokala strolled over to a photocopy machine like he had all the time in the world. *Stalling technique. I know that one.* He stared at the photo before making a copy, studying Terese's eyes—*Her eyes—certainly intoxicating to a guy—So Tokala's not immune to beauty. Perhaps he has a soft spot after all.*

It took a while for the copy machine to warm up. Tokala continued to stare at Terese before putting it face down, reverently on the top tray. When he finished his little ritual, he handed the photo back like he was returning to me a precious work of art. With his eyes boring into mine—a fox studying its competition—he winked. "You be careful, Ms. Seraphina..."

"Will do." I choked. His concern took me by surprise. *He knows more than he lets on...about a lot of things...*

We shook hands. I wiped my sweaty palms on my thighs. *Dead giveaway.Authority triggers that effect on me...*

I can't totally figure Tokala out. I think the intimidation factor interferes with my sensory channels. I'd hate to cross him. Glad I spilled my guts—Anxiety level going down...I can breathe again... Definitely would not like to be on his bad list...Tokala has a way of finding things out. Good sheriff. Astute detective. He's on to me...I know. I can live with that small detail... or so I surmised, like a smart aleck at that moment. But moments pass and Time figures out a way of transforming good intentions into catastrophes.

Chapter Twenty-Four

The short shuttle flight from Kodiak to Anchorage made me think I'd lose my breakfast. Major turbulence…Shot nerves. Plus the fact that I thought we might crash into Barometer Mountain on take off. Walter reassured me that we only have a chance of crashing into it on landing, not takeoff, because it is at the end of the runway...

Simmering annoyance over Walter's marvelous intellect, his carefree ability to deal with turbulence, near plane crashes…and Tokala—and my own cowardice in the face of adversity—kept me from losing my marbles. *Sometimes anger serves a good purpose. I don't know why Walter makes me so mad…probably because I love him. There. I lay that on the table. Don't think I'll tell him for real. Yet.*

After we deplaned at *Ted Stevens Anchorage International Airport* and ran to our connecting flight—on to our final destination—*Seattle-Tacoma International Airport*—I decided I'd sit back, relax and explore the contents of Father Caine's envelope. Alas, flashbacks of sweaty palms prevented me from playing detective—me…still, a nervous wreck. If I were home, my feet would be pacing the floor. *Here on the Boeing 757, with the seatbelt sign continuously on due to the inclement weather, my body is held captive—Trapped—under siege…stuck to thoughts that I'd rather escape.*

Flashbacks from my youth begin to take hold of me and will not let go. I look at Walter. No help there. He sleeps like a baby up here in the sky. Probably having sweet dreams. The cad. Rats...I hate it when he's relaxed and I'm going nuts. I close my eyes and start my deep breathing. It doesn't work. Good thoughts desert me...Just my childhood staring me in the face...I open the door to my past—and that little girl who doesn't have a clue about being different from the other kids, emerges.

My mother, Marianna, always impressed on me to tell the truth...but when I did, the other kids laughed at me. I wasn't so good at hiding my gift back then and would say whatever came into my mind. Wrong approach. I remember the time my second grade teacher said, "Boys...which one of you stuffed the roll of toilet paper down the commode? Mr. Carney, our custodian, told me what a tough time he had...getting the lavatory back to normal...so the rest of the boys could use it."

Being seven and sympathetic to old Mr. Carney...and knowing nothing about peer pressure, I blurted out, "Timmy did it."

My teacher, Miss Plum—who by the end of the year became know as Miss Prune Face—raised her left eyebrow and started twitching. She closed one eye and stared at me with the other...the whole time hovering over me. "I didn't know you were in the habit of using the boys' restroom, Angelina."

I blushed. I felt shame for the first time in my young life. I choked. I couldn't talk. The other kids roared—Timmy being the loudest—the beast.

That was the last time I tried to help a teacher.

Teenage years grew worse. No way I would open my mouth. I knew who'd be prom queen—never me. I knew who did drugs—not me...who cheated on their boyfriends—not me—I didn't have one. Dating became impossible—I always saw through a guy's line...I knew his intentions...and they freaked me out... No foreplay to warm me up. I took out a code of silence and pretended not to care. I think the other kids viewed me as stuck up. I pretended to do the shy bit, but teenagers are perceptive. They pick up on phony. I might as well have worn a sign that read: Odd. Many kept their distance. More than once I heard kids snicker, "What's her problem, anyway? What a dork!"

No sympathy. Just cackling.

I became the silent avenger. "Some day you'll be sorry you did this to me," I would whisper under my breath. Then one night on late-night television, I saw a movie...all about a teenage girl wrecking havoc on her tormentors—and the consequences of her actions...and it scared me to death. My weird thoughts of revenge are going to destroy me, I decided.

I leveled with my mother the night of my last horror movie...waking her from a deep sleep. She wasn't upset I woke her up. She hugged me and told me she loved me. Then she got up from her warm, cozy queen-size waterbed—which I sometimes slept in when I was sick or skipping school—and turned on a switch to allow the soft light from the lamp on the bedside table to enter the room. My mother hated overhead lights. She only used them when cleaning—which I must say she did rarely... She'd rather spend time with Bryan and me...that's where I get my tolerance of dust...

Mom put on her robe and led me downstairs to the kitchen. A night-light glowed by the stove—All quiet and serene. She opened up the pantry and flipped on the light switch, hunting for something...loose tea...in an old tin that used to belong to my grandmother. Then Marianna turned off the light, came back into the kitchen and put the kettle on the stove. She motioned for me to find a place in the breakfast nook... "Angelina...it's time I told you about Nagymama."

I nodded and stared at my mother as she began her story. "You know, Angelina, you're a lot like your grandmother. Your father and I named you after her—Angelina Marie. She insisted. I could never say no to Nagymama when she had that look in her eyes—that look that said I would break her heart if I didn't abide by her request."

"I remember that look."

"It's a look you give me sometimes, Angelina."

"I do?"

"Yes. In some ways, you are a lot like her. Remember when you pleaded with me to take you to that hateful concert...The....

"Pelviks?"

"Yes...that weird punk rock band. I almost broke my eardrums. I could hear nothing but bass. Not very musical."

"I could have gone alone..."

"You were twelve."

"Oh yeah...Jail bait."

"You're still jail bait."

"I'm fifteen. Plus I have better taste in music now."

"Angelina, I planned to wait until you were sixteen to have this talk..."

"Mom, we already did the facts of life...We did that at ten. Remember?"

"No...this is about your nagymama...and what you share."

"Nagymama's dead. How can I share anything with her?" I started to tear up.

"Don't you ever feel a connection to her?"

"I used to...We loved each other—I could talk to her about anything...She understood me...I miss her in my life...Sometimes I dream about her...It seems as if she's trying to tell me something...like tonight...to quit the revenge stuff and do some good with my life. I think I'm a big disappointment to her."

My mother brushed the hair out of my face. "Of course you're not. You're just confused." She left me for a minute, poured the boiling water into the loose tea in the teapot and removed two cups and saucers from the cupboard. She brought everything over to the kitchen booth, turned on the small side lamp and went back to the refrigerator for some cream. Then she scooted into the booth under the window, next to me and looked out into the night sky.

I put my head down on the table and started to cry.

Mom poured me a cup of my grandmother's tea. She stroked my hair and hugged me. "Drink this. It will make you feel better."

I picked my head up, wiped my eyes on my grey frayed sweatshirt sleeve and after dumping three teaspoons of sugar into the strong brew encompassing my grandmother's old china tea cup, did what she requested. I took a sip. I never before noticed the delicate green and gold leaves surrounded by violet and pink flowers dancing on the brim. Nagymama had an eye for fine art.

"Thanks, Mom." I downed the rest of the brew, leaving a few tea leaves in the bottom of the cup. I filled my stomach and depleted my anxiety.

"Angelina...Tangie...Turn your cup over, please."

"Mom, now you're being weird." I looked at the clock. Three a.m.—Here we are in the kitchen—playing with teacups. "Okay, Mom."

I inverted my teacup and placed it on the matching saucer...then I lifted it up like a grand chef. "Voila! Tea leaves. Now what?"

"Look closely, Angelina...Do you remember? Your grandmother used to tell your fortune in the tea leaves."

"Sure, she used to play that game with me every day after school, when you were at work and Bryan did his kiddie gymnastics."

My mother smiled at me.

"Once she told me that someday I'd have a little white dog...That's never happened. Then she told me I'd be sad for a while but that grief would make me stronger...and...she told me when I was all mad at Bryan that someday I'd appreciate him...Like that's gonna happen."

"Maybe you have to be patient. Maybe she wasn't playing games with you. Maybe she knew."

"Yeah...well she told me I'd love two young men...and that the first one would disappoint me but not to give up on love. So far there's not even one man."

"Tangie, you are only fifteen. Give yourself some time."

"Maybe...maybe she's right...Strange...the last thing she said to me...I remember clearly: Angelina, never give up on love...just follow your heart..."

I sighed and put my hands on my chin. "Mom...how did she know these things?"

"She knew. She read them in the tea leaves."

I looked into my mother's eyes, shining at me with kindness and love...She knew about me. How I loved her warmth and understanding. I felt dumbfounded...but then I realized I would not be alone anymore. I took a deep breath and relaxed... I looked down at my saucer. Nothing. Then the leaves began taking shape and pictures started appearing in my mind. I could swear I heard a dog bark...A little white one...Then a school. "Seattle University—my college—my first choice—Excellent!" I jumped up and began shouting cheers that could wake the neighbors.

I gave my mother a high-five and hugged her. Soon we were both dancing around the kitchen. "Mom...you're right...you are so right!"

I went back to the table and put my cup over the saucer. Enough. I didn't want to know anymore.

I studied my mother who simply smiled...and stared at me with a questioning look in her eyes.

"Mom, come back to the table...sit down...turn your cup over and then lift it up...I want to read your tea leaves."

Giving a sigh of relief, she grinned. "I thought you'd never ask!"

I felt my world shake. The plane...then the wheels—dropping. At last...we're landing in Seattle. I looked out the window. Clouds embraced the jetliner. *"Thanks, Nagymama,"* I whispered. I glanced at Walter sleeping...a soul without a care in the world—or so it seemed at the time. I leaned over, kissed him on the cheek and whispered in his ear, "Sweetheart, we're home."

I think Pebbles gets the award for being the most elated—when we arrived at my mom's house and I shouted, "We're home." He would not stop licking me. He even got my mouth when I wasn't looking. "Ugh..."

Mom hugged me...and Bryan did too--who just *happened* to drop over with Andee and the twins. Jason and Jeffrey wrapped themselves around my knees like Christmas elves. I'm glad I made Walter stop, on our way to the Kodiak airport, at the only gift shop open. I pulled two stuffed Kodiak bears out of a shopping bag and handed them to the boys.

"Auntie Tangie, Auntie Tangie," Jason yelled and scrambled up my body to kiss me.

Jeffrey pulled him off and grabbed me. "Can we come over, can we, can we?"

I sighed. "Maybe later, guys. Auntie Tangie just got back. I'm a little tired from my travels."

Andee intervened. "For heaven's sake, boys, let Auntie Tangie breathe for a minute."

I smiled at her with gratitude in my eyes and extracted myself from their octopus-like hold on my body. I put Pebbles down on the floor and flopped on my mother's soft-cushioned sofa.

Pebbles ran to Walter and nuzzled his leg and prevented him from moving. Walter—held captive by my family—and liking it. A warm fuzzy feeling consumed me—like toast and tea on a rainy day. Walter smiled and signaled me with raised eyebrows. I snapped into polite mode.

Grinning at my family, I introduced my *secretary*. "Bryan, Andee, Jason, Jeffrey...This is my friend, Walter."

"Is he your boyfriend?" Jason giggled, as he hugged the Kodiak bear.

I giggled along with him. "Could be."

Walter's eyes brightened. He extended a long strong hand grasp to Bryan and then to Andee, who hugged him in return. "Great to meet you all." Then, my love focused on the twins. "How old are you guys?"

Jeffrey spoke first. "Four."

"Four and a half..." Jason added. I'm the oldest...by three minutes.

"Four is good. Four and a half is even better." Walter grinned as he stooped down to peer into their inquisitive eyes.

"So how was Alaska?" Bryan asked.

"Cold. No bears. Not even one." I got up off the couch and joined Walter on an overstuffed chair...squeezing myself close to him and putting my arm around his shoulder. "Very scenic."

Bryan looked at Walter. "How'd you get the black eye, buddy?"

Bryan always notices things like that. When he was little he drove me nuts with his quiz mode. *Now I appreciate his concern. A step in the right direction—My brother cares about me—and the one I love... I'll have to pay closer attention to all the advice Nagymama gave to me...She was trying to tell me something...all along...and I didn't know...*

Walter responded to Bryan without batting an eyelash. "Oh, just a minor skirmish on the way to the lodge. Ran into an *undesirable.*"

"Well, at least it wasn't a bear." Bryan smiled at him...trying to make light of the situation.

My mother gasped. *One thing she owns is a great imagination.* "What about you, Tangie?"

"Oh Walter took all the blows. *Liar, liar, pants on fire.* "I'm fine." *Good thing I have a scarf around my neck. Horst's marks haven't faded yet...*

My mother relaxed. "Thank goodness. And thank you, Walter...for watching out for our Angelina. I'm glad she found you."

Walter grinned. "Me too."

I could swear she winked at him.

"So my dears," Marianna announced, "Let's all of us eat. I fixed something special for your return, Angelina."

The seven of us sat down in Mom's library/dining room to Thai takeout...*my favorite*...and my mother's home-baked contribution--rice pudding with whipped cream and cherries on top—*doesn't get much better than this.* We drank wine and sparkling cider, coffee and tea...I dove into the meal like a person who just returned from being stranded on a desert island. Breakfast seemed light years away.

After midnight, Walter and I climbed the steps up to our humble abode. *Home.* I checked voicemail. Fifteen calls. They could wait.

Tomorrow comes soon enough. Walter walked into my office and gave me a hug. "Think I'll take Pebbles out for his evening stroll."

" You go ahead." I yawned. "I'm exhausted."

He gave me a lingering goodnight kiss...I responded, gently kissed him back.

I yawned. "I can hardly keep my eyes open, Walter...too tired to join you..."

He smiled back at me...and I caved—overcome by his charm. *No way I could stay angry with my man. Let's say, he's irresistible when his eyes sparkle in a certain way—Kind of like the center part of a flame—very hot.* As I watched him leave to walk Pebbles...I felt electricity beginning to pulsate in my exhausted body. I tore off my clothes and thought about running after him...but the power I felt extinguished itself before it caught fire...The flame would have to burn another night...I climbed into bed, too tired to put on my *jammies*—just grateful to be home again—*safe*...in my Ballard by the sea.

Chapter Twenty-Five

I awoke the next morning with Walter's hand on my breast and Pebble's body crushing my ankle. I felt the need to stretch, but enticed myself to remain entwined in the embrace of my roomies. Sure beats living alone. I could hear the phone ring in my office. I tried ignoring the annoying whining and succeeded—By the fourth ring it stopped...Gotta love voicemail. I leaned over, planted a kiss on Walter's ear and shook Pebbles off my foot. My foot. "Ugh..." Nothing's worse than a foot that's asleep. Gotta move and walk around. Darn that dog.

Walter awoke. "Good morning, Angelina...Something wrong with your foot?"

"He speaks! What happened last night?"

"Nothing happened. I don't make love to the comatose. But you know, you are wonderful to caress."

As he kissed my neck, I noticed Walter wearing his pajama bottoms, confirming the truth of his statement—*What a boy scout. Me—not even a dream to remember the night. Out cold.*

I kissed his waiting lips. "Um...you taste wonderful...Thanks for being so nice to my family."

"An easy task...I like them." He started kissing my neck.

I sighed..."They like you."

"I know."

I smiled at him and pushed him away. "Don't be so smug."

"I'm not. Just being honest. Want some breakfast? I haven't played Julia Child in awhile."

"Love some…but what's to cook?'

"Oh, Pebbles and I walked to the all-night deli during our stroll last night. I can whip up some bacon, cheese omlets and orange juice—if you do the cappuccino..."

"Sounds heavenly...I'll feed Pebbles first. He's giving me that look... but perhaps I should take a turn and walk him right away..."

"Remember to put some clothes on first."

I chuckled. "You'd like that, huh? Me going out naked?"

"Only in a private setting…like the tropics…on the beach…Hum… Yum… Angelina…Can I ask you a question? Did you ever have a cat when you were little?"

"A cat? Where did that one come from? I never had one of my own, but my grandmother—*Nagymama*—came to live with us when I was young—she had one... Furry beast...Don't know why, but he liked me. Nagymama called him *Tzigane*—which means—*gypsy*—in Hungarian. The name fit—Such a beggar."

"Did you like him?"

"Sure. He roamed outside going from house to house looking for morsels—Usually got 'em too. Tzigane was a cat with charisma. But he embarrassed my grandmother—she would say, *Tzigane, bad kitty...Don't I feed you enough? You're getting too fat. Why you wanna be a beggar?*

Say Walter, why are you asking me about Tzigane?"

"Oh I was just wondering..."

I noticed as Walter averted his eyes from mine and ambled off to the kitchen to do the chef bit. *He's hiding something…Maybe he's got a cat stashed away somewhere…I'll get it out of him—after breakfast—First things first.*

When I got back from my mini-stroll with Pebbles—no more snow on the ground, but still bitter cold—glove weather—my office phone started ringing…first one call and then another—*more yadda, yadda, yadda. They can wait. I have my priorities.*

I sat down to breakfast with Walter and everything seemed normal again. I poured the orange juice and then got up to make us some cappuccinos. Yes—the simple life—I could go on like this. I would if I could stop time.

After breakfast, the phone resumed its annoying ring. "Take it," Walter said. "I'll clean up. Tell Santigo something to put him off a bit."

Of course Santigo answered the phone. *Walter knows stuff too. Full of surprises...or psychic...One of these days, he's gonna have to level with me... thinks he's fooling me. He's not.*

I turned my attention to my caller. "Hi Mr. Santigo."

"Call me Fred."

"Fred."

"Did you find anything?"

"Fred, we have to talk."

"Where? When?"

"This afternoon. Seattle. *Ivar's Fish and Chips Bar*—at the Waterfront. Outside."

"It's freezing."

"It's cold...It's winter. Plus it's warmer than Alaska. It's private and they have heaters on the deck...and I'm bringing my secretary."

"I prefer to meet alone."

"Then you won't see me."

"Have it your way then."

"Two-thirty p.m.—Order something for us. I like clams. If we get there first, we'll do the same."

"I prefer shrimp."

"You would," I thought...but I said, "See you then."

Walter gave me the once over as I stormed out of my office and slammed the door.

"So, Angelina," my partner-in-crime asked, "Not a happy camper? You're not going to start throwing things, are you? Should I duck?"

"It's not you, Sweetheart... it's Santigo. Look at your eye. Look at my neck." I pulled off the white silk scarf I had wrapped around my wounds and displayed the remnants of Horst's throat squeezes. How will I explain these to my mother? She worries about me enough as it is... plus...they look like hickies."

Walter grinned and tried to reassure me. "I worry about you too, Angelina." He stopped drying the last of the dishes, took off his apron and hugged me nearly crushing me with his strong arms. I didn't want to move. I wanted to stay in his embrace forever—Secure, loved, cherished.

Walter crooned a familiar tune in my ear. Seems he has perfect pitch. "I like it when you call me *Sweetheart*, Angelina—Sounds like a song."

"You could make a song out of anything," I whispered and brushed his black eye with my lips.

"Remember to focus…Tangie, my love…Santigo didn't do these things. Horst did."

I pulled away from Walter, reluctantly…brushing a tear from my eye. "Yes, but you know it's Santigo's fault."

"For loving his wife?"

"For putting all of us in danger...and for being a fool. I'm gonna give the bastard a piece of my mind. He'd better tell us the whole truth."

"Are you sure you need me to go with you?" Walter grinned. "You're scaring the hell out of me just listening to you rant about him."

"Of course I need you. You keep me calm. You protect me. Plus I feel safe with you. You're like...a good luck charm."

"That's me…the lucky Irishman…all I need is red hair."

Red hair…I wonder. "Say Walter…"

"You are wondering what'll we do with Pebbles?"

"No…not about that…I'll just get his tartan vest out of the closet. He'll be our guard dog. He loves *Ivar's--outdoors*—and clams and seagulls..."

"Great…I'll get him ready for you…Go finish up in your office and we'll be waiting."

I nodded like a robot, went into my office and checked the last of my messages. Three from Suzy, saying: "We never do anything together anymore. Let's go shopping...Let's do lunch...Let's go to a movies... Anything...Call me back!"

There were two from Jean. First one: "Are you all right? Need anything?"

"Yeah," I mused. "How about a flight to the San Juans...You can take Walter and me to Rosario Resort on Orcas Island...in your Otter...One way..."

Her second message got my attention. "Listen, Tangie, I'll be out of town for awhile. Have this fancy client that wants me to take him to Orcas Island. Gotta run. Oh…I fed Spike…and I met your next-door neighbor, Mr. Jarrick. He's rather cranky. He yelled at me over your fence…told me not to feed his cat…He made it clear to me…he wants to be the one to do that...So I guess you're off the hook...Oh…and don't worry about Spunky…My mom is watching him…I know you're busy…"

Lucky gal. Getting paid to hang out at *Rosario Resort* with some fancy client. And Spike is loved! Seems we're no longer foster parents...

Next call: *Electric Company. Pay or else…*At least I have until Friday. I erased all the ones from Santigo without listening to them. The next one hailed from a Mr. Benson, asking me to call him at a certain number and ask for a Mr. Peter Jones in Room 212. Where did I hear the name Benson? Benson…Benson...Ah…yes...the airport...the porter…I jotted the phone number down and pushed the buttons...my hand began to shake.

"Renton Memorial Hospital. How may I direct your call?"

I sat down.

"Do you have a Mr. James Benson there?"

"Let me see...No. No Mr. Benson."

"Oh...just a minute, please…" I looked at my notepad. *He said to ask for Mr. Jones...*

"I'm sorry. I meant to ask for Mr. Jones. Mr. Peter Jones in Room 212."

"Yes, Miss. I will connect you."

I stood up and paced the floor. Something smelled rotten.

"Hello?" A feeble voice at the end of the line answered...then I heard a man clearing his throat. The voice became clearer but remained frail. *Benson*. "Who is this?" the voice asked.

"Hi Mr. Benson. This is Angelina Seraphina. I am returning your call. Are you all right?"

"Well, I'm alive."

I sat down. "What happened?"

"Well I've got three cracked ribs, my left arm's broken and my right eye is swollen shut. Otherwise, I'm dandy."

His voice got deeper and louder as he continued talking—Reassuring me, but I still felt the panic rise in my gut.

"Mr. Benson…I'm sorry."

"It happened right after I saw you…That dude…That dude you were asking me about...*Horst*...He came back and beat the living daylights outta me."

"I feel so bad. Responsible..."

"Don't worry, Miss. I'll live. I told that bully nothin'. Ya see, I got this here heart condition...I passed out. The fool thought I bought the big ticket to the sky. After I hit the floor, airport security took over and chased 'em. They told me the honkie took off running…a black *Mercedes* limo picked him up…outside those automatic doors…and security lost him.

"Well, at least they saw the car…so we know he has an accomplice. Did security see the driver?"

I didn't see nothin'…I was kinda out of it…as I told you…but security told me the windows were black, but they could have sworn the driver was a woman…with blond hair…"

"Did they get a license number?"

"Well, they got a reading…but the license turned out to be fake—stolen…"

"Kind of a dead end…"

"Well, not exactly. I can identify the goon."

"Ah…that's why they have you in a secure room…"

"Yes, indeedy. The police put a guard…outside my room. He stands watch night and day…they keep me here under an assumed name. Maybe you should go to the authorities, Miss…"

"Well, I did, Mr. Benson…in Alaska…and I'm gonna do the same here. That same creep attacked me and a friend, up north…but we—my secretary and I escaped with minimal damage."

"You are one lucky, gal. Be careful. He plays dirty."

"I know. So…you gave the police a description?"

"I did. They made up a flyer and gave me one, not that I want to see his ugly mug again."

"I understand. Say, Mr. Benson, could you send me a copy? I could use one."

"Sure, Miss. I'll have my wife do it. Millie's good like that. She works in an office. She'll make you a copy—She can fax it to you...I still have the business card you gave me."

"I'd be ever so grateful." I pictured James Benson in his hospital room and an uncontrolled sob spilled out of me.

"Hey, Miss Angelina...Don't you go being sad. One good thing came out of this whole fiasco. *Alaska Airlines* offered me early retirement... due to my pain and suffering...and a good settlement—But what a way to go."

"Yes..." I recited after James Benson..."What a way to go."

I closed my eyes, visualizing Mr. Benson lying in bed, all bruised up, broken body parts, but with a smile on his face. *What a guy.*

"I 'd love to come visit you, Mr. Benson...But I don't want to put you in harm's way again. That Horst guy may be following me...watching me. When the police catch him, I will contact you...Would you mind giving me your home phone number?"

"Sure...but don't call too early, Ms. Seraphina...I'll be retired when I get home from the hospital. I'll be sleepin' in."

"You deserve it, Mr. Benson. Again...I'm sorry...and thanks... " I jotted the number down. "I'll be in touch."

"My pleasure, young lady."

I put down the phone, as sobs crept up out of my throat...I could no longer contain them. "What a dear, sweet man." *James Benson doesn't deserve this—to be thrashed by a ruthless thug. I gotta send him flowers—the least I can do...Something is seriously wrong here.*

My teeth started chattering as the telephone rang...again. I let it ring. Walter came into the office and noticed my white face. He picked up the phone.

"Yes, I understand. Could she call you back later? She's all in from the trip. Can't wait? Okay."

Walter handed me the phone—with sorry written all over his face. "Sheriff Tokala," he whispered.

"Oh, no." I couldn't breathe. My knees started twitching down to my toes. I put my right hand on my knees and took the phone in my left hand, grateful that I was 1500 miles away from *da' Man*. "Hello, Sheriff."

"What exactly is going on Ms. Seraphina?"

I took a deep breath and reached for a box of tissues on my desk. "I'm looking for a missing person...Therese Santigo. I told you that."

"Well, did you have to get a priest nearly beaten to death in the process?"

"What?" I stood up and started pacing.

"Father Joe. Gus found him all battered and bloody...with a broken leg to boot. Gus entered *Saint Francis Mission* to go to confession and almost tripped over Father Caine's body. Good thing Gus has a guilty conscience—*unlike you*—or Father Joe would be a goner today."

I sat down. Walter sat down next to me. I leaned against him for support."No, Sheriff…this can't be happening!"

"Oh, yes...and it appears your *Horst* did it."

"Horst? No…I can't believe it! Sheriff, he's not my *Horst*. I don't know why the thug would do that…Why?"

"I thought perhaps you could give me a motive."

"Oh...This is just awful." I groaned…I could feel the bile rising in my throat. To Walter, I whispered, "I'm gonna be sick." Walter got up and disappeared. I heard water running. In less than a minute, he reappeared with a cold washcloth and placed it on my forehead. The coolness helped lower my body temperature. I felt my stomach settling down a bit and I could go on.

"Sheriff Tokala...please…listen to me…Father Joseph Caine has no connection what so ever to Horst."

"Really. Am I supposed to take that as an explanation?"

I felt the sarcasm sting my red-hot cheeks. He didn't have to be next to me to have that effect on me. His words traveled.

"Sheriff Tokala…I believe Horst followed Walter and me to Alaska… He thought we would lead him to Terese. I didn't know that…until… until he attacked Walter and me. When I went to see Father Joe, the goon must have thought the pastor knew where to find Terese. Of course Father Joe knows nothing. I visited the padre about a totally different case...but apparently Horst doesn't know that…He's like a wild boar… charging anything in his path…"

"So you put Father Joe in harm's way."

"Not intentionally. Believe me, I feel as bad as you do about what happened. I didn't expect Horst to follow us...let alone find us in Alaska—and beat up Father Joe."

How many cases do you have in Kodiak?"

"Just two...it's a coincidence that they overlapped."

"Some coincidence."

"Please, Sheriff...could you tell me where is Father Joe now?"

"Right now, he's here with me...in the emergency room at *Memorial Hospital*...in Anchorage...We airlifted him from Kodiak Island. After surgery he'll be transferred to a private room. No visitors. No phone calls for three days—and that means you—especially you."

"Could you please tell him I'm sorry...and that I'll call him as soon as I see Clancy? He'll know what I'm talking about. Believe it or not, it may cheer him up. Please. Will I be able to call him at the hospital after three days?"

"I suppose so. But call me first. I will have to give you the necessary codes. He's under police protection and he'll be here for at least a week, I'm sure. I'll give him the message. But wait a week. He's heavily sedated right now and he will need to rest after surgery. Call *me*—I'll give him your messages."

"Thank you, Sheriff. I will. I appreciate you letting me know. Could you please do one more thing for me?"

"Does it involve Horst?"

"Well, another person is in need of protection from him...Terese's sister—*Simone*—could be Horst's next target. She teaches the children on Akhiok Island...Remember the place Walter and I traveled via float plane...before we visited Father Caine? Could you make sure she's okay? Her last name is Royale."

"Now, Ms. Seraphina...you expect me to go flying around on company time?"

"Please? It's important...I'm worried about her...As Terese's sister, she may be Horst's next target."

"Lady, you're trouble."

"I've been told that before."

"No wonder."

" Sheriff Tokala...I can send you a flyer with Horst's mug on it—compliments of...the *Sea-Tac Police...*"

"Now that would be appreciated...I'll look for it on my fax. Good luck on your cases."

"Thanks, Sheriff." With gratitude, I disconnected *da' man*. My guilt started taking its toll on me. I began shaking and tears welled in my eyes.

Walter came over to me and took me in his arms, rubbing my back and whispering sweet phrases to me, telling me in time, everything will be all right.

I can always predict that I will fall apart...if a loved one treats me tenderly...when I am upset. Right now was no exception. I buried my head in Walter's chest and started to sob, heaving my shoulders. I began hiccupping. I felt a sinking pain in my gut. While gasping for air between hiccups, I blurted out, "This case...is hurting too many innocent people...this is all...going beyond you...and me."

"Bad news in Alaska?"

"The worst. I feel like a criminal—I caused all this. Two innocent men...attacked because of me...First, James Benson—the porter I spoke with at *Sea-Tac*...and then that poor priest—Father Caine...up in Kodiak...Father Caine...knows nothing of Terese..."

"Quit beating yourself up, Tangie. You are not responsible for these acts of violence. Be mad at Horst, not yourself."

"Oh it goes beyond Horst, I'm sure. I should have...caught on sooner. Horst is the enforcer. I've looked into his eyes—they're empty. No conscience...a bully...but he just follows orders. No brains. Just muscle."

Walter released me and took my hand, "Tangie...calm down... please. Come in the kitchen...I'll pour you a glass of wine to warm you up...Listen to me...I thought that before we meet Santigo, we could stop off at the police station. At least we would be doing something to stop Horst...not just waiting for him to hurt someone else."

I sipped the glass of wine Walter handed me. "I kinda thought you'd say that...my love...that's why I told Santigo two-thirty."

"That's my girl. Great minds...stick together...How about I dry your tears?" Walter crooned as he kissed my wet cheeks...and resumed his strong hold on me. "You go take a shower. I'll wash your back..."

"Um...sounds wonderful...I'll take a shower...a long hot shower... but alone...otherwise we'll never make it to the police station...and we *have* to go there..."

"You know, Tangie...playing hooky from the police would be okay with me..."

I ignored his remark...knowing where that would lead..."Another question, Walter—totally off the subject—Why do you want to know about me and cats? Be honest."

"Oh...it's no big deal. Later, Angelina...I promise...Go on and take a shower...alone if you wish—before I change my mind and follow you."

"Yeah right... we go to the cops...get the dirty deed done...I understand...duty before pleasure...but you know I'll get my answers—one way or another. Don't worry...I'll be ready in a flash."

I raced to my tiny bathroom hoping to shower the words of Santigo and Tokala down the drain...but they remained tattooed in my brain. *Bad memories have a way of putting a stranglehold on my psyche.*

Chapter Twenty-Six

The *Seattle Police Department* didn't feel as intimidating as Sheriff Tokala's office—Probably because we brought information voluntarily and Walter did most of the talking—like he knew the guys...on a first name basis.

Me, I'm never at ease in these places, but I did an incredible job of not showing my discomfort—And I did not stutter. I told the police about James Benson and Father Caine. They listened intently and thanked me for coming in to see them. Both the first detective and the second, whom I thought was his partner. He came in halfway through our visit...and informed us they'd be in touch and that they would fax a police drawing to Sheriff Tokala immediately—after they requested and received a fax from the *Sea-Tac Police* on Benson's case. I smiled in gratitude—That would make it official...and relieve me of the duty. The detective—darned if I can remember his name or his partner's—One I remember was Steve something...Walter's *friend*...my mind being in a haze—trying to block out the surroundings from my consciousness. Well, the first detective—*Steve*—got the fax in a few minutes and showed Walter and me the copy of the police sketch from the *Sea-Tac Police*—a sketch which did look remarkably like Horst. Mr. Benson ID'd him well. *Thanks, Mr. Benson. You got me off the hook with Tokala.*

Fortunately my shaking didn't resume until we left the detective's office. Walter and I squeezed into the elevator heading down. When we got off and headed towards the security door, I started hyperventilating. I began running and caught the guard at the door staring at me but I didn't care. I didn't breathe until I got outside. I put my head down and then lifted it up slowly…smelling the fresh air. Ah…warmth that I hadn't felt in two seasons greeted me…and a bright light shone in my eyes—Sunshine! Where'd that come from? When we first entered the building, the air felt cold…and fog surrounded us. What a difference an hour can make…new life! I breathed in—exhaling a little breath at a time. I could smell the change—Spring! Ah…sweet spring in the air. I opened my purse to search for sunglasses. Wonderful...to be warm again...The first time in months...Yes! A few short weeks until the flowers bloom—the daffodils, lilacs, and tulips…then come the roses, peonies and daisies...*I am so ready for it.* Shoot…I may become a gardener after this trauma…I am so ready for a peaceful existence…

I put my arms up in the air and just stood there looking at the sky. Walter smiled at my trance and led me down the steps to my canary *Escape*. The sun blinded me. I could not find my sunglasses and I almost mowed down two street people standing near my mini *SUV*. One moment I'm conversing with Walter and the flowers and the next thing I know I'm plowing into these two panhandlers. I tripped over the woman's ankle, which appeared rather hairy—I noticed—as I went down. Walter helped me up and at the same time, pulled a twenty-dollar bill out of his pocket. The woman didn't fall, but her body slumped against a parking meter. Her companion steadied her and gave her back her cane, which had fallen on my head—Pretty heavy for a cane—made of some strong metal, like a lead pipe. Guess this woman didn't get picked on much…on the sunny streets of Seattle.

Walter gave the woman the twenty dollars. "Sorry for your trouble, Senora. Perhaps you could get some lunch with this."

"Muchas Gracias." The disheveled woman whispered like she had a cold. Shabbily dressed, with an old army jacket covering a patched dress, she wore clogs without any socks. *She must be freezing—It's still winter, despite the sun.*

I pulled a five out of my pocket, my only money, and gave it to her. "Maybe you could get some socks." I didn't know what else to say.

She grabbed the money and grunted. I noticed she didn't have any gloves on either. *It is getting warmer outside, I guess*...Her enormous fingernails grasped me—each about three or four inches long and curved, like claws. On the right index finger, instead of a claw, a thimble adorned the appendage. Creepy. Maybe she worked as a seamstress in a previous life. Clean hands, I noticed...not the hands of a street person...and a colorful woven bracelet decorated her wrist. She took pride in her appearance, however shabby.

The man who assisted her took her arm. "Are you all right, Senora?"

She nodded and tapped her cane on the pavement and pointed to the corner of the street. As the two of them sauntered down the street, the man tugged at his knit cap and pulled on his black dirty jeans as if they belonged to someone else...Probably did...probably stolen. He wore working boots encrusted with mud and a faded denim jacket with torn plaid lining and about two sizes too small for him.

A disturbing feeling possessed me, like I used to get at horror shows...movies I relished as a kid...but I never go to them anymore... Just thinking about these two characters made me shudder and I dropped my purse. I bent down to pick it up and when I looked up again, the pair evaporated from sight.

"Funny..." Walter commented. "Panhandlers in front of the police station."

"No doubt scanning the place—or seeking to cause trouble for someone."

"Yes. Strange bedfellows. Those two would scare could scare the dead."

"You're frightening me, Walter."

Walter took my arm and kissed my cheek. "Come on, Tangie. We don't want to be late for Santigo." Walter opened the door of the *Escape* for me. I noticed his body quivering a little as he shut the door. *He must know something I don't know.*

Walter started the car and I turned on the heat. The sun continued to shine, but I started shivering. *What is wrong with me? And Walter... Why is he distressed? We're both a mess.*

Walter cruised a few blocks down James Street to the waterfront. On the way, he reached in his pocket and gave Pebbles two pieces of bacon—the pooch's reward for waiting in the car. No dogs allowed at *Seattle Police Department*. Walter thought of everything. *That's why I love him. There. I said it, One of these days I'll say it to his face. Really.*

I studied Walter's profile as he slipped into a parking spot under the Alaskan Way Viaduct, surrounded by dead weeds and old withered blackberry branches, that will come back to life in a few months, like the rest of the plants around the city...*The Viaduct*...soon to be torn down and made into a tunnel...if city plans don't change again...either way... it's gotta come down...Can't stand another earthquake.

I dismissed that thought and smiled at my driver. At this moment, Walter, with his chiseled face resembling that of a Greek mythic hero... appeared perfect to me—catching me off guard.

Grabbing my hand, he smiled tenderly at me. "Ready?"

"Ready...ah...Walter..."

"Yes, Tangie?" Walter's eyes quizzed mine...matter of fact...still in business mode.

"You have beautiful eyes."

He softened and started joking with me, after my compliment. "Ah...*Angelina. The better to see you with, my dear.*"

"I'm serious."

"Me too. Come here." He growled in a low voice and pulled me into his embrace, giving me a long, lingering kiss. I melted and returned his caress. Our gestures of affection went back and forth for about ten minutes—or longer...I lost count of time. The windows steamed up... Pebbles started barking and whining. Finally the pooch jumped into the front seat and started pawing me—and then Walter. We pulled apart, reluctantly.

I looked at Walter...lipstick on his collar...on his cheek...on his ear... on his...

He frowned. "Next time, we leave the dog home."

I couldn't help laughing out loud. "He thinks you're the *Big, Bad Wolf...*"

"A wolf, maybe, but not bad. Tangie, you better comb your hair—I'm afraid I messed it up..."

"Here's a handkerchief, Sweetheart." I gave him a package of *Kleenex* from my purse. As he wiped the lipstick off his face, neck and other body parts, I reached into the back seat and grabbed a black cashmere scarf. I wrapped it around his neck. "Voila. You're presentable."

I took my spare makeup out of the glove compartment and redid my makeup and brushed my hair. *Why do they call those storage areas glove compartments? I mean, who puts gloves in them? Guns, maybe. Makeup—like me. Maps, money, snacks...Maybe they should be called hobby chests. Think I'll write a letter to Ford Motors...*

I checked the clock below the dash...2:35. Late. *Oh well, Santigo can order the clams.*

Santigo sat at a table by the edge of the outside deck, huddled up to an outside heater. The sun continued to shine brightly over Elliot Bay, signaling a spectacular day. I'd give today a ten if I weren't so perturbed over meeting Santigo. I scanned the waterfront and watched the seagulls flying over the ferries crossing the Puget Sound. The Olympic Mountains stood at attention. Not one cloud to darken the day. *Sometimes nature is like that—Perfect. Too bad we need to do business with someone I view as crab bait. Despite his over abundance of cologne—to me—Fred smells as distasteful as the rotting turkey backs that fishermen use to catch crustaceans.*

He leapt up when he saw us approach.

"I got you clams."

"Thanks...Fred, this is my secretary, Walter."

"Walter Cunningham." My secretary extended his hand to my client.

"Fred Santigo."

I noticed Walter wiped his hand on his *Eddie Bauer* khakis as he sat down. *Santigo has the same effect on him.*

"So Fred," I began—speaking first. "Who besides you knew Terese was heading to Alaska?"

"Maybe my secretary, Marlaine...She knew Terese wanted to visit Simone. I asked Marlaine to check the airline rates in her spare time for me...She called a travel agent before Terese...*before Terese*...Oh Santa Senor! She must have..."

Santigo sat down and put his head in his hands. I could hear him trying not to sob out loud. *It wasn't working.*

"Why did Terese really leave?" I asked.

"She told me she had to clear her head."

"Why did she have to clear her head?" Walter asked. "Did you have a fight?"

"Something frightened her."

"What? Who? Did you do something to her?" Walter began to drill him. I think he liked playing bad cop this time.

"Look, Fred..." I interrupted, deciding to play good cop. "We're trying to help you find Terese, but you're making it very difficult. You aren't being honest with us."

"I can't tell you everything...It's too dangerous."

"For you, maybe. For us, it's dangerous not to know. We need to know who's following us...and why...Someone's going around beating up people...a priest, an old man, Walter, me. Who knows what will happen if *Horst* finds Terese."

"Horst...you met up with Horst?" Santigo cringed and wiped his brow with his napkin. "That's who has been tormenting me." His shrimp remained uneaten. "But it's not just Horst..."

"Is Horst taking orders from someone?" Walter began raising his voice, as he got in Fred's face. "*You*, perhaps?"

"No...I swear...not me. I'm just as afraid of him as you are."

"I'm not afraid of him," I bragged, trying to convince myself. "I just hate his guts."

Santigo continued, "You're right. Horst's a Cretin. There's no telling what he'll do. He'd just as soon wipe you out as look at you...but he takes orders. He's *The Enforcer.*"

I rolled my eyes and clenched my fists...*I figured that much out on my own, Santigo. We need more, you bozo.* I averted my eyes from Fred and signaled Walter for help.

Walter caught my glance and noticed my mounting frustration—making the connection. "*The Enforcer* for *who*, Fred?" He leaned closer towards Fred, getting in his face.

Fred wiped his brow, now covered with sweat—but not from the outdoor heaters.

The sun went behind a fast moving cloud and a cold wind picked up. *My hands are cold from the sudden dampness and chill in the air...and he's sweating.*

"Sargento." Fred whispered the name like a hidden curse.

"*Sargento? Sargento* who?" I asked.

Santigo looked around suspiciously. He whispered, "Actually there are two of them—Sylvan and Adolphus—brothers. *Twins*—but they look nothing alike. I met them three years ago when I operated a little shop on Aurora Avenue. The shop did good business... It made me a decent living. Nothing fancy, but I got along fine...until Sylvan Sargento walks in and asks if I'm interested in a partnership with him. I told him I wasn't interested—that I did fine solo."

I studied Fred as I rubbed my hands together...trying to thaw them out. "But that's not the end of his interest in you...and your business."

"At first, Angelina, he left me alone...but not before he buys a bunch of fancy plumbing fixtures and commodes, bidets and stuff like that and pays in cash...Has me deliver them to a fancy home in Broadmoor and hook them up for him. Then he comes into my store a month later and has a proposition for me. Sylvan..."

I rolled my eyes. "Lovely name—*Sylvan*..."

Fred didn't catch on to my sarcasm. *Not the brightest fish in the stream.*

He continued his story. "Yes...you see...Sylvan is everything his brother, Adolphus, isn't. Tall, tan, blonde and handsome...His hair is so blond it is almost white. He stands out. Plus he's charming, smooth...He could be a poster boy for suntan cream or something like that. Instead he's a front for his brother's operations—none of them are legal. Adolphus sends Sylvan in to smooth out the territory. Sylvan's the salesman. So he makes the pitch to me...One that is hard to refuse..."

"And you take the bait."

Fred nodded. "I wanted the American Dream...I wanted to buy an expensive car...Have the good life...buy an elegant home for Terese and me..."

"So you're going to blame all this on Terese?" Walter barked at him, as only one man could do to another.

"No...of course not. I'm not implying anything. She's not to blame. She just got caught in the middle of..."

"In the middle of what?" I asked.

"A *business* transaction."

I stared and Fred and tried to be patient. "Fred, slow down. Tell us about this Adolphus fellow…about what happened…and what made Terese run away from you…"

Fred looked at me…and then at Walter. He spoke slowly, as if he wanted to get things right. "I agreed to let Sylvan store some of his things in my storeroom…but he told me he wanted more space…that I had to move my business to a location that had more room…a place more convenient for him. I resisted. That's when Adolphus entered the picture. He came in with a check to buy out my business on Aurora. He gave me a fancy address—in Seattle—Told me to set up a luxury bath store...catering to wealthy clients. He assured me my business would go sky high. He put the squeeze on me…saying I should listen to him… that he has good business sense. But the real truth is, he can be downright scary…So I did what he asked. For a while, it seemed like I did the right thing, despite my reservations. And business boomed. The new shop...with the Sargentos' help…made me a rich man. Terese and I got married—I thought we could not be happier."

"And you closed your eyes to what they stored in your back rooms."

"At first, yes…Later, I had no choice…After Terese and I got married, Adolphus told me my success would all go away—my profits, my business, my wife—if I screwed up. Said he would ruin me if I quit on him. Told me we are *familia* now. So when he told me to hide the cocaine, the guns…and anything else he brought to me, I did."

"Great way to start a marriage," I commented. "You could have said no."

"It wasn't just the money. He threatened to turn me in as an illegal."

"Use your brain, Fred," Walter said. "He's dealing cocaine and who knows what else. Why would he turn you in?"

"Adolphus is really scary. Evil even. Trust me. You don't want to cross him. I believe his threats."

"Did Terese cross him?" I asked.

"Terese didn't do anything...She didn't know anything about him until…she…until she…I'm sorry…I can't go on…" Fred put his elbows on the table, placed his hands over his eyes, and his head down...unable to continue.

"This is going well," Walter whispered to me. He frowned and gazed at the vacant tables.

I got up and walked to the end of the deck to get some sea air and wait for Fred to calm down. I stayed there for a few minutes, trying to relax. I watched clouds moving into our fair city. I walked back in time to watch Fred raise his head and sip his coffee. His shrimp and fries remained untouched. Meanwhile, Walter sat at the picnic table, ravishing all his clams, his French fries and some of mine as well. Pebbles started begging for clams. I shared what was left of mine with him and took a sip of my coffee. Cold...like my hands. *Bad omen.* I leaned over the outdoor heaters, took off my thin leather gloves and warmed up my palms.

I returned to the table. Fred resumed his confession, in a voice that sounded like the moan of a wounded animal.

"The day before Terese left for Alaska, she encountered Adolphus for the first time. She came to visit me and walked into my office, looking for me. I didn't notice Terese...I was busy selling a porcelain tub...to an interested couple in the showroom. At about the same time, Sylvan strolled in the front door...and whispered in my ear...*Fred, get rid of the customers...pronto.* He ordered me to put the *Closed* sign on the door. So, I made some feeble excuse to the would-be buyers and hustled them out of the store. After I closed and locked the front door, I heard a terrifying scream..."

"This is not good..." I felt a pit in the middle of my stomach. "What happened, Fred...What is going on here...in your office?"

"Tangie...I thought maybe someone was injured. And then I recognize my wife's voice—saying, *No, no, no!* Then I heard, *How could you?* She said this over and over again. You see, she barged in on Adolphus—in my private office. My poor wife...Terese must have been scared to death."

"What was Adolphus doing? How did he frighten her?" *I didn't really want to know the answer...*

"Once in a while...he used my office to intimidate employees of his... this time, he roughed up a prostitute."

I stood up straight. "Oh...the worst...so he's into prostitution on the side. Nice friends you have, Fred."

"He's not my friend."

"No, he's your benefactor," Walter added.

"I'm telling you both, I'm afraid of him...what he is capable of doing..."

Santigo's hands started shaking and then his shoulders.

I thought he was going to start crying again. I sat down. "Fred... did you know Terese went into your office...when you locked the showroom door?" *I could not believe this guy's stupidity...his ability to justify his actions.*

"Not at first...But I heard her screaming—and then, I recognized her voice—her cries. I raced to my office but Sylvan held me back and stood in front of the door—his body blocking my path. I shouted to him...*Let me through...Let me through...* I had to know what was going on...if Terese was all right.

He strong-armed me, saying...*Relax, stay here...*"

"So you left Terese with Adolphus?" I asked.

"No...I kneed Sylvan, got past him and burst open the door. What I encountered, I wouldn't want to experience, ever again."

"Did Adolphus hurt Terese?"

"No...not physically. But he stood there, laughing at my wife—my love—she kept sobbing—and I saw what terrified Terese...A young girl, no more than seventeen, with letters and numbers burned into her arm... lying in my chair. Eyes open. Not breathing. I'll never forget those eyes—staring at me...Lifeless. I grasped at Terese's hands with mine... hoping to calm her. Her eyes bore into me with disbelief...She flung my hands back to me saying, *How could you? How could you?* Then she ran out the open door. She thought I knew what going on—that I contributed to that poor girl's death."

"Well, Terese saw the poor girl lying dead in your office—In your chair! What did you expect your wife to think? That you're an innocent bystander? Get real!"

I could feel steam coming out of my ears. I wanted to scream. Coward. What a coward!

What did you do with the dead girl?" Walter asked Santigo.

"I didn't do anything with her. Horst came in, picked up her body and took her away…out the back door..."

"Considerate of him," added Walter.

"Adolphus gives orders…Horst follows them…"

"Just like you," I said.

"I suppose you're right…I'm no better than him…and I don't deserve Terese…maybe I should just let her go…"

Santigo started wailing again…and I asked if there was anything else he wanted to tell us.

"Yes, Tangie…That poor girl—that Adolphus killed…The police found her…under the pier—near *Ivar's*...I know…she matched the description released to the news. Adolphus murders people and he laughs about it. Can you understand why I'm afraid? Can you?"

I can't understand how in the world I got drawn into this nightmare. I'm beginning to think I'm as crazy as Santigo. Worse. I should know better… Santigo's a chump. What's my excuse?

I didn't answer Santigo's question. I had no sympathy for him. Instead I asked, "What happened after Horst left with the dead girl?" My concern for Terese began to mount. I started biting my fingernails. *I haven't done that in ten years.*

"What did you do, Fred, after all this happened? Tell me." I spoke with a patience I didn't feel.

"Adolphus told me to get rid of Terese. I couldn't believe what he asked me to do. I cried…*She's my wife!* He smiled like…a hyena…and said, *Fred…that should make it easy, comprende?* He laughed at me...He *laughed* at me! I looked toward Marlaine, my secretary...who just stood there…leaning against the filing cabinet...She wouldn't make eye contact with either of us. Adolphus put the pieces together for me…He said, *You needn't be concerned about her, amigo…Marlaine's one of us.* That's when I knew he had me trapped. All of them together in this…surrounding me…I had no where to run…"

"What then? What did you do?" I had to know. My impatience grew and it showed in my voice.

"I pleaded with Adolphus…begging him to reconsider, saying to him, *Senor Sargento, Terese is my wife...I love her...I can't do this for you… Please, don't ask me to do this…I cannot…Anything but this…*I could not reason with him...He just kept saying, over and over, *I don't like witnesses...She's a witness. It's her or you. Do it or I do it for you...And then, you'll be next."*

"Nice guy, this Adolphus," Walter said. "How could you go into business with such scum? Don't you have any scruples?"

"I told you how I got trapped...Sylvan came into my Aurora shop as Mr. Charm...and then after Adolphus entered the picture, I found myself in an impossible situation...I didn't know how to get out..."

"All right...so just tell me, Fred," I asked, "What happened next... between you and the brothers?"

Well...before The Sargentos left my office...Adolphus told me they were going to their headquarters for a few weeks...and that I better get busy carrying out their orders. Adolphus snickered at me as he walked out the door. The man has no heart. Then Sylvan left, but before he did, he ordered me to close the showroom...so I told Marlaine, my secretary, not to come to work for a few days...to take a vacation.

I went home, not knowing what else to do. I discovered Terese... weeping in our bedroom. She gazed at me with such hate; I could not bear her disgust—her disbelief. I tried to convince her that I took no part in Adolphus' crime, but I'm not convinced she believes me to this day. She just kept screaming: *Don't touch me—Leave me alone!* She paced around the room, throwing clothes in a suitcase...refusing to look at me...or even talk to me.

I interrupted Santigo. "Can you blame her? She just witnessed a murder! Are you a fool or just totally insensitive?"

"Whatever you think of me, please, don't doubt my love for my Terese...I would do anything for her...I would die for her..."

"So what did you do?" Walter asked.

"I pleaded with Terese...saying, As *much as I love you, my darling, I have to let you go. You are right...you have to disappear...it's not safe to stay in Seattle, near the Sargentos. Take that trip that you wanted—to see your sister in Alaska.*

I called the airlines for her, got her an early flight and made arrangements for a limo to pick her up at five a.m....I promised her I would break free from the Sargentos as soon as I could and that we would move away...to someplace where they couldn't find us. I told her to stay with Simone until I contacted her—but she never got there..."

"You never once thought about contacting the police?" Walter asked.

"I'd be dead for sure if I did that...as well as Terese...there'd be no one to protect her."

"Haven't you ever heard of the *Witness Protection Program?*" Walter asked. "You have information the police want. They would negotiate with you if you testified against the Sargentos...you could get a plea bargain..."

"I think about that now...and it all makes sense...but at the time, confusion took over my thinking...and I feared...for Terese and myself... but now...I will do as you suggest. First though...I have to find Terese. I have to be sure she's safe. Then, together...we will approach the police..."

"You're the reason she ran away..." I reiterated.

"I know...I *know*...but somehow I have to convince her that I'm not one of them...that I'm not with the Sargentos...I *have* to...I'll do anything..."

"Where's Adolphus now?" I asked.

"I think Columbia...with Sylvan. That's where his headquarters are located—where he makes all his deals...but Adolphus has businesses in Argentina...as well as in The States...He used to have connections in Chile, but he got in trouble—the authorities know about him there. I expect him back here...in Seattle...in a week or so. He told me he wants to see Terese's body. Every day he calls me to see if I've done his dirty deed. How am I going to explain things to him when he returns...that I didn't follow his orders?"

"Well, at least you've got a week." Walter surmised the situation. "Perhaps I could help you. As I see it, you need a body. I have friends at the morgue. Perhaps we could loan you a body for a few hours."

I glanced at my secretary with wonder written all over my face. *More good news...I could feel my stomach rumbling. Walter! Are you bluffing or what?* He gave me that *don't-say-a-word* look and I bit my tongue 'til I tasted blood.

Walter continued his plan, explaining the terms. "In exchange for our help, Fred, you'll have to meet the Sargentos in a place where Ms. Seraphina, another policeman and I can watch and I-D them. *Price's*

Funeral Parlor comes to my mind. It's not far from the University District. My friend does business now and then with the owner. As long as Mr. Price gets paid, he obliges the customer. Money talks. We'll fix it so he'll think you're the grief-stricken widower. But, remember…we need your assistance to apprehend Adolphus, his brother Sylvan…and Horst—when and if they shows up."

"I can't. They'll kill me."

"They'll kill you anyway once your usefulness to them is over. We can protect you."

"You?"

"Well, the police," said Walter.

"What are you, a cop?" Fred asked.

I was wondering the same thing.

"No. But I know detectives who will give you safe haven. You don't have to do anything but lore the brothers to the funeral parlor, identify them to us, then testify against them, after they are apprehended."

"I don't know if I am strong enough to lie to the Sargentos—They figure things out—They're smarter than me."

Now…Finally…Something on which we both agree. Fred does not win the I.Q. award of the year. But perhaps his heart is in the right place. I almost feel sorry for him. Almost.

I looked at Walter. Maybe he could get to Fred, *man to man.* Walter looked at me and then at Fred. He read my silent cue and began working on Fred.

"You told me you love Terese...Do it for her." *Walter picked love as motivation…great choice.* "Think of your wife, not yourself."

Santigo looked up at Walter and nodded.

Suddenly, in my mind, all the pieces of *The Puzzle Walter* began to fall into place...*Musician, writer, undercover agent...What a duffus I am. Some psychic I am. Love is blind...or love is my weakness...Just like Santigo's love of Terese...He can't seem to get it right...and here he goes crying again…Just like me when I get all stressed out…At this moment I know how he feels. I don't think of him as scum anymore…I just have pity for him…Poor sap.*

Santigo interrupted my silent epiphany, with uncontrolled wailing. "How can I protect Terese? I can't even find her...You can't even find her!" He started weeping out loud. Some customers strolled by and noticed his ranting. Up until now...late afternoon, we had the outdoor eating deck to ourselves...but now the early supper crowd began filtering in one by one.

I hate to see a grown man cry, so I softened my approach, remembering the pain of love lost, my grieving for Don when he left me. Plus I didn't want any eavesdroppers. I lowered my voice and whispered, "Fred, we are trying to find her. We haven't given up. So far we haven't located her, but when we do, we'll caution her not to go near you. We know you're being watched and no doubt your home is under surveillance. Probably your home phone is bugged. As soon as we find Terese, we'll make sure she's in a safe place, call you and give you some code words... like, *I can't wait for summer*." For now, hold tight. Don't fall apart."

Walter ended our meeting with his plan of attack. He whispered, "Fred, we'll call you when we have things lined up. We'll meet at *Price's Funeral Parlor*, as soon as we can get a body double. I'll have my friend put your name on the deceased, so Mr. Price won't get confused. It will all be on the up and up...You just play the role of the grieving husband and we hope this time, the Sargentos take the bait."

Chapter Twenty-Seven

We left Fred Santigo in a dazed state, but he did agree to meet us at the funeral home one week from today. As we walked away, I looked back at him. He engrossed himself in feeding his shrimp and fries to the seagulls as tears continued to fall from his bloodshot eyes. He pulled out a handkerchief and blew his nose, then put his head down on the picnic table to block out the pain and fear that consumed him. I could say he brought all this trouble on himself, but I wouldn't wish this nightmare on my worst enemy.

"That went well, don't you think, Tangie?" Walter took my arm as we left *Ivar's Seafood Bar*.

I glared at him.

"I know, I know. We have to talk. I promise. Soon."

As we strolled north down the pier, Walter tightened his hold on my hand. He picked Pebbles up and tucked him under his arm. With an air of caution in his voice, he whispered in my ear, "Let's turn around and head south, walk very fast...Horst is over there...back at *Ivar's...* at the beginning of the seafood pickup line; he's watching us. Come on, before he can follow us."

We cut through the gathering throng of people around the bend—waiting in line to order their clams and fish and chips. We got more than one dirty look. Seattleites are serious about their seafood. The trolley that ran up and down the waterfront approached us. Walter whispered in my ear, "Run...Now!" We darted in front of the trolley, narrowly missing it's front bumper. The conductor swore at us. I froze when a car behind us in the adjacent lane slammed on its brakes to avoid hitting us. Then we crisscrossed in front of the rest of the traffic and made it to the other side. I was about to pee in my pants.

"Don't ever make me do that again, Walter." I began gasping as I bent over and started hyperventilating.

"I'm sorry, Angelina. Horst has a gun."

"You don't know that."

"Oh, but I do. It's strapped to his calf. He's on to us...Come on...let's get to the car before the creep spots where we're going. I think he'll wait for the traffic. Folks never want to hit a dog, but they'd make a pancake out of that thug for sure."

This time, Walter called it right. He's usually right and he knows it. I could feel myself ready to collapse from holding my breath and I really did need to use a bathroom. We raced to my mini SUV, hopped in the front seat, then slammed and locked the doors. Walter tossed Pebbles in my lap and gunned the *Escape*—aptly named, I might add—backwards, hitting a few garbage cans that were chained to the side of the parking area. *So I'll send the city a check. Business expenses.*

Walter drove south, towards Pioneer Square...then turned around and headed northeast towards Fifth Avenue and Union Street. Good diversionary tactics. If I weren't still mad at him for holding out on me, I'd congratulate him. We got a little stuck in the four p.m. traffic, but come to think of it, the masses protected us from Horst. *I don't know how one can be a little stuck, leaving the city...You're either stuck or you're not...no in-between, really...but that's the English language for you.* Getting stuck in traffic worked wonders on me...*reverse psychology*. Sitting through the same stop light for ten minutes gave me time to simmer down, exhale and do my deep breathing. I petted Pebbles who started shaking. *He senses my fear. Hates the bad guys as much as I do.* Walter took my hand and kissed it and then leaned over and kissed me on the lips. I lost my anger.

In the recesses of my mind, I heard a horn blasting. How long did that kiss last? Not long enough...*Things are getting complicated*...I looked at my blouse—unbuttoned...No wonder the guy behind us was leaning on the horn. Traffic jerked forward. Walter released his hold on me and dashed me that disarming grin...and I almost wet my pants for real this time.

Walter's hand resumed its place on the shift of the car and we cruised towards the Aurora Bridge and our little haven in Ballard. *Our home in the outskirts of downtown Seattle—A little craftsman two bedroom with a garden plot. Okay, so the garden is full of weeds and dog bones, but I have high hopes this spring. Ballard is a bit of Scandinavian charm clashed with the grunge scene in Seattle. Made for an eclectic neighborhood...Senior citizens--mostly Norwegian, Hippies--mostly my mother's age, groupies--of all races and creeds, yuppies--some married, some single and folks just trying to make a living staying out of trouble and doing their best--like me. Together we all enjoy a little bit of suburbia mixed with the urban environment that is Seattle. I love it...seven years good luck in my home. No complaints. No fears. Never even have to lock my front door—Nothing to steal anyway. Okay, the house is a little run-down. But it's classic. Today it's a fixer-upper. Tomorrow it will be in Seattle's Fine Homes and Gardens Makeover Section. I'm sure of it.*

Walter ground the gears as he pulled into my minuscule driveway. "Sorry, Tangie..." he said. "A thought occurred to me...Why don't we take a walk...to the park..."

"We just got home and you want to take a walk?"

"I know, but we need to *talk*..."

"Okay, but first I gotta use the little girl's room and give Pebbles some water. All that salt...All those clams...His tongue's hanging out."

"I'll wait on the porch."

"You do that, *Mystery Man*," I said, as I jumped out of the *Escape* and hopped up the steps taking them two at a time.

I went inside with Pebbles and raced into the bathroom. On the way out I looked in the mirror...windblown hair again...Make-up a mess. This time I didn't care a fig. I went back into the kitchen to get Pebbles, but only an empty water bowl greeted me. I filled it up and *went* searching for the pooch. I called him and he didn't respond...*Sometimes Pebbles reminds me of Walter.* I went into the living room and there my pooch laid, on the couch—Walter's bed. Like me, Pebbles likes Walter's scent. I laughed at my Westie as I viewed him spread out, lying on his back, feet up in the air...Dead to the world...Too much adventure for him today.

"Okay, Champ, I've got Walter all to myself. You'll be sorry!"

I strolled out the front door and took Walter's waiting palm. We walked hand in hand down the creaky stairs and onto the cracked sidewalk—Just two folks embarking on an early evening stroll to the neighborhood park down the street.

"Hey Tangie," Walter said, throwing me a curve, totally changing the subject at hand. "If you want, I could help you find Father Caine's sister. She's probably around here somewhere. Local I bet."

"How do you know?"

"Just a hunch...If you have her picture, I could have Paul—at *Seattle Police Department*—do an aging sketch for you."

"Now that would be excellent...I'll dig out her photo. There's one in the envelope Father Joe gave me." *Rats! I've completely forgotten to look into that lead...Seems I've been kinda busy lately...*

I grinned at my partner-in-detective work. "Thanks Walter." I kicked a stone on the sidewalk.

As we strolled arm in arm toward the park, we passed no people, but cars zoomed by us...one by one like clockwork...worker bees coming home from their jobs downtown...Supper time in Seattle. "Hey *Mystery Man...*" I decided now would be a perfect time to grill Walter. "Are you trying to take my mind off the Sargentos...or off your lack of being completely honest with me?"

"Neither. I'm trying to help...If you find Mary Claire, you can find Terese."

"Oh...The order of things..."

"Well, sort of...That's kind of it."

"Look Walter, I really do appreciate all you do for me—with my detective agency...but what about the dead body stuff? What are you into?"

"I told you. I have a friend...well...friends..."

"The police don't just hand over dead bodies."

"This particular friend does. I help him out. He helps me."

"Who is this friend?"

"Well, he belongs to a special branch of Seattle P.D...Hush, Hush."

"So that's why you are so closed-mouth about things."

"Well, sort of..."

"But you don't entirely trust me..."

"Now that's not true. I trust you...especially with this..." Walter pleaded...as he took my palm and placed it over his heart as if to validate his concern.

My eyes filled with tears...and I could not go on. I remember placing my hand over Don's heart and him taking my hand away. Walter is not Don. Interrogating Walter—my Mystery Man—Impossible. What do I ask him? "Do you love me?" Not the sort of thing you ask a guy. I love him, but I can't tell him...and he won't tell me...unless he's joking...or is he?

"Angelina," he continued. "I didn't tell you everything, because I didn't want you to get hurt...but it seems I can't keep you in the dark anymore...about me..."

"This isn't the time when you tell me you have a secret life and you are going to leave me, is it? I've been there before."

"Of course not. I'm not going anywhere."

I sighed. *Score one for Tangie. But I still don't know the real Walter. He may be staying, but he has a secret.* We opened the gate to *Finney's Park* and walked over to the swings. Empty. *Figures. What kid swings in the dark and at suppertime? Actually it's dusk and very beautiful outside. The sky is pink and the sun just setting. I love this time in the day...right before night moves in and takes over.* We could see the lights of the city in the distance beginning to twinkle.

Walter took my arm and motioned to the swings. "Care for a push?"

I sat down—Nothing like a swing to take your cares away. As my body moved back and forth, in rhythm with the ropes, playing them like strings on a violin...I gazed at the snow-covered Olympic Mountains beyond the city... towering over the rain forest and the Olympic Peninsula that stretched far away—invisible to my eyes--but the mountains, still visible as the sun set, reminded me of their presence. I felt the cool breeze caress my face. As my body came back to Walter for another push, he whispered in my ear, "I love you, Angelina..."

Angelina...Whenever he says my baptismal name, I feel special—warm, needed, loved. And...he said he loves me...I close my eyes and smile. Heaven is a swing.

I came to an abrupt stop. Walter halted my flight from the world's woes, lifted me off and placed me on the cold hard ground.

"Angelina…Tangie...we have to go home..."

"We just got to *Finney's*, Walter...It's lovely here." I pointed west. "Look at the sunset..."

"Tangie, please. Something's wrong!"

I glanced up at Walter and at once saw that fear…that same fear I saw in his eyes, that grabbed me our first night together. I snapped out of my reverie. *Business alert*. Walter encapsulated my hand tight in his and together we raced down the wooded path back to the sidewalk. We crossed the street and galloped the rest of the way home. My eyes targeted the front door as we approached the house...Ajar. I know I shut it when we left. My feet turned to lead. I couldn't move. I gasped, "Walter...Someone's in our home..."

Walter stepped in front of me. "Wait here." He tiptoed up the steps.

I ignored his words, regained movement in my legs, took a deep breath and followed him into the house.

Nothing looks disturbed in the living room, but no Pebbles asleep on the couch. Just some ruffled cushions. I proceed into the kitchen after Walter. The water bowl remains where I left it, but it's contents gone… spilled onto the floor...Nothing else visible on the floor...I look on the counters and out the window. My eyes fly to the center of the kitchen... Bull's-eye…Sharp…Dead center...A knife...not one of mine...but a hunting knife...serrated edge...and I don't hunt. Neither does Walter...He's like, for saving the polar bears...The knife stuck smack into my antique butcher block with a note through it's blade...and blood...Blood all around...dripping down the side onto the cluttered shelf below…ruining my cookbooks. The note, written in a barely legible handwriting, reads, "Look in the ice box."

Walter opens the doors to my refrigerator and freezer, which are plastered with photographs of Pebbles and my nephews. We take turns looking inside...first the freezer and then the cold food storage...fearing the worst. In the center of the meat tray rests a heart. My knees give way. I steady myself on the countertop. "Oh my God...Pebbles!" I shriek, "Where's Pebbles?"

Walter takes a hold of my body and caresses me. "It'll be all right, Angelina. We'll find him...He's around here."

Just then I hear a whimpering...The sound...coming from my bedroom. I race upstairs to the loft two steps at a time...with Walter just behind me...I could see Pebbles' head sticking out from under my bed. I start gasping. Again, I could not breath. Walter bends down, eases him out and hands him to me. I hug Pebbles—There's blood on his neck and collar...and in his mouth. I start to shake along with the dog.

Walter takes him out of my arms and examines him. "I think he's okay, Tangie. This isn't his blood. Probably drippings from the calf's heart in the refrigerator...or..."

I spot something white on the needlepoint rug alongside the bed...a piece a paper splattered with blood. I lean down and pick it up. Writing, in a neat block style printing, comes into focus, beneath the drops of blood. The note reads: *"Sorry I missed you. Next time I won't. Mind your own business--or else*!"

I drop the message on the floor and sit down on the bed, my entire body shaking.

Walter picks it up, reads it and tries to pull me to my feet. "We've got to leave, Tangie. Horst knows where you live. He'll be back...Come on...Please...get up...we've got to go."

I sit there in a trance—*So much for Home Sweet Home.* "It isn't fair!" I start to cry. "What did I ever do to deserve this? He comes in...invades my home...*our* home...and we...we've done nothing to him...or those... Sargentos!"

"No it isn't fair...What happened to James Benson, Father Joe and that poor girl in Fred's office isn't fair either. Look, Tangie—Face it—These guys are dirty. They're scum. Walter begins shouting...as he tries to penetrate my stupor. "We have to get out of here—Now!"

Walter never yells. He is the calm one. I look at him, tears streaming down my face. Then he leans down and pulls me up with one arm... Pebbles, in his other one.

"I'm sorry, Angelina, for raising my voice at you...I didn't know how else to get your attention..."

"It's okay...I'm all right now...I just lost it...Just give me a minute...I'll grab my laptop and a couple of files..."

I look around my bedroom...Father Joe's envelope...on my dresser. I grab it and stuff it in my hobo bag, along with my files on Terese and Clancy. I enter my office and pack my laptop.

"I'm ready, Walter. Don't you want to bring your computer?"

He holds up a flash drive. "I'm all set. Let's go."

Chapter Twenty-Eight

Walter leashed Pebbles and we walked out the house like any other couple out for an evening stroll. This time I stopped to lock the front door and sighed, "Walter, I don't have any other clothes...Maybe I should go back in and get some."

"No time, Tangie. "We'll get you some later."

I walked down to the *Escape* and open the door. Walter came by and took the handle from me...then shut and locked the door before I could get in the vehicle.

"Horst knows your car. Leave it here. Follow me."

Walking as in a fog, I followed Walter...choking back sobs—Back to the park. He carried my laptop and files for me and handed me Pebbles to walk...who perked up once we hit the fresh air...Doing his usual sniff, sniff, stop and lift his leg bit...and...eager...like he smelled adventure. *Maybe I have a psychic dog. Naw, he's only smart. I don't know what I'd do if anything happened to him. We've been through so much together. I am not ready to lose him.*

"Walter...Pebbles hid under the bed when he heard Horst come in. Strange how we all knew it was Horst...How did that creep find out where we live, anyway?"

Funny, all of a sudden, I don't think in the singular anymore. And I don't think I can go back to being a woman without a man...I've become too needy...and Walter knows it...I'm toast.

Walter led me through the gate of the park. Second trip there. Baffled would explain my thinking. *Maybe he wants swing again. I give up.* "Why are we here, Walter?"

"Come on…"

I didn't argue with him. I followed him through the side gate that bordered the doggie walk path. We ambled along, letting Pebbles take the lead. The dog knew where we were going before I did. He's been with Walter this way before. The path dead-ended into a parking lot. Walter directed me to a red wine *Porsche Cayenne* and pressed a keypad. *Voila*. The door opened. "Get in," he commanded in a soft voice.

In shock, I crawled into the passenger side and put Pebbles in my lap and Walter put my hobo bag with all my loot in the back seat. I opened my mouth to speak, but nothing came out except maybe *ga…ga…ga*. Must be dry mouth. Two bottles of water were waiting in the beverage holders. I opened one and took a swig and stared at Walter.

His eyes softened as he looked back at me. "This is my *safe car*…I store it over here *just in case*."

"I...I didn't know you had a car, let alone a *Porsche*...thought you relied on public transportation."

"I do and I do."

"Walter…Why are you doing this? What is going on? Why did you decide to help me?"

"I've never lied to you."

"Now you sound like a politician."

"Really, Tangie…" Walter groaned, then winced as if in pain. He revved up the engine and put his deluxe *SUV* in gear, backing out of the parking space.

I could feel its power. Must be a V-8. Strong—like him. I couldn't help myself. I had to know. "You didn't tell me the whole truth."

"No."

"Why?"

"I was trying to protect you..."

"Yeah, but what about us?"

"You and me?"

"Yes, you and me. Is that an act?"

"No. Of course not."

"If it is, I'm outta here..." I said, putting my hand on the door handle.

Walter reached over and grabbed my hand and kissed it. "Angelina... Just stick with me a little longer. We've got to get out of here. I'll tell you everything when I get you safe. Trust me."

Well, it's either Walter or Horst. You guessed it. Walter won. Hands down.

I sat silent in the front passenger side of the *Cayenne* and watched my mystery man put on his shades and drive out of my Ballard neighborhood. I pulled on the hood of my jacket and slumped into the ultra-soft heated black leather seat. Its warmth calmed my growing unrest, urging me to relax. Wondering what our next stop would turn out to be, I sunk into a reverie... *Will the real Walter please stand up...Nice guy...nerd... or scoundrel? Sure, they all have their appeal, but somehow, Walter is becoming more of the scoundrel here...and for sure I am determined to see for myself the real Walter--naked before me—and the world. I guarantee that I am going to strip him of all his multiple personae and see him for who he really is—if it kills me! And believe me, I can do it. Just try me.*

I pulled Pebbles close to me, scratched him on his head and caressed his neck. *Poor dog. What a scare.* I petted his nose and felt something hanging out of his mouth. It was stuck in his teeth. I pulled it off his front fangs and out of his mouth. He seemed grateful and licked me. I asked Walter to put on the compartment light. I examined the specimen. It was a bloody piece of a cuff—torn off a man's pant's leg.

"Good dog, Pebbles...very smart Westie!" I patted his head and practically jumped for joy, except that the seatbelt held me captive. "Hey Walter! I think we just might have some DNA here. *Horst the Enforcer* is about to go public."

Walter stopped his frantic driving for a minute and glanced over at me. I saw him smile for the first time since the break-in. He pulled onto a side street off of Aurora and parked the *Porsche* under some still bare birch trees. They looked naked, swaying in the breeze. "I love birches," I reminisced, momentarily transgressing, caught off guard by the beauty of the trees...and my love of nature..."Whenever I see these trees swaying, I think of Robert Frost's poem, *Birches*...my all-time favorite poem and the last line...I could rephrase that one... *We could do worse than be Seattle Detectives*...maybe what we do is important..."

Walter looked at me, nodded and smiled. "I love that poem too."

Yeah...Frost talks about going back to nature...but there is so much more going on—not spoken..."

"Yes, Tangie...kind of like us." Walter leaned over and kissed me. I responded. He pulled away first...and that concerned look came back on his face. "Angelina...I hate to stop...but...my mind is on business...I can't seem to shut it off—What about the DNA and Horst—What are you saying?"

I waved the swatch in the air and said to Walter, "Horst's...you like?"

"I like!" Walter exclaimed with a broad grin and then patted Pebbles, the Wonder Dog on his head. "Good boy!"

My crime-fighting partner pulled a plastic bag out of his glove compartment and instructed me to drop the specimen into it. He sealed it, picked up a nearby pen and labeled the bag with date and contents. Walter is so prepared. In my car, I'd probably contaminate the evidence by putting it in a *McDonald's* container. Walter leaned over and returned the plastic bag and pen to the glove compartment. Before he shut the compartment I noticed the barrel of a gun facing me. I shivered. Walter noticed.

"The gun is for protection, Tangie."

"I figured that one out. Things are beginning to add up...with you—*my secretary*. Anyway, Walter, score one for the detectives and a big zero for Horst...Two points for Pebbles—I'd say he's earned a month's supply of bacon, don't you think, Walter?"

"Mais oui, Mademoiselle."

"I love it when you talk French."

"Wait until you taste my French Kissing."

I grinned, remembering. "But first we have to take this to the cops, right?"

"It can wait. Right now, I'm bringing you to a safe house."

"I'm *safe*. I'm with you."

"We've got to sleep sometime and we can't return to your home—dangerous back there. Call your mom. Tell her not to go near your house. Tell her it's in quarantine—Make something up—Dry rot mold or something. Don't tell her someone broke in—That'll totally freak her out big time. We have to stop your mail..."

"You know, Walter, it's a good thing Mr. Jarrick decided to show a little love towards Spike...The poor kitty would starve if he had to depend on us...No time to catch him and bring him with us—That is, if we could catch him. He's a little on the wild side."

Walter smiled. "Now who's a softie?"

I shot Walter a grimace and took out my cell phone. Before I could push any buttons, Walter grabbed it from me, shut it off and deposited in a padded envelope he had above his visor. He sealed it and handed it to me. "We'll mail this to Steve for safe keeping. We can't take any chances—It may be compromised."

He pulled a small box out of his glove compartment. "Here...use this...It's a pre-paid cell phone. Only use this one. Not traceable. We've got to lay low for awhile."

Walter started the car up again, drove to the neighborhood post office and dropped off the package. He then steered the *Porsche* over the Fremont Bridge to *Seattle Center*...towards *McCaw Hall* and the theatre district. *Great. Now where are we going? The opera? Doesn't he know I'm tired? To say nothing of being scared...hungry...confused...I'm a mess.*

After we passed Mercer and the theater crowd milling around on the side of the street, Walter crossed over to Roy Street, pulled a left and then a right—heading up towards the Queen Anne neighborhood...driving all the way up Nob Hill Avenue before making a turn...onto a side street and then up Queen Anne Avenue. He continued heading straight to the top of Queen Anne Hill. He slowed down in a quaint quiet neighborhood, away from the hustle and bustle of the city, yet on the pinnacle of Seattle—like the place existed in the clouds. A breath-taking view greeted us as Walter slowed the *Porsche* down to a crawl. We could see all of *Seattle Center*...and the *Space Needle*...completely lit up in green lights...and the ferries twinkling and crossing back and forth across the Puget Sound...a little piece of paradise.

I think I'm gonna like this safe house.

Chapter Twenty-Nine

Queen Anne is an upscale neighborhood on one of the seven hills of Seattle. It is one of the "in" places to live within the city limits and borders *Seattle Center* and the theatre district--which houses *McCaw Hall*, where the *Seattle Opera* and the *Pacific Northwest Ballet* co-exist, along with the *Seattle Repertory Theatre*, housed in the *Bagley Wright Theatre*, next to the *Intiman Theatre*. Both theatres send a lot of their original works to *Broadway*. Here, the classics are part of the eclectic. The urban and suburban art aficionados mix. It all works. It's all good. I don't know exactly where I fit in, but I do know I love the ballet. I go every chance I get—My favorite art form. *I wonder if I could drag Walter? Funny, I never asked him about his culture fancies. Why not now?*

"Hey Walter? Do you want to go to the ballet sometime?"

"Sure. I've got season tickets. You can be my date."

"I never saw that one."

"What one?"

"I don't see you as the ballet type."

"What do you see me as?"

"Oh, the video type. Games...computer...*Wiz Kid*."

"That's just an act. I like classical stuff...and jazz, of course. I've been around it all my life."

Moment of truth.

"Walter...You've been holding out on me. Time to come clean. Look at me."

"I'm driving. Geez, Tangie...wait until I stop the car. We're almost there."

"Tell me something else about yourself."

"I play the piano."

"Good?"

"I'll let you be the judge of that—I play mostly jazz and classical."

"If you're good, you'll be a shoe-in for my mother...She loves piano players."

Walter pulled into the driveway of a handsome Queen Anne Dutch Colonial, with a perfectly manicured lawn and neatly clipped hedges. The outdoor lighting illuminated the stone walkway to the front door. I pictured tulips and daffodils bordering the path in the springtime. Right now I could see buds of crocuses trying their best to shoot up above the ground. April is not far away.

"What are we doing here? Visiting someone?"

"Yes. I want you to meet my friend." Walter pressed the garage door opener and pulled the *Porsche* into the detached two-car garage. The lights came on like magic and the door shut automatically—*a far cry from my dilapidated garage door in Ballard.* My mystery man exited the vehicle on driver's side, went around to the passenger side and escorted me out. "Come on, Angelina. I'll show you around."

We left the garage through a side door. Walter let Pebbles off his leash into to a wooded fenced-in yard that ran around the side of the garage and connected to the back of the house. Walter took my hand and guided me to a gate, opened it and showed me around to the front of the house...up to the main entrance. He pulled out a key, like he owned the joint. *He does own the joint. What a duffus I am! Clouded vision again. Strike Two! Better watch myself—Strike Three and I'm out.*

"Hey Walter…I'm a little puzzled here. I thought you sublet your apartment in the city...you know...the poor starving writer/teacher..."

"Well...I might have stretched the truth a bit.

"I'd say, just a bit."

He led me into the foyer. The seasoned dark-wood embraced me with its warmth. This house smacked of loving care and constant upkeep. The outside lights shown in through the picture window in the living room...beckoning me to enter. I walked in as Walter flipped on a switch creating a soft light by the fireplace. The elegance of this room captivated me. Two *Queen Anne* chairs—*like what else would he have in this home?* They framed a corner of the room and perched on an antique woolen Persian rug with beautiful intricate designs. The floors—polished cherry—showcased a baby grand piano that sat near French doors leading to the private courtyard. Well, private except for Pebbles—I could see his face peeking at us through a door window. He looked comfortable. Like he knew this place. *He's at home here. The traitor. He's been here and hasn't told me.*

Two wall-to-wall bookshelves surrounded the massive stone fireplace, ensconced in marble and hardwood...and nearby a club chair shared a spot with a library table—Walter's reading corner, no doubt. An open space caught my eye—where a couch used to be. I looked at the club chair and then back again. *Ah ha! Same fabric—identical texture—as the couch sitting in my diminutive parlor in Ballard...Deception uncovered!*

"Walter!"

"Hush...You'll scare Hildie."

"Who's Hildie?"

"My roommate." Walter went over to the French doors and let Pebbles in to race around the house.

The pooch slid on the wood floors and caught himself just before he fell over. Then he ran out of the living room, down the hall, continuing to slip and slide as he leapt...running as if on a mission...into what appeared to be the kitchen...swinging doors and all that...and I hear a commotion...which leads me to believe...

"Your roommate."

"My kitty."

"Hildie." I smiled. *I should have known. No wonder the concern for Spike...No wonder all the questions about cats.* "Bet she's a Maine Coon cat, right?"

"You're on to me—The cat lover."

"I bet she and Pebbles are long-lost friends."

"Yes...they love each other."

"You haven't been straight with me for a long time, have you?"

"You haven't been straight with yourself."

"Now Walter, what is that supposed to mean?"

"I haven't lied to you."

"Not in so many words...but your misrepresented yourself."

"And you didn't?"

"What?"

"I know, Angelina."

"Know what?"

"Know what you know."

"You're driving me crazy, Walter."

Walter took me in his arms, embraced me ever so softly and then leaned my body back and looked in my eyes. "I know that you see things. I know that you need help. I know that you need a man."

He stopped talking and gave me one of his really special lingering kisses. *Where is a couch when you need one?*

Walter, as if reading my mind, pulled me over to the club chair, which could comfortably seat two people. He sat down with me—half on his lap, half on his cushion—and studied my face while brushing the hair out of my face. *I love it when he does that…*

"Angelina, I wanted to tell you so many times..."

"Walter…Did you read my journals? Did you talk to my mother? Level with me."

I reluctantly push myself up off of his lap...I want to stay close to him...God knows I want to stay by his side…always…Let's just say I'm a magnet clinging to another magnet—Our forces irresistible.

Walter got up, took my hands and placed them alongside his cheekbones. "Look, Angelina...See for yourself. Please...Look into my eyes."

I closed my eyes. *I don't want to play this game.* Walter persisted. He pressed his body into mine. He made it harder for me to play tough. I began melting for the second time in this safe house.

"Angelina, come on...Let's go somewhere else...Come with me." He picked me up. Up until now, I didn't recognize his true strength. I felt light as a feather in his arms. He carried me upstairs to what appeared to be the master suite—*His* bedroom in *his* house. He shut the door and closed the blinds.

"The neighbors." He grinned at me. "They all have telescopes. Retired star gazers...Don't want to take a chance of giving one of them a heart attack."

Still holding me in his arms, he threw open the quilted down comforter on his four-poster bed, and placed me on his feather bed. Soft... Inviting...Then he took off his shirt and crawled in next to me. I gave up fighting him...not wanting to hold my desire back...just wanting to be with him...in this place...*safe*...

Walter's breathing echoed mine. The two of us ripped off any remnants of clothing ensconced on our bodies. Nothing would separate us tonight. Any lingering anger in my psyche evaporated with the closeness of Walter's heated skin next to mine...I held my breath for a moment and then breathed out...slowly. Paradise. Passion replaced doubt. Love replaced longing. Trust replaced fear. I may have forsaken Ballard by the sea...but...with Walter, I found my way home.

Afterwards, when the moon rose high in the sky and Its glory reached its peak, advertising itself through the skylight above our love nest, Walter leaned against my breast and kissed my neck...my cheeks...my eyes.

"You taste like salt. You've been crying, Sweetheart." He held my head in his hands. He looked into my eyes and would not let me look away. I felt more naked at that moment than I ever have in my entire life.

"Angelina. No more games. I promise. We need to be true to ourselves...and we have to trust one another."

"Walter, I know..." At that moment in time...feeling naked before the world, I knew I could trust him—with anything. *If this isn't love, then I don't know what love is. I just know he takes my fear away. I am safe with him—he will not desert me. He loves me...*Eternal gratitude kicked in and the tears began flowing once more.

Walter caressed my cheek. "Angelina, I'm sorry..."

"Oh Walter..." I took his hands in mine. "I'll look into your eyes... for real this time...I love you...I do."

Reluctantly at first, I stared at him...An eerie feeling crept over me. He bared all. I bared all. *No secrets. None. Not anymore. Then... a feeling of complete peace. Light, love, togetherness, compassion...I began to see what he sees...*

He's in love with me...He knows I'm psychic...He "knows"...No one told him...He knows...He knows! Walter...Walter is psychic too...but...behind the love is something else...The fear...the fear is still there...in his eyes...He takes away my fear... but his is still there...what does he fear? Santigo? Sargento? Adolphus? I can barely see it...I see clouds...and darkness...then red and black...Adolphus...and Santigo...I see Sylvan hurting someone...Who? Oh...no!...Adolphus is...Oh, no. Oh, NO! I panic...I scream...and let go of his hands and fall on the bed. The darkness takes over...and the moon disappears...

"Wake up, Angelina...Wake up!"

I hear Walter's voice...Bringing me back from my nightmare...I'm here. Safe...with him...in his bedroom...in our bedroom...I feel a cold washcloth placed on my face and Walter massaging my shoulders...I start chanting to myself... "I'm okay...I'm out of danger..."

"It's over, Angelina...I'm sorry...for what I put your through—But I had to do it...I know how hard it is for you...but you're with me...You're safe..."

I opened my eyes. "What happened?"

"We had a sort of...meeting of the minds..."

"And?"

"You fainted."

"That bad, huh?"

"It doesn't have to be."

"Walter...I remember...now. I know why I'm so afraid—You and me—We ...are going to get hurt."

"We'll stop them. I promise. It will not happen. I love you, Angelina. I won't let anything happen to you...to us."

"But I saw it. I always see what happens. Santigo...Adolphus... Sylvan..."

"No, Angelina, you saw what I see...Not what you see."

"You are totally confusing me, Walter." I took the glass of ice water he handed me, took a sip of the water and chewed on some of the ice cubes.

"Look, Angelina, I see what the Sargentos plan to do. We can stop them from carrying out their plans. We can stop them. We can stop the controller and his puppets. What you see will happen or has happened.

What I see is up for grabs. It's a gray area. Sometimes I can stop things from happening...if I follow my instincts the right way."

"The right way?"

"Yes, I have to stay totally focused...and then I am usually successful."

"Usually?"

"Most of the time. It takes discipline."

"How about courage?"

"That too."

"How do you know this stuff, Walter? How can you control your *gift?"*

"Well, I can stop things that I see, because what I get are warnings—signals—I've learned to listen to the signs."

"But you have to live with these horrible visions..."

"Until I stop them."

I grab a hold of Walter's hand and squeeze it. "You're worse off than me. If I were you, I'd have nightmares all the time."

"I think you have just what you can handle."

"How did we ever hook up?"

"Maybe it's fate... Remember, you prayed for help...when you thought about asking Don to..."

"Walter, you're an eavesdropper!"

"No. I told you I get signals. I got my first one about you on our first date...Don isn't around to help you...He's all wrapped up with his mission. I'm available."

"Don't tell me Don is psychic?"

"No. Don't think so. You and I would sense if he were...But you know, he's a good soul. That's why you fell for him. And he really does love you, in his own platonic way...But I'm more your type, Angelina...You and I have passion...I can give you what you need."

"Convince me, Walter...I need convincing..." I whispered, as I took the washcloth off of my forehead and lay down on the bed, feeling light and carefree for the first time in a long while. Walter lay down next to me and kissed my eyes, my cheeks, my lips, my... ah...I could feel my fears evaporating again...What joy...Warmth and passion embracing me...Walter and I...succumbing to our longing...our need to connect...to entwine our bodies together as one...*I know I would not feel this safe for a long time...but right now, Walter is here and he loves me...*

What else can I say? Just that I'm love-starved...and Walter is my feast.

Chapter Thirty

I pry my eyes open. Daylight. I look at the brass and oak antique clock next to Walter's bed. Roman numerals...Not a digital clock in sight. I listen as I hear the grandfather clock in the downstairs foyer striking eight. Good grief. We must have slept for eight hours. Ah...What a wonderful sleep...What a wonderful dream...What a wonderful...

I roll over. No Walter. Figures. He always beats me up—Well, I mean, gets up before me. Bacon. Do I smell bacon? Ah, yes. Reason to get up—My Walter—The Cook.

I slipped unwillingly out of the intoxicating refuge of Walter's down comforter that smelled like him...and placed my feet upon the plush white rug next to the bed and noticed fuzzy brand new maize slippers waiting for me, along with a pale yellow fleece robe draped on the bedside chair. I put on the slippers and held up the robe. My size. Walter does shopping. *Good thing I pay him well.*

A single yellow rose peeked out of the pocket of the robe. I picked it up, smelled it and put it with its friends...in the *Waterford Crystal* vase on the table not too far from the fireplace. *Fireplace? Walter has a fireplace in his bedroom! Figures.* I warmed my...*Oh, so naked body*...by the fire before draping myself in the royal apparel set out for me to make my descent down the staircase. *Walter knows how to entice a woman. No wonder Suzy became ticked off at me. Now I know. Walter dropped her...not the other way around. I'm beginning to see things more clearly now that Walter and I have leveled with each other.*

Let's see, I'll envision breakfast. Bacon. That's a given from the smell. Cappuccino—which I know I'll make. Walter's a great cook but no barista. Eggs? No. Crepes—his specialty...this time with raspberries and whipped cream—My very favorite of all time. Fresh fruit salad, with mangoes—Where the heck does Walter get raspberries and mangoes in winter? Perhaps I don't know everything about him. It will be exquisite finding out.

I raced down the stairs, eager to meet my prince, tripping on the last step...but Walter ran to the landing to catch me.

"I just happened to be on my way up to wake you."

"Some entrance, huh?"

"I love it when you fall into my arms, *Sleeping Beauty...*"

Walter tightened his grip on me and kissed my eyes, my nose, my lips...

I moaned. "Want to go back upstairs, Sweetheart?"

"No. First you have to make me a cappuccino...and I'll serve you breakfast. Don't worry, we'll have our dessert later."

Well, dessert lasted a long time. Around noon, Walter's bedside phone rang. I answered it just for kicks. "Steve somebody," I whispered, as I handed the receiver to Walter. I inched out of bed to get a drink of water—Dehydration setting in.

I sighed. "Ah...Water." I noticed a ray of sun peeking through the window showcasing a pitcher with lemons floating on water...greeting me, along with a bouquet of intoxicating yellow roses.

"Thanks, Sweetie," I whispered, as I poured each of us a glass. Then I went over to the fireplace and warmed my buns up by the fire as Walter talked to Steve. I glanced at him. His ears listened to Steve but his eyes digested me. For the first time since I arrived in my safe house, I felt embarrassed. I never saw myself as sexy, but I could see that Walter did.

I walked over to the window and peaked out one blind—Sure enough. The neighbors had their telescopes sitting on their second story decks. This room fit right into their vantage point. *Oh well, can't have everything perfect. So I can't open the window naked. Can't do that in Ballard either. Mr. Jarrick would suffer an apoplexy.*

Walter put his phone down and smiled at me.

I smiled back. "Sometime, Walter, let's go to a beach somewhere, where the sun shines all the time. *Maui...Fiji...* A place where we can open the windows and doors and be naked before the world."

"You've got my vote on Fiji. I've always wanted to go there. Maui's good too. I've been there."

"Alone?"

"Well, when I was younger—with my family—They're gone now..."

I snuggled next to him. "I'm sorry...do you want to tell me about it?"

"Maybe later."

I nodded, not wanting to pressure him. "So, Fiji's good?"

"Either place is good...we could go for our honeymoon."

"Are you proposing...or propositioning me?"

"Perhaps both."

I gulped. Walter—getting serious again. I handed him the glass of water I just poured...as if offering a love potion. We clicked glasses. "You really know how to smooze a girl."

"I'm serious."

"I know."

"I love you, Angelina."

Walter pulled me towards him and kissed me on my neck.

I sighed. "What about Steve?"

"Steve who?"

"Walter...tell me..."

Walter continued kissing my neck and graduated to my ears. "We have to meet him at two p.m. at the station."

"That's in two hours."

"Plenty of time."

I gave up talking. *Sometimes speaking is a waste of time.*

I opened my eyes and stretched my arms. *Ah...what a marvelous nap.* I heard Pebbles barking. *Poor dog. I've totally neglected him.* I rolled over. *Walter gone. Shower running.* I tiptoed to the door leading to the master bath. Opened it slightly...Lots of steam.

"Any room in the shower?"

"I was just about to scrub my back."

I scrubbed his back. He scrubbed my back. I washed his hair. He washed my hair. We laughed. We cried. We held each other. Things began to get insane.

"We have to meet Steve," Walter murmured.

"We?"

"Yes. He's the guy who gives us the body."

"Oh, Body-Snatching Steve. I get it. You really know how to put a damper on our love life."

"I promise I'll make it up to you..."

"I've heard that line before..."

"Tangie...I'm sorry." Walter sighed and switched into business mode. "We have to go to work. We're late...We were supposed to be at the morgue...like ten minutes ago. Bring your photo of Terese."

"Is what we're doing legal?"

"Well, sort of...It's..."

"I know, *hush—hush.*" *Like whom would I tell this to? Marianna—my mother? Don—Father Don? I don't think so.*

"Tangie, this is the only way to catch the Sargentos."

"Walter, I don't want to go chasing the Sargentos...Sylvan or Adolphus. They're evil. I don't do evil."

"The police will help us. We just lead them to the criminals and they take over."

"Yeah, but what if we get stuck in between the two?"

"We won't let that happen. We'll be careful." Walter tried his best to be reassuring.

Don't know if it's working.

"Here's the plan, Tangie...Let's drop this DNA over to headquarters. I'm sure the police would love to nab this guy, Horst. This will give them a positive identification. Then, we'll pay Steve a visit."

"Walter...I'm sorry...I have to ask...did you know about Horst... and the Sargentos before...*me?*" I looked into his eyes as I dried myself off on one of his Turkish towels.

Walter dried his hair with the other towel and then wrapped it around his waist. "Well, Sweetheart, as I told you, I knew something about them, but you completed the picture—with color and shape...and got them to appear."

"You sure you're not using me?" I hated those words as soon they left my mouth.

"Angelina...How can you say that?" Walter looked crushed.

And I'm an idiot. Gotta learn to shut my mouth...

"Sorry, my love." I put my hands on his shoulders and massaged them, as if penance for my hurtful words. "Sometimes I don't think... I'm just so insecure, sometimes..."

Walter took my hands and looked into my eyes—his steel-blue irises penetrating my soul...*God...how I love his eyes*...I kissed his lips...and hugged him...not wanting to let him go—ever. "I'm so sorry, Walter...I love you...I always will..."

Walter placed his cheek next to mine and whispered, "Angelina... Tangie...I know how you feel...please...don't beat yourself up." He wiped the tears running down my cheeks and led me into the bedroom.

We sat on the bed, dressed in our towels, as he began his explanation. "I didn't connect everything together until later...I just knew that somebody would be threatening you...and that you needed help...That night... When I came over—Your dinner invitation...the first time we ate alone together...I just wanted to look out for you...That's it...I stayed around to protect you...because I liked you...I didn't want you to get hurt."

"You quit your job."

"I was going to do that anyway. You gave me an excuse."

I put my arms around Walter's neck. "So you like me."

"Well, yes...before dinner and at the beginning of the evening...but by the end of night, I knew that I'd love you...and that you would love me...and I didn't want to lose you. So I stuck around."

"It all sounds so simple."

"It is." Wrapping us together in one towel, he crushed me in a passionate embrace. "True love, Angelina—hard to fight that one."

Walter picked up my towel, dried off my hair and wrapped it around my shoulders. "Get dressed my angel. While you napped, I washed and fed Pebbles. He's his ol' sweet-smelling self again. He and Hildie will keep each other company while we go to the police. There is a doggie door in the kitchen leading to the fenced-in backyard—Both pets can go in and out according to their whim. They'll be safe. Come on, Sweetie—we're twenty minutes late. Can you be ready in ten minutes? I'll call Steve and tell him we're running behind. I'll make up something."

"Ten minutes! What about my hair?"

"I like the wet look. Wear a hat."

"Hat?" Then I remembered. "I don't even have any clothes!"

Walter walked me out of the bathroom and pointed to louvered doors, around the corner from the fireplace at the far side of the master bedroom. "Look in the closet…I bought you a few things, just in case."

Walter was already putting on some gabardine slacks by the time I inched over to the walk-in closet. Two sides. One side filled with men's clothing—Walter's. The other side, woman's clothing. Shoes, boots, hats, underwear, bras, jeans, skirts, jackets—A trousseau! All new with tags on them—*Leave it to Walter. Not only does he shop…he has a personal shopper…from Nordstrom's no less. I like this guy!*

"Ten minutes," Walter chirped, handing me a scissors to cut off the tags.

I took the scissors, kissed him on the cheek, and cooed back at him like a grateful dove. "I'll be ready." *New clothes have a soothing affect on me—Like I'm a little kid in a candy store. No more hunger pains for my wardrobe in my Ballard house—I have a sweet tooth for great clothes…and these are delicious!*

Well, in ten minutes—almost ready on time…I had a crisis. Couldn't decide between the lace-up Moorland Hollace boots, picked as one of the *ten things you must have in your wardrobe* or the Italian red leather pumps. The boots won—warm and fuzzy inside—like Walter. Outside—still winter mode for two more weeks or so…*But the calendar says spring is coming…Ah…Spring—a good season for lovers…Walks in the meadow…Trips to the tulip fields…Sailing on the Puget Sound…*

I looked out the window. Yep, still winter. No leaves on the trees yet. I wrapped a white cashmere scarf around my neck and grabbed a black fedora hat from the other side of the closet. With a smile on my face, I placed it on Walter's head. "Let's go, Special Agent Cunningham. I'm ready."

"Where'd you get that hat, Walter?" I asked as we sat in *Walter's Porsche Cayenne* and crawled through the afternoon city traffic on route to the morgue.

Walter got all serious. "My grandfather—His favorite hat. He left it to me along with the house."

"I bet you miss him."

"Yes...I do. He practically raised me...he was such a great guy. We used to stay up late and talk about all sorts of things...He'd always wait for me to come home after school functions...and stuff like that...Always have a snack ready and be ready to listen to me tell him about what happened at school each day...what I was interested in doing..."

"Has he been gone long?"

"Almost two years. I remember his last words to me in the hospital: *Follow your heart, Walter...and you won't go wrong*. Now I know what he meant...because I've found you..."

"I'm glad you took his advice...and I'm glad we found each other..."

Walter took my hand and squeezed it. I melted, leaned into him and kissed him on the cheek, getting a warm feeling all inside me. " *Walter...* My grandmother...Those were her words...before she died."

"Our grandparents, up in heaven, must be having a few chuckles... about us getting together." Walter's mouth widened into a grin—*God, how I love to see my sweetie smile.*

He shifted his *Porsche* and zoomed up a hill not far from Pioneer Square, as traffic opened up. "Almost there, Tangie."

"I'm in no rush, Sweetheart...Believe me. Tell me...is there anyone else in your family?"

"Well, I have an aunt on the East Coast. I see her about once a year, when I head back there to visit her. She's a kick—Aunt Hattie...My mother's older sister. She runs a small art gallery in Newport, Rhode Island.

"Sounds high brow."

"She is...sort of...but she's always been kind to me. She never married. Someday you'll meet her. Say...you can come with me when I go back to New England to visit. We could go sailing around Newport bay."

"Where'd you go to college?"

"*Brown University*."

"Ivy League, huh?" *Figures*. "So why'd you come back here?"

"I love it here—This is my home. When I was back East, I missed the mountains, the Puget Sound...the rain. Plus my grandfather needed me...after he got ill he needed help getting around...I'm glad I came back when I did...we enjoyed some special time together—he and I..."

I noticed tears swelling up in Walter's eyes. I clasped his hand for a moment.

He leaned over and kissed my cheek. "You know, Tangie, I just feel more connected here. I'm a Northwest guy."

"And I'm your Northwest gal."

"*And...so easy to love...*"

Walter started singing a familiar sappy tune. I joined in and we didn't stop until we reached police headquarters. Then he reached over and pulled out a permit from his glove compartment, which I noticed he kept under his concealed weapon, and placed it on the dashboard. *Clout. Figures*...He got out and went around to open the door for me. It started raining again. *Glad I'm wearing my warm fuzzy boots.* I start to shivered—*don't know whether due to nerves or the cold. Probably both.*

"Tangie, Let's go down to the morgue."

"Gee...my favorite place..."

"Come on...we'll get it over with first." Walter smiled, showing his brilliant straight teeth. *Methinks he had a good orthodontist when a young boy. I have a weakness for brilliant teeth as well as brilliant minds. Walter has both.*

"Steve's waiting there for us, Tangie...Come on, you can do it. That's my fearless detective..."

"It's only because of your pearly whites that I have come this far."

Walter grinned, took my hand and sensing my hesitancy, continued chatting business tactics. "After we see Steve, we'll go upstairs and turn in the DNA sample from Pebbles' good deed."

"What about Mary Claire's photo?" My memory kicked in at last. "We needed to multi-task...Remember? The aging process...from Clancy's case?"

"We'll take care of that also."

"Thanks, Walter...as you can see, I'm not as comfortable around here as you."

Walter caressed my hand and brought it to his lips. "So I've noticed. Stick with me, kid."

I must admit I like his vocal imitations. I smiled and could not help relaxing. "As long as you do most of the talking."

I followed his footsteps... *Walter, like me, has a fondness for those old back and white movie classics...Hum...maybe we could watch one when we get home... Our reward for all this sleuthing.*

As requested, Walter did most of the talking. *I've come to appreciate that in my secretary. He's the Go-To Guy.*

He introduced me to Detective Steve Winters. Steve—The big burly body building type. I noticed he has the kind of skin tone that looks tan all year long...A real pin-up kinda guy—Broad shoulders, thin waist, about six-feet tall. A girl's dream date, if you like the strong, silent type. He wore his curly black hair short, except for one curl falling over his brow. His penetrating brown eyes could cave a person's guilty conscience—I'm positive. *Probably is a good interrogator. Glad he's on our side. This cop could take on Horst. Only trouble is Horst doesn't have a conscience.*

Steve informed us he could help with our dilemma. He flexed his muscles as if on cue and leaned back in his chair. "Walter...Tangie... As you know, we've been wanting to nab the Sargento brothers for a while—We've known about their dirty deeds for the past two years. But until you encountered their henchman, these sleazebags have managed to elude us. You have put a time and a place where these criminals can be spotted. Plus, we now have a strong reason to arrest them...and something we can make stick. Good work."

Steve seemed as eager to find the brothers-in-crime as we were to find the missing Terese. I handed Steve the photo of Terese.

He studied the recent photograph and asked me her height and weight. I gave him approximates. He got up from his chair, went to the color copy machine and made several copies. He handed me back the original and said he'd get a make-up artist to help him and he'd keep his eyes open for a body to match her looks. He made it sound so easy. The coldness of the surroundings haunted me. Just knowing that bodies of people—people no longer alive, lay all around us made me shiver. It didn't seem to bother Steve. If it bothered Walter, he didn't let on—*Tough Guy*.

Walter shook hands with Steve Winters and patted him on the shoulder. "Thanks, buddy. I owe you."

Steve the Cop nodded. He turned to me and grinned. He took my hand and shook my sweaty palm. He winked at me. "You're all right, kid."

"I'm twenty-seven. Not exactly seventeen, anymore."

Funny, I don't mind if Walter calls me "kid" but when Steve does, it annoys me. Go figure.

Steve gave me the once over. "I can see that you're not a kid, Tangie. I bet you're trouble."

"I can be." *Bluffing again. Why do I do that?* I stood up straight, faking a confidence I did not feel. "You know, I've been told that before."

Steve smiled. "I'm not surprised." He turned to Walter. "Looks like you've got your hands full...buddy. I'll see ya in a few days. I'll give you some advance warning when we have the stiff ready...at *Price's Funeral Home.*"

"Thanks...much appreciated." Walter concluded the meeting and became rather sober as he shook Steve's hand.

I grimaced. I wasn't used to being callus about the dead. Even people I don't know. All these people have family...friends who cared about them at one time. Well, most of them.

As we road the elevator to the fifth floor, Walter took me in his arms and hugged me in a gentle embrace. "You okay? I'm sorry...Steve can be, at times...well, you might say the guy needs some sensitivity training."

I nodded. I would have kissed him—I was so grateful for his tenderness...but the elevator door opened up and greeted us with a sign that leaped out and grabbed my emotions—*Homicide...Drug Enforcement*...All that bad stuff. Walter led me out of the elevator and down the hall to an office with an inscription on the door that read: *Private.* Walter knocked, then grabbed the doorknob and led me into the room. A tall, rather thin man, wearing horn-rimmed glasses, turned his attention away from talking on the desk phone and motioned us to sit down. He finished his call and hung up.

Walter shook his hand and began introductions. "Tangie, this is Detective Barry Cardoso.

I extended my hand to him. "Pleased to meet you, er...ah...Detective Cardoso."

"Call me Barry."

"Yes, sir, Barry. Call me Tangie."

This being the extent of my brilliant conversation, I sat down on a chair and shut my mouth. *I just can't seem to get beyond the stammer when I'm faced with folks who have the power to incarcerate me. I don't know why they have this effect on me. I'm not a criminal—The worst thing I've ever done is to steal a few road signs. Okay, so I went through a stage in my youth...Hum...I wonder if my mother ever threw that No Parking sign and the blinking light out from the garage? I'll check the next time I visit her. Can't help to look—Gotta get rid of the evidence. Never know when your past will come back to haunt you.*

Barry Cardoso hung up the phone and asked Walter about any new developments...any more information or leads for the department. From the gist of Walter and Barry's conversation, I took it that Walter previously worked with Detective Barry Cardoso. Barry spoke freely in front of me. *Either he forgot I existed, or he has a not so subtle way of recruiting me. I could see through his tactics—I know he studied me and analyzed my presence in his office... and he knows I surmise his motives for checking me out. Smart cop...*

don't think Walter told him anything about me...Barry has good intuition—a real asset for a cop. I start to squirm. Soon the sweaty palms would appear. I looked at the clock. Four-forty five. *Almost closing time. Good. We'll be gone soon. Unless this place never closes. Which is probably the case.*

Walter handed Barry the evidence. Horst's bloodied cuff that would give us the DNA sample.

Barry smiled. "Do you have a police dog, Ms. Seraphina?"

"Yeah, Pebbles—All eighteen pounds of him. Actually, he's a West Highland White Terrier—And would you call me Tangie, please?"

"Of course. Tangie. Are you in?"

"I've always been *in.* " I smirked...getting braver. That seemed like the right thing to say, but misgivings crept into my mind. I embellished my answer. "But remember—I'm just a private detective...I look for missing persons."

Barry didn't laugh or smile, or argue with me...He remained serious, saying, "We'll deputize you."

"That sort of thing still goes on?"

"Yes, to some people it's still *The Wild West* out here. We still have it on the books so why not use it?"

"Well, I'll work on this case, but don't consider me a regular, like Walter."

"Oh, Walter isn't a regular. More like a consultant. We couldn't afford him any other way. We call him when we are desperate."

"So do I." I laughed and smiled at Walter. My courage returned just in time, along with my sense of humor.

Walter winked back at me with a look of relief on his face and then turned to Detective Cardoso and asked if his sketch artist could do an aging process/computer photo for me, of another missing person.

"I owe you one, Walter...Tangie. Sure. I'll call Paul." Cardoso picked up the receiver and punched a button on his desk phone.

Father Caine's sister, Mary Claire. I would have forgotten...that tells you how stressed out I have become without even knowing it. Thanks, Walter. I almost lost my wits along with my memory. I took a deep breath while Walter handed Barry the leather folder with Claire's picture inside. *He remembers everything. I used to be able to juggle three cases at once. Now two are getting to be overwhelming. Good thing I have a secretary.*

The door opened and in walked a medium-built young man—fair-haired, with streaked red-dyed locks hanging over his face. He could be an undercover cop…but Barry introduced him as Paul Scribner, the sketch artist. He took Mary Claire's photo from Barry, sat down at a computer and went to work. A minute after closing time (turns out Paul leaves at five), he finished his assignment, printed a copy and handed it to me…*Voila*! Mary Claire aged sixteen years in sixteen minutes. I thanked Paul and Barry for the new photo/picture of the older Mary Claire. I felt the excitement building inside me—*I have a chance to close up my first case of the year. That is a good feeling. Thanks, Walter…Thanks, Barry…Thanks, Paul…* Suddenly I felt hungry pains. My stomach grumbled as on cue.

Walter noticed. He got up and shook hands, first with Paul and then Barry, thanking them for their help. I got up from the chair that my rear end seemed glued to for the past half hour, and also shook hands. *I'm a good parrot.*

As we approached the door to the outside world, Walter announced, "I'm taking Tangie to the *Union Grill*. Care to join us, Paul...Barry?"

Barry spoke first, saying, "Sorry, Walter, another time perhaps...My son's got a basketball game this evening. You two have fun."

Paul looked interested at first but then looked at me…with my arm through my honey…and then at Walter, who stood there grinning. The sketch artist smiled. "You two go ahead...I'll catch you the next time. Have fun. Enjoy your dinner...Remember to stay in touch."

Next time? Stay in touch? I just met these guys. How deep is Walter in this police business? These guys act like his buddies. And how in the world did I allow myself to be deputized? Now I'm da' Fuzz! This time I really am getting in too deep. Too involved in my cases. I am breaking my resolutions. So what else is new? I just gotta learn when to draw the line…and say no to da Man…No way, no how…and as they used to tell me in school…Just Say No!"

I remained quiet on our short elevator ride down to security level… out the doors and into the street. Outside the rain stopped…giving us a reprieve from the nasty weather.

Walter squeezed my waist. "A penny for your thoughts."

"You don't want to know my thoughts right now."

"I know you don't want to be a cop."

"You're on to me."

"Come on, let's walk to the *Union Grill*. We can use the fresh air."

I put my arm through his and my hands into the pockets of my new burgundy leather jacket and felt the fleece lining. I leaned against Walter, nodded and smiled. *I couldn't agree more.*

Chapter Thirty-One

I've eaten in the Union Grill a few times—Great food...interesting people to watch...hip...expensive. The last adjective is the reason I don't frequent this establishment on a regular basis. I meet most of my clients at hamburger joints or Starbucks...just in case I have to pay. Cheap would be a good way to describe me. Somehow with Walter, I don't feel cheap—Probably because he always pays. I guess everything's relative. Cheap to one person is expensive to another. Growing up, he and I traveled in different circles...but that doesn't seem to matter to either one of us. We're past such things.

Our waiter appeared, tall, husky, wearing a bow tie, white shirt and vest. "Welcome to the *Union Grill*. My name is Newton. I will be your server this evening. Might I suggest our excellent Filet Mignon with Portobello Mushrooms?"

Walter nodded. "Sounds good to me. Medium-rare. How about you, Tangie?"

I stalled for a moment as the image of *Fig Newtons* came to my mind. "Oh, I'll have the Cobb Salad...No ham, please...with Bleu Cheese dressing...on the side."

"Excellent choices," piped Newton. "Anything to drink?"

Walter answered for the two of us. "A carafe of red wine—Let's make it *Guenoc...Petite Sirah*."

"Another excellent choice, sir."

"And bring us some water, please."

"Of course."

I chuckled as Newton scooted off. "Even in the *Union Grill* you have to ask for water."

"That's Seattle. The city of conservation."

"Hey Walter...I didn't see any excellent Figgy Pudding on the menu."

"Cut it out, Tangie...The guy can't help what his name is."

"Okay, Walter...I'll be good...but don't get mad if I get a midnight craving for cookies. I unfolded my napkin. How about you finish telling me about your grandfather. I'm curious. You just began when our visit to Steve and company interrupted your storytelling...I'm interested..."

Walter stared at me for a moment, and then looked up at the ceiling. For a moment I thought he'd say, *forget the whole thing*, but instead he wiped his eyes, took a deep breath and continued his story where he left off. "I'm his namesake. He and my grandmother had no sons, just two daughters—my mother, Analise...and her sister, Hattie. When I came along, he bragged about me to no end—to anyone who would listen; he overwhelmed me with attention. I spent more time with my grandfather then I did with my own parents. You see, my mother and father—being classically-trained musicians...and employed by the *Seattle Symphony*—worked nights as well as days...and they left town frequently...touring with their quintet when not with the orchestra."

"What about your grandmother?"

"I never met her. She died before I came on the scene."

"I'm sorry, Walter. "How about your grandfather? Was he a musician, like your parents...and you?"

"Part-time...A pianist...He used to play in supper clubs in his heyday. He also taught at the University—Professor of Comparative Literature...and Jazz. But he always made time for me. I could ask him anything. He considered me his priority. When I turned five, he retired from teaching but kept playing once in a while in clubs. He spent more time with me...pinch-hitting for my parents when they traveled... whenever they left me. He taught me the piano, took me to *Mariners* games and enrolled me at *Lakeside* School, his alma mater. He fed me homemade cookies and milk after school and did all the things parents usually do."

"You didn't spend much quality time with your parents, did you?"

"Music took center stage in my parents' life. They didn't know how to fit me into their schedule. They were home for the holidays—well, most of them...and then again for a few weeks in the summer, but otherwise they occupied themselves with their concerts...they traveled around the world...*jet setters*..."

"Hard for a little kid to understand."

"I didn't know any different. I loved them, but they became more like distant relatives than parents. My grandfather remained my father figure...He showered me with love, provided for my education and gave me a sense of security—which every kid needs. When I turned fourteen, I moved in with him—permanently. He pressured me to do just two things: Practice the piano and do my schoolwork. Good thing. I have a tendency to be laid back."

"So I've noticed...but in a good way. You always calm me down when I get crazy."

"You're not crazy, Angelina."

Newton brought our water, each glass with a slice a lemon on the top, opened the wine, pouring each of us a small amount to taste, and smiled at me in a leering way.

Walter noticed and cleared his throat. "Thank you, Newton...that will be all for now...until our dinner is ready." I could imagine my honey clenching a fist under the table.

Mr. *Fig Newton* got the message and hustled away to get our main course. Good thing. If he lingered any longer, I could vision Walter coming to fisticuffs with him.

We sipped our wine and held hands...I told Walter I loved being with him in restaurants...that I loved being with him anywhere...As I leaned over to give him a gentle kiss, I noticed tears glistening in his eyes. Even though he closed his eyes, I could see them...*I could visualize a little boy about five sitting by a fireplace late at night, staring at the embers, waiting for his parents to come home. He misses having a mother. No wonder he gets along so well with my family. He sees what the little boy lacked at home... He probably identifies with Clancy.*

As I leaned over to kiss Walter a second time, Newton stumbled on the scene with our entrees.

The clumsy waiter placed the food down like a pelican diving for food...but this pelican left the food...some of it on Walter's shirt. He apologized to Walter and attempted to wipe his errors off Walter's clothing. Walter waved him away and handed him the empty wineglass that he, Mr. Figgy, spilled all over the tablecloth. I noticed Newton making contact with Walter's hand by mistake...dropping the glass as he did so. Luckily the floor was carpeted under our table and the glass did not break...but the red wine will leave a stain.

Walter leaned under the table, picked up the glass and after handing it to Mr. Figgy, glared at him as he stumbled out of sight. I watched Walter as he closed his eyes once more and then opened them with a glazed look of extra-sensory awareness. I noticed beads of sweat forming on his forehead. He picked up his napkin, wiped his brow and caught me staring at him.

"It's only wine, Walter."

He regained his composure and took my hand. "I'm sorry, Tangie."

I squeezed his hand and noticed a familiar look in his eye. "Nothing to be sorry about, Walter. Sometimes it sucks being a psychic. What is going on? Are you able to tell me?"

Walter nodded. "Tangie...It's just that I know...I know...that... that guy's planning to go home and beat on his girlfriend...I can see him doing it...So what if she's cheating on him...she probably has a good reason...Newton's a creep. I hate creeps."

"Maybe you could talk him out of becoming violent—You know... stop it before it happens. You told me you could do that...sometimes..."

"Like talking to that moron would do any good."

"It might."

"All right. I'll give it a shot—for you...and for his girlfriend. But... on the way out...for now, let's eat...I know you're starved."

I picked at my Cobb Salad...it didn't taste right to me—Newton forgot to tell the cook to leave out the ham. I pushed the salty meat aside. I took a few bites of lettuce and put my fork down. My stomach churned...my hunger subsided. Concern for my partner-in-crime-fighting took over. "I'm sorry, Walter. Your parents—I'm sorry they left you. How could they leave you—you at such a young age?"

Walter took a few bites of his steak, chewed slowly...thinking... then put his fork down. "It happened...later...when I turned fifteen... shortly after I moved in with my grandfather...The only comforting thing to me, right now, is that they were together when it happened...They were always inseparable. Grandfather and I got word two days before Christmas—A plane crash—In Italy. Mother and Father planned to play at a concert engagement in Tuscany, after a short holiday for their Twenty-Fifth Anniversary. We expected them to be home for Christmas Eve...but they never made it...Grandfather and I planned their funeral instead.

"I'm so sorry." *Now I'm the one with tears in my eyes.*

"My parents were married ten years before my mother gave birth to me...they married late in life...each involved in their careers. Me, the *late-in-life* baby...and they never really got used to me...but I loved them...just as they were..."

"And they loved you...but they didn't know what they missed... they missed your childhood." I leaned over and kissed his lips...without interruption this time.

Walter kissed me back, placed his napkin on the table and with urgency in his voice, whispered, "Let's go home."

Tears streamed down Walter's cheeks...and mine as well. He picked up the cloth napkin and dabbed at his eyes as he rose from the table. He helped me out of my chair, motioned to the maitre'd...and asked him to summon Newton.

Walter motioned to the bench by the front entrance. "Angelina... wait for me over there, while I have a chat with *the creep* before we leave."

I walked toward the doorway, alone, blowing my nose as I did. I wiped my eyes and thought to myself, *Life isn't fair. It isn't fair at all. Rats. I am becoming unglued—not a good sign...of things to come.* I sat down on the bench by the revolving door and felt the cool evening breeze. I closed my eyes and took a deep breath. As I breathed out, I felt a sudden urge to rise up and rush to the entrance, sensing someone in need. As I did, a lone customer struggled through the revolving door, and almost fell on his face. I helped steady him and handed him his carved wooden cane with a silver tip, which had fallen to the ground. He nodded in appreciation. The maître'd appeared, thanked me and greeted the white-haired gentleman—who looked to be about eighty-five, wearing a tweed jacket, beret and horn-rimmed glasses. I thought to myself, *He's probably a retired professor—of art history, no doubt*...or he's a curator at the *Seattle Art Museum.* He chatted with the maître'd about the days events, the weather and the Monet exhibit at the *Seattle Art Museum—he must be a regular.* Before he hobbled off to his table by the front window, the elderly scholar smiled, then winked at me. I waved and smiled back, thinking about the Impressionists...and Monet...my favorite...

I would have loved to meet Walter's grandfather—just as I would have loved my father to live longer...I miss my dad being part of all my milestones—like graduating from college and meeting Walter...I especially miss him at our family gatherings—Picnics, Mom's dinners, birthdays...Christmas...gosh...Christmas without Dad...difficult...for all of us...the worst. Dad loved Christmas...I remember that last holiday with him the most...such special memories...

I felt tears streaming down my face, again...I could feel myself becoming consumed with all the sadness of the past...I distracted myself by glancing in the direction of Newton and Walter conversing. Well, mostly it was Walter talking and Newton listening. I spied Walter placing a large bill in Newton's shirt pocket and saw Newton shaking Walter's hand. I faintly heard the last of Walter's advice to *the jerk...*

"Buy your girlfriend some flowers. Respect goes a long way. Treat her right. Be the good guy. A girl likes dependable...someone who cares about only her. Trust me...it will work out."—*Walter's words of wisdom. I hope Newton takes his advice. If the big lug has any brains at all, he will. If not, he will join the ranks of abusive men who wind up losers in life.*

I didn't say a word to Walter when he met me at the door. *Sometimes I do know when to shut up.*

Silence consumed our ride home. Walter—reliving the pain of his youth and grieving the loss of his parents and grandfather all over again—Me—dwelling on my losses instead of my blessings. Until I met Walter, I played the tragic heroine—always on a collision course with men—the ones I cared about always left me. Sitting in the warmth of the car, near my constant companion, I started listening to that old tape again...*The one where everything I do is wrong...That I ruin things for myself and those around me...Why did I open these old wounds—His and mine? I tell*

myself that I need to develop patience. Not one of my virtues. Things will get better again... Walter said so. I have to believe that. Otherwise, I will crack up.

Walter pressed the automatic door opener to the garage of our *safe* home on Queen Anne...we got out of the car, left the garage and entered *Home Sweet Home...* Pebbles greeted us, jumping up and down in the air like a circus dog...and Walter's Maine Coon kitty strolled into the foyer, rolled on her back and meowed. Then she came over to me and rubbed up against my leg. *She likes me!* Walter smiled at the two of us. Overcome with happiness at our return, Pebbles and Hildie started running in circles all around the downstairs, chasing each other and then they graduated to jumping on and off all the furniture...coming to rest at our feet... brushing up to us, begging for attention.

"They really do seem like old friends." I ruffled the fur of first Pebbles and then Hildie.

"I have a confession to make, Tangie. At night, when I took Pebbles out for a walk, I drove over here to feed Hildie, check up on the house... and to play the piano. Pebbles came here a lot."

"I thought as much. I knew you were up to something, but I just didn't know what."

"You're okay with that?"

"I'm okay with you. *I love you.*" I went over to the baby grand and opened the keyboard. "Play something for me, Walter."

Walter flung off his coat and tossed it on the side table. He sat down on the ebony bench and began playing. I slumped in his club chair and closed my eyes...and listened to Walter—*The Accomplished Musician.* Add that to his list of identities. No doubt he played this selection—*The Warsaw Concerto*—a piece full of passion and pain, on his dark days. I got up and put my arms around him as the last chord sounded. Walter's shoulders shook. I kissed away his tears...pulled him up to me, and put my arms around him. Then I shut off the downstairs light and led him up to our bedroom, with only the moonlight to guide us.

I could hear the wind and rain pounding on the windows, waking me from our early evening retirement. I sat up in bed and looked down at Walter, who smiled at me, content.

"You know, Walter...I've only seen your bedroom, bathroom, kitchen and couch-less living room. Maybe you could give me a tour of the rest of my living quarters."

"Later…I promise." He grabbed me by my shoulders and stared into my eyes. "Thanks for tonight, Angelina…you took me out of my dark mood."

"You're welcome…anytime."

"Are you hungry?"

"I was...three hours ago."

"Want me to cook something?"

"I love a man who cooks."

"I love to watch you eat."

"How about we eat in bed?"

"Okay. You stay here and I'll be right back."

I rolled over, closed my eyes and fell asleep...*A girl's gotta get her beauty rest when she can.* Forty-five minutes later, I heard Walter playing a jazz piece on the keyboard...Sounded like, *Take Five*…Then a doorbell...I closed my eyes and rested, content…happy. I lay in bed another ten minutes until I felt Walter caressing my shoulder.

"Dinner is served," he announced.

I opened my eyes just as Walter placed a tray on a rolling table he pulled up near the bed. "Walter! You cook *Thai!"*

"Well, not exactly—Your mom's not the only one that does *Thai Take-Out*."

"Yum, yum!" I licked my chops and picked my head up from the pillows, and spun my feet out of the bed. I could hardly contain myself… as I viewed the feast spread out before me. Spring Rolls. Phad Thai. Coconut Soup. Garlic Prawns. Orange Beef...All of my favorites! And in the corner of the display, I spotted dessert—Black Sticky Rice.

"I made the tea," Walter exclaimed proudly, as he poured the steaming liquid out of a porcelain teapot, decorated with blue flowers and birds in flight.

I inhaled. "Jasmine...my favorite. I love you!"

"I know."

"Hey, Walter...How about tomorrow we find Mary Claire. We've got that aged photo now and maybe we could head over to *Our Lady of Peace...* in Edmonds...I've got a good feeling we can make some tracks there...and then the next day, we could hunt for Terese. We've only got a week before the Sargentos reappear."

Five days, to be exact."

I jumped to my feet. "Holy Mary! We've got to get to work!"

"Slow down, Tangie." Walter came over to me and led me to a chair by the bedside table. He kissed me, briefly, on the lips...Tomorrow will come soon enough."

"Promise?"

"Promise. Tonight...tonight is for lovers," Walter whispered, as he pulled me up to him and kissed me until I could not breathe.

"Close the blinds," I gasped, after I came up for air.

"Walter released me and went to the windows. "Consider it done."

I heard his stomach growl.

Walter smiled. "Ah, Angelina...A guy's gotta eat..."

"Okay, Walter. No more skipped meals."

I put my sweet dreams on hold...and surrendered to the meal my beloved set before me. I sat on a Windsor chair—with a floral needlepoint cover—that Walter pulled out for me a second time. Stark naked—I felt like Eve in the Garden of Eden... *Walter is my Adam. Good thing there is a fire going in the fireplace.*

Walter spread our late-night supper on heirloom Wedgwood plates and handed me a cloth napkin. *This guy has class. My Adam* pulled up a nearby desk chair and sat down next to me. He dressed more elegantly than I—he wore an apron—*his fig leaf.* I giggled at his thoughtfulness as he expertly used chopsticks to place a spring roll in my mouth. I fed him a garlic shrimp with my fork. We continued to chow down the rest of the food like lovesick savages—not leaving even one morsel for Pebbles or Hildie. I sighed.

"Not to worry," Walter said, reading my mind. "I fed the pets some Chicken Satay—minus the peanut sauce."

I envisioned our furry friends, well fed...asleep on the club chair, together...near the warmth of the downstairs fireplace.

"Thanks, Walter. You know, sometimes life is wonderful for everyone you love."

After dinner, our black sticky rice…and our second helping of dessert—the one not on the menu, I heard the clock strike twelve...I began to dream...such wonderful dreams...they lasted all through the night... long after we fell asleep, exhausted and entwined in each other's arms.

Tonight is a gift and I love to sleep with my new present.

"Thank you," I remember whispering to my sleeping Walter... kissing his closed eyes and listening to the March rain that began to fall...pitter pat, pitter pat...beating against the window, beating along with the rhythm of my heart.

Chapter Thirty-Two

The next morning I transformed myself into the person I always wanted to be—an early riser. I reluctantly left the warmth and safety of my new sleeping quarters, beside Walter...and got out of bed before daylight... *For me, that's a record.* I let my sweetie sleep. He looked peaceful as a kitten that's been hunting all night long...and I knew he needed to catch up on his Z's.

I entered the expansive closet in the corner of the master suite and pulled out a green jogging suit I found on *my side*...along with a pair of expensive running shoes and soft, comfy alpaca socks. I looked in a chest nearby and found a sport bra and some exquisite silk underwear—my favorite brand. After I dressed myself, without a peep, I went downstairs, leashed Pebbles and together we ambled out the front door to walk around the neighborhood and explore the surroundings. I noticed Hildie peaking at us through the window. Wonder if cats like to take walks? Must ask Walter about that one. The sun began to rise, but I couldn't see much as the fog enveloped everything...I felt like Pebbles and I were strolling through a cloud—which of course, we were—so we didn't venture far...we just ambled around the block. I began to get used to the steep hills Pebbles seemed to know so well...He stopped at every tree... at least I imagined them to be trees...I couldn't see them. When we returned to the front of our safe house, I picked up the *Seattle Times*, and turned around, pausing to look at the fog looming all over the city in the distance. The fog began to break in sections...allowing Seattle to look like a distant planet with twinkling lights peering through the clouds.

I smiled at the eerie view and bounded up the front steps two at a time, following my leader—Pebbles—through the massive wood door. I tiptoed through the foyer and into the living room and put the newspaper on the coffee table for Walter. My man is the early morning reader. I'm the early morning thinker.

I unleashed Pebbles and petted Hildie—thanking her for keeping watch over the house while Pebbles and I took our walk. Then I strolled into the kitchen, filled the teakettle with water and placed it on the stove. I'd make tea, as I didn't want to make noise with the coffee grinder. When Walter arose from the dead, I'd make us some cappuccinos. The teakettle started whistling; I grabbed it before it started any high-pitched sounds. I discovered a small white English bone china teapot in the cupboard and made myself a brew—*Tazo English Breakfast*—with a smidge of raw sugar. No cream. Yum...Warm—Hot—Sweet—Just the fix to get me going.

I fed Pebbles, who gulped his food down like it was his last supper, and Hildie, who meowed a note of thanks for her breakfast. I petted her, whispering I loved her too. I poured myself a second cup of tea and walked into the living room. Sometime during the night, Walter arranged the logs in the hearth—all set up for a morning fire, so I lit a match and started a small blaze. The warmth soothed me. For the moment, I felt safe and secure. I sunk into the oversized club chair and stared at the manila envelope Father Joe gave me up in Alaska. It sat next to the newspaper. *I am almost afraid to open it. Don't know why...Probably because I know I'll find closure in it and I am always hesitant to come full circle... Why it scares me I don't know. Perhaps it's the memories...I feel like I'm eavesdropping on other peoples' lives...but what else can I do? It's my job.*

I picked up the stuffed envelope. In my state of mind, it seemed as heavy as the boulders I see along mountain trails...like it carried secrets and longings and disappointments too difficult to handle. In reality, the oversized manila envelope weighed five pounds, tops. I undid the clasp, took the items out and spread them on the coffee table so I could examine each one. An antique prayer book—with alternating pages of Latin and English translation—probably a heirloom...used by Father Caine's grandmother—before the padre's mother. It had two gold inscriptions on the front...One with the surname of Caine and another name, which had worn off—I could only see partial letters. A photo in an expensive gold frame of Father Joseph Caine and his sister Mary Claire, as children...and two adults I presumed to be their mother and father in happier times... The photo taken thirty years ago.

What I took out next shone in the firelight...a beautiful blue pearl rosary affixed with a solid gold crucifix. *No doubt belonged to Father Joe's mother.* I picked up the prayer beads—Soft and smooth to the touch—They offered a feeling of serenity...Peace. Perhaps this rosary showered Clancy's grandmother with relief from her constant physical and mental pain.

I studied the photo of Father Joe, his sister, mother and father, rubbed my fingers across it and closed my eyes. I pictured a family torn apart...Denial, mistrust, rebellion...all present...but something else too. Underneath all the lack of communication and heartache, I could feel love. Love lost, love forgotten, love wanted. I opened my eyes and looked at the faces before me...A sad family gathering—a portrait of a family that didn't get it...They didn't know where to start...No one willing to change...to reach out...to be honest...

I saved examining the small prayer book for last. I opened the cover and began reading some pages...remembering the prayers of my youth and my visits to church with Don...I looked at the turned-down pages. Some passages were read over and over...especially those written by St. Terese—*the Little Flower.* I could see somebody struggling with forgiveness—Clancy's grandmother—a sad, bitter woman. I could feel something more here...more than just a little prayer book. I patted the leather cover with my thumb and looked inside the torn binding. Tucked between the cover and the book, underneath the lining lay two scraps of paper...a letter...torn in half. I held my breath for a moment and then searched in the back of the book.

Like in the front of the book, the lining of the back cover appeared slightly torn and something else emerged—hidden from sight, all these years...I stuck my finger in it and carefully eased out a photo. What I saw brought back the utterances of Selene Russo...when she repeated Clancy words, *"I want my mommy"...* for in the tattered photo sat Clancy, as a small child, *staring at me...*dressed in his blue suit, holding a blue blanket. He sat on the lap of his mother—Claire—*Mary Claire.* A few words and a signature graced the bottom of photo. It read: "*To Grandmother...with love...from Clancy and his mommy, Mary Claire.*" I turned back to the front of the prayer book and pulled out the torn letter and pieced it together, *like a puzzle.* It read:

Dear Mom,

I am sorry I have not written or called in a long while. I was afraid you wouldn't see me. I miss you so much. I am so sorry we had to fight all the time.

I just didn't understand what it was like to be a mother then. Now that I am a mother—myself—I understand what you were trying to do. I hope you can forgive me.

Mom, you were right about Rick—He's so wrong for me. Things are so bad here...I am forced to leave him. I have no choice.

Would you please write me at the address on the envelope? Tell me if it is

all right if I come home for a while? I don't know what else to do. Rick won't stop drinking and he's doing drugs again and he's been hitting me. I don't mind for myself so much, but I am afraid for Clancy. I read that if a man hits his woman, he will start beating on the child. I don't want anything to happen to Clancy. If you don't help me, I don't know what I am going to do.

I love you and I am sorry for all the trouble I caused you. I know you would love Clancy. I told him all about you.

Your loving daughter,

Claire

Well...now I know why Mary Claire abandoned her son. In her mind she had no choice. What she did, she did to keep Clancy away from harm—from Rick. Apparently her mother never answered her daughter's letter...

Not knowing what else to do, Mary Claire went to seek help from her brother—Joey—Father Joe...Thinking he still ministered at *Our Lady of Peace Parish*...Perhaps she meant to come back for her son...Perhaps not... but at least she placed his welfare before her own. It probably killed her to leave her son.

If I were a mother...in Claire's situation, I don't know what I would do... But of one thing I am certain—Claire left Clancy at the church—to protect him. I leaned my head back on the chair and closed my eyes. *Mary Claire is nearby...I'm sure of it. To her way of thinking, if she is close by, she can keep a watch out for Clancy. She is staying in the Seattle area for her son—should he ever need her...*

I became so wrapped up in my thoughts I didn't see or hear Walter walk in the room. He tiptoed behind me and put his hands around my eyes.

"Guess who?"

I jumped out of my chair. "Walter! You scared me!"

"Sorry, Babe. Didn't know my touch had that effect on you."

I turned around and hugged him. "I'm sorry, Sweetie...It's just, I'm working...I'm intense..."

"I like you intense..."

"I know." I stood up, shook my upper torso and gave him a lingering good morning kiss. "Ready for some espresso?"

"I thought you'd never ask."

I left Father Caine's mementos of his mother on the table, glad for the break. I zoomed into the kitchen and began the ritual of making our morning cappuccinos while Walter popped some bagels in the toaster. He took some cream cheese out of the fridge and put some raspberry pepper jelly and some smoked salmon on the table, along with some fresh-squeezed orange juice, he just happened to whip up. *Yum! Looks delicious.*

I finished off the espresso with swirling foam, placed two *Dansk* oversized cups, with matching saucers, on the table and sat down alongside Walter in the window booth. I glanced at the garden in the backyard and spotted daffodils beginning to push up through the cold, damp earth. *Spring is on its way. Finally. It's been a long winter.*

As we feasted on bagels, prepared Pacific Northwest style, I questioned Walter. "So, my love...do you wanna go up to Edmonds with me...seeing as I have no car? As you know, it's being held hostage with the Ballard house. I could take the train, but I'd rather go with you—if you're up to it. I want to follow up my hunch about Mary Claire...It's a good one...We've already stopped by S.P.D. and Paul Scribner did that photo enhancement for us." I let out a breath. "What do you think?"

"I think, yes. You know I'm always free for you, Angelina...Besides, Pebbles and I need to keep an eye on you...You have a knack for getting into trouble..."

"Yeah, I'm trouble."

"In a good way, Sweetheart. Maybe after your *hunch* we could walk the Edmonds waterfront...we could watch the ferries, the fishermen and the waterfowl. I'll pack a picnic lunch."

"You do fried chicken?"

"Well, the Colonel does. We can stop at KFC."

"Solid plan. Okay...*Our Lady of Peace Church*, then we walk on the beach...picnic...and maybe we could..."

"Tangie, save Terese for tomorrow. Too complicated for one day."

"It's just that I'm so excited...I feel so empowered today."

"I wonder why?" Walter put his hand under my hair and caressed my neck.

I smiled. "Nothing at all to do with you...or last night."

"Nothing?" He kissed my neck.

I caved. "You win...you have the magic touch, my love."

My attention turned to *Felix the Cat*—the clock on the wall, striking...or I should say, meowing nine a.m.—Time to get to work. I gave Walter a kiss on the cheek... and proceeded to play lady of the house. I picked up the dishes, put them in the dishwasher and cleaned out the espresso machine. Then I announced, "I'm gonna take a quick shower and beautify myself for our trip to Edmonds."

Walter wiped his mouth with his cloth napkin and grinned. "I'll join you, Angelina."

"We've got to stop meeting this way, Walter."

"I know...I know...I'll be good. I promise."

Walter turned on the cold water and chuckled as I shrieked and hopped out of the shower, dripping water all over the bathroom floor. I picked up a heated towel, dried my body and raced out the door—determined to be dressed and ready before him. *Another record if I can pull it off.*

Pebbles could not contain his furry self, jumping all around in circles when I put the leash on him. The pooch knows when he's going on a car ride. Unfortunately, his nose tweaked out of joint when we stopped at

Our Lady of Peace and left him all alone in the *Porsche Cayenne* . Although there's a statue of St. Francis—patron saint of animals—in the garden area of the church, a sign—*Service Dogs Only*—is posted at the entrance... *poor Pebbles.*

Walter and I entered the parish center adjoining the church and waltzed down the corridor like we were members of the congregation. I peeked in the office door and called to the parish secretary like a long lost friend. "Hi Adrianne." Walter held the door for me, and together we walked into her office.

I introduced Adrianne Cooper to Walter and told her I had some new information for her.

She told me she had a few more minutes with the task at hand. "Please...have a seat...I'll be right with you."

A parishioner stood by her desk with bundles in his arms...apparently dropping off some expensive donations for the church's rummage sale—I saw the advertisement for this coming weekend's sale posted on the door...*Rats, if I had known, I would have brought something...but then again, I am no longer in my home...*I rummaged through my purse and produced a twenty-dollar bill. That should do it.

Adrianne thanked the parishioner. "See you on Sunday, George." After the *Good Samaritan* left, I got up and handed her the twenty for the rummage sale. She smiled at me. "Thanks, Tangie. How have you been?"

"Well, pretty good, lately. I wanted to catch you up on my progress."

"On Clancy?"

"Yes—on Clancy. I went to see Father Joseph Caine—in Alaska. Together, he and I have determined that he is Clancy's long-lost uncle. We believe his sister, Claire, is Clancy's birth mother."

"Well, that's a relief...That's a good thing...I think. Mystery solved."

"Well, not entirely...I just have one more request...Would you mind looking at some more photos for me?"

"Not at all. I'd be glad to help."

I presented to Adrianne the cherished photo hidden by Clancy's grandmother—the one of Clancy as a four-year old with his mother. Next, I showed her the age-enhanced photo of Father Caine's sister, which Paul Scribner created for us.

She studied the first one. "This one certainly is like the little boy left at the church...and this must be his mother holding him. I don't recognize her."

Then she glanced at the second picture and gasped. "Why it's Mary Dolores!"

"You know her?"

"She works in our nursery school on Sunday morning. She watches the children while their parents attend Mass. The little children love her. Her son and daughter assist her in her ministry with the preschoolers. Her husband plays his guitar in the Spanish Mass Saturday night...they attend that Mass together. Do you think Mary Dolores might know Clancy's mother?"

"She is Clancy's mother. She's Claire."

Adrianne stared at me, speechless.

"Her name is...was...Mary Claire Caine."

"No, this is Mary Dolores. You must be mistaken."

I took out the picture Father Caine had given me of Claire and showed it to Adrianne. "This is Father Caine's sister as a young girl. We had the police do a photo enhanced-aging process on it. As you can see, she is aged to look like your Mary Dolores."

"I don't know what to say..."

"Could you help us locate her? If she's been in this area a long time, she probably did so to stay close to her son...whether she realized it or not. My guess is she would like to be reunited with Clancy...as much as he would like to find her...Father Caine is also anxious to get in touch with his sister. He has been out of touch with her, since before Clancy appeared on the doorstep of the church...He never knew anything about his nephew...never knew he existed...until a few days ago..."

Adrianne nodded and whispered, "All I can tell you is...she works at *Top Foods*...here...on the outskirts of Edmonds...Highway 99...Aurora Avenue. She's a very sweet person. Her husband is a kind and gentle man...I can't believe this..."

"Sometimes people act in certain ways because events in their life are out of their control. I think she meant to protect Clancy...You know... like *Moses in the Bulrushes*."

Adrianne nodded. "Please...if you talk to her...tell her...Oh never mind...I'll tell her myself...my heart goes out to her...and Clancy." Adrianne dabbed her eyes with a tissue from the box on her desk.

"I understand, Adrianne. Please know that I am very grateful to you. . .for all your help."

Adrianne nodded. "Let's keep this latest bit of news between us for the time being...but please. . .let me know how everything works out, okay?"

"Yes, I will. I promise...and keep in mind..."

"Keep what in mind?"

"We found Clancy's mother with your help. . .Without you. . .I don't know where'd we'd be right now. . .Certainly not prepared to reunite a mother and son. . .Thank you again."

Adrianne nodded, started to tear up again and could not speak. Walter and I shook hands with her and started to leave. As Walter opened the door, I looked back to see how she reacted to the news when it finally hit her. The office phone began ringing, but she ignored it. She put her head down on her desk and started sobbing. As we tiptoed out, I watched Adrianne take the phone off the hook and disconnect the caller.

We hopped into the four-wheeling *Porsche* and traveled to *Top Foods*—a short distance from the church—Up the dry ski slope hill and through a few green lights. *I remember when I slid down this hill in the snow. Not scary this time.* When we got to the supermarket, an idea popped into my brain. "Hey Walter, how about we get our chicken at *Top Foods*. They're sure to have take-out there. Save us a trip."

"Sure, Tang." Walter exited the *Cayenne*, went around, opened up my door and extended a hand to me. "I get the message. I'll get the chicken—and I'll make it baked—healthier. You cruise the store. . .looking for Mary Claire."

"It's a deal." I smiled. *I can feel the excitement in my pulse and heartbeat. . .we are so close to finding Mary Claire.* "If you can't find me, Honey, look in the bakery...I have a craving for something warm and sweet."

"So do I." Walter stroked my cheek and kissed me good-bye after we walked through the automatic doors.

I sighed. *Gotta love my man...Walter makes the hardest tasks easy.*

Before I embarked on my quest to the bakery, I cruised the bargain isle, then the fruits and vegetables. No Mary Claire. I surveyed the dairy department...All I spotted, besides the cream and eggs, was a guy wearing a white jumpsuit and green nylon jacket. He stopped his chore of unloading milk cartons and asked, "Can I help you, Miss? Need anything?"

"Oh I'm just browsing." *Now what kind of person browses in a grocery store, a budget one at that, with no shopping cart? Someone on the prowl—That's me.*

I found myself in the northwest part of the store and smelled cinnamon. The bakery. My heart started beating. *All at once I could envision Mary Claire pulling loaves of bread out of the oven...sourdough, rye, wheat...and blueberry muffins, cupcakes, sweet rolls...donuts...Yes...My sense of smell directed me...Why, I don't know...Maybe it's my weakness for sugar...maybe yeast, may be Mary Claire likes comfort food, like me.*

I saw Walter walking down my isle with a box of chicken tucked under his arm. I went up to him and put my arm in his and led him over to the bakery section. We looked just like an old married couple out for a stroll in the store. Except for having no cart, we fit the part. I peered into the refrigerated glass case and looked at the Boston Crème Pie—my favorite bakery dessert, next to sweet rolls. I heard a soft voice speaking, as if in a dream.

"May I help you find something?"

I shook myself out of my sugar trance and glanced up—seeing Mary Claire staring me in the face. A black hairnet garnished her long hair, a green apron with the *Top Foods* emblem circled her body, and plastic gloves adorned her hands. *Not a roly-poly dough girl, this beauty—Mary Claire is still fit and trim. She probably works out with her husband or spends many hours playing with her children...or working hard...Probably all of the above.*

"I'll have the Boston Crème Pie."

I didn't know what else to say. Walter peered at me and came to my rescue, adding, "I think we'd like some of those sticky-nut sweet rolls too."

"How many?'

"How about four?"

He struggled too. *What a pair we are. Don't think I ever saw him stall... Walter's probably following my lead on this one.* I took a deep breath.

Mary Claire boxed the cake and tied it up with a string. Then she put four sweet rolls in a paper bag and sealed it, placing a price label on the top of each package.

"Will there be anything else?"

"Do we pay up front?"

"Yes. At the cashier."

"Thank you, very much."

"You're welcome."

Mary Claire shared a beautiful smile, with perfect teeth, that reminded me of Clancy's. I watched as she turned to disappear into the racks of muffins and gourmet breads.

"Wait a minute," I piped up. "Come back...Please..."

Thank you, Jesus. My nerve returns!

Mary Claire turned around to face us once more.

"Are you Mary Dolores?" I whispered.

"I'm sorry, I don't think I know you."

"I'm sorry too, I hate to bother you, but...I know your brother... Father Joseph Caine."

Mary Claire put her hand on the counter to steady herself. Her beautiful smile evaporated and her face turned white.

"I'm sorry...I didn't mean to upset you."

"No, It's all right...It's just that it's been so long...I haven't seen him in so many years...Is anything wrong?" Mary Claire's voice became a little higher in pitch. She started to tear up...reacting like a patient anticipating the worst possible diagnosis. "I just about gave up on ever seeing him again..."

"He hasn't given up on you. Say...Ms. Dolores, could we talk somewhere?"

"Yes…definitely. Go to the *Starbuck's* just outside the store, across the parking lot...I'll get Margaret, my co-baker, to cover for me. I'll meet you there in five minutes."

I noticed tears in her eyes, as she removed her apron and gloves. Then she did disappear behind the racks of baked goods…but this time, to find her replacement, Margaret.

Mary Dolores arrived at *Starbucks* exactly five minutes after Walter and I secured a table and ordered espressos. Walter, ever the gracious gentleman, rose from his seat and pulled out a chair for our guest. "Welcome. If you'd like, I'll get you a latte."

"That would be wonderful…Thank you...a hazelnut would be great." She looked relieved to be sitting down. She took off her hairnet and revealed a thick crop of red hair—hair that matched Clancy's.

"Where did you meet my brother?" Mary Claire began.

"In Kodiak, Alaska." I reached out my hand to her, and continued my introduction. "My name is Angelina Seraphina...and Walter Cunningham, my secretary, just went to get your latte. Actually, he's a little more than my secretary."

"I can see that." Mary Claire cast me a smile. Her entire face lit up as she did so.

Walter walked up to us, grinning and placed Mary Claire's Grande Hazelnut Latte down on the table. "Well the truth is out. Pleased to meet you, Mrs. Dolores." He grasped her hand in his. "If you'd like, I could wait outside."

"No…Walter…I don't mind if you stay. It's all right."

"Thank you." Walter pulled up a chair from another table. I could smell the chicken Walter purchased—its strong odor flowing out from the box under his arm. He set it down on the adjoining table. *Funny. Chicken seems so out of place here in Starbucks, the land of lattes, scones and sweet delights, although in most of their establishments, they now sell sandwiches.*

I began to explain my mission to Mary Claire. "Ms. Dolores, your brother would like to see you. He's been hurt. Someone attacked him at his church."

"Oh my God! Is he all right?" Her smile turned to panic.

"He's getting better. He's a mission priest…up in Kodiak, Alaska—*Saint Francis Mission*. He's been there ever since he left *Our Lady of Peace* in Edmonds.

"So that's where he went…I never knew." Mary Claire leaned forward, intent on every word coming out of my mouth.

"Well…some thug beat him up…and the sheriff had your brother airlifted…to a hospital…in Anchorage for treatment. Father Caine made a request of me—the last time I saw him—to tell you he never forgot you...that you are in his thoughts and prayers every day...and that he is sorry..."

"Sorry for what?"

"Not helping you. He didn't know..."

"Didn't know what?"

"He didn't know about *Clancy*...and he didn't know what happened to you…when you disappeared...he didn't know anything…"

Mary Dolores closed her eyes. When she opened them again, she whispered, "That was such a long time ago…but every day, it seems like yesterday to me. You know about Clancy?"

"Yes, I've met him."

"You *know* my Clancy?" Mary Dolores regained her full voice.

"Yes. He's quite grown up…A college student…and…He's looking for you...He hired me...You see, I'm a private detective." I handed her my new business card, with my photo and secure cell phone on it—*compliments of Walter…he had them made up for me…my secretary thinks of everything*. "Your first born son…Clancy…wants to see you...He wants to be reunited. So does your brother…Father Joe."

Mary Dolores' shoulders shook…then her hands started trembling. She reverted to whispering, "This is all so overwhelming..."

"I know." There I go…fumbling for words again…*not really knowing…and not having a clue what else to say to comfort her.*

"Ms. Seraphina, It's very hard for me to believe what you've told me... It's like I've been in a desert and you've just thrown ice water on my face...Holy Mary, Mother of God!" Mary Claire regained her voice with this ejaculation. "I've prayed every day...for years...for my Clancy…I've prayed to the Blessed Mother...for her to watch over my son…If it weren't for Miguel, I don't know where I'd be today…When he met me I was such a wreck…On a crash course towards self-destruction. Depression set in—I didn't care if I lived or died...but I'm doing okay now—Thanks to Miguel and my angels... *Clancy…*Clancy wants to see me!"

Miguel...He is your husband?"

"Yes. Miguel helped me get my life together...and distance myself from Rick. Miguel protected me...Rick scared me to death—made me frantic…I was so afraid Rick would come after me...and after I lost Clancy…I just wanted to die…I hit rock bottom…I wound up in a women's shelter...in Mountlake Terrace, after...after..."

"After *Social Services* took Clancy?"

"Yes. After I left Clancy to wait for his Uncle Joey...at *Our Lady of Peace*...I didn't plan to abandon him...I left him there—I thought for a little while…to be safe…I thought my brother knew...You see, I traveled five hours from Portland...It was getting dark and I didn't know my way around...and I thought Joey was the pastor at *Our Lady of Peace*… My mother never told me he moved...Here I was…all alone in a strange place. I didn't know what to do...I had no food, no money...I ran away from Rick...and I was afraid for Clancy...I couldn't think straight...I hadn't slept in days...and I thought my brother knew…I didn't know my mother kept Clancy's birth a secret from him…"

"Why didn't you come back?" I hated to ask this, but I had to get the answer.

"I did...but it was too late. Clancy was gone…No sign of my brother... and Rick was still on the hunt for me and Clancy…I panicked…I didn't know what to do…so I went to Mass at *Our Lady of Peace* church…and questioned a couple of parishioners—Kind of matter of fact like…though it killed me inside…They told me Clancy was placed in foster care...and then shortly after that...A respectable, professional couple adopted him... They told me to look in the church bulletin...So I did. I read an article that informed me how everyone in the parish prayed for the abandoned child and…that the poor child found a home. No one surmised he was my child…I alone knew the truth…and I went into hiding. Claire Caine disappeared."

"How did you survive?"

"Well the staff at the women's shelter helped me get my life back. They gave me clothes, counseling and a will to live. They helped me find a job. I started using my given first name...*Mary*...Leaving the second part out...and I started working near the church...right here at *Top Foods...* as a stacker...then as a checker. I worked myself up to baker. Then I started going to *Our Lady of Peace* on a regular basis. Going there helped give me comfort for my loss...and for the terrible thing I did to Clancy. I've been living in the Edmonds area ever since. Never went back to Portland...Nothing for me there."

"What about Rick—Clancy's father?"

"Rick died of an overdose...A year after I left Portland...and...he's not Clancy's father."

The plot thickens...I always wanted to say that.

"Do you want to tell me who Clancy's father is?"

"It's hard to talk about him...I only had ...I mean...I was fifteen when it all started...He was my science teacher...in high school. I had a crush on him. Rick hated him. Sometimes I don't blame Rick for the way he acted...He was so jealous all the time...He had reason..."

I thought of Mary Claire's mother...and the letter...but thought better of bringing that subject up now. Shame does strange things to people...Even when it isn't their shame. Mary Claire was abused and she took all the blame.

"Does anyone else know about Clancy's father?"

"I told my mother, but she never believed me...and Rick knew...I turned to him...when she called me a...I can't go there anymore..."

"I understand. It's all right...you don't have to...Where did you meet your husband?"

"I met Miguel at the *Center for Battered Women*...the one in Mountlake Terrace. He visited us weekly as a guest counselor and motivational speaker. He used to play the guitar for us. He helped me trust people again—men especially. He made me believe in myself...and I stopped looking at myself as a bad person. When I moved out of the shelter, we kept in touch...and...

"And you fell in love with him..."

"Yes. I love him very much. We have been together for fourteen years...and we have two beautiful children." Mary Claire took out her wallet and showed me a picture of four smiling people content to be in each other's company. The daughter looked like her father, slender with dark eyes and dark brown hair. The son, the younger child, had auburn hair and resembled Mary Claire...and Clancy.

She continued. "They are my angels. Their names are Serenity and Peter. Serenity's my peace and Peter's my rock. I love them more than my life...but I want you to know that not a day goes by that I don't think of Clancy...and pray for him—my first-born son—my child in my heart."

"Do you ever go by *Mary Claire*, anymore?"

"*Mary Claire* died when she gave up her baby. Mary Dolores took over."

I reached out and patted Mary Claire gently on her shoulder. "You are too hard on yourself...Please...don't be. At the time, you did what you thought was best for Clancy...You acted out of love."

"That's what Miguel says."

"He knows?"

"Yes. We have no secrets between us. I found out what secrets can do to people—They cost me my brother's love and my mother..."

"If you give others a chance, you will see that they too, will understand. Your son—Clancy—will...and your brother—Father Joe—feels a great sadness remembering the terrible times you encountered growing up. He knows you are hurting...He didn't know back then...No one told him...but he has never stopped loving you...You can't fix things with your mother, but you have a second chance with Father Joe...He wants to see you..."

Mary Claire put her hands together as if in prayer and bent her head down. I heard her whispering to herself. This time I could not make out the words.

I placed my hand on her clasped fingers to comfort her. "What do you think? Would you like to be reunited with your son...and your brother?"

"More than anything...if they want me...It would be my dream come true..."

"Sometimes dreams become reality. I could set it all up for you...How would you like to go to Alaska...with Clancy...to visit your brother?"

"Alaska? I can't believe it! Alaska! Miguel and I have always wanted to go to Alaska...and now...with Clancy! Could I bring Miguel? And my little ones?"

"I think your little ones will be the centerpiece for a wonderful family reunion."

I grinned as I placed my hands over hers.

Walter looked at the two of us, smiled and broke his silence. "I'm very happy for you...Mary Claire Caine Dolores..."

"Thank you...I don't know what else to say." She stood up and shook both of our hands, her tears flowing freely down her face. "I'll never forget you and how you helped my son and brother find me...I am beyond grateful. I don't know how to repay you..."

I smiled at her. "Just be happy. Look, I'll talk to Clancy and Father Joe and get back to you. I know Clancy would like to accompany you to Kodiak and meet with your brother. There's a part of him that never gave up on you."

"I've prayed for this day for sixteen years."

I leaned over and gave her a hug. "I know. If you give me your phone number, I'll call you as soon as I get things set up."

"Yes...of course." Mary Claire retrieved a pen and a business card—engraved with her husband's name, Miguel Dolores—out of her purse. She wrote her home phone on the back and handed it to me.

"Thank you." Mary Claire began sobbing. "I will never forget you... both of you...for your kindness."

Walter wiped a tear from his eye. "Are you sure you will be all right? Can we do anything else for you?"

"No, you've done so much already...I'll be fine. But I think I will go back to *Top Foods* and tell the manager I am taking the rest of the day off. This is a day to celebrate. I am going home and rejoicing with Miguel and the children...I cannot wait to tell them...That Clancy is found... and...Serenity and Peter...I can tell them...I can tell my children they will meet their older brother."

We said our good-byes and left Mary Claire meditating—leaning against the table in *Starbucks*—as if it were a pillar of strength. She stood there for a moment, transfigured... with a radiant smile on her face...

holding her latte, tears of joy streaming down her face, washing away her makeup. I envisioned Clancy's mother—no longer haunted by painful memories, but armed with a growing hope—hope that would extinguish her anxiety and guilt—and replace them with peace and contentment. Clancy—her saving grace.

Chapter Thirty-Three

The sun came out strong, the afternoon being a precursor to spring.

Walter looked in our take-out bag. "Well...we've got chicken."

I looked in the bakery bag. "And Sticky-Nut Sweet Rolls...and let's not forget Boston Crème Pie."

"I think we have some water to wash it all down, in the car."

"The car! Pebbles must be going crazy!"

"I'll reward him with a chicken wing...The breasts are for me." Walter smiled.

"Just take the bones out before you give it to him."

Turns out, Pebbles lay sleeping...Rest assured, we would wake him up in no time. "I'll race down to the waterfront," Walter announced as we got into the car. Pebbles smelled the chicken. An ear twitched. There'd be no peace until we reached the beach and gave him his morsels. Pebbles thrives on chicken—The greasier the better.

"Hurry, Walter...The pooch is losing it," I cried, as Pebbles jumped over the seat and descended into my lap.

Under expert guidance, the *Porsche* sped the few blocks to the waterfront park and Walter pulled into a space right in front—A rare find, even in winter. We hopped out with our bags of protein, fat and carbs and grabbed two bottles of water from the back of the *Cayenne*.

After we walked through the park, climbed over the rocks and driftwood and followed the path to the beach, I unleashed Pebbles. He refused to move until he got his chicken. Once fed, he took off, running wildly and gave us a little peace and quiet...time to enjoy the lapping of the waves and the chatter of the waterfowl. I sat down on a driftwood log as three familiar white-winged scavengers swooped over me. Uh oh... Seagulls.

"Walter! How are we going to eat our picnic lunch?"

"Fast! Don't exhale. Just eat!"

We ate like prisoners on the run...until the seagulls started haunting us to death, Walter put the remains of our lunch in his backpack and pulled out a *Frisbee* and sailed it in the air towards Pebbles, who caught it in mid-flight. Then our furry friend took off for parts unknown. Soon he disappeared completely. No way he was giving anyone—bird or beast—a chance to grab his new toy.

Walter smiled, "I'm all yours, Angelina."

"You've always been all mine."

"Don't get too sure of yourself."

"I am sure of my *Mystery Man*—I know you're here to stay."

We walked about a mile down the beach, arm in arm, enjoying the Olympic Mountains staring at us—and the ferries—cruising by us like easy-going messengers doing their errands back and forth across the Puget Sound. The sun warmed my face and the gentle breeze caressed my face.

"Say, Walter, I feel so peaceful now...Thank you."

"Say, Tangie, you are welcome." Walter stopped walking, brushed the hair out of my eyes and took me in his arms. "I hate to interrupt our escape to nature, but I have a question...How do you know Clancy wants to go to Kodiak with Mary Claire?"

I hugged him, took his hand and led him to nature's bench...a log of driftwood. "I *know*. One of those news flashes I get in my head. Look at it this way...one more mystery solved.

Walter kissed my cheek. "One more to go, *Sherlock*."

"*Watson*...please...Don't overwhelm me...I need at least an hour to be grateful. When we get home, I'll call Clancy...give him all the news... and help him make arrangements to meet with his mother first...and the entire family after that..."

"You think Father Caine is well enough for visitors? He's just been beaten to a pulp."

"Are you trying to make me feel bad? It's working."

"Of course not...Just asking...I'm sorry, Tang..."

"I've thought it over, Walter, really I have...It will take a few days to make the arrangements...Father Joe will be on the mend soon...and, I'm sure you agree, my dear Watson, that reuniting with his family is the best medicine anyone could give the missionary priest..."

"Yes, I do. Angelina...Did I ever tell you...you are a crackerjack detective?" Walter enveloped me in his arms. "Life's too short...We've got to enjoy every moment. *Carpe Diem*..."

"I know...I know...but I keep thinking that the Caine family has a lot of missed days to seize."

"So do we. I wish we met in grammar school."

"You wouldn't have liked me then, Walter."

"Try me."

"I was really strange."

"I was strange too. We could have been strange together."

I kissed him lightly on the mouth and he returned my kiss with passion. I melted. "We are good together," I murmured.

"Like *Paris and Helena*..."

"Like *Orpheus and Eurydice*...

"Like *Tristan and Isolde*... "

"They met a tragic end..."

"Okay, we're not like them..."

"Say, Walter, I think I'll call Clancy tonight about getting reservations to Alaska... Try to coincide the reunion with the University's Spring Break, so he...and his Jessica don't miss class.

"That's a good idea."

"I'm sure Father Caine will be back at the mission on Kodiak Island by then."

"Why are you so anxious, Tangie? Don't you want to wait until the snow melts to go back to Alaska?"

"That might be June. And remember...Kodiak is milder than Anchorage...The weather is similar to Seattle. That blizzard was a fluke... Sheriff Tokala even said so. Just like the back-to-back snowfalls in our neck of the woods this year...but maybe I'll wait a couple of weeks. By then, the *Terese* case should be wrapped up..."

"If we're lucky." Walter nodded...but no smile appeared on his face.

Pebbles came up to us with a half-chewed up *Frisbee.* Our quiet interlude exceeded the price of a flying saucer. Our furry beast dropped it at our feet and took off chasing seagulls that descended upon us in their search for food—thinking the *Frisbee* represented dinner. *Dumb birds.* I picked up the frayed plastic disc and tossed it down the beach as far as I could.

Pebbles gave up the chase when he saw a large dead fish, torn apart and surrounded by scavengers, mostly crows. He proceeded to roll on his back all over the carcass.

"Yuck! What is it with you, Pebbles?" I cried. "Get off that dirty dead thing…Right now, Pebbles…or else…" Pebbles ignored me and kept rubbing up against the enormous stinking fish. I pulled him off and fastened on his leash.

"Walter…Know any dog groomers around here? Pebbles…you reek!"

"Yeah, right...Hey Tangie…there's a guy over there with a sign…*Will Work for Food…*Maybe he'll wash Pebbles for the leftover chicken."

I groaned. "I don't think so."

"Well, Mr. Pooch is not coming in the *Porsche* smelling like that."

As if reading Walter's mind, the smelly beast slipped from my grasp and tore down the beach like an escapee from the chain gang. Walter took off running, grabbed Pebbles' leash before he disappeared beyond the pier and dragged the pooch back to me.

"Drastic measures are required here... I'll just drop Pebbles in the drink to wash him off."

"You can't Walter. He'll freeze!"

"Serves him right, the dirty dog. Besides, the water temperature is about the same now as it is in the summer. Don't worry, Tangie..."

I laughed, despite my anxiety—triggered by my Westie soon becoming a *Popsicle.* Walter took off his jacket and handed it to me, kicked off his hiking boots and socks, rolled up his pants' legs with one hand, lifted Pebbles up high in the air and wadded in the water…with the dog in his out-stretched arms.

"Pebbles, you stinky dog…hold still…"

A maverick wave hit them both. "Yeow!" Walter dropped Pebbles, and the two of them plunged in the Puget Sound. They raced out together but before Pebbles could roll his back on the sand—this time to dry himself off, Walter scooped him up, took his own fleece jacket from my arms and wrapped my shivering Westie in it. *What a guy.* As we jogged the distance back to the *Cayenne*, I laughed and Walter shivered—I noticed his feet beginning to turn blue.

Out of breath when we got to the car, I had to stop and bend over. Pebbles' tongue hung out—Thirsty. Probably from all the chicken... and whatever else he ate on his excursion. Walter poured a bottle of water into Pebbles' travel bowl, which the pathetic pooch drank in its entirety—without stopping. Walter started to shake. He slipped on his socks and hiking boots, took off his soaking shirt and said, "Hop in the car, Angelina...I'll turn on the heat and we'll cruise home, against the traffic...so it won't take long..."

"Good deal."

Pebbles and Walter stopped shaking...I twisted Walter's shirt out the window to get the water out and put it in a plastic bag I just happened to have handy, left over from our bakery treats. Then I put a blanket I found in the back seat under Walter's pants so the Porsche wouldn't get soaked and he could dry out a bit. The warmth of the heater kicked in immediately. Pebbles lay down on Walter's jacket in the back and went to sleep. Already steamed up from running, and overcome by the heat, I took off my shoes and jacket, and then stripped down to my tank top.

"Yum." Walter rolled his eyes and smiled. "I'm so looking forward to summer..."

"Ah, summer...Me too." I grinned, staring at his naked chest. "Don't forget we are going on a vacation...to someplace warm..."

"Remind me..."

"You've got to remember, Walter...Any place with a beach, where we can open the door of our room and look out...naked to the world..."

"Ah, yes...Fiji!"

"Yes...Fiji."

"Right after we find Terese...and..."

And...What Walter didn't say...What he couldn't finish...I know...*I know...our collision course is set...We have no choice...We have to face Adolphus... and that is not gonna be pretty."*

When we arrived home, we gave Pebbles a quick warm bath in the over-sized sink...in the laundry room off the kitchen—and set him down to play with Hildie. Walter peeled off his pants and socks and as he promised earlier, took me on a tour of his home. He started with the solarium and hot tub, where I stripped off my beach clothes, with some assistance from Walter...and together, we put aside the events weighing upon us and enjoyed a long soak in the Jacuzzi. I looked up at the skylight. The sun peeked in as it made its descent...*some days just fly by... especially the ones you want to keep.* I looked around at the exotic greenery surrounding us.

"How do you have time to care for all these plants, Walter?"

"It's a hobby of mine. Helps me relax. See these rare varieties? Favorites of my grandfather—It's a way for me to stay connected to him."

"Wow! Orchids...Our own little *Garden of Eden*," I said.

"Yes, *Eve*," Walter grinned and gave me a devilish look as he climbed out of the tub and picked a fragile yellow bloom. He returned to the water, placing the orchid in my hair.

"I'm glad I found just the right spot for that one," he said, as he kissed the top of my head and snuggled in beside me.

"Amen to that, *Adam*. Thanks for a great day."

I leaned up to return my horticulturist's kiss, just as Pebbles came charging through the door of the solarium with Hildie, who kept her distance from the tub. *Don't think cats like water. Hildie is no exception.*

I got up and put on a white fleece robe, which rested on a heated rod on the wall. "Okay, pets...almost time for the rest of the tour." I picked up two waiting wine glasses, one for me and one for Walter. I filled the glasses for us with white Sangria concocted earlier, by a mystery ghost. Then I handed one to Walter and clinked his glass, toasting him and taking a sip.

"Hey Walter...I love your *Sangria*...just a hint of sweetness..."

"I hope you'd like it...It is my special blend...I call it *Tangerine Wine...*"

"So, that's your secret ingredient."

"It's no longer a secret. I think I'll shout it to the world."

"You know the old saying—*Be careful of what you wish for...*"

"Angelina, I have what I wish for..."

Walter brushed my lips and then, in perfect pitch burst into song.

"*You make me so very happy*...Happy in a crazy sort of way," Walter crooned, as he snatched his waiting robe, climbed out of the Jacuzzi and poured each of us another *Sangria*. "My dear, you owe me for the orchid in your hair. It took me a year to grow that one."

"You think I'll do anything for flowers, don't you?" I winked as he clinked his glass with mine.

"It's worth a try." Walter smiled at my bantering. He picked up my hand like he grasped his prized flower earlier, and urged me on. "*Apres moi.*"

He escorted me out of the Jacuzzi and solarium, down three stairs to a wide hall. On the walls hung watercolors done by local artists...I recognized their names...Some famous, some just starting out...I saw treasured street scenes of the local color in Seattle...*Pike Place Market*, The ferries, *Yakima* and *Nisqually* crossing the Sound, and *Pier 66* at the *Seattle Waterfront*. Walter led me into the adjoining library, which faced the secluded backyard. Floor-to-ceiling bookshelves dominated the room and showcased first editions, current magazines, reference books and today's newspapers. Under the window, on adjoining desks sat two laptop computers—one a PC and one a *MacBook*. One desk—mine; I know, because an engraved wooden marker displayed my name...and I recognized the computer on that desk as my own. *Walter thinks of everything*.

"How did you get my computer set up? When did you have the time?"

"You like?" Walter grinned at me. "I thought it was the least I could do for you, as you let me share your office."

"I like. It's all right, Babe—A wee bit larger that our office in Ballard..."

"Ballard is good...Intimate..."

"That's us...*Intimate*...Any more surprises?"

"Well..." Walter pointed to another hallway. "Down here...there's the kitchen, where we've already been..."

"Yes...I love our breakfasts together..."

"And through that door is the dining room..."

I peeked inside. Graceful antique furniture—Royal Doulton in the china closet— Fresh flowers on the sideboard—Original oil paintings of flowers and fruit on the walls—Coffered ceiling—which framed the hand-carved myrtle wood table in the center of the room.

"Quite a formal room."

"You can change it if you like."

"No, I like it, Walter. You have good taste."

"Just family pieces..."

"Yes...and they are lovely." I touched his cheek and looked into his eyes. "You and I are...like...family now..."

"That's why I want to share my home with you...*You are my family now*...Let's go upstairs..."

"Walter, you promised..."

"*I know*, Angelina...I want to show you the other upstairs rooms...the den and the guest rooms."

"Promise?"

"Of course. I always keep my promises."

We walked up the stairs with Pebbles and Hildie running behind us. They didn't want to miss anything. Walter opened the closed door across from the master bedroom. The den. Complete with a high-definition television screen on the wall, equipped with a DVD player and *Bose* surround stereo. Two mocha leather recliners, a loose pillow-back plaid sofa and an oak bookcase with *Seattle Seahawks* memorabilia on the shelves. *Come spring, Walter will probably replace it with Mariners stuff. The twins would love this room; however, they'd probably trash it. Somehow I don't think that would bother Walter.* I looked over to the other side of the expansive room...where an enormous aquarium with Betas, Angel Fish, Clown Fish, and Bottom Feeders highlighted the corner.

I wonder—when does he have time to feed the fish?

Then, alongside the home for the fishes, stood a wall-to wall-bookcase with board games, DVD's, CD's...but no video games. Come to think of it, I never saw Walter play video games. I just assumed he did. Wrong again. *Some psychic. I'd flunk if there were a school for psychics. I used to think I was good at what I did. Wrong again.*

We went back onto the landing and Walter led me to the guestrooms at the end of the hall. Inside *Door Number One* I viewed dormer windows, a walk-in closet and another door that led to an inviting bath. Designed for comfort. I strolled through the bathroom, which had all the necessary amenities and noticed that it connected with the other guestroom—Mirror images of each other—Both decorated in grays and blues, with French Country light wood furniture. Each room possessed a dresser, end tables alongside a queen size bed, and a desk under one of the windows. I peered outside the dormer windows and zeroed in on the backyard garden. The garden surrounded the brick patio, and outdoor lighting embellished the exterior summer living space. I spotted cherry trees beginning to bud.

Professionally landscaped—a stark contrast to my weeds in Ballard.

"Gee, Walter, if you get hard up, you could always turn this into a bed and breakfast."

"I was thinking more of turning this area into a nursery and a playroom...*in the future...*"

I looked at him and my eyes filled with tears. *Maybe I am maternal. Maybe one of these days I will abandon my birth control and embrace motherhood...but for now, I will just learn to enjoy life...and to be grateful for my newfound love. The future will sort itself out.*

"Tour's over." Walter smiled and wiped away my tears. He took me into his arms and gazed in my eyes. "Angelina, tell me...Which room is your favorite?"

I slipped my robe over my shoulder, and tiptoed down the hallway, stopping at the master bedroom. Walter smiled and followed me. He swept me off my feet and through the threshold, shut the door with his foot and carried me into the boudoir. He kissed my forehead and whispered in my ear, "You made the right choice, Sweetheart."

Chapter Thirty-Four

Next Morning...Starvation set in. Walter lay next to me in bed, sleeping like a baby. *Okay. I can do this. Get up first—again. Walk Pebbles—again. Feed Bam Bam...I mean, Hildie. Hildie...What kind of name is that? Almost as dumb as Pebbles. Maybe Pebbles and I can walk to that bakery down the hill and get some sweet rolls. Now that is worth getting out of bed. I'll do the entire breakfast today. Surprise Walter.*

I heard the clock strike six. *Okay, so I've turned into a morning person. Stranger things have happened.*

I sighed as I removed Walter's arm from my waist and climbed out of bed as quiet as a titmouse. I tiptoed to the closet, shut the door and turned on the light. Picked out some jeans and fancy lace underwear... grabbed a Seahawks hooded-sweatshirt and got dressed like a squirrel in her den—pulling on my fuzzy boots, after slipping on some alpaca socks. I like Walter's concern for my comfort. I could get used to this. I shut off the light, snuck out of the closet and tiptoed downstairs.

Pebbles greeted me with a yawn and Hildie with a soft meow. I couldn't help smiling at them, curled up together in the club chair, taking in the warmth of the embers still burning in the hearth.

I grabbed Pebbles' leash. He jumped up and stood alert on his feet, waiting for me—That jingle always gets to him. I hooked Pebbles secure and petted Hildie...telling her we'd be back soon and I'd give her a treat when we returned. She scrunched up her nose, and her stare seemed to say, "You are one crazy lady to be conversing with a cat this early in the morning." Having condescended to me, she yawned, curled up and closed her eyes.

Pebbles and I scampered down the front steps to the stone walkway and turned right at the sidewalk. A brisk, clear day greeted us. I could see the *Space Needle* and the twinkling lights of the city coming to life. Pebbles led me down the hill. He knew when to turn left and head down the hill. He took this walk before...with Walter...I'm sure. He knew the way better than I did. When we got to *Raycine's Boulangerie*, I picked out four hard rolls, two Napoleons, three apple turnovers, one loaf of rye bread and one loaf of French bread. The smell, ah...the smell... so intoxicating this early in the morning—Everything in the bakery... fresh and warm to the touch. Who needs booze? Just a little cappuccino and irresistible raised dough do it for me. The baker spoke with a French accent. Don't know whether he's for real or fake, but he sounded romantic. Thoughts of Paris came to me...*Walter and me in Paris...It could happen...Two Americans in Paris...Maybe for our second honeymoon...or our first...No...not the first...No place to stand naked on the balcony in that city... Maybe the French Riviera would be it...but Fiji is still my first choice...*I gave the baker the money for my breakfast collection and he smiled at me with one gold tooth reflecting the sunlight. He didn't seem to mind that a dog visited his bakery. *I'll remember that.* A bell rang as I opened the door...I waved to our friendly neighborhood baker as I exited, eager all of a sudden to get home to Walter.

Pebbles and I raced up the hill—not an easy feat. Some of the hills in Seattle rival the ones in San Francisco. Queen Anne is no exception. We took the same route home, just stopping for Pebbles to water a few trees. When we returned home, I put the goodie bag up high so Pebbles couldn't get into it and opened the drawers of the side board, looking for a tablecloth. I found one on the third try...A blue-checked one that looked just right for the occasion. I spread it on the table nestled into the window seat overlooking the garden. I yearned for fresh flowers to go with my little bit of formality. I went into the living room and found a pot of African violets. That would do the trick...I carried it back in and put it in the center of the table. The table prepared, I went to work on the cappuccinos. I foamed the milk and put two glass mugs side by side to fill with my morning elixir.

I paused from preparing our morning repletion to tend to the pets—feeding Hildie, then Pebbles. *Don't want them begging while we're delighting in our culinary treats.* While they were busy with their morning meal, I ran upstairs to wake Walter.

After our breakfast, our shower together and our *morning dessert*, I told Walter my plan for the day while dressing for the second time since my rising. "How about if we put on our ski jackets and cruise up to Crystal Mountain?"

"Tangie, the slopes are closed. The snow is melting in the Cascades."

"Oh, yeah. Hope we're not too late."

"We are. No more skiing."

"I don't wanna go skiing. I want to find Terese."

"And you think she's a ski bunny?"

"No, Walter. The way I figure it is...She worked as a waitress when she met Santigo. I think she might be hiding out at the ski lodge...waitressing there."

"Why there?"

"Santigo and the Sargentos don't ski...I'm sure of it...They're warm weather guys...and Terese knows that too...Plus her postcard to Simone had a Bonney Lake postmark. That's just a hop, skip and a ski jump from Crystal Mountain."

"Sometimes you are too clever for your own good—Don't you ever get tired?"

"My brain is on hyper-drive today, for some reason...You'll come, right?"

"I'll come...and I'll drive."

"You're terrific, you know? An answer to my prayers." I stood on my tiptoes and kissed my big hunk. It's a deal, Detective Cunningham."

Walter returned my kiss...first on my eyes and then on my lips...and then...I pushed him away...No way was I getting dressed a third time.

Compact snow greeted us on the road to Crystal Mountain. Dark clouds. Wind. Eerie. Not difficult traveling with Walter's super-charged SUV, but I felt a chill rising in my upper torso. I shivered as we cruised along the snowy path...I don't know whether it was a foreboding to the weather or our mission.

I looked out the passenger window as we cruised along. "Hey Walter...I thought you said the snow is melting...It still looks like winter around here... You should see the snowpack on the side of the road... Must be eight feet!"

"On the morning news, they used the "A" word...*Avalanche*...It's supposed to get really warm tomorrow...Can't you feel it warming up?"

"No. I just feel cold."

Walter grabbed my hand and put it to his cheek. "I'll keep you warm, Babe. Stick with me, kid."

"I think you're stuck with me, whether you want me or not."

"I want you. Always have, always will."

"You didn't always know me."

"Yea, but I know I always wanted you. Since I was little, you have been imprinted on my heart and soul."

"Umm...soul mates...I like that...Too bad we're working." I leaned over and kissed Walter on the ear. With all my might, I resisted temptation and sighed. "Back to work...What else did the news say?"

"The *D.O.T.* doesn't want to take any chances...It's good we're heading up the mountain now...Tomorrow the *Department of Transportation* is closing the roads. They're going to trigger some small avalanches to control the risk of larger, uncontrolled dangerous ones later on...that could come crashing down on cars...and people. "

"It will be a zoo here tomorrow...Miles and miles of backups..."

"Yes..."

"I gazed out the window. "This is our last glimpse of the snow for the year...I'm gonna miss it." I memorized the portrait forming in my mind...stately cedars blanketed with the last snowfall of the season...The last of the old growth timber...evergreens so majestic they resembled cathedrals reaching to the sky.

As we rode along the winding road approaching the official *Crystal Mountain Ski Area*, my senses mingled with the waterfalls here and there...I saw gigantic icicles melting...flowing down over the rocks, bringing the cool, fresh water to the lakes and streams below...beginning life again... *Maybe next year we could take up skiing... Walter and me in a private ski chalet—I could dig it. So what if I don't ski. I could take lessons... or just snowshoe my way around the place...or Walter could teach me. He knows something about everything...I'm beginning to catch on to his talents...*

Walter pulled the *Cayenne* into one of the several available spots in front of *Crystal Mountain Lodge*. "Here we are."

Silence all around us...No cars, no trucks, no people. Just one lone snowplow that stood locked in place, having finished its past call to duty.

Walter got out and went around to open my door. *I could get used to this chivalry...La vie est belle...*

I hopped out. "Follow me, Sweetie." I caressed his hand and smiled, giving him a familiar grin. Walter donned the role of secretary...*We've got our game down pat.* I switched to the strong-willed detective part... *but Walter knows the real me...and I know the real him. That fact can get me through almost anything.*

We opened the front door of the lodge and walked over to a section that had a sign posted on the front desk. It read: *Closed for the Season.* I ignored it and walked in the restaurant, with Walter behind me as backup. A woman around forty years of age, slim but curvaceous, with dyed-red hair, wearing reading glasses, and a low-cut angora sweater sat at a booth by the window sorting receipts and counting money.

She stopped what she was doing and looked up at her intruders. "Sorry...we're closed. Do you need something?"

"Hi. My name is Angelina Seraphina...and this is my secretary, Walter Cunningham. We're sorry to disturb you."

"Are you selling stuff? I don't have the time."

"No, nothing like that." I emphasized that statement with a shake of my head and a smile. "I know you're busy. We won't keep you long. We just want to ask you a few questions."

"I've gotta get these papers in order before sunset. My boyfriend's picking me up then and he don't like to be kept waitin'."

"Please...I wouldn't bother you if it weren't important...We've driven three hours up here to speak with you." *All right...it was only one and a half hours, but I can count stopping to walk Pebbles, can't I?*

The manager studied me first and then Walter. I guess we looked harmless enough to her...so she nodded. "Alright...I was gonna take a break around now anyway. Want some coffee?"

"We'd love some," chirped in Walter. He was not one to turn down caffeine.

"I'm Sally...the manager of this here café." She rose from the booth and went over to the counter. "What can I do for you?" This she said more to Walter than me.

I'm glad I brought him along. Bait for the fish.

I spoke up. "We're looking for a friend of mine..."Terese Santigo."

"Never heard of her." Sally poured three cups of coffee. Strong. Black. "Do you want any sugar? Cream?"

"Yes, please. Both." *I'm such a wuss. Can't take my coffee straight.* I thanked Sally for our beverages and decided to get down to business. "Terese may be using her maiden name...She in the middle of a divorce. Would you mind looking at a couple of photos?"

I showed her Terese as a raven-haired beauty and the doctored-up photo with Terese as a blond.

Sally pointed to the raven-haired beauty and tapped the picture with her index finger. Her nails looked like she visited a manicurist regularly. *Odd...where does one find a nail shop on a ski slope? Maybe Terese did nails on the side.*

Sally tossed the picture back to me. "This is Terese. Around here, she goes as Terese Seabrook. She worked here until yesterday. She picked up her last paycheck and split. No forwarding address."

I groaned inwardly. "Did she say where she was going?"

"Why the twenty questions?"

"I'm a friend of hers...I wanted to see if she needed any help. I know the divorce proceedings are taking a lot out of her." I *had a feeling if I invented a messy divorce, that might endear Sally to me...Women are like that... Camaraderie ran deep in a crisis situation.*

"Well, Terese is an excellent waitress...I'll give her that...and she attracted the customers. Plus, she never complained...except about that louse of a husband of hers..."

Bingo! I chose the right ploy. "Yes he wasn't the right man for Terese... He didn't understand her at all."

Sally nodded. "He sounds like a rat to me...I wish I could have done more for Terese...But this work is seasonal...I told her I could definitely use her next winter, but that I didn't have any work for her until next November. The poor girl looked crushed. Ya know—she started tearing up and all that. I loaned her my phone to call her sister, way up in Alaska.

"She called her sister?"

"She called her sister. Why is that so odd?"

"Ah..." I stalled for a moment and kicked my brain into working. "Terese doesn't exactly get along with her sister...Plus she's hard to reach. I haven't spoken with her sister in awhile, either...She's rather distant."

Sally gave me the once over and then looked at Walter. After studying us a minute, she decided to continue.

"Well, *Terese* got a hold of her sister...but after she returned my phone, she started getting all weepy again. I'm thinkin' her sister said no dice to Terese staying with her in Alaska...that she couldn't put her up. What kind of sister is that—not willing to help out her own family? I just don't understand."

"Terese and her sister have been at odds with each other for a while... They aren't very close." *Well, here I was fudging a bit, but they were distant in space. I do know Simone told Terese it wasn't safe for her to come to see her in Alaska with Horst prowling around there...Hum...I wonder if Horst gets frequent flyer miles for all the trips he makes back and forth between there and Seattle...*

Sally woke me from my thoughts. "Thanks for clearing that one up...that explains all the weeping and carrying on. Terese was in such a state...saying she didn't know what she was going to do...that she had no place to go...So I told her about some guy I know who recently bought a restaurant...His place is open year round. He probably could use a good waitress...I told her to use me as a reference and gave her my business card and wrote the guy's name and number on the back...Terese said she didn't know if she wanted to go to Seattle... but she took the card I gave her... then got on the final bus out of here. That was the last time I saw her."

"Where did you send her?"

"Well, I don't know for sure if she went there, but this friend of mine manages a café...well, it's really a pretty big restaurant...I think it's called the *Last Stop Café* on Capitol Hill...located on the corner of Broadway and...John Street. People in our business are always lookin' for good servers."

"Thanks, Sally. You've been a huge help."

"Anytime." She spoke to me but eyed Walter, like he was a juicy steak, and smiled at him with her pearly white veneers.

Walter and I finished the coffee and brought the mugs over to the counter. I told Sally we'd come back as customers next winter. She nodded, as if to say, *"I'll believe that when I see it,"* and put her glasses back on. Break over. We left Sally immersed in her pile of receipts and money counting.

As we walked out, Walter opened the door for me, but I did a little dance and motioned to the restroom—done in by Sally's strong coffee. Walter grinned at my dilemma and nodded. "I'll walk Pebbles and meet you back at Dodge—that is the car."

On the way down from *Crystal Mountain*, my cell phone rang. *Mother.*

"Tangie! Are you all right? Why do you have a new cell phone? Why can't I see you? When are you coming over?"

"I'm fine, Mom. I told you. I left my phone in my house, which is being fumigated for bugs."

"I thought you said *mold.*"

My mom's sharp.

"Either way, I don't wanna go into it."

"Is Walter with you?"

"Of course. He's my secretary."

"Good. At least you're not alone. I've been worried."

"Sorry, Mom. Really, I'm okay. Walter and I just cruised up to the mountains in his four-wheel drive…to see the sights."

"Oh no! Avalanche warnings are all over the news…Tangie, you didn't!"

"We're on our way down...No avalanches until tomorrow…and… Mom…I'm staying at Walter's for a few days."

"Well, that's a relief. Tell Walter *Hi* for me."

I turned to Walter, "My mom says, *Hi*."

Walter grinned and kept his eyes on the windy road.

"Mom, I gotta go...I'll call you soon. I promise. I'm working on a case. I'll tell you all about it when I see you...It's almost done."

"Be careful, Angelina."

I detected the *I'm still worried about you* tone in her voice...but I knew she was trying really hard not to sound overly-distressed.

"I will, Mom. Love you."

"I love you too, dear. Remember...call me."

"Will do...Bye, Mom."

I closed the phone and wiped the tears from my eyes with my scarf.

"I hate lying to my mom."

"I know, Sweetheart." Walter pulled the car over to the side of the road and fastened the brake. "Come here." He took me into his arms and hugged me and then kissed my eyes and cheeks.

"You're salty."

I started shaking uncontrollably and cried, "We should have come up here yesterday. Terese was *here*. We just missed her."

"You'll find her, Angelina...I know you will. It will all be over soon."

"How soon?"

"Soon."

I snuggled into Walter and stayed warm and safe, wrapped in his arms until the car windows steamed up. I dried my eyes with my glove, looked up at him and attemped a smile. "I'm okay now, Walter. I think we can go on."

"You sure?" Walter said as he handed me a handkerchief from his breast pocket.

"Yes." I said, blowing my nose. "Just a panic attack saying: *I don't want to do this anymore*."

"Hunting?"

"Yes. It's exhausting."

"Angelina...You're strong...you're beautiful...you're..."

"A wreck. No more compliments, please. They weaken me. We've got to get to work. Home, *James*."

"At your service, m' lady," Walter said as he gunned the SUV, advancing our trek down the mountain.

We hit the hills of Seattle as twilight approached.

"Do you wish to visit the *Last Stop Café* for an early supper, Ms. Seraphina?"

"I thought you'd never ask."

Walter turned off the freeway into the Capitol Hill neighborhood and headed up Broadway. Sally mentioned The *Last Stop Café* was on the corner of Broadway and John Street…not too far from Seattle University as I remember...probably a lot of student clientele strolling down Broadway this time of night to study, eat and unwind. I rolled down my window looking for the *Last Stop* and noticed a restaurant with a neon sign in the shape of cowboy hat in a front window and around it's doorway, blinking red and green lights pulsing in time to up-beat country music. *That must be the one.*

"That's it, Walter…Pull over as soon as you can…I'm sure we'll find a parking spot nearby."

Walter slowed the *Porsche* and two blocks down the street, eased into a tight spot with expertise. I know I would have banged into one of the cars Walter sandwiched between without blinking an eye. But that's Walter—*Expert Parker*. Before we got out of the *Porsche Cayenne*, I called the director at Simone's school and left a message that ended with..."Please…have Simone call me...at this new number. The old one doesn't answer...It's very important. *Spring* is near and I am moving." *I hope she remembers "Spring" is my code for Terese.*

I mustered up some belief of discovering Terese…I could sense her close by… as I crawled out of the *Cayenne*. The air smelled clean…

Crisp...Seattle air. Unspoiled. Rain started falling...contributing to the fresh scent I embrace. *Some people hate the rain. I cherish it. I love to walk in it...No umbrella...Just my Pacific Northwest Parka and my cozy rain boots...I especially like walking along the ocean in the rain... Ocean Shores, here I come...When this is over...Walter and I...at the mile-wide beach...listening to the waves...letting Pebbles bark at the crashing waves... and the sandpipers...*

I heard a Ka-chink—Walter putting some money in the metered parking...*Back to reality*...We've become two soldiers marching uphill toward the *Last Stop Café—The Last Hurrah*...or so I thought...*before things would get really ugly.*

Capitol Hill is edgy...The place to go for action. On one of the brick buildings, I noticed an advertisement for the *Seattle Film Festival*...advertising a screening in the nearby *Broadway Performance Hall* for an avante garde flick, *Nobody Loves You When You're Down and Out*. I pointed to the over-sized poster and smiled at Walter. "Ain't that the truth..."

We passed *Eddie's Tattoo Parlour*. Next door to that den of body art, on the left side, glowed *Love Nest Apparel*. A pulsating crimson light beckoned us. Walter lingered a bit before I pulled on his arm. Before our approach to the café, we encountered a soap and scents vendor marketing his wares on the street. He opened a bottle of pirated perfume to give me a whiff. A policeman trotted by us on a horse, and the salesman disappeared. The cop nodded to Walter as he passed us. *Is there a cop in the city Walter doesn't know?*

We stopped in front of a bakery. We always stop in front of bakeries. This one had an electric sign above its window that read: *Simple Pleasures*.

"I just love window-shopping with you, Walter."

"Maybe we could stop here for dessert," Walter said..."After we hit the café."

I smiled and motioned to the cookies in full view. The display case featured anatomically correct gingerbread men and women.

"Bet they do a good business," Walter laughed, put his arm around my waist and squeezed me.

I giggled. "You can get me some, next Valentine's Day."

"I'll remember." He grasped my hand in his and led me up the hill. I spotted a gay pride banner serving as a curtain draped over a second floor window. The wind kicked up and it became a flag, waving in the breeze through the open window. Two guys, one bald in a macho tee-shirt, wearing large chains around his neck and holding a wine glass in his hand...and the other with green spiked hair, no shirt and a beer in his hand...leaned out and toasted us as we passed by. I smiled and waved back to them. Friendly people live here on Capitol Hill—Weird, but friendly.

As we approached the entrance to the café, a man selling bracelets, beads and necklaces beckoned us to his makeshift stand. The vendor lifted up a piece of beaded jewelry and dangled it in front of my eyes. "This is from Uganda, Missy...Is it not beautiful?"

The beads mesmerized me as the salesperson moved them back and forth. I saw these beads before. "Yes." Then I turned to Walter. "You know, Walter, Pebbles' Vet sells jewelry at her office... She raises money for an orphanage...in that same country in Africa...I have a pair of ear-rings that would match this bracelet."

Walter pulled out a twenty and gave it to the vendor.

The vendor shook Walter's hand. "Thank you, sir. You are very wise...Also...you are helping the children in the orphanage." He turned his attention back to me. "The children made this bracelet just for you, Missy. It will bring you luck."

"Yes...perhaps it will." I smiled at the grateful hawker. "It's wonderful."

Walter took the bracelet and fastened it on my wrist. I held up my arm and admired the green and blue beads, tied with leather and woven into an intricate mosaic design. "Thank you, Walter...This will be my good luck piece. I'm not going to take it off until we are done with this case."

I smell Chicken Curry. Thai food! My favorite! Coming from...the Café—I look up at the entrance to the restaurant and notice a small sign situated next to the over-sized neon cowboy hat —and guess what? Last Stop Café seems to be the Lone Star Café. Oh well, close enough.

I heard a tune being played by a country band, about a lovesick cow-boy and the girl who left him, wafting out from the bar area. I noticed people strolling in and out of the place wearing Stetson hats. Cowboy boots...clacked along the floor...college students rushed to get in...to drink, dance...and consume Thai food. The smell of ginger, red pepper and garlic overtook my senses. I started thinking to myself...*On Capitol Hill, diversity rules—why not a Taste of Thai in a cowboy bar? I am thinking Chicken Satay would be just about perfect right now.*

I grabbed my honey's hand. "Hey, Walter...I think I'm gonna like this place." I did a little two-step in time to the music and tightened my grip on him.

We ducked further into the crowded restaurant. I tried not to lick my chops. Hunger pains set in. I began salivating.

"Country music...you like?" Walter asked.

"It goes with the territory...but this place is not a café...and not a last stop drinking hole. It's Texas in Seattle."

Walter studied the patrons. "Probably the owners inherited the name...and decided to keep it to lure in all kinds of people. Businesses today need to be creative."

"Yeah and maybe to cash in on the late-night drunks and give them a good meal." An inebriated older gentleman grabbed my rear and tipped his over-sized cowboy hat to me. I gave him a quick slap on his hairy hand and watched him teeter-totter to his next victim, an older woman with bleached blond hair, sitting by the bar...*Who knows, maybe he'll get lucky.*

"You know Walter, they probably threw in the music to lure local cowboys roaming the streets."

"Seems to me, Tangie, some of these cowboys come from Ellensburg... Rodeo country—Can't envision them catching a bus on a daily basis in cowboy boots. They probably are visiting the *big city* tonight...and are out on the town.

I looked around and studied a vivacious group of college students and a few urban professionals on the small dance floor alongside the bar. "Kind of a yuppie crowd tonight, hanging out with the obvious cowboy types, don't you think, Walter? I wouldn't exactly call this a redneck bar."

"You know what I really think, Tangie? I surmise most of the cowboys in this bar are what you call all hat and no cattle. The bar is crawling with the upwardly mobile...and wealthy college students."

"Isn't that an oxymoron? Wealthy-college student? All the ones I knew in college were poor—extended college loans—broke parents—nest egg depleted."

"All the ones I knew made me feel poor."

"Ah...That's right...*Brown University*. You, my love, are an Ivy Leaguer."

A thin young man interrupted our banter and introduced himself as Lee, the host, and asked if we wanted a table. He wore a cowboy hat, riding boots with spurs, plaid shirt under a suede vest and wrangler jeans. All he needed was a rope. Walter nodded, holding back a smile. Lee bowed and apologized and told us there was a twenty-minute wait, but that we could relax in the bar.

Walter nodded. "Sure, but could we please speak to the manager while we're waiting there?"

Lee winced, led us to the bar and excused himself. Walter ordered us two beers. Seemed like the right thing to do. The bartender placed them on the bar before we blinked twice, along with a bowl of rice crackers and peanuts. Lee came back lickety-split with the manager, who didn't look like he was from Thailand...or Texas for that matter. New York City...would be a good guess...Definitely not Asian...not close... not redneck...not even a cowboy from Montana...maybe Italian...maybe Jewish...maybe Middle-Eastern. He looked about forty-five...hair graying at the temples...in a blue pinstriped suit that looked hand-tailored. His black, silver-streaked hair, immaculately styled—slicked back and shiny—gleamed in the dim light of the bar...and his nails looked freshly manicured. He appeared to be someone who liked to spend his money. Tall. Dark. Handsome. Cosmopolitan.

"Is everything to your liking?" He began speaking in a commanding voice. When he talked, people listened. *I bet Sally has a crush on him. It probably killed her to send Terese to him, as Terese is such a looker...Sally must be a good sort to share her cache of men.*

"Oh yes," I piped in. "It smells heavenly here. We just want to ask you a few questions if you don't mind."

"Absolutely."

"Why is your restaurant called a café...specifically, the *Lone Star Café?*"

"Previous owner. I never got around to a name change. Hey, are you from the *Times*? Will you be reviewing the place? We could use some good press."

"Oh, no. Just interested customers—Locals."

"Well, my partners and I changed the menu and the ambiance of the place when we purchased the *Lone Star*...We hired some new help. Seems the old chef was drunk all the time...and the waitresses were...well, I don't want to go there...The best chef we could find cooked Thai...So we went for it...The bet paid off...We've got a hit on our hands."

I smiled. "I can see that...congratulations to you. The crowd is hopping for a weeknight."

"You should see the weekends. Standing room only. I had to hire more help."

"That brings me to *Question Number Two*. Terese Seabrook. Is she working here?"

"Why do you want to know?"

"Well, I'm a friend of hers...I know she's having some tough times...I could offer her a place to stay if she needs it...She's kind of proud...She won't ask for help."

The owner looked at me...studying my answer for a bit. "Well, young lady, as a matter of fact, I just hired her. She's gonna start on Friday. Poor kid. I felt sorry for her. I gave her an advance to help her get settled. I hope she doesn't stiff me."

"She won't. She's been going through a lot with her abusive husband, but she's dependable. Thanks for helping her. I've been trying to get in touch with her, but since she moved, I can't seem to locate her...She's been traveling around. If she comes in before Friday, could you give her my card?" I took out one of my *hot off the press* business cards...This one displayed only my name and new phone number on it. Then I continued. "I'm a friend of hers...from high school. Her sister and I are worried about her. Tell her if she needs a place to stay, I've got room. She could crash with me for a while. Tell her I have a new, larger home."

The manager smiled at me and nodded as he took my card and put it in his jacket pocket.

"Please tell her, I have a new phone number...probably why she hasn't called me."

Mr. *New York City* smiled at me. "Will do, Sweetheart. Anything else?"

"No, we're good."

"Unfortunately, I have to get back to the kitchen. We're short on help this evening. It's been a pleasure kibitzing with you."

Thank you for listening...Say, what do you recommend for dinner?"

"Sweetie, here it's all hot...but your friend..."

"*Walter...*Walter is my partner."

"Walter. Pleased to meet you." The manager extended his right hand—I noticed an expensive diamond ring on his right ring finger and a Rolex watch encompassed his wrist. He continued in his commanding voice. "You'll like the Orange Beef, Walter. We do that up great."

Walter matched his strong handshake. "Thanks, Mr. Ah..."

"Call me Paul...Paul Dimon."

"Okay, Paul. Will do that."

I nodded in agreement and placed my hand on Walter's arm, as a sign of my affection towards him.

"I hope you enjoy your meal...and come again." Paul Dimon, looking directly at me, gave me the once over...*I know that look. Paul Dimon struck me as a wolf...a wolf that softens his prey and then delights in pleasing them. Strange dude. I'm sure his last remark was meant for me alone...He's the kind of guy that gives your mother nightmares...I remember that type from high school...I never told my mom about Billy Rosa...he roamed through the hallowed halls of learning morning, noon and night...and delighted in capturing innocent young maidens...the more the merrier.*

Lee, our host, came up to us. "Your table is ready." He smiled a toothy grin and winked at me—*probably glad we weren't filing a complaint.*

I shook Paul Dimon's hand. "Thank you," Mr. Dimon."

"Bon appetite." Paul held my hand, a little longer than necessary and then bent down and kissed it, before disappearing into the kitchen.

Must be the New York City way. I could feel Walter steaming through his jacket, but he put a lid on it...for the moment. He doesn't have anything to worry about with me, but I sense an inner struggle going on within him. Walter's one of the Good Guys—but it's hard to figure him out sometimes. He knows I'm his girl...and he's my guy...I do feel flattered he cares enough to get jealous—I never confronted his... or my basic instincts until we became a couple. All I know is, Walter brings out my MoJo and I love that about him.

We devoured our meal. Walter's appetite surpassed mine. That's a first. Usually I win the prize for starving patron of food. I licked my fingers, polishing off the last of my black sticky rice and sighed. "You know, Walter...You and I eat Thai take-out all the time...But this is the first time we've chowed down together *inside* a Thai restaurant."

"Well, this is a Thai Restaurant in food only...There's authentic one on Roy Street, a block from *McCaw Hall. Bahn Thai...*Atmosphere plus... I'll take you there, when we go to the ballet. It's totally Thai... and as it's on Queen Anne, we could walk there from our home."

"*Our home*... I like the sound of that... and I'd love going there...It could be our new hang-out."

"I'd like having a hang-out with you."

I leaned over and brushed his lips. He tasted like garlic prawns. I felt hungry all over again.

"More dessert, Angelina?"

"Maybe later." I winked and started playing footsies with him under the table.

That did it for Walter... He leaned over, breathing heavily, and whispered in my ear, "Let's go home." Then without another word, he put down his napkin, took my hand and lifted me up from my chair.

Home... to Queen Anne...no longer Ballard—which seems far away from my life now. As we left Capitol Hill, I thought of the seven hills that constitute Seattle. Seattle, like Rome has seven hills... *Ah Rome... another romantic city... Walter and I must go there sometime...*

Come to think of it...*Queen Anne Hill is my favorite of all the hills in Seattle—the perfect place to live...It's near everything...The Space Needle, the twinkling lights of the ferries, the theatre district...Seattle Center and all the cultural fairs and festivals—like the Northwest Folklife Festival in May and Bumbershoot in September—the last free-for-all of summer...and now—best of all—Walter.*

Riding home across town, Walter took the northwest route and drove along the sound, the ferry docks and the waterfront shopping area, which was comfortably asleep at this hour. We rode in silence. I looked out at the Puget Sound as we cruised and spotted a lone ferry approaching Seattle from Bainbridge Island. The boat glowed as it approached land—a beacon of light in the evening sky...It brought back thoughts of Terese...A woman in the early bloom of her life... alone in the darkness of her fear. *I could feel her presence. . . nearby...*

I'm sure Terese has a week's worth of hotel stays in her pocket. After that, she will be hurting for dough. I have to find her before she does something stupid—like contacting Fred Santigo. If she does, the Sargentos will find her...I know they are watching Fred...They aren't going to give him any slack.

I hate playing the waiting game. Tomorrow will come soon enough. That means Walter and I have time for one last fling before getting in the body-snatching business.

At Broad Street, Walter turned right—heading up towards *Seattle Center*, then turned towards Queen Anne Hill...and our home in the clouds. I leaned back and sunk into the heated leather seat, which enveloped me like a long-lost parent. I would not feel this safe in a moving vehicle for a long time to come.

Chapter Thirty-Five

"Ring, Ring, Ring..." The landline sounded downstairs as the grandfather clock struck eight...as if in chorus with the phone. No one answered the phone, but I could hear Pebbles barking...probably didn't like waking up either. Then, a minute later, I heard Walter's cell...squealing an annoying tune...Loud...with lots of drums and bass. Walter rolled over and picked up his phone on the bedside table. "Un huh. Un huh. Yeah. Okay...You da' man. Thanks. We'll be there."

I pushed my head up from my cozy down pillow—no longer dead to the world. I looked out the window...*Sun's up. Ah...What a night...Walter and me...Me and Walter—in the shower...in the Jacuzzi...on the rug, by the fire...brandy...wine... and the four poster bed—All night...no interruptions... until now...*

"Hey Walter...Who, besides you...is da' man? And where are we gonna be?"

Walter tuned out my questions, jumped out of bed, picked up his jeans, draped over the chair by the fireplace, and put them on. "I'm off to walk Pebbles...I hear him whining."

"He's always whining. Answer my question."

Walter grabbed a sweatshirt hung on the bedpost like a flag. "Want to come? I'll tell you along the way."

He leaned over and kissed my nose, and then my mouth. "Thanks for last night, Angelina."

I groaned. Who needs answers, when you can have a kiss like that?

"Come on, Tangie…" Walter pulled off my covers, coaxing me out of bed. "We can hike down to *L' Boulangerie…*"

That did it for me. "Yum!" *Apple turnovers, chocolate éclairs, cinnamon twists…*

"Yes…wait for me, Walter…I'll be dressed in a flash."

We walked back up the hill from the bakery with our arms loaded with our favorite carbohydrates and refined sugars. I anticipated sipping my home-brewed cappuccino and a sugar high as Walter explained the morning wake-up call. "Steve called me…this morning."

"Steve…the cop?"

Walter nodded, stopped walking and squeezed me tight. "Now don't get alarmed, Tangie. I know how you are."

"No…how am I, Walter? Tell me."

"Well…in bed, Angelina…you're great." Walter kissed me on the lips and tightened his grip on my waist. "But you have a tendency to worry about things in the real world…that…well—you know…"

"Things I don't wanna do, you mean…"

"Yes, Tangie…you can't help it—I know…it's hard."

"So I'm a psychic…big whoopee deal. So tell me already…I'm a big girl now. I can handle it."

"Okay…here goes. Steve...Steve's got a body for us. Says he'll bring it to *Price's Funeral Home* tonight...around five-thirty…after hours…less suspicious. He needs it back by the a.m. shift or people will be asking questions..."

I looked at Walter and tried to act cool. My hands started to shake, so I put one in my pocket, grabbed firmly onto Pebbles leash, and started my deep breathing…all the time trying to appear as cool as the air around us. Then my wheels started turning again. "I'll call Santigo and let him know."

I let out one breath and groaned, no longer hungry. "No rest for the wicked," I muttered to myself, as I handed Pebbles' leash to Walter and took out my cell. I pressed Santigo's number while we trudged up the steep slope.

Santigo picked up after two rings.

"Fred?"

"Who is this?"

"Me. *Tangie...*Angelina Seraphina." *Time to talk in code...Santigo better catch on...*"Fred, I'm so sorry to hear about your wife, *Terese.* Is it all right if I attend the viewing tonight at Price's Funeral Home?"

"Tonight? I'm sorry, I..."

"Please...I know it's a private viewing—just family, but I'd really like to pay my respects to Terese. She was my friend."

"Well, perhaps you could come early, around...say...6:30 this evening?"

"I will do that...Thank you, Fred. It means a lot to me."

"See you then."

"Oh...and Fred...Her sister says she's so sorry, she can't make it...she can't afford the airfare."

"I suspected as much. If I had thought of it, I would have sent her some cash, but this is so sudden...It happened so quickly...no warning..."

"She understands...I'll see you tonight."

"Thank you."

"My sympathies." I hung up, feeling like an idiot.

"You did good, kid." Walter took my head and leaned it into his chest as he embraced the rest of my body.

"I did? I'm not really the acting type."

"Give yourself credit. You're a natural."

"I am? Why do I feel so tense?'

"You're new at it...I've got to hand it to Santigo. He catches on."

"Yeah...I guess you're right..." I looked up at the sky...I could see specks of blue peaking out of the clouds...*Maybe today would be a good day, after all...Maybe we'll get one step closer to finding Terese...It could happen.*

I smiled at Walter and touched his cheek with my gloved hand. "Look, Walter...I know business is calling...but first...breakfast!"

My appetite resurrected itself, stabbing me with an intense desire for caffeine. I took Pebbles back from Walter. Pebbles continued pulling on his leash...leading us forward...knowing a meal awaited him when we returned home. I've said it before and I'll say it again, sometimes I wish I were a dog. Dogs live in the present and aren't concerned about what's coming around the corner—Such a luxury...

I gave him free rein on his leash to race up the last block towards home...*I don't know which one of us ran faster, but I do know that nothing keeps me from my cappuccinos. It's my drug of choice.*

After breakfast, I stood up from the table and took the dishes to the sink. "So...Walter...What are we going to do for the rest of the day? I'm gonna go nuts, waiting for our six-thirty showdown."

Walter bit into the last remaining éclair and took a sip of his second cappuccino. "I thought we'd visit your mom."

"She'd like that...I'd like that."

I loaded the dishwasher and cleaned out the espresso machine. "She'll probably ask us questions...when we show up in our basic black—funeral attire."

"Yes...but you are good at answers, my love...and..." Walter began twitching his nose...like he was about to sneeze. "We can't get dressed until after we give Pebbles another bath...He smells. What did he roll in this time?"

I sniffed the air and then the pooch. "Maybe the cat litter. He's a sucker for all things unmentionable."

"Yuck." Walter he put down the last bite of his éclair. "What that animal will do for attention astounds me."

"Yeah, but he clean ups good."

Walter got up from the table and brought his coffee cup to the sink. "Before we head over to your mom's, I'll leave plenty of food for Bam Bam...I mean Hildie...see you've got me calling her that weird name."

"I kinda like *Bam Bam*...and it's no weirder than *Hildie*."

"Tangie, remember I'm not the one who named my cat *Hildie*...my grandfather did...after his favorite opera singer. Hildegarde something. What can I say?"

"Respect your elders..."

"I hate it when you are right all the time." Walter took me into his arms and hugged me as he began to talk business—frightening me all over again. "I think it's a good idea if Pebbles is in safe hands...while we wrap up this case. Let's ask your mom to watch him for a few days...He needs constant attention. My housekeeper can watch over the house and Hildie...She comes in every other day...I'll leave her a note...but Pebbles will go nuts if we don't come back right away. Dogs are like people. They need constant reassurance."

Walter squeezed me tighter, taking my breath away and ending his embrace with a kiss that tasted just like a chocolate éclair.

"Um...you taste scrumptious, Walter." I pulled away from him with reluctance...feeling a yearning for his body that would not go away. "I kinda thought a housekeeper took care of your home. No guy is this neat."

"You know me so well," Walter grinned. "And remember...this place is *our home*."

"Our home," I whispered...then kissed him on the cheek. Just as I began to relax, an unwelcome vision tugged at me trying to ruin my happiness...flashing at me like a camera bulb...taking me somewhere I didn't want to go. I closed my eyes forced the vision from my mind. I murmured to Walter, "Home Sweet Home..." and tried to relax in the nearness of his presence. I wanted to return his smile...and thank him for his thoughtfulness...but I couldn't...That same familiar chill took over my body...tapping my senses into a place I only visited in my nightmares.

I quivered. "It's gonna get ugly, isn't it?"

"It might...and I know you, Tangie...You'll be worrying about Pebbles...and what if we get tied up tonight?"

"Literally or figuratively?" I chuckled—trying to be funny—but it wasn't working. Even my dark humor couldn't get me out of this one. My quivering turned to shaking...first the hands and then the knees.

My body continued to shake. I could not stop it. "I think I'll put on a sweater, Walter...and then I'll call my mom."

My stomach started competing with my limbs…it started doing the old up and down movement. *Bad sign.* I walked away from Walter, into the foyer and ran up the stairs to get my cell.

My mother answered after one ring. "Tangie! So good to hear your voice… What's wrong?"

"Nothing's wrong."

"Well, I just talked to you, yesterday. Something must be wrong. You never call me two days in a row."

"Mom, relax...Walter and I are just wondering if you could watch Pebbles for a few days...We're finishing this case...and where we're going, we can't take a dog..."

"This Walter thing is getting serious, isn't it?"

"Yes, Mom...but that has nothing to do with Pebbles...I just need a place for the little pooch...Really...We're working."

"Honey...I'm sorry...I didn't mean anything...I'd be delighted to watch darling Pebbles. The twins are coming over for a few days...They will love to play with him..."

"Thanks Mom. But don't let Jason or Jeffrey feed Pebbles their supper...Last time he threw up hot dogs all over my bed."

"I'll keep my eye on them and Pebbles...I'll do Italian this time. They love the pizza delivery man...They fight over who pays him."

"Pebbles will get constipated if they shove mozzarella down his throat."

"Now, Angelina...I told you I'm watching the boys...You are getting over-protective. Wait until you have kids..."

Kids…hadn't thought about that one in a long time…until two days ago… and now…somehow the idea doesn't seem so foreign to me…I even kind of like the idea. With Walter…kids would be wonderful…

"Angelina…are you there?" I heard my mother's voice as if far away… but coming from the phone…

"I'm here, Mom…Sorry...I think I'm stressed out over this case. I just want it done."

"I understand, dear...I know how you like to finish what you start… it can be stressful…I can't wait to see Pebbles...I'll have to remember to hide my underwear."

"Good idea." I smiled and my body stopped shaking. *She knows how to humor me...*"Mom...we'll be over before rush hour...about one or two this afternoon."

"Great...Oh...I almost forgot...I wanted tell you...I heard from Don... He called me...said he couldn't reach you...Said you weren't answering your phone at home...or your cell phone. I told him you moved out... temporarily. I didn't know exactly what else to say to him."

"Thanks, Mom. You're awesome."

"You should call him, Angelina. He's still your friend. He sounded worried."

"Yeah, I will, Mom...I promise. Thank you."

"See you soon..."

"Can't wait." I closed the phone. *My mom—tender loving soul...always concerned about what I'm doing. Wish I could level with her this time, but she'd really freak out. Don—my ex-fiancé, the priest—I haven't called him in months. We usually call each other every week or so...we talk...we chat. Being as he's a missionary in Chile, he's a safe distance from me...but despite the odds, we have become good friends after all. I still confide in him...I ask his advice...He gives me pep talks...We discuss his ministry in Chile...but...since Walter...I've ignored him...Several weeks at least...No wonder he's calling my mom. My ol' Catholic guilt is kicking in...*

I went back downstairs and strolled into the living room—stalling. I peered out the window...and noticed fog taking over the city...*So much for my hopes of this turning out to be a good day*. I opened my cell and pressed Don's number. He picked up on the first ring.

"Father Don speaking."

"It's me, Don."

"Yes...of course...Tangie! How are you? What's up? You worried me when I couldn't get in touch with you."

"I've been good, Padre. Really...It's just that I've been working on this case. It's complicated."

"Oh...okay...so you don't want to talk about it. I understand. How's Pebbles?"

"Still has a craving for lingerie, but otherwise good. Feisty as ever."

"I thought you like him feisty."

"I do. But now he's into playing guard dog." I thought of Horst and shivered.

"Are you sure you're all right? Is there anything I can do for you?"

"Actually I'm great. And Padre…I've got a boyfriend. After seven years, I thought I'd take another chance on love."

A silence enveloped our conversation for a while. I heard a sigh on the other end and then Don, in a brisk voice—hiding his emotion, asked me, "Is he good to you?"

"Very." This time I smiled like the Cheshire Cat, momentarily forgetting my panic.

"In that case, I'm happy for you…but Tangie...what's this about the new phone number...and leaving your home…what exactly is going on?"

"Oh Don, I had to leave home...because of…my case. Walter and I are working on some hush, hush detective stuff...We're sort of going undercover. Don't tell my mother. She worries."

"I worry too. Who's Walter?"

"He's my secretary...and my boyfriend."

"Your secretary?"

"Well, it's a cover...It works well."

"Why do I feel like you are not telling me everything?"

"Hey Don, you may be a priest, but I am not making a confession."

"Sorry, Tang, but I'm concerned about you."

"Don't be...You are beginning to sound like my mother..."

"Sorry…"

The light bulb switched on. "Hey Don...Could you do me a favor?"

"Anything, Angelina…You know that…"

"Would you mind asking around your village...in your casual way... See if any of the locals have heard of Fred Santigo...or the Sargento brothers—Aldolphus and Sylvan."

"I could do that. Who are these guys?"

"*The good, the bad and the ugly*. See if they have any ties near Santiago... They grew up in South America...I am sure at least one of them is from Chile."

"How sure?"

"Well, I know Fred Santigo comes from there...I'm not so sure of the Sargento brothers...I never met them..."*and I really don't want to meet them...*"See if you can find any stuff about them...if they're wanted by the police in Chile..."

"I could drive the jeep over to *La Guardia...*"

"That would be great...Could you please get back to me ASAP?"

"I'm on it. I'll call you pronto."

I recited my new cell number to Don, and waited while he wrote all the stuff down. I thanked him, and inquired about his life at *San Pedro Mission.* He told me he finds his peace at the small mission...that he and the *Sisters of Charity* are helping to educate and feed the forgotten poor there... A lot of young women...many with small children come there—they have no other place to go...He and the nuns and a couple of lay people are teaching the mothers computer skills...so they can find work...These young mothers have no husbands...and the children—no fathers...The forgotten poor...the outcasts of their society.

Sounds like a rewarding and humbling experience for Don...He is saving these young girls from the likes of the Sargento Brothers...He is doing something positive to help them...unlike me—seems I just follow dead ends here and there... not getting anywhere...

Don spoke my name and I didn't answer right away...engrossed in pictures in my mind of innocent young women, hurt and tortured by life. I could feel the pain, the fear they endured. I held my breath and sat down on one of the Queen Anne chairs, near the fireplace...almost collapsing as I did. A worried tone in Don's voice brought me back to our conversation.

"Tangie...are you there?"

"I'm sorry, Don...Yes...I'm here...you know...I was just thinking... about your mission. I'm grateful for you...the sisters...and...what you are doing for those young women...you are saving lives...

"Thanks, Tangie, that means a lot to me...I'll share your words with the sisters—They appreciate any support—it's hard for them here—but, like me, they love their mission. Say, listen, Angelina...I'll be in Seattle for a sabbatical this summer...

"That's great, Don..."

"After my time of reflection, I hope to return to San Pedro on a more permanent basis...I'm going to request reassignment to Chile when I journey home."

Like a dork, I nod...like Don could see me when I nod over the phone.

He continued, "I hope I can see you before I return to my ministry. After September, it may be a while before I'll be in Washington State again. San Pedro has become my home—Life has brought me here...I feel like this is where I am supposed to be."

"I am glad you found your peace, Don." I wiped the tears that began flowing down my cheeks. I coughed and sighed, trying to remain calm—the images of young women, in pain, crying for help, started flashing before me once more...

I shook off my mounting panic and said in a reassuring voice, with a reassurance I did not feel myself, "You know, Don, you are doing more good than you realize."

"Thank you, Angelina...I appreciate you saying that..."

"And...yes, I do want to see you again...I've missed you...Plus, you can meet Walter when you return to the Pacific Northwest...We'd both like to spend some time with you...Walter is a great chef...and I can sort of cook now, myself..."

"I look forward to that. You take care of yourself..."

"I will. Call me again soon...or I'll call you..."

"Peace."

"And to you too, Father Don." I disconnected the phone and gazed out the window, noticing dark clouds taking over the foggy mist.

*Fireworks this summer...but in a good way...Don meets Walter. Walter meets Don. I should feel like the cat that ate the canary...but I don't. I just feel relieved...Don is where he is supposed to be...I am where I am supposed to be... wherever that may be...I've been moving around a lot lately...*I took a deep breath and looked around the living room and my eyes settled on Walter.

Walter sat slumped across from me... in his club chair...studying me. I walked over to him and eased myself onto his lap. "Thanks for starting the fire. I appreciate it...and you. I told Don about us...and a little about what's going on...He's gonna do some checking on the Sargentos for us."

I ruffled Walter's hair up and placed a kiss on his forehead, and leaned against him, feeling the warmth of his body.

"I heard the gist of your conversation." Walter squeezed me around the waist. "Yes...we could use all the help we can get."

"You approve?"

"Of course." Walter smiled, as he kissed me on my neck. "I'm not jealous of a priest...I'm actually grateful to him...I look forward to meeting the famous Father Don."

"Curious?"

"Of course. How he could give you up is beyond my understanding."

"A higher calling."

"So be it. I will never complain. Thank you, Jesus!" Walter put his hands up in a salutatory manner.

I grinned at him, and forgot my panic and the dark clouds pressing in on us, surrounding us…refusing to let us go. But, at this moment, at least, my visions ceased and I could relax.

Walter lowered his arms, squeezed me once more around the waist, picked me up and carried me to the plush furry throw that he had placed on the rug in front of the fireplace. The pillows and brandy were still there from last night.

"Angelina," Walter whispered, as he kissed my ear. "We have time for one more *voyage au paradis* before we dress in our basic black."

"You know me so well, Walter." I began to gasp for breath…*Walter always takes my breath away. Halleluiah! He knows so well how to reassure his woman.*

Church bells…*ringing…and ringing and ringing…*

Coming from my cell phone...on the floor…Oh my God...I fell asleep! Walter fell asleep…*Oh, but what a nap...*I pushed aside the brandy glasses and picked up my cell before it went to voice mail...

"You're going to need more than my prayers, Angelina..."

"Father Don…"

I sat upright…awaken from my revelry. "What do you mean?"

"Tell me, Tangie...What kind of case are you working on?"

"A difficult one...a missing persons..."

"All your cases are missing persons..."

"Yes, but this one's complicated."

"I have a feeling you will be the missing person…if you keep working on this one."

Tell me about it. "Do you have something for me, Don?"

"Well, not on Fred Santigo. He's clean."

"I figured as much…Fred's kind of strange, but doesn't look dangerous. I'm looking for his wife…she's the missing person…"

"The Sargentos are another story. They operated out of Chile until they got themselves thrown out of the country. Anything illegal, they did...Drugs, prostitution, loan sharking, smuggling...They're also wanted for murder—That bit of information came out after they took off for parts unknown—The police combed the streets for them...but the brothers already skipped the country...compliments of a few corrupt politicians—friends of the Sargentos..."

"So that's why they went to Columbia..."

"How do you know that?"

"Fred Santigo shared that bit of information...but The Sargentos have been spotted…in The States—around the Seattle area."

"For the love of Mother Mary! Angelina...Please...Avoid them at all costs! Promise me you'll keep away from them..."

"Don…I haven't run into them and I don't plan on meeting up with them." *Okay, so I didn't tell Don about Fred Santigo doing business with them... or our meeting tonight with the dead body...Besides, I'll just be watching...Don't think that counts.*

"Promise me you won't go looking for them…My God…Please…"

"Don, that's a job for the police. If I find anything or anyone…I promise, I'll let the *Seattle P.D.* take over."

How bad can I be, lying to a priest?

"Angelina, I'm serious."

He's on to me. Rats.

"Don, *Father Don,* I do promise...I'll be careful."

"There's a bounty on them here in Chile. The police in Seattle can contact Senor Constable Pedro Rodriguez...if they apprehend the criminals. *The Guardia Santiago* would love to get them into custody."

"I'll notify the *Seattle Police Department.* It'll be easier for the cops to arrest them if they're known fugitives...Thanks a lot, Don."

"You'll call me again, soon? Let me know how things work out?"

"Of course. You're a peach."

"Haven't been called that in awhile."

"Well, I appreciate you, Father Don."

"I'll pray for you, Angelina. Be good. Stay out of trouble."

"I will...I promise...and thanks for all your prayers..."

This time I mean it. I hate to hang up. I know it would be sometime before we spoke again. I think Don felt the same way.

"Peace be with you, Angelina."

"And you too, Padre."

As I closed my phone, Walter rolled over the pillows spread out on our fireside love nest. He kissed the tears that were flowing uncontrollably from my eyes. "It's hard...I know, Angelina."

"I'm lying to everyone..."

"Not to me...and not to yourself..."

"No...not you...but Walter...you don't know me...I'm a phony when it comes to being brave."

"You could've fooled me, kid."

I sighed. "Time to face the music..."

"Rap or Flamenco?"

"Walter, cut it out. I'm serious."

"I know..."

He took me into his arms and kissed my hair, then my cheeks and my lips. "You taste like a pretzel...Come on, Angelina...how about you and I take a shower...It's almost two o'clock...Your phone will be ringing—your mom wondering what's up. We're late...again."

"Oh Walter! We'll be stuck in rush hour..." I hopped up and gave Walter a shout as I cruised up the stairs..."Twenty minutes, my love...I swear...Just give me twenty minutes. I'll be ready."

"I'm right behind you, my love. Save me some hot water..."

Chapter Thirty-Six

My mom called as we were crossing *State Route 520*...cruising over the *Evergreen Floating Bridge* on route to her home in Kirkland. She owned one of those stately old middle-class homes, way up on a hill overlooking Lake Washington...the kind that developers love to get their hands on, tear down and put up million dollar estates in their places. So far Marianna's resisted all offers to sell. When the taxes go sky high and she gets hounded enough, she'll cave. But for right now, she enjoys her garden and her view of the lake and the lights of Seattle in the distance. She loves singing in her local choirs and of course, there's Charles.

I put my phone on speaker phone as my mom crooned, "Angelina... You and Walter are still coming...aren't you?"

"Of course, Mom...Sorry we're late...We're stuck on the bridge."

"Oh that's all right, dear. Just wanted to let you know there's been a change of plans. No pizza. I would like it if you and Walter could stay for an early dinner, before your appointment. Charles is here...and the twins—We're both watching them...and my Charles is barbecuing chicken and salmon."

"Charles on the grill?"

"Yes, isn't it wonderful?"

"Much better than pizza, Mom."

I began to salivate. *Need protein to fight off the bad guys—Sort of a Last Supper.*

"Mom...we can stay for dinner...but we have to leave by six."

"Charles and I will have everything ready...so when you get here, we can sit down to the table..."

"You're great, Mom. See you in twenty minutes, tops!"

Warm fuzzy time at my childhood home—spring flowers on the table...Jason and Jeffrey clowning around with Walter...Mom and I in the kitchen...Charles serving up his barbecue. I love a man who cooks. Apparently Marianna does too.

We all sat down together in my mom's library/dining room and said *Grace* before the meal. I found it difficult to suppress my tears. Walter squeezed my hand and kissed my cheek. That helped. My mother poured each of the adults a glass of champagne and the twins, sparkling apple cider.

I looked up at my mother and pleaded, "Mom...I'm working."

"This is a special occasion...Not to worry, my dear Angelina...I just poured you a little bit...and we'll have coffee later..."

Pebbles sneezed and nodded his head. He sat up straight and look at me. Seems even the dog knows something is up. Either that or he's begging for chicken. Jason threw him a piece of his thigh meat. Jason hates skin...and he knows Pebbles loves it. I groaned.

My mother took her place beside Charles and smiled at me, showing her wonderful set of pearly whites and winked at Walter..."Now, Tangie...and everyone...please, listen..."

Walter grinned. He knew. *The rat. Why didn't I know? I bet he's blocking my signals. He must have more hidden talents I have yet to discover...*

My mother sighed, looked at Charles and took his hand. "Angelina, Walter, Jason, Jeffrey...*My Charles*..."

My mother always refers to her boyfriend as My Charles...

"My Charles has proposed to me...and I've accepted."

I chugged the champagne...forgetting to wait for the end of the toast. Walter stood up and kissed my mom on her cheek and shook Charles' hand.

"Isn't this great, Angelina?" Walter said, as he squeezed my arm and tried to pull me up. I stuck to the chair like a hen roosting on her nest.

In slow motion, I inched myself up off my chair and gazed at my mother. She radiated joy like the sun poking out after a gloomy storm. Her glow lit up the room consuming me with its warmth. I steadied myself on the arm of the chair and then went over to my mother—my lifeline, and hugged her...clinging to her, wanting her warmth, her strength, her love to flow through me.

I turned to Charles and gave him a hug and wished him all the best.

Charles took my hand and kissed me on my cheek. "I didn't think the news would make you cry, Angelina. I am hoping you'll be glad for us..."

"Oh, Charles...I always cry when I'm happy." *Bluffing again.* "I'm delighted for both of you."

I looked at my mom, who proceeded to wave her arms and move her feet side to side...as if on a dance floor.

"Does Bryan know?" I whispered in short breaths.

"No, Angelina...You...Walter and the boys are the first to know... after me." She giggled. "I'll tell Bryan and Andee when they pick up Jason and Jeffrey..."

The twins, seeing their chance as the grownups chattered on, started shooting scalloped potatoes at one another. Jason got Jeffrey in the eye. Pebbles licked Jeffrey's remains off the floor. I poured myself another glass of champagne and chugged it.

"Wait, there's more," my mother announced, after kissing her fiancé and spinning around like a top...or a ballerina on Prozac.

Walter refilled his glass, then mine and clinked our glasses together while raising his eyebrows and shrugging his shoulders.

Charles grinned and provided us with what he thought would be pleasing information. "We'll be moving to Whidbey...this summer..."

I looked at my mother...searching her face. "Mom...Whidbey Island? That's in Island County..."

"I know, Sweetheart." My mom patted my cheek. "It's a beautiful island...and it's not the end of the world."

"We'll never see you..." I began to cry...feeling out of control with my life and my family.

"Oh, Tangie...Instead of driving over that crowded *Evergreen Floating Bridge*...or *I-90* every time you visit, you can relax on the ferry—you love ferry rides...No traffic...Just the seagulls to keep you company... We'll be a short distance from the dock...outside Langley. There will be so much for us to do when you visit—Walk the beach, browse in the antique shops...and don't forget... the gourmet restaurants—the Penn Cove mussels...the wineries..."

"Sounds inviting, Marianna." Walter tightened his hold on my waist, urging me to speak.

I looked around the room...feeling lost—Everybody but me smiling. I started grasping at straws. "What about your books?"

Charles answered me. "Marianna can take them with her...There's room in my home for a library...and we really do have room for all of you...Come up...stay for the weekend...for weeks...as long as you want... You'll always be welcome. It's quiet, it's peaceful...on the water."

"You have beachfront?" I felt my mouth drop slightly...like a fish without his gills.

"Well you have to hike down to it, but yes."

"This is all so sudden..."

My mother spoke up. "Well, *Carpe Diem*, Angelina."

Walter chuckled.

"Yes, Mom...Walter and I were just saying..."

"*Carpe Diem.*" Walter nodded and smiled at my mom. "Mrs. Seraphina, you are so right." He grabbed my left hand and patted it, waking me up to reality—and my civil duties as a daughter.

"Yes, Mom...*Carpe Diem.*" I echoed Walter's speech...wiping the tears from my face with my sleeve. "Congratulations to you both. When is the wedding? August?"

"How did you know?" My mother's eyes widened, then she smiled, remembering.

"August it is." meowed Charles.

This time he's the cat who caught the canary.

Walter took my right hand in his and brought it up to his lips. "Soon," he whispered in my ear. "Soon...our time will come, Angelina... Be patient...Our case is almost over...everything will turn out okay for us...you'll see—Don't sweat the small stuff, Sweetheart."

Walter put his arms around me and gave me a needed hug. I closed my eyes and leaned into him, trying to relax. Instead, I started to tear up again. I didn't want to sob in front of my mother—Too late. Marianna noticed. She came over to me, took my quivering hands and looked into my eyes, saying, "You are happy for me, aren't you, Angelina? It's been a long time..."

"I am...really I am, Mom...I'm just getting all emotional...Everything's just been piling up...you know, work...stuff like that...That's all."

"What's for dessert?" Jeffrey yelled at the top of his lungs.

"Finish your dinner, first, Buddy." Walter smiled, and ruffled up Jeffrey's hair. He seemed grateful to the little guy for the diversion. He poured me another glass of champagne and whispered, "I'm driving, Angelina...calm down...relax..."

Relax. Easy for him to say...but even in my stupor, I gotta say...I love this guy. He's good to me. My mom thinks so too...She keeps winking at him...

Marianna announced, "Come on...Let's continue our dinner. And I want to thank Charles, my favorite chef, for preparing us a gourmet feast...Grilled Salmon with lemon and wine...a little barbequed chicken on the side, asparagus...with hollandaise sauce...and more...Yum... Let's eat before it gets cold."

We all cheered for Charles. We ate. We drank. The twins devoured their dessert—chocolate cake and ice cream—and on a sugar high, proceeded to chase Pebbles all around the house. Their noise made no impact on any of us, except maybe poor Pebbles, as we laughed and cried over past memories and plans for the future. I carefully avoided thinking about the present ordeal looming over Walter and I. Despite all the happiness drifting around the room, I felt drained. My efforts to cloud the visions drifting out of my subconscious into reality exhausted me.

I heard my grandmother's antique mantle clock strike six times. Time to say good-bye...*Time to drive to Price's Funeral Home...Back to 520... over the Montlake Bridge...through the U. District...off to the neighborhood near the Arboretum...I can see the place...and I don't want to go.*

Walter pried my claws off the chair. After he did that, he started to tremble himself. He whispered, "How about if you stay here, at your mother's home...enjoy the party...I'll go meet Santigo...alone..."

"No...he's expecting me...he trusts me. If I'm not there, he's liable to bolt...but thanks...Walter...You're my main man." I looked in Walter's eyes and saw his fear—mounting fear, getting stronger...taking over.

"Walter...I'm sticking with you. You're the shoe...I'm the gum...We're the pair of gumshoes...and we're in this together."

I swallowed my last sip of coffee. *Bitter. My mother never makes bitter coffee. Why now? What's going on?* I hated to quiet the high spirits exploding all around us, but I had no choice. I turned to Marianna as my knees and arms started shaking. "Mom, We have to go. I'm sorry...We're out of time...We have to get back to work..."

I kissed her cheek and hugged her...giving her one of my extra-tight hugs I used to give her when I would leave for college. I could feel the warmth of her body and I didn't want to let go. I forced myself to smile and release myself from her loving embrace. I turned to Charles, shook his hand, then thought about his love for my mother and gave him a hug.

"Best wishes, Charles...Be good to my mom...She's special..."

"I know, Angelina." He returned my embrace with a bear hug.

Strong. Man of few words. I like that about him.

I called to my nephews as they raced around the living room couch with imaginary swords. They always make me smile, no matter what mood befalls me. "Jason, Jeffrey...Come...give me a hug...Be good for your Mimi. Be nice to Pebbles."

"We will...We promise, Auntie Tangie..." they answered in unison, as they pretended to drop their swords.

We all hugged one last time...Walter shook Charles' hand and whispered something in his ear...*Probably something like, "Good luck, old sport"—Walter loves to quote F. Scott Fitzgerald...and Charles no doubt understands his intent or pretends to...*

One minute we stood there...all smiling and saying good-bye and the next, we evaporated...into the night...No stars to lead the way...only darkness...and the cold chill of winter, not wanting to release its grip upon us...even though spring fought to take over. I could see the crocuses pushing their way up through the ground in my mother's front yard...but icy diamonds strangled their stems and choked their blossoms. Sometimes it's hard to go gently into the freezing night.

Chapter Thirty-Seven

Halfway to *Price's Funeral Home*, as Walter drove through the March winds, and I navigated, with tree branches blowing all over the place and a few smaller ones landing on our car, we reached the cut-off to the Montlake Bridge and entered the University District. My cell rang. *Simone calling.*

"Angelina?"

"Yes...Simone! What's happening?"

"Terese contacted me."

"Simone...I'm so glad. But, please...call her back. Tell your sister to lay low. Tell her under no circumstance should she contact her husband. Someone's watching Fred's home and workplace."

"I think it may be too late. I tried to talk some sense into her, but she's panic-stricken. She wouldn't listen. She said she has no clothes and she needs her outfits for her new job...She told me she plans to sneak into her house when Fred is gone to get her stuff...Terese is a clothes-horse...It's killing her to live out of one suitcase...she told me she needs her western apparel, of all things...you know—cowgirl boots and hat...I don't know what she's thinking..."

"Simone...Listen to me. I'm just a day away from contacting her and bringing her to a safe house. I know where to find her now. But if she goes home...she'll get hurt."

"Tangie...I'm scared..."

"We both are. Try to call her...or if she calls you back...tell her...No dice going home...Maybe she'll think twice. Please...make her listen to you...She can't contact Fred...She can't go home..."

"What if she already has?"

"Then, heaven help us."

Walter took his eyes off the road for a moment to give me a reassuring look, but it didn't work. I began to panic.

I spoke into the phone, with some confidence, but feeling helpless and in need of a good cry. " Look Simone...I'm doing all I can to protect her, without knowing her…without meeting her...If she calls you before I find her, tell her to go to a woman's shelter...the police...any place but near Fred Santigo or his home. He's under surveillance—by the bad guys. Got that?"

"I do. Help her, please….Find her. Promise me…She's all I have in the world."

"I'm trying…I will…I promise…and I'll contact Sheriff Tokala in Kodiak to keep an eye on you. You can trust him."

"What's to worry about up here in Alaska?—I thought perhaps since you left…the danger is over here…"

"No, Simone…no…that guy—in Kodiak...Remember…the brute that beat up Walter and got his mitts on me? He may still show up in Akhiok…looking for Terese…or you. He still doesn't know where she is…yet. Be careful. Lock your doors. Tell Pete and Michel to stay with you...until this is over...Don't handle the creep alone..."

"Does this creep have a name?"

"Horst. Horst Blouzer. He's dangerous."

"I'm a sitting duck."

"Please…keep your friends near. They'll protect you. Horst doesn't like to be double-teamed. He'll back down."

"Thanks for the warning. I'll try to reach Terese…right away… before she does anything foolish…Then, I'll knock on Pete's door… and before I return this satellite phone to my school director, I'll call Michel...I know he'll help me...He's always telling me to call him if I need anything…"

"Good. Take him up on it, Simone…and please…remember to…"

"Remember what?"

"To keep the faith. This nightmare will all be over soon."

"We should be so lucky," she said, as she sighed and said goodbye.

I pictured Simone sitting on her daybed with her quilt draped around her shoulder for warmth. Staring out the window. Looking for answers. Praying for her sister. *My hope is that Simone doesn't catch on that I am shaking in my boots. How can I operate this way? How can I reassure her when I'm a mess myself? She probably senses the desperation in my voice...*

I called Sheriff Tokala. Voicemail. *Okay...So I'll be coy.* I left a message. "Keep an eye on Simone." Then I elaborated...telling him I thought Horst returned...or never left Kodiak. *At least I didn't have to give my sources...The only source I have on this last bit of information is me... While I conversed with Simone, I kept having visions of Kodiak Bears and Horst. I just know he's there...Ready to pounce. He's getting anxious. He'll show no mercy. Somebody's got to stop him.*

The *Porsche Cayenne* pulled up to the curb. I could feel my heart pounding. "How'd we get here so soon?"

"I drive fast." Walter fastened the emergency brake and took a deep breath.

Price's Funeral Home—Place of death...a place I'd just as soon avoid.

Walter got out and opened the car door for me. He took my ice-cold hand and led me towards the well-kept stately Victorian home, now a reception area for the deceased. Foggy outside. *Fitting. Spooky. Could be Halloween for all we know—Cold enough for ghosts and goblins. Would spring ever get here? It's on the calendar...but who'd believe it?*

Walter—*Hopeless Romantic*—took my hand and kissed it and rubbed it with his...trying to warm me up. "I love you, Angelina."

"I love you too, Walter. Let's go home."

"Come on...We'll go in together...Just two grieving friends, paying our last respects." He lowered his voice. "Remember...Steve will be in the next room if we need him."

"That's some small comfort."

"Ready to go undercover?"

"I'm not a cop."

"No, but you can act."

"Walter...my knees are shaking. I can't walk."

"Lean on me. Play the grieving friend. I'll balance you...Your fear will be your grief."

I took a deep breath and with Walter's help, hobbled up the steps.

I hate funeral homes. As a seven-year old kid...in my dreams, I saw my dad die. I saw the car wreck...I saw his lifeless body...and I remember his funeral—The meeting place—Larson's Funeral Parlor and St. Catherine's Church... Then...the cemetery—St. Francis Eternal Place of Rest. Death. It's a hard reality for a little child to comprehend. I get flashbacks of my father's death, whenever I enter a place where bodies are laid out. The worst is the sweet smell of flowers...so out of place in this house of grief and mental anguish. Claustrophobia engulfs my being and the familiar nauseous feeling steam rolls inside me as my world starts spinning.

Tonight proved to be no exception. Same anxiety. Same fear. At the entrance, I tightened my grip on Walter's arm. Walter put his arm around me and opened the heavy wooden door, which shut automatically after we entered. We tiptoed into the first room on the right and inched over to the casket set up in the corner, near a wealth of carnations and lilies.

An elderly lady slept peacefully...on her way to her eternal rest.

"Doesn't she look gorgeous?"

I must have jumped a foot, not expecting the high-pitched voice... I pulled my eyes away from *Sleeping Beauty* as a painfully slim man, about six-foot six, dressed in pinstripes, spoke to me. He bore a remarkable resemblance to Icabod Crane. I relaxed when I read his nametag: *Glenn Price, Funeral Director.*

He took my hand. "Are you the granddaughter?"

"No. My grandmother is already dead, buried and up in heaven... *Praise the Lord*...I mean...err...We must be in the wrong room. We've come to see...err...Terese Santigo."

"Oh, Terese Santigo...the poor girl..."

"Yes...the poor girl..."

Walter spoke up. "Could you tell us where she is laid out?"

"Yes, of course. She is reclining in the next room—our *Room of Roses*. Just go out into the hall and turn left... She's right next door...resting by the fireplace. You can warm yourself up there."

He must be referring to the icicles that used to be my hands.

"Thank you, Mr. Price." Walter nodded, took my hand and led me out the door.

I stumbled down the hall. "For a...a...mo...moment, I thought Steve decided to play a s...s...sick joke on us." I started to chuckle, feeling like I was trapped in an avant-garde play production. *I often think that emotions are connected in a very strange way—Love/Hate...Tragedy/Comedy... Fear/...*

"*Comic relief*," Walter replied, reading my thoughts. "How's your stomach?"

"Better. Thanks, Walter. The churning ceased when I started laughing at Mr. Price. He's so serious."

"That's his job, Tangie...and...you know what our job is. Be careful. Try not to panic, Sweetheart."

"I promise...Stay close to me, Walter. Don't let appearances fool you. I'm still a train wreck."

Walter took my hand, kissed it and led me down the hall. He didn't seem to mind the coldness that he grasped. He just squeezed my hand tighter. We entered the *Room of Roses*. True to its name, it inhumed heavenly scents. *Roses*...They used to be my favorite flowers...*Don't know now.*

Terese's body double—lay in a casket next to the fireplace. As expected... cascades of pink and white roses overflowed on and off her casket...On the mantle, yellow and white blooms flourished...On the table...near the door...red and lavender-blue petals. The room smelled expensive. I spotted Santigo—decked out in a wool black suit, white shirt and red tie—sitting in a chair as if in a trance. Walter went over to him, tapped on his shoulder and shook his hand. Santigo got up and whispered, "*Mi Dios*, I'm scared to death."

I frowned. "Get a grip, Fred. This isn't easy for any of us."

"When do you expect the Sargentos?" Walter asked.

Santigo glanced at his watch—a *Rolex*. He wore his gold wedding band studded with rubies and diamonds, and kept twisting is as he gulped, "In about five minutes."

I studied the body in the casket. *Jane Doe...peaceful in death—A prostitute...I imagine...a runaway from a rotten home life. Young. No family to mourn her—No one to say a final farewell to her—except for us—strangers.*

I knelt down at the side of the casket and recited a prayer for the victim. I reflected that in her death, the poor girl is extending the life of another young girl in trouble...*Uncanny how much she looks like the photo of Terese. Probably shook up Fred too. Steve's guys at the morgue do exception work...or perhaps Mr. Price is the one to thank...*

Santigo started crying. I stopped my meditation and rose from my perch. His sobbing started to get on my nerves. My nervousness turned to annoyance at him. He stirred up my anger, giving me courage. I stopped shaking. *Weird.*

"Be the grieving husband, Fred," I barked at him. "Walter and I will sit over there... on the other side of the room. I'll say a rosary for this poor girl. You do your part."

"*Si*...I will give it my best...for *Terese*...and...this poor girl," he muttered as he wiped the tears from his eyes with a red silk handkerchief. *Fred knows the Sargentos...knows their evil...He witnessed their dirty deeds. I didn't—I guess he has a reason for his uncontrollable cowardice.*

I slumped down in one of the straight back chairs reserved for friends of the deceased and stared at my beautifully crafted rosary—a relic from the past—an early present from Don. For the last seven years, I kept it in my purse—unused. I touched the pearl beads—blue and soft to the touch...I started murmuring prayers...*Glory Be to God* and the *Hail Mary*—Prayers I learned as a child. They came back to me like a flood... and I started to cry uncontrollably. Walter put his arm around me and I buried my head in his chest.

He leaned over and whispered, "You're doing a great job as the grieving friend, Tangie, but you don't have to overdo it."

I looked up at him and watched his smiling face turn to panic. He grasped that my tears didn't happen to be the crocodile variety. Tears swelled up in his eyes. "I'm sorry...I'm sorry Tangie...for everything... I'll take you away from here..."

I squeezed his hand. "No. It's okay. I'm all right—You can't know everything, Walter...It's just...I don't...I don't want to lose you..."

"I'm not going anywhere..."

"Promise?"

"Yes...I'm a keeper."

My body relaxed and my shoulders stopped heaving. I looked over at Santigo. He appeared to be unraveling at the seams. He got up from his chair and started pacing and pulling on his hair. He looked strung out on electricity—only no glow. He glanced over at me. I motioned for him to sit down. He put his hands up in the air and then sat down in a soft pillow back chair near the coffin and started tugging on his tie as if it choked him. He unbuttoned his suit coat and patted his forehead with his handkerchief. Not a calming effect. Fred continued to sweat even after he wiped his brow.

I continued to feel frostbitten. I put my fingers on the beads of my rosary...willing them to thaw out...then I closed my eyes, trying to block out this house of horrors and my role in the whole fiasco. As I started the fourth decade of my *Hail Marys,* I heard the outside door open and shut. Footsteps...One heavy...tramping its way to us. The other, staggered, as if the person limped...or dragged an object. The roller coaster resumed, churning its way up and down in my stomach. Next would be the hyperventilating. I started doing my deep breathing. Walter caressed my hands. His warmth took the chill off my body. *I could do this...I could be a witness—piece of cake—Yeah...a piece of cake with dynamite inside of it.*

A solitary figure appeared in the doorway to the *Room of Roses*. He walked in slowly, dragging his left leg as he did so. He carried a cane looped over his arm. Thin, with a bit of a hunchback on his right side, he wore his black hair long... slicked to his head—looking like an ad for *Brillcream*—he fastened his greasy hair in a pony tail behind his back. You could tell a professional tailor altered his clothes—his suit fit him like a glove— not an easy task considering his uneven build. Under his grey suit jacket, he wore a pinstriped vest, white shirt and black tie. I noticed on the light wool jacket a gold pin in the shape of a wolf. *Funny, I didn't take him for the outdoorsy type.* He carried a black topcoat next to his cane and wore shiny black leather gloves. A white cashmere scarf adorned his shoulders. I sunk my eyes to his feet. Elevator shoes. *Figures. Napoleon complex. "He doesn't look like much of a threat...Just a professionally dressed, rather homely individual,"* I thought...That is...until he reached out with his gloved right hand and shook Fred's waiting hand. His high-pitched voice scratched my ears as he spoke. I detected a distinct Spanish accent, "So, Fred, have you been grieving the loss of your wife?"

More than the creepy tremble of his voice, his eyes gave him away. They penetrated everything and everyone in the room...Beady eyes... sharp...like the steel tip of an ancient sword. *This guy has done some dirty deeds. Don warned me—Told me to keep my distance from him—I must remember—Let the police handle him...*

Fred received Napoleon's hand and responded like a servant answering a king, begging for mercy, "Adolphus...This has been very hard for me." He released the clasp as soon as he was able and I noticed that he rubbed his hand as if it received an injury. For a lean guy, this *Adolphus* packed a heavy weight's punch.

I positioned my head to the side, so I could eavesdrop with ease.

Adolphus glared at Fred. When he spoke, his voice reminded me of fingernails scrapping the blackboard at school. I shuddered as I listened to the conversation.

"What are you going to do next?"

"I don't know. I can't think clearly."

"You should leave the thinking to those who have the brains. Let me have a look at your wife; then we'll talk."

Adolphus followed Fred over to the casket and studied the Terese look-alike. "She looks good...Price does remarkable work. I'll remember that."

Santigo nodded, unable to speak.

"Lift her head up for me, Fred. I want to look behind her neck."

"Fred lifted the body up as Adolphus Sargento looked behind the corpse's neck.

"So that's it," Adolphus croaked. "*Or not.*"

Fred looked around the room—panic-stricken. He glanced in my direction. I averted my eyes, not wanting Adolphus to get a glimpse of me. Fred went back to his chair by the casket, sat down and put his head in his hands. Adolphus pulled a straight-back chair from the crowd of invisible spectators. Except for us, the visitors' section held no captives. As Adolphus grabbed the chair, his eyes traveled around the room like those of a buzzard. He zoomed in on Walter. Not eager to catch Adolphus' gaze, Walter kept his face buried in a copy of *The Bible* he found on a nearby table. Adolphus switched his focus to me—this time like an owl doing his night vision hunting.

I dropped my head, dabbed my eyes with a handkerchief Walter gave me, and placed my hands on the rosary. No escape…I could still feel his eyes penetrating my person. I could feel his breath and sensed him digesting my body. I thought I would throw up—I could feel my last supper rising up to my throat. I kept my head frozen…down…out of view. No way did I want to make eye contact with this repugnant reptile. When Adolphus resumed speaking to Fred, I assumed my leaning over position. I could hear him confronting his next target. I may be scared to death, but I am earning my keep.

I studied Santigo. *Poor Fred…"Mama's hung you…in the closet…" Why in the world is the title of that old avant-garde play—"Oh Dad, Poor Dad…" coming into my mind? I'm losing it. I'm exhausted. I am so ready to give up this fight. As I contemplate how to make my flight, Adolphus opens his crooked mouth. He shows a set of pearly-white jagged teeth. Hollywood would seek him out...for their latest horror flick. If he ever gives up crime, he could find work in the movies.*

"*Mi amigo*, Fred...*mi hermano*..." Adolphus cawed like a crow and put his gloved hand on Fred's neck. "Sylvan had to go out…*uno momento*. We wait for him...then we talk."

Fred nodded, unable to speak. I could hear him making choking sounds. *Bad omen. Doesn't look good for him. He's got to get a grip on himself…or Adolphus will do it for him.*

Adolphus turned around in his chair and pointed his cane at Walter and me. "Who are those two gringos?" he hissed at Fred.

"*Amigos*...friends of Terese."

"Well, at least your *puta* has some mourners," he said, while chuckling under his breath—*A real sicko. Not the guy you want to meet in a dark alley.*

I glanced up at Adolphus Sargento...Sarcasm, anger and suspicion resonated in his voice...I could feel his anger…Hidden…He kept it under wraps…not allowing it to rise to the surface. Not good.

I grasped my rosary and found the fourth decade…anything to get my mind off thoughts of death and mayhem. I forgot myself and spoke aloud… "Holy, Mary, Mother of God…"

I kept my head down until I finished the final decade…and a second caller thundered into the *Room of Roses*. A tall, elegantly dressed man with a crop of white-blond hair crept over to Fred and Adolphus. He moved like a demented panther ready to strike...and snarled in a low-pitched voice, "Adolphus…"

No respect for the dead.

Adolphus left his chair, put his hand on the panther and resonated in his sinister *fingernails scraping the chalkboard* voice, "Sylvan...We're in a funeral parlor. Show some decency. Look at poor *Terese*. Do you want to call attention to yourself?"

Sylvan leaned over and whispered something in his brother's ear.

I couldn't hear that one. Probably needed that piece of information, too. Rats.

Adolphus patted Sylvan on the arm…he couldn't reach his shoulder. "I'm not surprised," he answered. "Good work, *mi hermano. Muchas gracias*."

Then Adolphus turned to Fred. He placed a death grip on the poor chump's arm and dictated, "Now we talk. Outside. Suppose you walk with Sylvan and me to our limo. We don't want to disturb your guests."

Walter and I kept our heads down as Sylvan seized Fred and escorted him out the door and down the hall. Adolphus, no longer limping, followed the two of them out with a sharp gait. The ornate cane used for walking transformed—into an ornament—or worse…a weapon of torture. *Poor Fred.* A sense of doom consumed me. *Curtains. We've got to help him.*

Walter and I rose simultaneously and walked gingerly out into the hallway…just as we heard the entrance door shut. We scrambled over to the heavy carved wooden door adorned with stained glass. We peaked out through the clear part of the glass in the door, seeing only a blurry picture. Walter opened the door a crack and peeked out first, then me. I could see Fred being pushed into a black limo parked under the only street lamp. The car shone like a tomb in the moonlight. Adolphus crawled in after his brother and motioned to the driver, a young curvaceous woman with light blond hair, who wore a lot of eye make up. I didn't recognize her. She did look familiar, like I had seen her or someone that looked like her, once before.

"We've got to follow them," Walter whispered. "We don't want to lose them—We've ID'd them...We can't let them get away..."

"What about Steve? What about the police?" I felt the panic rise in my voice.

"Don't worry, Tang...Steve will be right behind us—He's in the next room...He'll radio for help...We have to hurry...Fred's in a pickle...I think the Sargentos suspect Terese is a fake..."

"Oh no...Not good for Fred. Damn...What else can go wrong?"

"Don't ask, Sweetheart."

Walter started deep breathing...*self-talk...willing himself to go on...He knew...and it's bad. My rock. Crumbling. We're toast.*

Walter leaned underneath the car and put something under the front fender. *Tracking device, no doubt. At least my boy scout is prepared.*

"Steve will follow us. I activated our signal," Walter reassured me.

"He'd better."

"We can't go into this situation alone, Tangie. We need the help of the police."

"Now that's the most comforting thing I've heard in awhile." I hurried into Walter's *Porsche SUV* and buckled my seatbelt.

Walter rolled the vehicle out of its space, pulled out his phone and pressed one button. "Steve, we're out of here. Follow us. Pronto. Call for backup—The Sargentos have Fred—We've got to catch up to them before..."

Walter closed his cell phone, gazed at my eyes in the dark and handed me a miniscule device. "Put this in your purse. Wrap your purse around your neck...In case we get separated."

"Walter, don't leave me."

"I have no intention of leaving you...ever. This is insurance."

I studied the tiny metal circle with a light glowing in the center and made a feeble attempt at humor. "Beam me up, Scottie,"

Walter sighed. "Seriously, Tangie...This device is designed to protect you...You have a way of wandering off..."

I tried to reassure him. "Walter. I'm sticking with you. No way I'm gonna leave your side. No way." I looked at the road ahead...very few cars out tonight. "Where are we headed?"

"Looks like the limo is turning in at Broadmoor. Gated community. Figures. Nothing happens in gated neighborhoods."

"Till now."

"Great cover."

"Walter...how are we gonna get in?"

"We've been deputized, remember?"

"Oh yeah...Tangie—The cop. Walter—The vice detective—Seattle's in trouble."

"I have a badge."

"Clout."

When we made our approach to the gate at Broadmoor, Walter, good to his word, pulled out a badge and showed it to the sentinel on duty. "Good evening, sir."

The guard smiled. "Oh...Good evening, officer. Out for a patrol?" No doubt, the guard, a man about Charles' age, probably used this job as his retirement gig—Keeper of the Gate.

Walter nodded his head and put his hand to his lips. "We're undercover. Hush, hush."

"Anything I can do to help?"

"Do you know where the limo—that just passed through the entrance—is headed?"

"Well, I saw Mr. Santigo in the back seat. He didn't look so good. I guess he's being driven home...But...strange...He left earlier in his own car."

"Maybe he had too much to drink," I added.

"Could you tell us where he lives?" Walter asked. "We need to speak with Mr. Santigo about a complaint."

The guard nodded and got serious in his speech, like he didn't want any trouble. He picked up a clipboard that had been hanging on a hook and recited, "He lives at 324 Red Vine Maple. Follow this entrance street for five blocks and then turn left. Fifth estate on the right."

"Got it. If another policeman comes by, flag him in immediately."

"Certainly."

I looked at the nametag on his uniform. "Thanks a lot...Mr. Sweeney. Keep up the good work."

"Will do, Ma'am." He tipped his hat to me. *Maybe I have clout too. Just not as much. I am beginning to feel like a cop...So far, not so bad.*

"So...We're officers now," I remarked to Walter, as we drove through the gate.

"Whatever works."

"It's hard enough being psychic...Don't know if I wanna be a psychic cop."

"It's only temporary, Tangie."

"If it lasts longer than tonight, I'm taking jujitsu lessons."

"That's fine with me, Tang...but I have a feeling this will all be over after tonight."

"Is this a good feeling or a bad feeling you are having?"

Walter never answered me. He slowed the car down and pulled the car over to the curb. "Uh oh..."

"Uh oh, what?"

"Tangie...Something's wrong."

"No kiddin'."

"I'm serious...Look..."

I looked out my window and saw a massive Georgian Colonial. Not my taste, but it reeked of money. Emerald green grass...Manicured... Outdoor lighting illuminated the lawn and the entrance to the door...The door...The door was ajar...with an arm sticking out of it. My eyes zeroed in on the hand...and then the fingers...I could see Santigo's diamond and ruby ring on his wedding finger...twinkling in the bright light of the massive carriage lamp...the lamp glowing like a vigilant gargoyle over the front entrance...The immobile hand, wearing the familiar jewel, beckoned us into its lair with a death grip on the door.

"Stay here," Walter commanded. "Lock the car doors." He stepped out and scrambled up the walk.

I opened my door, jumped out of the front seat and ran after Walter. "Walter, you can't play the *Lone Ranger* without *Tonto*. I refuse to stay in the car. Remember...you aren't gonna leave me."

"Tangie...Please," Walter pleaded—fear pulsating from his eyes. I could feel his panic...I could not leave him.

"Walter, I can't help it. I can't stay alone...even in a locked car...I promise...I'll be careful." I followed after him...up the stairs to the doorway.

Walter tried to open the door. Stuck. He reached inside the door with his foot and pushed the body over—clearing the entrance.

Walter took my hand and together we went inside the house. The foyer appeared empty except for the body. Walter rolled over the figure of a man...a man whose identity I knew before his face appeared. Santigo. Walter bent down and felt Fred's wrist and then his neck.

"He has a faint pulse, Tangie." Walter gasped as he touched the body. Then, he leaned down to listen to Santigo's heart and next, he put his ear by Fred's mouth, searching for a breath. "No air coming out."

Walter ripped open Santigo's shirt. I could see a burn mark on his chest—a recent burn—practically steaming...Someone branded his skin...I could make out initials...and numbers...*AS1SS2...Where did I see that mark before? Somewhere...*

Walter began performing CPR...First the pressures...then leaning down...still no air..."Call *911*," he yelled, between pumps on Santigo's chest. I took my cell out of my purse and peered out the doorway...I heard a rustling noise...Then a tree branch snap against the window...the March wind...Not a car in sight...I turned back to watch Walter frantically trying to save Santigo's life...I saw Walter leaning over Fred's body and listening for a heart beat...Fred's face...chalky white. Eyes...staring—wide open...His hair—still sticking straight up—as though struck by lightening. The poor guy had a look of frozen panic upon his face...as if he beheld Medusa in his gaze, or some other strange beast of folklore.

I shuddered and pressed *9-1-1* while Walter resumed pumping on Fred's chest. As I took my finger off the send button, I felt a crushing weight on my shoulders, an iron stronghold on my mouth and neck...then a sickening, sweet odor. I could feel the phone being squeezed out of my hand and my feet being lifted up and my body floating out the door...towards the rear of the house...My vision blurred...I could see a fading blinking light in the distance...before the darkness consumed me and I felt nothing, nothing at all.

Chapter Thirty-Eight

Bump. Bump-pity bump—A sound...reminiscent of the *Tilt-a-Whirl* at the old *Seattle Center Fun Park*...Only I am face down in this ride. *Where am I?* I try to lift my head, but cannot. I try to open my eyes but I cannot. I try to remember where I am but I cannot...I hear a humming sound...a motor...There is a lump under my waist. I feel the floor... it's a rug...a coarse rug...like in a car...a car. That's it...I'm in a car...I remember! Walter! Pumping Fred's chest...but what's happened to me? I feel all squished...like a sardine in a can. I put my hands down and pushed up off the floor. I try to focus, but everything in my field of vision remains blurry. I sit up on the floor and squint. I see ten curved, elongated fingernails—sharpened like little knives. *Where did I see them before? ...Outside the police station...That woman...that woman I tripped over...*My vision becomes clearer...No longer an abstract painting...but the fingernails belong to a man this time...a man in a dark coat...with a pony tail and a cigarette holder...*Sargento...Adolphus Sargento.*

Sitting next to him is a picture of a raven-haired beauty...*Terese*... only this picture is real! *I found her!* I open my mouth to speak her name but before I can get a word out, I feel a crushing blow to my head...and darkness consumes my world again.

When I come to the second time, I do not open my eyes...Scared of the consequences...or a fast learner. Now I lay on a flat surface...Cold concrete greets me... and kisses my face. No movement, no vibrations. Guess they threw me out of the car—the Sargento Limo. I smell gasoline. *Must be in a closed space. Cold. Damp.* I want to move, but dare not budge. I want to get up off this garage floor—It's freezing...and the smell makes me nauseous—but I know better. I try not to breathe audibly. *Tough...Next to impossible.* I want to gasp and scream. I listen to the voices swirling around me. First the sound of Fred's secretary—haughty—unfeeling—hard...I recognize her German accent...her condescending tone. Laughing at me. Taunting...

Then I hear her flirting with Sylvan, Adolphus' brother; he joins in her laughter...and responds to her affections toward him.

I hear moaning. Then silence...

I lay on the garage floor wondering when they will force my eyes open as I squeeze them tight and hold my breath.

*I sense Sylvan, the panther growling, ready to strike...*I hear his voice, guttural this time conversing with his brother. "So, Adolphus...what do you want me to do with these two putas? How about if I brand them?"

"Later, Sylvan..." Adolphus answers. "I'm not in the mood for the screaming. I have to think. Put that hot iron down! Listen to me...for the last time. We need these girls to work for us. Horst is never around when we have a deadline and someone has to load our shipment—might as well be them. We've got to vacate this place, pronto."

"They're weaklings."

"If we beat them, they'll be as strong as we want them to be."

"Then what?"

"Perhaps we'll take them with us...to our American compound... you know...the one outside Coeur D'Alene. We owe them a visit. From there we go to *The Summit* in Columbia. These beauties will fetch a pretty price in South America. New blood. Exotic. *Bellissima.*"

"*Si*, Adolphus. We could sell them to the Terrorists—They're always looking for new prostitutes. And they pay good money. What shall we do with Marlaine?"

Marlaine interrupts, snarling...her tone changed...no longer that of a loving spouse. "I'm your wife, Sylvan! You owe me." *Somehow I don't think her caustic remark will endear her to him...Yep, I'm right.* Sylvan turns his impatience, about not branding Terese and me, towards Marlaine. I hear a face being slapped...then a choking sound.

"I owe you nothing," Sylvan shouts. "You're here, because we let you stay with us."

I think to myself, she should let it drop, but she keeps hounding her husband, raising her voice, saying, "I help you get into dis country. I hide you in der Fatherland when you need to get away. You stay with my family in Munich. They feed you...and take care of you—like you are der blood...and dis...this is how you pay me back?"

"Look, Marlaine. *Comprende*—you're nothing to me. Just a—what do they say in America? Just a piece—You've served your purpose."

"To think of what I give...what I gave up for you..."

"You gave up nothing you didn't want to lose...only thing is, I don't know who would want you now...and when I'm through with you, I don't know anyone who would touch you."

Adolphus interrupts Sylvan's tirade. "Later. We've got unloading to do. Idate prisa!"

I felt a kick in my side, and a prodding with a hard object—Adolphus's cane—Then a sickening, sweet voice beckoning me out of my self-enforced darkness.

"Wake up, Angelina, my little nightingale."

I resisted, not wanting to visualize my fate.

"Sylvan, get the salts."

Ammonia. Stuck under my noise. I sneezed as two strong arms grabbed me and stood me up, as the scent forced my eyes open. Sylvan held me under my arms as Adolphus stroked my hair with his fingernails. I wanted to throw up. I became the despondent character in a horror show...but this was no movie. Without any will of my own, I cringed. Instinct told me showing emotion would make things worse for me.

Adolphus stared at me with his ferret eyes. "You don't like us."

"I don't know you." My throat parched, I could only talk in a whisper.

"But you know about us," Adolphus snarled and touched my check with his index finger.

I found it hard not to scream. I began to have an inkling of what drives people mad.

"We have to keep you, my sweet one," the Ferret continued. "You know too much. But don't worry. You won't be with us long. Alas, the ones to whom we sell you are the monsters. They will treat you worse than we do. Count on it."

Then he laughed—His cackle being worse than his speech. Maniacal. Panting like a wild animal, he kissed me hard on the lips, pressing his fingernails into my arms, pricking them. I let out a silent scream, which turned into a whimper.

"I think you will talk to us. Tell us some more of what you know… after we brand you. The others all talk after the iron. You will too. We'd like to know where your secretary lives. You see, I don't want to poison you, like the others—To kill you would be a waste of beauty. You talk—we let you live."

Adolphus unscrewed the thimble that was attached to his right index finger. He took out one white capsule. "If you give us any trouble," he growled, "We give you one of these. *Death comes quickly*."

"Like Fred…"

"*Like Fred*."

I swallowed and felt a rush of a dinner…from a long time ago, rising to the surface. I took a deep breath and held it in and then let it out slowly, trying to calm myself.

Adophus, noticing my distress, continued his harangue, without hesitation. "The chump…wanted us to let Terese go. Had to fight us. That's impossible. No one fights us and lives. You aren't going to fight us, Angelina, are you?" he crooned in his high-pitched scratching voice… as he twirled my hair with his fingertips.

"No…I will work for you." I cringed inwardly and thought…*Hard labor will buy me some time.*

"Good girl. That is the right answer," Adolphus smiled and showed his jagged white teeth…up close and personal. I gasped. He pulled my hair back and I screamed in silence as kissed me hard on my lips. I tasted blood. This time the terror consumed me...Bile rose in my throat. Any courage reserved in any part of my psyche, evaporated with the ferret's touch.

"Now, Angelina...Keep your mouth shut. *Silencio*...until we question you. *Comprende?* I don't like conversation."

I nodded. *No way did I plan to have small talk with this monster.*

Adolphus turned his attention away from me and barked an order at his brother. "Sylvan...Get Terese up. She's had enough rest. Be a gentleman. Give her a handkerchief."

I looked down on the floor and zeroed in on Terese lying in a grease spot near the limo, bleeding from a jagged cut on her left cheek and a cut over her right eye. *Poor girl. She probably didn't want to wake up either. Not much to look forward to around here.*

Adolphus acknowledged Marlaine, as she slumped on the concrete floor, leaning against the limo. "Marlaine, if you behave, we may keep you. You're a good secretary. Come with me. You can teach the pretty girls what we do around here."

Marlaine nodded, defeated. She pried herself off the cement floor, straightened out her dress, fluffed up her hair and then glared at Terese and me.

Adolphus motioned us to follow Marlaine.

Sylvan put a death grip on my left shoulder, squeezing me until I cried out involuntarily in pain. It came out as a moan ...I didn't want to make any noise to stir up Adolphus' wrath. *Survival Skills. So what if I turn into a whimp. When in Rome...*

Sylvan spoke directly to me for the first time, as he kept his hold on me. "Such a pity...you'd be a good woman...*for me*...if you weren't such a snoop."

"It's my job," I whispered, defending my honor.

"No job for a pretty *puta* like you."

Marlaine's eyes continued to glare at me. I clamped up. No chance of sisterhood with her. She still loves the jerk, even though he abuses her.

Sylvan turned his attention away from me and started kicking Terese in the side. She groaned softly, like a wounded fawn. Like me, she knew better than to scream.

Adolphus turned around and smiled at his brother. "Ease up on Terese, Sylvan. I have plans for our little treasure."

"Ah, *mi hermano*...I just pushed her around a little..."

Adolphus feasted his piercing eyes on Terese, grabbed her hair and cackled. "Hey, Terese...Show me your butterfly tattoo. Funny...your body double didn't have one. Your husband, Santigo—*the fool*...thought I wouldn't notice. Hah...I notice everything. But Santigo—not too sharp—your famila...didn't even notice the brand on the double's arm—*My brand.* Sure, Senor Price covered it up with makeup, but I knew it was there. Santigo...Ha! Lacking in the brains department—the traitor... Imagine planting a body, a body that I extinguished...and he thought I wouldn't know...wouldn't know it wasn't you...Wouldn't recognize my own kill. I will say she looked a lot like you...she had great looks... Bellissima...That's why I took her in the first place...I called her *My Belle*...But she wouldn't cooperate—wouldn't give me what I needed... Maybe you can be her replacement...Yes, I'll keep you for myself...You can be my little butterfly."

"I'm not your anything," Terese yelled back at him, squirming from his grasp, losing a few hairs in the process as she collapsed on the cement floor.

"Hit her again, Sylvan. She doesn't understand."

I closed my eyes. I heard a scream and then quiet sobbing.

Adolphus' voice echoed delight in Terese's torment as he continued to jeer at her. "*Comprendes mi belleza?* You belong to me now. No more independent American...Just my dutiful puta. No more the little butterfly that flies away."

I opened my eyes to see Terese dabbing her cheek and her mouth with the handkerchief, blood soaking into the thin material. This time Terese did not take Adolphus' bait. She remained silent, with downcast eyes.

Adolphus grasped Terese, pulling her close to him, forcing her to look in his eyes and smiled his nightmarish grin. Then he released her and pushed her forward, commanding her in his sinister voice..."Follow Marlaine."

He glared at me and hissed, "You too, *detective*."

Like prisoners facing a firing squad, Terese and I marched in a straight line out of our *holding cell*...led by Marlaine. As we did so, I glanced furtively at our surroundings...Over-sized garage. No windows. The Sargento's black limo—taking center stage, parked alongside a Silver *Hummer*—no doubt a getaway car. The environment—dark—a dim light shining overhead, like a unwilling moon—and a strange...strong odor...of kerosene...swirling around—making me woozy...making me surmise their plans for us...our future doom.

Adolphus barked, "Pronto, pronto...my pretties...you have much work to do."

I averted my focus from Adolphus to Marlaine and forced myself to follow Sylvan's wife. Marlaine strutted ahead of Terese and me, wiggling her hips and clicking her high heels on the concrete floor. She caught up to Sylvan, who began ascending a flight of stairs ahead of all of us. Terese and I stayed in our single line and proceeded after Marlaine and Sylvan. Adolphus stepped aside to watch us from the rear. When Sylvan reached the top landing, Adolphus tossed him a key, and Sylvan unlocked a door, pushed it open, went through and then motioned us to enter. We obeyed. *What else could we do?* Terese and I found ourselves surrounded by plumbing supplies...and a neon sign flashing *Numero Uno Bath Boutique.* I looked out the front showroom window...I could see Pike Street in the distance...and downtown Seattle. *I knew our location!* Somehow that little bit of knowledge comforted me.

I sighed.

Adolphus shut the door to the garage and came over, past me, to the showroom window and pulled the plug on the neon sign. He turned and his eyes penetrated mine. "You recognize this place?"

"I've never been here before," I whispered—*That's the truth...I just know the location...Maybe Walter would put two and two together—It's possible. The tracking device! In my purse! Where is my purse? Rats. Probably lying next to my phone on the floor of Santigo's house. Santigo...Poor guy...Dead, no doubt...and I don't think I ever told Walter the name of Santigo's business...How could I be such a lame brain?*

I sensed Adolphus reading my thoughts. *His radar is up. Great—An evil psychic—as if I don't have enough on my plate...God, if you hear me, please...I can't handle much more of this...*

"Funny little *detective*...praying..." Adolphus chuckled, in his evil sardonic way. "You think you can get away. We found your tracking device. It's on a *Metro Bus* as we speak…riding around the city. Maybe it will wind up in West Seattle or Renton, if we're lucky. Your *secretary* will have fun with that one. He'll never find you."

The chuckle turned into a manic-choking sound and then coughing. Adolphus' beady eyes looked like they were going to pop out of their sockets. Sylvan joined in the hoopla and patted Adophus on the back.

As they hooted and carried on like malevolent fiends lost in their madness—Sylvan, the chimera and Adolphus, the gorgon—both appeared to be creatures from the netherworld—with Sylvan wiping tears from his eyes in manic laughter and Adophus doing an insane jig.

Terese tapped my arm and whispered, "Thank you for trying to help me."

I glanced at her and noticed the poor beauty studying me through uncontrollable tears. I observed that—despite two bloodshot eyes that began to swell up and streams of blood oozing from the wound on her cheek and lips—she could pass as a goddess. Terese didn't deserve this treatment. She played no part in Fred's stupidity—his association with these psychopaths.

I wiped the tears from my eyes with my sleeve and tried to account for my actions. "You're welcome, Terese—but I didn't do so good…I'm sorry about Fred. I tried to support him...but everything went wrong at the last minute…"

"I'm the one that's sorry…I never should have gone to the house—for what? Clothes? Don't beat yourself up. It's not your fault…you almost pulled it off…we almost got away…but now…there's nothing." She cried softly, like a kitten whimpering for its mother.

"Please…don't give up, Terese…please…I need you to be strong." I encouraged her with a confidence I did not feel.

"No talking. Silencio!" Adolphus advanced towards us and struck me over the head, with his cane.

A lead balloon—Now I know the meaning of that term. Sometimes you have to be hit on the head to understand things…What a dummy I am…If I ever get out of this mess, I will know better…I promise I will never... I closed my eyes. I could see stars. *Really. It's not just an expression.* When I opened my eyes, the room started spinning. Terese held onto me. "Don't fall down. It will be worse for you."

My eyes became slits as I leaned on her, trying to focus...everything around me started to get blurry...even Terese. Shaking consumed my body and I took a deep breath, trying hard not to faint.

Adolphus shouted at me, "Angelina!"

I opened my eyes wide and willed myself to stand, despite the room spinning around me. Vertigo took a hold of me and would not let go. I ignored it and started walking towards him, abet unsteady.

"Hurry over to those commodes," he commanded as he waved his cane. "Put your hands inside them and pull out the packages. Don't forget to put down the seat when you are done." Adolphus' last order amused him...He forgot his anger towards me and started laughing like a hyena. "Put the packages by the front door."

I complied with his orders as bidets and toilets kept floating around my head in circles. I stiffened myself upright and began serving my sentence—unloading from the porcelain displays the packages—Cocaine and cash, no doubt.

"Terese," Adolphus snarled. Go to the sinks...the vanities. Search beneath them. Take the bundles out and go with Angelina over to the front doorway. Stack them. Be careful with them. Pronto."

He turned to Marlaine. "Marlaine, you go supervise. I need to rest... I need time to think."

"Ya, Herr Sargento." Marlaine lowered her eyes for a moment, turned her attention on Terese and me. "*Mach Snell*," she barked, like a sergeant at arms. "Let's get to verk." She marched us into the showroom, depositing us at our workplace among the plumbing fixtures.

Adolphus motioned to Sylvan and handed him a cell phone, saying, "*Mi hermano*, get Horst on the phone." Then he went over to a desk in the center of the showroom and sat down on an overstuffed chair. He perched himself there like a grey spider spinning his web.

Sylvan pushed a button and handed his brother the phone, saying, "Adolphus, I got Horst on the line."

"Put him on speaker phone."

Sylvan pushed another button and sat the phone on the desk in front of Adolphus.

A deep voice called out, "*Gutten abend.*"

"Horst!" Adolphus yelled. "Where the hell are you?"

"Still in Kodiak. You know vat, Adolphus...you sent me on...how do they say it in America? A...a vild goose chase."

"Well, come back. You're finished there. You don't have to go there anymore. We're going back to Idaho...to our compound there... *Adairwolf*...You know where...if you can't get there in a week, meet us at *The Summit*...you know...in Columbia...Hurry. We need your help... to help train these *putas*, among other things.

"You have new prostitutes?"

"A couple. One of the *putas* is Terese...she fell into our arms—We didn't even have to look for her. The other one, you'll recognize when you see her."

"So you got Terese?"

"*Si*. You can forget about her sister. She's no use to us anymore. Unless you want a woman."

"Not that von—Too much verk. I already paid her a visit. Put the squeeze on her. She vould have talked too, but dez two guys burst in... just as I vas getting up close and personal...One an old geezer vith a shotgun and den some young punk vaving a board at me. They took me by surprise. But I punched der lights out before I left...but now der sheriff's looking for me."

"Stupido."

"Don't vorry. I've got it covered. I'm a hiding in zee voods...Reminds me of der Black Forest. I'll-a drive back, but I got to vait it out a day or two. My plan is to catch da ferry to da mainland. Den, I get a R.V. in Anchorage and take da highway to Canada...Den I catch da plane. First, I got to lose dez guys. They'll-a be tailing me if I don't vatch out."

"Where are you now?"

"Some place...they call *Kodiak State Park*. Camping...like a touristo...sittin' out under da stars, cookin' mein sauerbraten."

"There are no tourists in April. Watch out for bears."

"Yah, yah...Any Kodiaks come near me, dey get shot."

"Unless they get you first. Ever encounter a bear?"

"Yah...in Germany...They have bears. We Germans train dem to dance. Ever been to der Black Forest?"

Sylvan, chuckled, "He thinks he's in the zoo, Adolphus."

"*Silencio*, Sylvan...I can't hear Horst." Adolphus glared at his brother and then continued his phone conversation.

I listened intently, a fly on the wall, as I labored under Marlaine's watch. I looked at my prison guard. Like me, Marlaine seemed spellbound by Horst's voice on the speakerphone—all ears—holding onto every word Horst uttered. She forgot to watch me. If I weren't keen on protecting Terese, I could have slipped away...out the front door...

Adolphus completed his orders..."Horst, remember...meet Sylvan and me in Columbia—if you're longer than a week...and go to *The Summit*. We'll only be in Idaho for a few days...just long enough to unload our supplies...If you get here early...go to *Adairwolf*. Late... Columbia. Got it?"

"*Yah, yah, Herr Sargento...Numero Uno*...Augh...Helppp...No... Nine!"

I hear a blood-curdling scream, then static...then a growl that will give me nightmares for weeks...then nothing.

The speakerphone dies along with Horst's voice. An eerie silence ensues in the showroom. I shudder and look at Marlaine. I cannot read her face.

Adolphus glared at Sylvan. I forced my head down as I slaved away, but continued to sneak peeks and eavesdrop on any future dialogue between the brothers.

Adolphus turned his phone off, started pacing back and forth, like a panther in distress, then growled at Sylvan, "Neither Horst nor that satellite phone is worth the money I shell out..."

Sylvan nodded. Then he smiled. "Horst is...*was*...a fool."

"Worthless piece of..."

Sylvan interrupted Adolphus' ranting. "Adolphus...want me to get the suitcases?" The ferret returned to his seat and nodded. "*Si*...They're in the Hummer." He reached in his pocket, took out his keys and tossed them to Sylvan. "Drive the Hummer around front and bring the suitcases in the front door...Our little *putas* will fill them up...Hurry...*Pronto!*"

Adolphus left his perch and walked over to the door leading to the garage, let Sylvan out and then relocked the door. He came back to us and zeroed in on Fred's secretary. "Marlaine...I thought you were one of us."

"I am."

"Then remember to keep your place, and your mouth shut."

"I understand, Adolphus...I will. But please, tell me how is Horst... How is mein bruder?

"Horst? Bear meat before you see him again," Adolphus cackled.

Marlaine turned white and cried, "No! Not *mein bruderlein*!"

Adolphus started his maniacal laughter again. The horror show continued. Adolphus resumed his place at the order desk and continued to stare at us, while playing with a gun in his lap, and periodically would aim the pistol, a Glock, at us. We labored in silence, unloading small packages and large bundles for a half-hour. Marlaine continued to watch us through glassy eyes and motioned to us now and then, pointing what direction to go in and urging us not to stop *verking*...but somehow, I knew her heart wasn't in bossing us around. My back began to hurt from the bending. The packages didn't weigh much, but there were tons of them. Terese had the heavy bundles. I don't know how she did it. She didn't look very strong. She must have built up her muscles waitressing all winter.

Some of the packages were wrapped in red, some in green. All the larger bundles were white. Each package and bundle was neatly tied up with string. When stacked together, they could pass for Christmas presents...except it's April...That's what Adolphus said...Funny when I left my mother's home it was March...March 31st...*It must be after midnight now...April Fools' Day. Here we are...in a house of fools. But nothing's funny.*

Sylvan opened up the front door with a key and dragged in four oversized American Tourister suitcases. Adolphus left his perch at the desk to confront us...waving his Glock and shouting orders at Terese and I. "Hey...*Dos prostitutas entender*? Time to start loading the merchandise."

Terese and I stored the cache of packages into the four suitcases until we ran out of room. Sylvan came in with two footlockers. We packed half of the bundles into them.

Adolphus barked some orders at Sylvan. "Sylvan, get the limo. We'll load the rest of our *supplies* into plumbing crates."

Sylvan raised his eyebrows. "Will they fit in the limo?"

"We'll make room; don't question me. Just do what I say."

Sylvan shrugged his shoulders and departed. I could detect some words coming out of his mouth in German, but I could not make them out.

Adolphus shook his head. He tossed another set of keys to Marlaine. "Marlaine...You...you will be my driver. We'll change the plates on the limo before we leave. But first go into Santigo's office. Get the boxes, crates and a screwdriver. The crates are folded. Unfold them and bring them out here."

Marlaine left without a word...leaving Adolphus to torment Terese and me—his eyes piercing us with an icy glare...like a hyena stalking its prey. No emotion except the thrill of the hunt. The two of us stood in front of him and leaned against the wall, afraid to speak.

"Now it's time for you to carry these suitcases outside," he said, in a matter of fact tone. "Carry them to the Hummer." He aimed his Glock at us. "Don't try anything. I'm an excellent shot."

His trigger finger was free of a curved fingernail. *I believe he could shoot us both without blinking an eye.*

Terese and I dragged the suitcases to the Hummer, one by one. Together, we hauled them up, loading them into the back of the getaway car—just as Sylvan drove up in the limo. Then at Adolphus' insistence, we went back into Fred's former showroom and almost bumped into Marlaine, who appeared out of nowhere with two boxes.

Adolphus smiled and his face took on the appearance of a snake. I shuddered and looked at Terese. She simply looked at the floor. Better not to make eye contact with him. *She's a fast learner, unlike me.*

"Now, *mis gatos*," Adolphus whispered—deliberately speaking softly, as if to confuse us—"Load the boxes and put them in the limo."

We put our heads down and went to work. Marlaine announced, "I need to get the last of the crates...there are two still left in the office."

Adolphus dismissed Marlaine with a wave of his left hand as he spotted Sylvan leaning on the doorway, awaiting orders. With a triumphant tone in his voice, *Numero Uno* announced to his brother, "Sylvan, it's time to light the fire."

Sylvan nodded as Adolphus tossed him a key to the back exit door. Dutiful brother—*Numero Deos*—unlocked the door and disappeared down the staircase.

Terese and I scrambled to the front entrance, dragged the two boxed, lead weights out the doorway, to the car and, lifting them together, heaved the backbreakers into the rear of the limo. Adolphus leered after us with his Glock in one hand and his lead poker cane in the other—with which he continually beat upon our shoulders, shouting at us, "*Apuro, apuro*!"

Upon finishing loading the boxes into the vehicle, Terese and I shut the limo door while Adolphus hustled us back into the showroom, hurling curses at us—insults being his drug of choice. He became the prison guard and we became the criminals. *Everything's relative in the world of crime.* As we trudged obediently back into the showroom, to load the last of Adolphus' loot, I caught Marlaine in the corner of my eye—Marlaine marching towards us with the last two crates...and something else in her hands.

Adolphus...consumed with taunting Terese and me, ignored Marlaine. He continued waving his Glock at us, telling Terese and me to stand against the wall.

I suppose we could be facing a firing squad. I can't imagine saying goodbye to my family...to Walter. I lifted my head up and closed my eyes for a moment...saying a little pray for Terese and myself. *If we ever needed help, now would be a good time.*

Adolphus glanced down at his Glock and started patting it, like it was his pet. I cringed and averted my attention from him to Terese. Terese's eyes were shut tight, her lips muttering inaudible words. *Shutting out the inevitable, no doubt.* Adolphus grinned at me, showing me his complete set of jagged teeth—like he was proud of them...a wolverine ready to pounce. He observed me as I unconsciously began touching the beaded bracelet Walter had fastened on my wrist—outside the *Lone Star Café*—the bracelet I called *my good luck charm.* He flipped a switchblade out of his pocket, reached over to me, and with one swift movement, cut my beloved bracelet off my wrist. The beautiful blue and green beads scattered all over the floor of *Numero Uno Bath Boutique.* He laughed at me as I cried out, knelt down and tried to salvage the beads, placing the ones I could find in my pocket. He grabbed my arm, pulled me upright against the wall and fastened on my wrist a woven multi-colored bracelet... *Where had I seen this bracelet before...with the initials AS1SS2 engraved on silver beads in the center?*

I closed my eyes and groaned. *In my nightmares...the bracelet...just like the one that poor girl wore—the girl found dead under the pier...*

Adolphus cackled as he squeezed my wrist. "Now you are mine, little bird...and your *secretary* is history."

Crying in the stillness of my soul, I turned my face away from Adolphus, and glanced at Terese as she moaned and choked out barely audible sounds...her hands clasped together...no doubt praying for a way out of our nightmare. Around her right wrist...I noticed an identical bracelet—compliments of Numero Uno. *We are doomed...we are in this hell together...The Sargentos are going to start a fire and leave us here...or worse...take us to Columbia.* I slumped to my knees and started praying with Terese.

Through my silent prayers, I heard a door creak in the rear of the showroom.

Chapter Thirty-Nine

Adolphus spun for a moment to look at the door leading to the garage. Sylvan had forgotten to lock it and it swung open. Adolphus, not losing his hold on his Glock, pointed his weapon at our faces and called for Marlaine.

"Imbecile," sneered Adolphus.

Rising anger resonated in his voice. His eyes twitched and he cursed in his native tongue. Before he could turn around to lash out at Marlaine to lock the door, a box of metal pipes came crashing down upon his head. The Glock flew out of his hand, unfired, and went soaring out the front door like a bat escaping from its cave. Terese and I looked at each other and she let out an uncontrollable sigh. I did the same.

Behind Adolphus, stood Marlaine—hovering over our tormentor... staring at him, as he lay crumpled on the tile floor with blood gushing out of the side of his head. She held her hands high in the air in a victory salute. A triumphant smile crept over her face, as she remarked, "He never knows when to stop."

I stared at the scene in disbelief, frozen in place. Terese stood alongside me, with her cheeks stained with mascara and her eyes, swollen from crying and stretched wide-open. She looked like a raccoon that got an unexpected treat from a coyote.

Marlaine pointed her finger at us. "Run." She poked Terese on the shoulder. "Snap out of it, beauty. Go...get out of here! There's no more time!"

She waved her right arm at the two of us and then steered her finger to the entrance of *Numero Uno Bath Boutique*—our escape route. We followed her lead and rushed outside the doorway. I noticed Marlaine pick up Adolphus' Glock, tuck it under her blouse, and roll up her sleeves. As she did so, I saw the initials branded onto her arm...*AS1SS2*...the same letters and numbers branded onto Fred's chest...*Adolphus Sargento Number One...Sylvan Sargento Number Two. Control Freaks. Both of them*...Marlaine finally saw the light—*Lucky for her—and for Terese and me.*

We watched as Marlaine re-entered the showroom and dragged the limp body of Adolphus behind the over-sized desk, like a lioness hiding her kill. Then she carted the two remaining crates outside towards the waiting limo. She showed more strength than either one of us... but then, she wasn't injured...except for the slap across her face...and a few marks on her neck. An ugly bruise began to surface right beneath her right eye, which appeared swollen and half-closed. She looked like a prizefighter that wouldn't give up.

Terese and I stood there motionless, beside the doorway—staring at her. Marlaine scrutinized the two of us and shook her head. "Vat...Are you crazy?" . "You vant to be dead? Vamoose. Get out of here! It's your last chance."

My eyes widened. "We can't leave you alone with them."

"Don't vorry. I'm a big girl. I got the key to da limo...and I got to leave now. You two—Run...Get out of here! *Mach schnell*!"

Marlaine smiled at us for the first and last time, a broad, energetic, beautiful smile, then jumped in the Sargento's limo and gunned it. Before I blinked twice she zoomed halfway down the block. The next second, she disappeared out of sight. I regained my senses, grabbed Terese's arm and dragged her across the street. We squatted near an alley, behind a restaurant's trash bin. Smells lingered from the past day's meals. I spied Sylvan come running up to the door of the showroom. He glanced inside and saw no one. He came back out and leapt into the Hummer. He drove the speed limit, with no lights on...slow enough for me to memorize his license plate, under the light of a lone streetlight.

Strange—They were the same numbers and letters as the marks on all of the Sargentos' victims—*AS1SS2*. Talk about being creepy. The Sargentos give creepiness a whole new definition...

It seems to me that when Sylvan drove away in the Hummer, he assumed Adolphus was in the limo heading to Idaho, with Marlaine driving. Funny thing, I don't think Marlaine steered the limo in that direction. My guess, she's cruising up I-5 to Blaine, Washington and then over the border to Vancouver, Canada. After that, she'll probably catch a hasty flight back to Germany—Back to her hometown—Munich—after things calm down. Good for her...She wised up. Plus she saved our lives.

Some people surprise you.

I studied Terese...*She made little choking sounds...Poor girl...still in shock...unlike me—Yeah, right...I'm holding on by a hair.*

Trying to rev her up...trying to give her energy that I couldn't muster up myself, I shook my companion in flight and pulled her to her feet. "We've got to get away from here. What if Sylvan comes back?"

Terese shook her head back and forth like a puppet. She managed to speak. "I'm so tired. I can hardly walk."

I motioned to the lights in the distance, urging her to move, "Come on, Terese...let's go...just up the street a few blocks..."

She stared back at me with half-open eyes—eyes that started rolling around in their sockets when she tried to focus. *Terese is fading fast. I wonder what drugs Adolphus pumped into her?* Her blouse hung in shreds over her shoulder and dried blood covered her eyebrows, cheek and neck. I noticed a nasty bruise forming on her neck, and another on her upper arm.

"Terese, lean on me. Together we can get to a phone. We can't remain here any longer. We've got to put some distance between us and that place...before it blows up..."

I put my arm around her and together, we started walking in the opposite direction that Sylvan took with the Hummer.

Terese and I made it halfway down the block. The street, lit by one working lamppost seemed a mile long. Not one soul passed us. The entire neighborhood...deserted...*Come to think of it, who would want to hang out around warehouses at night?* Not even a street person in sight. Two more blocks and we'll be near The *Smokin' Moose Saloon*, a late-night hangout. In the distance, I could discern music erupting from the open doors...a little jazz playing on a piano...and a sax taking the melody...

and the drums—calling us to safety...*We are so close...to people...to a phone...to help.* That thought kept me going another half-block.

Terese let out a sigh and slumped in my arms.

"Terese...please!" I stood her up, shaking her slightly. "You've got to stay awake...Please—we're almost there—Stand up...I'm not strong enough to carry you..."

A bright light shone like a beacon—or a warning—up the road, a distance from us. I continued to drag Terese step by step along the sidewalk, with her arm around my shoulder. We walked along like two skiers stuck together on a jagged slope. Two giant headlights appeared...coming towards us...they blinded us...*Could be the police...* Before I could react, I heard a door open and slam shut...Two large hands grabbed Terese out of my arms and threw her on the pavement... She lay there lifeless. I didn't know if she was dead or faking it. She didn't look so good.

Sylvan's voice trumpeted, as he screamed at me and crushed my arm. "Where's the limo?"

I gasped, "I don't know..."

I couldn't tell what hurt more...His screaming in my ear, or my arm, upon which he placed an iron stronghold—his strength being even greater than Horst's. Sylvan did not let up on me—he continued to beat me while hurling diabolical curses...His erratic behavior terrified me... without Adolphus reigning him in, he became a loose cannon firing out of control.

Agitated by my answer, Sylvan grabbed my throat. I couldn't stand his yelling. My right eardrum popped. He continued cursing at me and questioned me like an inquisitor preparing torture. "Adolphus doesn't answer his cell. Where the hell is the limo? Do you want me to break your other arm?"

"No...Really...I swear. I don't know where your limo is. *Your wife... Marlaine* took off in it." My voice broke as I sobbed in pain.

"Do you expect me to believe that?"

"It's the truth."

His grip on me tightened, I could feel the cartilage in my shoulder tearing... Sylvan continued screaming at me—twisting my arm...*Oh*

God...I can feel myself passing out from the blinding pain—I can hardly see... Sylvan is spinning before me...If I just close my eyes, I can escape from the pain...

Sylvan shook me, as if delighting in my torture....forcing my eyes open. "Tell me...where's Adolphus?"

"Your...brother...is in there..." I whispered, pointing with my good arm...across the street...and down the block...to *Numero Uno Bath Boutique.*

"You bitch!" Sylvan snarled, slapping me hard across the face. I cringed, shielding my good arm from Sylvan, trying to get away, but I couldn't maneuver the other side of my body, not even an inch, without excruciating pain. I slumped to the pavement, unable to move.

"Hit her again and you're a dead man."

I heard a voice from another world...from my past—Walter! And then, Sylvan's sarcastic humming...taunting my love...as I feel myself, once more fading...the pain...it is too much...for me...I close my eyes...

"Oh, the little secretary is threatening me."

My eyes flicker as I force myself to open them..."Walter!" *I scream...but my voice is mute...I cry silently, almost fainting. Thank God! It's real...It's not a dream. Walter is here...He's come to get me. Wait...Walter is alone. Where's Steve? Where are the police? Sylvan will kill him!* "Walter!" *I manage to yell in a whisper to my beloved. I try to get the words out.* "Walter...Watch out! He's got a...gun...No...No! Sylvan...Leave him alone!"

I try to shield Walter and myself, as Sylvan removes a pistol from his jacket with one hand and clasps onto my waist with the other. I struggle one last time with my good arm to get away. I fight to remain conscious...feeling a sudden burst of energy, I kick my tormentor—trying to knock the gun out of his hand, to no avail—Sylvan is too strong for me...I cannot fight.

Like an angry tiger, Walter leaps at Sylvan, forcing the tyrant to release me from his death grip. I fall to the ground and roll over...struggling to ignore the pain...I see Walter...wrestling Sylvan to the ground...He knocks him down to the sidewalk and tries to release the gun from Sylvan's grasp...The whole time the glaring lights of the Hummer blind my limited vision...I can't see everything that is happening...

A loud boom shatters the stillness of the night.

I quiver on instinct and feel instant crushing pain in my shoulder as my body shivers—over the top pain—compliments of Sylvan Sargento. Mind-numbing pain. I take a deep breath and force my eyes open, catching the view across the street. Smoke...Fire...Sylvan's gun doesn't fire...but Santigo's plumbing supply house does...I hear the sound of glass shattering and objects being blown onto the street—and I can feel the heat of the blast ...Numero Uno is no more.

The explosion startles Sylvan—long enough for Walter to pin the beast to the ground and hold him immobile. I listen in disbelief as I hear another loud blast and then another...This time the gun does goes off—again...and again—and Walter slumps over Sylvan's body like a blanket.

"Oh my God! Walter..."

I cry hopeless tears, as I crawl over to my beloved...leaving my bed—my concrete cushion...Walter does not move as I draw closer to him... he lies sprawled out...with Sylvan's lifeless body as a pillow.

"Somebody help us!" I scream at the darkness—like a wounded fox crouching in the forest. Only this forest is concrete buildings...and unforgiving...unfeeling. Stone...Cold stone...The lifeless forest...I freeze as the fire from the eruption across the street illuminates the sky...I throw my arm up in the air like a flag and wave it wildly...refusing to retreat...

Terese moves her head—The noise of the barrage revives her...She rolls over to one side, coming to rest on her back—cradled on the pavement like a smashed sparrow...She turns her head towards me and says, "I want to help you but I can't move my legs."

"It's okay, Terese..." *I whisper...trying to reassure her...even though I am ready to give up...I can hardly move, let alone speak...* "The police will be here soon...I'm sure of it. Someone will hear...the explosion...and find us...Just rest..."

Terese smiles at me, grateful our nightmare is over, and closes her eyes. "I'm so tired," she says...*and then I hear nothing more from her...for a long time.*

A calm sensation runs throughout my body and I can feel the pain subside. I start reciting...prayers from my childhood—no longer afraid. Walter will be all right. I am sure of it. I cannot envision my life without him. We will be together again. I can see palm trees and iridescent blue-green water...Fiji at last... Walter and me on the beach...gentle breezes...my hair blowing as we walk along the surf...Walter with a lei of flowers around his neck...me with a flower in my hair and no pain, no Sargentos...just...Walter touching me and telling me how much he loves me...

I push myself up to my knees. I can crawl the two blocks to the bar…I can get help…Wait… Walter's cell phone must be in his pocket…Yes! It's within my reach…I manage to straighten my body half-way up and, with my one working arm, crawl over to my savior…I touch Walter's cheek with my lips…Warm…His eyelids…flickering…I reach into his pocket…and as I do, I feel a crashing blow to the side of my face and my vision vanishes. But I can hear sounds…an engine running…and then clicking noises… very close to me…a man crying…a grieving voice saying, "Mi hermano, mi hermano!"

A change in mood…a change in voice…a familiar maniacal laugh and cold claws, with sharp fingernails, jamming what tastes like a bitter pill into my parched, dry mouth.

Adolphus…He's here...He's trying to poison me…I hold the pill under my tongue until I hear his clumping footsteps fade in the distance…and the sound of an engine fading away…Then, with all my might, I spit his death sentence out on to the sidewalk.

I lay on my stone bed, smelling blood and death all around me. I sigh as the wind blows across my battered body and caresses my face. I lay there, trying to stay alert, waiting for help. I hear sirens…in the far distance…like coyotes howling in the night, calling to their mates…I call to Walter, and then to my mother…speaking my undying love for them…I gasp a final deep breath…and sink into the all consuming darkness…The darkness… waiting for me…as the pit opens and swallows me…

Chapter Forty

Death does not win this time. I can feel a dull, throbbing pain coming...and going like the beat of a clock. I cannot move. My eyes will not open. I can feel bandages on one of them. I listen to the sounds surrounding me. I can hear humming and a steady beat, like a bird's heart pinning for his lover. Soft voices...then the voices evaporating like a gentle breeze. A warm presence always surrounds me. And sometimes my mother...sometimes Bryan...and somehow, I can sense Walter, nearby. I can feel them sitting and standing...touching my hands, my cheek... but I cannot not speak. I cannot see. But I can sense them and I can hear faint sounds. I want to move, but nothing moves in my body. Not even my fingertips. Strange...I'm not nervous or upset. Just very tired. Sleep, welcome sleep comes again and I drift off. I remember the first time I woke up in myself—I thought, "I'm alive. I'm alive!"—And I could feel myself smiling, even though I could not move.

Nighttime is...cooler in the room...and voices—speaking quietly—like being at a funeral...my loved ones...dozing nearby...I can hear their deep breathing. I lay there, content and grateful to be near them and then slip back into my seductive sleep.

"Angelina, Angelina...Can you hear me?"

I hear an unfamiliar, yet kind voice calling me.

I can hear but speaking is difficult. I try to move my mouth. I cannot form the word, *"Yes."*

I feel someone prying my eyes open and a light shining into one and then the other. The darkness begins to disappear. Warm light. Wonderful light. A faint breeze from an open window brushes against my face! I can feel again! I am coming home!

My pried eyes stay open. Heavenly light...Faces in the distant. The sensation is exquisite. Like being born again...A return from the dead... Sure enough. Mom—right beside me—I recognize her. Tears roll down my cheeks and she wipes them off and kisses my eyes. Warm, gentle touch. She is holding my hand...

I form the word, *"Mom,"* with my lips but I cannot hear any sound coming from my mouth. A gentleman dressed in a white coat reappears and gives me some ice chips—Wonderful coolness for my parched throat. I mouth the words, "Thank you."

"Don't try to talk, yet, Angelina. It will come soon enough. Welcome back. You've had quite a rest."

"How long?" I mouth the words again, this time very slowly, very intently.

Funny. The gentleman understoods me...I think he is my doctor... and he must be used to brain-challenged folks like me. Some kind of specialist in this field, I'm sure.

"Eight days," the doctor answers me.

My eyes widen. *"Walter..."* This time I shape the word slowly and breathe deeply as I talked. Some sound came out but it wasn't language. Still the doctor understands me.

"Angelina...Please...Don't worry about talking now. You're weak. We induced you into a coma, due to the swelling on your brain...but you are doing fine now. Don't worry. You will recuperate. You will get well. Right now you have to rest. You've had quite a trauma."

"Walter..." I insist. *I have to know.*

My mother gets up from a nearby chair. She understands. She caresses my hand and says, "Walter is in a nearby room...here in the hospital, dear. He's very near to you."

The gentleman speaks. "I'm Doctor Gibbs. Like your mother says, Walter is in the next room, recuperating. We wheel him in here every day to visit you…He insists.

My eyes widen. The doctor understands. I sigh.

Doctor Gibbs smiles, "Don't worry, Angelina. He's doing well. He didn't have a fractured skull, like you. He's alert. We expect him to make a full recovery…as will you."

I smile back. I would nod my head, but it feels like a steam engine just ran over it. Excruciating pain if I move. Jesus! Please I don't want to be like Humpty Dumpty…Maybe the folks here can put me back together again. One could hope.

"I know you just woke up," Doctor Gibbs continues, "But you still need lots of sleep…Rest, Angelina…relax…get well. The next time you open your beautiful eyes, I'll make sure Walter will be here for you."

I smile up at him, squeeze my mom's hand and close my eyes. I hear the doctor's murmuring and my mother crying softly. I try to tell her not to cry but I cannot open my eyes again. Darkness takes over.

I wake up again at three...in the morning...I know 'cause it is dark in the room. Alert. I know the exact time because I can see the clock, which hangs over the night light glowing underneath it...reflecting it like a beacon in a storm. *I can see.* Clearly. Funny, I don't have to go to the bathroom. No doubt I have a catheter in me, along with all these other tubes. Just noticed them—a tube for everything. At least I'm breathing on my own...Don't know if I was—*before.*

Life is good. I turn my head to my side…no pain…and no other patients. Must be intensive care. I notice one chair in the room. Tears form in my eyes as I focus on my mother…sitting on it. Sleeping. Poor thing. She should go home and sleep. When I can speak again, I will tell her that.

I try to stay awake, but it's difficult. Either I am tired or they have designer drugs in this hospital. Probably both. Perhaps, I will be able to talk in the morning…maybe I'll be able to eat breakfast…maybe…I'll see Walter—my Adonis—my love—my best friend…

I spend a lot of time in my world of dreams. First, dreams about food. Then riding bicycles with Walter. Funny. We haven't done that yet...but it's been winter. It's spring now—I remember the month—April...We'll have to ride around Green Lake when we get out of here...Spring...I'm missing the daffodils...and all the blooming plants and trees flowering—the dogwoods and the cherry trees... The magnolias...Maybe they'll wheel me outside for awhile if I beg...Maybe I'll be better soon...Yes! And Walter and I...we can tiptoe through the tulip fields up in Mount Vernon...There's so much I want to do...

It is the tenth day and there is no sign of Walter. The doctor comes in...takes out his light and looks into my eyes and smiles.

"You're looking good today, Angelina."

"Call me Tangie." The words slip out.

This time, the doctor's eyes widen. "I can understand you!"

"Well that's a relief!" I say. "Where is my mother?"

"I sent her home. The poor woman was getting cramps in her legs from dangling them in a chair for over a week."

"Thank you, doctor. I tried to tell her to go home but nothing came out."

"Wow! I am surprised. You won't even need therapy for your speech."

"Promise?"

"Yes. It's what we call in medicine, a miracle."

"Well, I do believe in them...Please...I need to know...Where's Walter?"

"In recovery...More surgery on his leg. His gunshot wound wasn't healing the right way...so we had to go back in and do some repair work. That's why he wasn't in here yesterday."

"He came here the day before?"

"Yes."

"And I missed him. Let me guess. Dreaming."

"Just like Sleeping Beauty."
"When can I see him?"
"Tomorrow. I promise."
"And my mom?"
"She'll be here after your breakfast."
"You mean I get to eat today?"
"Yes. If you can talk, you can eat!"
"Hallelujah!"

As I sat up in bed, eating the last of my toast smeared with butter and raspberry jam, my mother came into my room, carrying a latte. She almost dropped her container when she saw me munching on my food like a little bird.

"Mom, you look great!"

This time she did drop the latte. Leaving the mess on the floor, she ran over to my bed, hugged me and cried. Sobbed even.

"Mom, it's okay. I'm going to be all right. Isn't that great?"

"Yes, dear. It's just that I've been so worried."

"And this is the first time you're cried, right?"

"Right."

"So let it all out—Just cry. It's okay with me."

"Oh, my dear sweet, Angelina...I am so happy." She stared at me, sighed and started sobbing all over again. I leaned over with my good arm and tried to hug her. She hugged me back.

"Hey Mom...Could you do something for me?"

"Anything, Angelina."

"Could you get me a cappuccino from the coffee shop? Also get another latte for yourself."

"I will, my darling girl." She looked at the floor. "My goodness... I've made a mess of things, haven't I? Oh...who cares? The only thing that matters now is...you're better! I can't believe you're talking. It's unbelievable! The doctors told me...months...speech therapy..."

"I'm glad I can see again..."

"You had us so frightened..."

"I'm sorry, Mom...really. Thanks for staying by my side all those days and nights. I knew you were here. I just couldn't communicate. You helped me through the darkness."

"And...I'm sorry I wasn't here, Angelina...for your return to us..."

"Mom...don't worry...I just woke up...before breakfast..."

"Last night...was the first night I took a shower in over a week! It felt so good."

"I know what you mean. I don't even want to look in a mirror."

"You look beautiful."

"You'd say that if I was an orangutang."

"Probably. But I mean it."

"Hey, Mom...On your way to Latte Land, could you stop by and see Walter? The doctor said he can't come in here until tomorrow...but you could go see him, right?"

"I can and I will. Don't you worry about him...He is healing just fine."

"I love you, Mom."

"I love you too. Welcome back to your family."

My mother came back later with a latte for herself and a cappuccino with just a hint of raw sugar, for me. I took a sip, closed my eyes and smiled—transporting myself to my little love nest with Walter...thinking *oh such wonderful thoughts of us together*. I opened my eyes, wanting to stay awake. I could feel sleep beckoning me and I had to fight it. I wanted to ask my mother so many questions. I sipped the last of my coffee elixir and placed it on my bed tray.

"Mom...how is Walter...really?"

"Tangie...Walter came through surgery fine. He is sleeping at the moment...he seems peaceful."

"Ah...my sleeping prince."

"I noticed a young man sitting by his bedside...I introduced myself... He told me his name...*Steve*...and said he's a friend. Do you know him?"

I winced..."*Steve...Steve the Cop*—some cop...some friend."

My mom didn't get it...Probably a good thing.

She continued, "Oh...well, then the nurse came in and told me Walter would be out for a while...so I left."

"My dear sweet Walter...I love to watch him sleep. You know, Mom...people sleep a lot around here."

"Part of the healing process."

I nodded. My head did not go into pain mode when I did. *What a relief. I could move again...and my mother didn't even flinch when I alluded to sleeping with Walter.* I looked at her and smiled.

"Mom...how is Bryan...Andee and the boys? And Pebbles? *Poor Pebbles*...I've neglected him..."

"Everyone's fine, dear." My mother leaned over, kissed my forehead and smiled like she just opened my Christmas present to her. She brushed my cheek with her hand. "You are not to worry about anyone or anything...Just concentrate on getting well."

"I guess I can do that..."

"Yes...and Bryan and Andee are fine...they have been here every day checking up on you."

"I heard them...when I was...dreaming...Please, Mom...tell them I appreciate them hanging out in my room."

"I will...and...my dear, sweet Angelina...Pebbles is not poor. He is still your same old snoopy pooch—but I can tell he misses you...He sits by the door waiting for you to show up."

My mother is a mind reader. She knows I worry about my furry friend. She takes great care of him, I am sure...or Charles does...He's a good soul—got more than he bargained for when he signed up with our family.

"Mom...thank Charles for me...for feeding Pebbles and..."

"I will, dear. He's a great help to me—to us...I think he and Pebbles have bonded. You rest now..."

I tried answering my mother, but I couldn't move my mouth anymore and the words stopped. I smiled at her, as my eyelids fluttered... then closed. I leaned back on my soft pillows and could feel my mother brushing my hair to the side of my head. She began singing my favorite spiritual to me—the same one she used to lull me to sleep as a child...

"Swing low, sweet chariot...Coming forth to carry me home...

Swing low, sweet chariot, coming forth to carry me home..."

Home...where is my home? Ballard? Queen Anne? My mother's home in Kirkland...or Mom's new place...with Charles...on Whidbey Island?

I guess it doesn't matter...as long as I am with Walter...and my family... I'm home.

Chapter Forty-One

The next evening, I'm sitting up...leaning against the pillow in my raised hospital bed, munching on chocolate chip cookies—my bedtime snack—No longer, critical. No tubes, No I.V.'s. I'm eating now and tasting things...I just love orange juice. Drink it for breakfast, lunch and dinner. Tonight I asked to be served breakfast for dinner. The hospital cook complied. What a surprise. The staff must be happy with my progress. I just love breakfast—Reminds me of new beginnings, new days to live. So, in addition to my late night snack, I am eating pancakes and bacon in the evening. Not bad. Pancakes are syrupy sweet. Bacon crispy. Coffee—decaf—watered down. Terrible. I need a latte! Where is Starbucks when you need them?

My left arm is in a sling. The doctor told me, broken. Three places. He informed me my shoulder was nearly separated, and my biceps and rotator cuff both needed repair. Arthroscopic surgery fixed the problem, and with physical therapy, both would heal. Doc Gibbs assured me my arm has *clean breaks*, but my shoulder, which is giving me the most pain—rather intense without the meds—will take longer to heal. My memory is improving daily as the swelling on my brain is completely gone. I still don't like loud noises and I get dizzy when I stand up. The doctor assures me that *this too will pass,* as well as the headaches that creep into my brain and debilitate me. The ringing in my ears is gone—no more vertigo—Don't miss that at all.

For now, the only walks I take are to the little girl's room, with the nurse's help. However slow and dependent I am at present, I am grateful

I can talk and walk. I know I am making progress. Everyday is a new adventure and I look forward to every morning when I awake, I cannot stop smiling.

So here I am, chomping on a piece of bacon and not feeling any guilt over the fat content, as Walter cruises into my room in a wheelchair.

"Walter!" Overwhelmed, I take a deep breath and start choking on the bacon. I haven't mastered eating and talking at the same time yet. What is it all mothers say to their children? "Don't talk with your mouth full, dear." Well, I take a swig of water and that does the trick.

"Walter…" I say, without going into spasms.

"Yes, it's me." My sweetheart holds up a cup adorned with a *Starbucks* label. "Sorry I made you choke. Didn't know I have that effect on you…"

With a smile, I accept my lover's gift of cappuccino and repeat like a parrot, "Walter!"

"It's so good to hear you say my name, Angelina…"

"I'm so glad you're alive, Walter. In my dreams you were…but I wasn't sure."

"I'm alive and well, Angelina."

"Come here, my love…Let me touch you…"

Walter wheels over to my bed, moving my tray out of our way. My smile widens into a grin and I lower my nest and invite him in. He scoots himself out of his chair, not without difficulty, and plops himself down next to me on my bed. I touch his face. He *is* real. I smooth his hair to one side, peer into his eyes and whisper, "I love you, Walter…I've missed you more than you could imagine…I am so glad you are here…"

After those few words, I cannot talk. I feel the tears welling up in my eyes and I can hardly breathe…

Walter presses his cheek against mine and I feel wonderful tingling… up and down my spine. Warmth spreads around my face and waist as I feel Walter's hand touching my body—kindling a fire that remained dormant for two weeks.

He whispers back to me, "I know, Angelina…I've felt the same way…I want to hold you so bad, but I don't want to hurt you…"

"I want to hold you, too…my one side is good—you can hug me there," I say, as I place his right hand under my good shoulder.

"Walter complies and gives me a gentle squeeze. "How's that?"

"Heavenly...I know I should be feeling some pain, but I don't...not any..."

"Angelina...you know I love you, really love you?"

I answer with a kiss, which Walter returns, soft at first and then our dance begins and the kisses get longer and harder and we both have to come up for air...I breathe in and out and whisper to my beloved, "You are real."

"One hundred percent real."

"Don't ever leave me again..."

"I don't intend to...I love you so much," Walter whispers and proceeds to kiss my neck and my ears and the back of my spine, which always makes me dizzy...and I don't want to stop...and I don't think either of us would have, if Nurse Sheridan didn't walk into the room at that moment.

She reminds Walter he is not supposed to be steering his own wheelchair and informs him that he has ten minutes before his physical therapy appointment. "I will be back to wheel you there."

"At night?" he asks his faithful nurse, who is giving me a stare—like I stole her patient.

"Morning, noon and night," she mumbles, and clomps out the door. She may have intended to stop us but she did not put a damper on our party. I gaze into Walter's eyes and encourage him, kissing his cheek and his bandaged forehead. He looks like a mummy with moveable arms, and one moveable leg, but to me he is the handsomest man on the planet.

Walter returns my gaze and kisses my sore shoulder with a tenderness that feels like a bird's wing fluttering alongside me. I sigh, feeling light and warm...not at all injured.

Walter touches my hand with a gentle caress and places his lips on mine.

"Angelina, I'll have to get to work fast."

"Work?" I squinted my eyes at him, trying to understand.

"I mean—I came in here to...act on something that cannot wait... not one more minute."

"Oh, Walter..."

Feeling intense warmth and compassion for my lover, I regain my voice. "Please...don't be worried. I'll be back to my ol' self—You'll be back to your ol' self...and..."

"And we'll never be apart again. I promise."

"Promise? I like the sound of that...I love you so much, Walter..."

"Yes...Angelina...and I promise to love you for the rest of my life."

Now I feel tingles way down to my toes and my shoulders begin shaking a little and then my knees...as Walter pulls out a ring...a very expensive-looking ring with an old-fashioned setting and a lovely diamond centered with little diamonds all around it. He slips it on my ring finger...a perfect fit.

"I want you to wear this...as a sign of my love for you..."

I look in Walter's eyes and my lips curl up in a smile...I feel an uprising of joy in my soul and I find it hard to breathe.

He kisses my lips gently. "I've been holding this ring—It's been wearing a hole in my pocket...since...before...well...Angelina...I can't wait any longer...I want you to marry me. I don't want to waste any more of our time together—joking around...wondering...roaming around without direction. Drifting in and out of each other's lives...like dandelions scattered by the wind...I want us to be like...fragrant roses... winter roses—with deep roots—that survive the bitter frost...and go on blooming. Every day is precious now...to me...and I hope to you. I want to be with you...only you...all the time...not just on cases..."

"Roses in winter—Yellow roses—for sunshine on cloudy days... the two of us...always. You will be my husband." I stop speaking and breathe in and out...I find it hard to get out all the words I want to say...I am stunned...but not surprised...I am surrounded by warmth and I visualize brilliant colors swirling all around me...And I feel light and peaceful.

"Yes...and Angelina...you will be my wife..."

"And we will grow old together..." I sigh.

"Yes...*come with me and be my love...*"

"I will go with you, anywhere...*your home will be my home*...and I will marry you, Walter...I will love you forever..."

And then there are no more words...we remain locked in an embrace that remains timeless to this day...whenever I am sad or down, I will remember this embrace. I will never be alone.

Nurse Sheridan comes in and taps Walter on the shoulder. I open my eyes. Walter doesn't say a word, but kisses me softly on my lips and stares into my eyes, which say without words, *"Later, Love."*

My beloved lowers himself into his wheelchair, with Nurse Sheridan's help and I touch his hand once before he is led out of my room. *"Later, Love..." I whisper. I know my voice is inaudible, but I know he hears me.*

I hear his voice ringing in my ears the rest of the night and as I fall in and out of my dreams...I can smell the roses—the yellow roses of spring...New life beginning again.

Chapter Forty-Two

After our engagement, Doctor Gibbs permits Walter to visit me all day long. I guess he considers my fiancé family. So in between rehab, doctor visits, and nurse check-ups, Walter and I talk for hours...we hug...we kiss...and spend a lot of time just holding each other.

I lean back on my pillow, daydreaming of the time Walter and I will be well...and we are swimming on a deserted island...Ah...heaven on earth. My eyes drift to my bedside table...I can smell yellow roses that someone placed there, this morning—while I lay asleep...I lean over, take one stem out of the vase and put the rosebud next to my face, and am once more transported to a love fest with my beloved.

I hear footsteps...not the people variety...I look down from my bed and see Pebbles standing before me. He lets out a bark and I start to cry. My brother Bryan walks in the door behind my pooch and says, "Gosh, Tangie...I thought he'd make you happy..."

"Oh, I am happy, Bryan...I'm just emotional...that's all. Place him on my bed, if you don't mind..."

"Of course, Sis...anything your say." Bryan placed Pebbles next to me and gave me a kiss on the cheek. "Love ya."

"Love you, too, little brother."

"I got one of those doggie vests engraved with...*Therapy Dog*...so I didn't have to smuggle him into your room. Clever eh?"

"You are a genius, Bryan."

"Thanks, Tang...Glad you appreciate me."

"Of course I do. And I love, love, love my pooch." I snuggled Pebbles with my nose and petted him with my good arm. "It seems like ages... since I held him..."

"I'm gonna meet Mom for lunch...in the cafeteria...I'll leave him here with you...then I'll come back to see you and pick the pooch up."

"Great, Bryan...Tell Mom to eat...I know she's been skipping meals..."

"I will...see you in a bit."

I smiled at Bryan and nodded...trying hard not to start crying again. "Thanks, Bryan...Be good."

I lay in bed for about a half-hour with my pooch, chatting with him—my trusted companion of seven years—*I could swear he understands my every word...and he looks so cute in his new vest.*

I heard footsteps in the hall. They came closer and I could hear a person entering my room. A solitary figure opened the door in the shadows, unannounced...walked in... and shattered my sense of safety and calm.

I sat straight up in my bed and continued petting Pebbles. "I don't want to talk to you, Steve. I'm not a cop. I'm a private citizen...and I want to be left alone."

Sensing my growing anxiety, Pebbles growled at my intruder. Steve put his hands in the air and cleared his throat. "Tangie...ya know, whatever...you're gonna have to talk about what happened sometime."

"Not today...and not without Walter."

Pebbles echoed my sentiments with a bark.

"Okay, Tangie...but soon."

"Don't count on it."

"Actually...I stopped by to tell you I'm sorry...I'm really sorry about...what happened...I'll check in with you tomorrow."

"You do that." I refused to make eye contact with him. A lot of pent-up anger towards him and unresolved thoughts of blame crept into my being. I rolled over, hugging Pebbles and pretending to fall sleep. I heard Steve's footsteps as he left the room and the door closing. I could hear voices outside...dim, unrecognizable. Then the painkillers took over and I did escape...into dreamland...until Walter and my family appeared once more in my foggy vision. I smelled the mixed aromas of hot food in the hallway—almost suppertime. I slept the afternoon away.

Oh well...Stay awake and deal with flashbacks and excruciating pain that strikes me without warning—or nod off...Think I'll choose sleep.

I pried my eyes open, feeling rested from my long nap, but still in a wretched mood after Steve's visit. As I stretched my good arm, I noticed Walter and my family all sitting and standing around my bed watching me. I reached down on my bed...feeling for my furry friend. Pebbles—gone! And there stood a guard—posted at my doorway.

"Why the police? Animal control?" I quipped. "Is Pebbles in trouble?"

"No, honey, Pebbles is great." My mother fidgeted a bit and took my hand. "Although he did leap off your bed after you fell asleep this afternoon. Wearing his fancy vest, he visited all the patients in your wing. They all seemed grateful...except one lady—Mrs. Burns—she shooed him away. Turns out she's allergic to fur...or maybe Pebbles annoyed her."

"That's my Pebbles...He likes to have his presence known." I laughed, forgetting Steve for the time being. I smiled, thinking, *it feels so good to hear the sound of my own laughter*. My mother smiled back at me. My laughter must have the same affect on her.

Bryan grinned at me. "Mom and I found Pebbles waiting by the elevator when we came back from lunch...so I called Andee...She and the twins came and took your pooch home...hope you don't mind."

"He's like me. Hates hospitals. Thank Andee for me."

"Good news," Walter jumped in.

Well, spoke up...He can't quite jump up...still wheelchair bound.

"Tangie..." Walter grinned. "In a few days, you can go home."

"What about you? I'm not leaving without you."

Marianna intervened. "Angelina...as your mother...I have to speak up. You are not well enough to go home on your own. Neither is Walter. You need our help."

"Really, Mom..."

"I mean it. Charles has offered his home on Whidbey to us. It has lots of room...and it's all on one level...When you feel better you can walk the beach with Pebbles."

"I can do that on Alkai...or along the waterfront park...at the end of Broad Street..."

"Andee, Jason, Jeffrey and I will come visit—we promise..." Bryan said.

"I guess you've all decided—before you even spoke to me. Let Walter and me discuss this first."

Marianna nodded. "Think about it, dear. Please. We think it would be best for your health. Charles is looking forward to your visit...He thinks it will be a good way to get to know everyone. You know, Tangie, in a few short months we'll all be family."

My mom took my ring hand and placed her ring hand alongside it. "Two weddings this summer...Father Don will be busy!"

"Father Don? Who contacted Don?"

"I did." Walter smiled like a little boy in a candy store. *The sneak.*

I raised my eyebrow--The other remained bandaged.

Walter kissed my cheek and held my hand, so I couldn't be mad at him. "Tangie...*Sweetheart*...I just thought...I thought Don should know everything—since he'll be here this summer...Why not? Who else would you like to officiate?"

"You devil...you're the cat who swallowed the canary."

"Hey, he's overjoyed to marry us...Trust me...He says to tell you he's relieved you are doing better. He's been praying fast and furious...Last time I talked to him, he said he'd continue his offerings...He's got all the nuns in his mission praying for us...We can't lose."

"Oh, so now the two of you have an ongoing dialogue."

"Just the past two weeks...you see, you weren't able to talk to him. And the poor priest seemed so distraught...and for some reason, he wants to marry us. He's elated we're engaged."

"Sounds like Don, all right. Doesn't want any of us living in sin. Either that or he's had a guilty conscience all these years. Now he can put both of those thoughts aside. Okay, I accept Don as our officiate, if you respond to the following requests...There are two."

Walter smiled, wheeled closed to my bed and kissed me on the cheek. "That's my Angelina...feisty as ever...Okay, Sweetheart...What are your requests?"

"Number One: Pebbles has to be at both weddings."

"That's a given, Angelina," Walter nodded, took my hand and kissed me again...on the lips...a warm, soft, inviting kiss. I sighed.

"Pebbles is family," My mother interjected. "I'll even make him a special collar for the occasions...and a black tie."

"Great, Mom." I smiled at her and giggled like a schoolgirl. *God, it felt good to laugh.* "And Walter, my love...of course Hildie's invited, but I think cats hate crowds...she'd just hide somewhere."

"Bingo." Walter nodded. "But thanks for thinking of the fat cat."

Then I got serious. I straightened up as tall as I could in my hospital bed and spoke in my best authoritative voice. "Number Two: Walter... answer me...for real this time. Why is there a guard posted at my door?"

Walter's smile froze and then disappeared like ice melting. "You have to talk to Steve about that. He'll tell you."

"Steve again...*Rats*...it's bad, huh?"

"Well, perhaps you and I can help fix it."

"How?"

"By meeting with Steve. He needs our help."

I started hyperventilating. Walter leaned over and rubbed my back. I started to groan as my stomach churned—not from hunger pains. Another familiar feeling crept through my body. Nausea set it. The room started spinning. I grabbed onto Walter for support.

"Tangie—We don't have to do anything, go anywhere...we just have to talk to him."

"I don't know...I am so pissed at him...He got us into this mess... and then left us to finish it. You almost got killed...I almost got killed..." *It's all coming back to me*...I put my hands on my head and closed my eyes. The spinning stopped. When I opened my eyes again, I saw the concerned faces of my family. *God, I hate to see them worry about me.*

"Walter, I do have one more question...

"Sure, Sweetheart."

"Where's Terese?"

"I don't know, Angelina." Walter sighed. "Steve does; I'm sure of that."

"Then, she's not dead..." I opened my eyes wider, relieved. I remembered my last picture of her...in my mind...her tormented body...lying there on the pavement...

"Steve knows more than we do...about *after*—After we both lost consciousness...I think talking to him will help us both—You know, *closure.*

Angelina, please...I am concerned about you...and your recovery from this nightmare. You are the only one that matters to me."

Walter squeezed my hand and gave me a look of intense love that melted my resistance to facing my demons.

"I believe you, Walter." A sob crept up out of my throat. "You can invite Steve in...but I'm not making anymore promises."

Before Marianna and Bryan left for supper, Walter asked them to please not return to my room until after our session with Steve. My mother nodded and let out a familiar sigh. A look of anxiety crept over her face. She tried to suppress her concern, but I noticed she couldn't help letting her guard down. She looked at me, and then Walter...tears forming in her eyes. She nodded. "All right, Walter. Please call me... when Steve leaves. Bryan and I will wait in the cafeteria downstairs."

"Will do, ah..."

"Call me, *Marianna*."

"Yes, Marianna."

I don't think I ever saw Walter squirm before. Sometimes my mother has that effect on people.

Bryan didn't help the situation. He murmured to Walter, "I hope you know what you're doing."

"I do, Bryan. Trust me." He grasped my baby brother's hand and shook it.

Baby brother...all six feet four inches of him...Bryan...transformed from my annoying bratty brother to my defender. The thought brought a smile to my face. *He's still adjusting to me having a boyfriend, let alone a fiancé.*

Walter followed Marianna and Bryan out the door in his wheelchair and escorted them as far as the elevator. Eavesdropping on their conversation, I listened as I heard my fiancé say, "Thank you both for understanding." *Walter—the peacemaker.*

When Walter returned to my room, he stared at me, quizzing me—like a professor setting up an exam. "Ready?"

I nodded. "We better see him right away, before I change my mind—What the heck, Walter... You're a trickster... a fox—you know I love a mystery—and Terese is missing... *again*."

Walter picked up his cell phone and pressed one button. "Steve—We're ready."

Chapter Forty-Three

Here we sit in my hospital room...Walter in his wheelchair, me in my bed, and Steve, in the stuffed fake leather chair...healthy as can be, but then again, he deserted us—left us to our own devices—yet we survived...and we seem...all chummy again. I don't feel particularly close to Steve, not having known him very long, but at least my anger towards him has subsided and curiosity has taken over. I take time to study him. Some girls might see him as a hunk, others, as a brute. At this moment, I see him as a cad...Perhaps he's just a guy who likes to be in control.... Guess that's a requirement at the police academy.

Steve speaks first. "Tangie, I know you're worried about Terese. Please...don't be...She's in hiding—We have her in police protection. I personally kept watch over her—until after she buried her husband, Fred Santigo...and then we put her in a safe house."

"Hum...that's one funeral I missed. Poor Fred...and Terese—to think what she's been through...So...you put her in hiding?"

"We had no choice but to put her in protective custody. You see, at first...after the explosion, we thought Adolphus would no longer harm her...She told us...absolutely he died in the fire—But it turns out he didn't."

"And you never caught him...I'm guessing. How long did it take you to figure out he was alive?"

"A few days. The fire department waited for the ashes to settle...It's too dangerous to go in immediately after a fire...Santigo's business... well what's left of it, got sealed off...until after the fire marshal searched

Santigo's showroom...The investigators couldn't find Adolphus...or any body."

"Adolphus..." I whisper...and close my eyes. "Our ordeal...it's not over..."

"No, it's not, Tangie...I'm sorry." I hear Steve pacing the room.

I open my eyes. "I remember now...Steve..."

Steve stops pacing and takes out a pen and notebook.

I close my eyes again. "Walter—bleeding...lying on the ground... over Sylvan...and I thought, dying. Terese—out cold...and me—screaming...*Help!* And then the dark figure—*Adolphus*—taking the keys out of Sylvan's pocket...I can hear him jingling them...I can't see him... He's the one...He clobbers me over the head...He tries to poison me... but I fool him...my mouth is so dry, the pill doesn't dissolve...and I spit out his elixir...he fails in his mission to kill me and then...I hear the coyotes..."

"Coyotes?" Walter asks me as I open my eyes.

"Must have been the sirens," Steve interjects, as he pulls a chair close to my bed and sits down. .

"Sounds like coyotes..." I explain. I begin to shake, uncontrollably.

Walter squeezes my hand. "It's all right, Angelina. You're here with me—you're safe."

"That's why the EMT's couldn't feel your pulse..." Steve whispers... "He drugged you...I found the capsule...you spit out...I put it in a bag and brought it to the hospital...The capsule helped the doctors determine what traces of poison you had in your system. Powerful stuff—You are lucky only a fraction got into your blood stream...any more...and..."

I look straight ahead. "He wants me dead...I play dead...Terese does too. *Walter*...at first...I think Walter's dead...shot by Sylvan...but... Sylvan..."

I almost gag...as I say the next words, "Sylvan—what a miserable excuse for a human being—he's one dead man I'll never miss...not in a thousand years."

"Like his brother, he has a long rap sheet..." Steve says. "The authorities in Chile are appreciative we...er...you caught him—They're not the least bit sorry he's dead."

"I didn't catch him...Walter did...and Walter's alive...*Thank God...*" I reach down and hug Walter. "My love, I'm so grateful Sylvan's a lousy shot."

"Me too," Walter whispers back to me. I see tears forming in his eyes...He clears his throat, dabs at his eyes with his sleeve and for a while he cannot talk.

He regains his composure and smiles. "He only got my foot...my leg...and he clobbered my head...No spring skiing up in the mountains...but I'll be okay—*We both will.*" His eyes light up and he tenderly massages my good arm. I begin to feel warm again.

Steve...playing the dutiful cop, remains unflappable—he knows he's on a roll—he doesn't want to stop his interrogation. "Tangie...when we questioned Terese, she told us Adolphus was in the building when it exploded...she didn't see him come out—she slipped into unconsciousness before he attacked you..."

"Yes, Steve. I guess I'm the only one who saw him after the explosion...well, I didn't see him...I heard him...I felt him—the ferret..."

"I'm sorry, Tangie...Can you tell me anything else?"

I close my eyes again. "I remember but...it's like I'm looking through a fog...*I see Terese lying lifeless on that pavement...I am thinking, she'll be dead if she has to wait much longer for help...We are living in this nightmare...They drugged her...they beat her...she couldn't take much more...*"

I open my eyes. "How is Terese? Please, Steve, tell me...is she recovering?"

"Yes...she is, Tangie. The doctors and nurses cared for her non-stop...No head injury...like you...but they kept her under constant watch because of all the drugs she ingested...Doctor Gibbs kept her in critical care for two days...After three days, she bounced back to the living—once the drugs were out of her system. She's looking and feeling like a different person—vibrant, even."

"Thanks, Steve...That's great news." I heave my chest and take a deep breath. "When can I see her?"

"As soon as it's safe."

"You mean, after we find Adolphus and disarm him..."

Steve nods.

I stare at Steve—looking straight in his eyes. He does not divert his attention from my gaze, but listens intently to my words. "Did I tell you Adolphus took the Hummer? I remember the license plate number... *AS1-SS2*...Easy to remember. Same logo as their branding iron."

"Branding Iron?"

"You don't wanna know."

Walter squeezes my hand and closes his eyes as if wanting to stop the disturbing images appearing in his mind. *I understand his suffering.* Steve casts his eyes down and nods.

I continue. "I memorized the license plate when Sylvan took off in the Hummer first time...And then he came back the second time...looking for Adolphus...Well, Walter knows that part...except for the next part—about Adolphus coming back and cackling like an old witch... and...*Old Woman...Oh no! That's it...*I shiver uncontrollably and feel all the pain in my body taking over—I couldn't go on.

Walter lifts his hand up and signals Steve to stop. My fiancé leans up on my bed, with difficulty, standing on one leg and takes me in his arms and hugs me, as he chokes out his words. "Angelina, I'm sorry...for what you went through—for what I put you through..."

I sigh, feeling loved and warm...and grateful. "Walter...my love, you didn't put me through anything...I'm here...I'm all right, now... and so are you—We're together—we're alive—We bit the bullet—and... you...you saved my life..."

Steve interrupts. His usual terrible sense of timing takes over and he plods on. "I hate to ask you to finish, Tangie...I know you're tired and want to quit, but it's important—We need the rest of the information... as soon as you can give it to us..."

"Yeah, yeah...I know..." I look at Walter and grasp his hand. "It's okay, my love...I can go on now...Just hold me..."

I close my eyes, forcing myself to continue, and I start to sink into a trance-like state of consciousness, as a form of protection from my nightmare. I begin to speak in a matter-of-fact tone. I feel my body relaxing and my mind becoming clearer.

"After Walter comes and saves me from Sylvan—all alone—with no help from the *police*...I might add...well...Walter passes out—after Sylvan shoots him...and I think maybe Walter could be dying and there's nobody here to help us...We just lay there...bleeding all over the street... and before I can do anything, Adolphus shows up and cracks me on my face with his cane...and I told you about the poison thing..."

Steve closes his notebook and puts his pen in his pocket. "So that's it..."

I open my eyes, and push a button to raise my bed. "No, Steve. There's more..."

Steve opens his notebook and takes out his pen. "Go on, Tangie..."

"Adolphus disguises himself as an old woman—one of the homeless. He likes to do that..."

I turned to my fiancé..."Remember that pair by the police station, Walter? The lady I tripped over?"

"Oh yeah...That crazy old woman with the younger dude...What a pair—They looked like they could take the shirt off your back if you let them...I gave them money to get rid of them..."

"Well, that was no lady...and that was no gentleman beggar...I didn't catch on 'til later...that Adolphus and Sylvan disguised themselves as two homeless souls...so they could...spy on us..."

"No sh..."

"And I think Adolphus, with Marlaine in tow, followed me...when I went to the airport...the first time...checking on Terese...They were dressed as an odd elderly couple."

Walter raised his eyebrows. "They've been watching us since the start..."

"Yes...and...Walter...Steve...I'm afraid that by now, a homeless person is lying dead in the street somewhere...under a bridge or in an alley...poisoned for her clothing... Adolphus is hiding out...waiting for his Hummer to be painted. It's possible he hasn't changed the plates... the extra ones were in the limo."

"The limo? Do you mean the same limo we followed from the funeral home...the one Adolphus used to kidnap Fred?"

"Yes...Santigo's secretary...*Marlaine*...took off in that limo...after she clobbered Adolphus...She told Terese and me to run...She tried to help us get away...right before she hopped in her get-away vehicle...and gunned the engine for parts unknown...but I think probably Canada. Say, Steve...did she escape?"

"Marlaine?"

"Yeah, *Fred's* secretary...did she get away?"

Steve thinks about my question for about a minute, and replies, "I haven't heard anything about a limo being found—or this Marlaine character...but then again, we didn't know who was in possession of it...or where to look...Now, we can alert the Canadian/U.S. border crossings."

"But you knew about the Sargentos' limo."

"Yes, but at the time, we thought the Sargentos both bit the dust... so we didn't put out an A.P.B. on their vehicle..."

"Figures..."

"Tangie...please...cut us some slack...I know we let you down...I let you down...and for that I apologize. I'm sorry we screwed up...I'm asking you to give us another chance—We won't let you down this time. I promise. Absolutely...we promise."

"We?"

"Me...and my boss...Barry Cardoso."

"Ah...I remember Barry. Didn't know he's your boss."

Steve puts his head down, like a penitent child. Poor guy. I almost feel sorry for him.

Walter pulls himself up out of his wheelchair and plops himself next to me on my bed. He takes me into his arms and hugs me. He kisses my nose and then brushes my lips. "Are you okay, Angelina?"

"I am now...but when I saw you lying there...draped over Sylvan... you looked like a corpse, with blood dripping down your face...I became terrified...If I lost you then...I wouldn't have the will to live...I would not have recovered..."

I let out a sob as Walter squeezes my hand and caresses my face. "I'm not going anywhere, Angelina...I'm right here...with you...always..."

I nod and squeeze his hand back. "I'm okay now, Sweetheart."

I look up at Steve and say, "So tell me Steve...Do you think Marlaine got away?"

"Marlaine?" Steve looks puzzled. His eyes are glazed over and he appears to be in a different world.

"*Marlaine*...Fred's secretary...who drove the limo..."

"Oh yeah...Sorry, Tangie...I keep having this image of you...on the sidewalk..."

"Steve...Listen to me...*Marlaine Blouzer Sargento* is another casualty of the Sargento Brothers. As well as being Fred's secretary, she's Horst's sister and Sylvan's wife...well, his *widow*..."

"Oh...now I understand...I think...No, we haven't found anyone else connected to this case...but now we have someone else to question... about the Sargentos...and their world of crime."

"Don't count on it, Steve. I'm sure she's left the country...I'm thinking after she drives to Canada she'll try to hop a flight to Germany. She has a lot of cash in the limo. I'm sure she'll dump the drugs...Dangerous merchandise when crossing the border...Easier to explain cash than drugs when trying to get into another country. Before or after she gets to Canada, she'll dump the limo also. She's no dummy."

"We will put an A.P. Bulletin out for her."

"If you do find her...cut her some slack. She helped us in the end. You know...her freedom for her cooperation. Terese and I would be dead meat or worse, if it weren't for her...She's a victim too—Adolphus branded her—She has a *tattoo* on her arm...*ASI-SS2*..."

"Like Fred..." Steve says.

"Like Fred. I nod in agreement...remembering Santigo's chest. A nauseous feeling stabs me in the stomach. I take a deep breath and start reciting a silent mantra: *"I can do this, I can do this...No one will hurt me again..."*

Nurse Sheridan walks in and places two snacks on my tray and announces that she has to take my blood pressure. I nod.

"Sweetie, your blood pressure is a little high. Are you resting?"

"Well...I have been, but this evening is a little stressful..."

"You take it easy, girl...we don't want you getting upset."

"I'll try to keep her calm, Shirley," Walter answered. Shirley nodded at him and cruised out the room.

"I can come back, tomorrow, if you want, Tangie..." Steve says.

"No...I'm all right, Steve...Can you tell me more about Terese?"

"Well, we found her heavily drugged—just like you said. She didn't remember a whole lot…she became terrified when we questioned her. I think she blocked a lot of the memories out of her mind. She has a small fracture…her left arm, like you—but not as severe—and no torn shoulder like you suffered…"

I winced, remembering my injuries and those inflicted on Terese. "Sylvan manhandled her."

"That's evident—She looked like a broken doll when I discovered the three of you—she couldn't move by herself and her speech was incoherent. Terese endured a lot of abuse…the Sargentos left her with a lot of bruises and abrasions on her body…which turned out to be superficial… They are healing…"

"How about her face? She's so attractive."

"The plastic surgeon says her scars will recede…that she will look her beautiful self when she heals…Doctor Gibbs is not so sure about her mental health."

"Steve…she was with the Sargentos longer than me…every second there is…was…a nightmare."

Yes…she's been through hell…and now her husband is dead—*murdered*."

"And his murderer is on the loose." I shake my head. "No wonder she's terrified."

"Terese thought you died on that street, Tangie. She became hysterical when the medics revived her…as she lay on the sidewalk…She saw what appeared to be your lifeless body next to hers…and she freaked out…Later, she told me that you kept her going…that she would have given up if you weren't there…urging her on…"

"When did you find us, Steve?"

"I arrived…after Adolphus got away…too late to stop him…"

Walter interrupts our dialogue. "Angelina…Look at me, Sweetheart…I know you're still mad at Steve, but you know, neither of us would be here talking if he didn't find us when he did…He called the medics…They stopped my bleeding…and gave us first aid immediately…Who knows when we would have been discovered if he didn't search for us…We were across the street…and a block away from the explosion…"

I study Steve. He busies himself pacing back and forth on the small path between my hospital bed and the door…He keeps getting up and sitting down. I'd say he doesn't know how to react to us. He seems uncomfortable to say the least. He looks like the *Sad Sack* in the old funny papers my dad used to read to me.

"I guess I should thank you, Steve."

"No, Tangie…You have all the right in the world to be angry. I should have listened to Walter…I should have gone with him… but…I thought you were somewhere else…that's the only reason I wasn't with him…I know words are hollow..."

I take Steve's hand when he paces back in my direction. "It's okay, Steve…I think I understand. Don't beat yourself up. I won't yell at you anymore. I promise."

"That's a load off…Thanks, Tangie. So now you know why…we posted this guard by your door, just in case…and when you leave, he'll go home with you."

"Whatever you say, Steve."

"Thanks for understanding…for not fighting me on this request."

"Steve…Please…would it be possible for me to speak with Terese?"

"Not right now, Tangie. But I can bring you a *safe* phone…later. I'll set it up for you, when I come the next time. Terese keeps asking about you. You'd be a welcome surprise for her. Although her physical health is much better, I think she's sinking into a depression."

"Wouldn't you...if someone murdered your spouse…and if someone took away the life you are living—your peace in the world—your ability to feel safe?"

"Yes, Tangie…I don't know…"

"Put yourself in her place…What if someone did something horrible to your wife?"

"Definitely—I couldn't deal with it…but I'm not married."

I start thinking to myself…Steve needs a woman. A good woman—to find that soft spot that he hides so well. I'll introduce him to Suzy. Who knows? Weirder stuff has happened. Suzy may want to settle down to one man. It could happen…and Steve is kind of a hunk…

And, being the dutiful cop, Steve is back on target. "Could you tell me anything more about Adolphus, Tangie? I need any information you remember about him—Anything—however small..."

"Well, Steve, I told you I think Adolphus is laying low in Seattle. He's ditched the Hummer but will come back to it later...Check out all the garages and chop shops...He likes to double as a street person... Like I told you...he may have killed some poor unfortunate woman for her clothes...promising her drugs...and feeding her poison...If you want Adolphus, look for a *woman* or man with long fingernails...and long black hair. Adolphus killed Fred with his elixir...He likes to poison his victims...*like a spider*...with a lethal dose of his *Death Comes Quickly* capsules...He keeps his cache in a thimble, attached to one short fingernail on his left hand. He also has a short fingernail on his right hand...on his trigger finger. All the rest are abnormally long. He's a very weird monster."

Steve raises his eyebrows and sighs. "Toxicology said Fred died from a lethal dose of poisoning...same stuff that was in that capsule you spit out." He shakes his head and stands up... *I can see him trying to take in the information without seeming disturbed.* "We've got to find him, Tangie..."

I nod and close my eyes. I force myself to see Adolphus again. *Not an easy task. I want to forget everything about him.* I grab Walter's hand and squeeze it till I stop trembling.

Walter puts his free hand on my head and caresses my temple and massages my neck—trying to calm me down. He whispers, "It's okay, Angelina...I'm here with you—don't worry...there's no one here to hurt you...you're safe...I'm here, Sweetheart..."

I feel myself fall into a safe spot, warm and cushioned with love. Tears trickle down my face. I tend to cry when treated with overwhelming tenderness. I take a few short breaths and let them out slowly. Then I can continue...As long as I have Walter's hand in mine, I can remember...I can open that door.

I lean back on my pillow and try to focus on the pictures flashing through my mind. "Adolphus has friends—associates—comrades... near Coeur d'Alene...Idaho...at some compound...I can't remember the name of it...but give me a minute...I see something...in the distance... in the fog...but it's becoming clearer ..."

"Take all the time you need, Tangie," Steve whispers, not wanting to disturb my inner thoughts...my flashes...my premonitions...

Walter enfolds me in a soft embrace, brushing my hair with his hand. I relax and start breathing slowly...in and out, in and out. I try to remember something in my subconscious. Keeping my eyes closed, I continue forcing myself to breathe...in and out...staying focused as the pictures start coming into view. "*Adolphus*," I speak aloud. "Adolphus is in a green and brown Hummer now...*Camouflage*...He's driving into a woodsy area...a logging road or something like that...I can smell the trees—like in December—freshly cut pine and cedar. He is turning left...right before a large covered bridge...he comes to a gate—There is a wooden sign with a wolf pasted on it. *Camp Adairwolf*...A-dare-wolf...Maybe he gave these directions to Marlaine when I passed out... Whatever...I can see them...Anyway...the damn compound's named after him...Adolphus—Adairwolf—Wolf camp...He's their benefactor...Maybe I heard them talking...or I dreamt this...He's in cahoots with the Neo-Nazis there...He's their Columbian connection...*I know now*...he's the descendant of one of Hitler's henchmen...and so is his brother, Sylvan—*Numero Dos*. His mother is native Columbian...his father, German...His father hates his son, Adolphus, because he resembles his mother—a prostitute. But he loves Sylvan—who looks like his father—*a true Aryan*. But Adolphus has the brains—He set up his Neo-Nazi camp there in Idaho...He started the operations in Columbia... Argentina...and until recently...Chile...The organizations all support each other—Neo-Nazis—*I hate those guys*..."

"Tangie," Steve whispers, "What else do you see?"

"It's becoming clearer...what's going to happen..."

"What, Tangie? What's going to happen? What do you see?"

"Adolphus—at the gate...of the compound...dressed like a woman—The guard does not want to open up the gate—Doesn't recognize his benefactor. Another guard comes up and tells him, "It's okay—It's *Adolphus—Nummer Eins*—our leader...Open the gate...we are ready for him..."

Steve stands up. "So we're gonna have to storm the camp..."

I open my eyes, release myself from Walter's embrace and sit up. "You believe me?"

Steve smiles for the first time this evening, as he closes his notebook and pockets his pen for the last time. "Tangie...Sweetheart...I let you down the first time. I don't intend to do it again. Last time, I went by police protocol. This time I trust your instinct, your vision, your memory—whatever you call your gift. I let Walter down—I blew him off the night the Sargentos kidnapped you...and Terese... Like a fool, I didn't listen to him...but I don't intend to repeat my mistake...I believe in you...and I'll convince Barry to do the same. You see, with what you've told me, we will be able to locate this camp. This time, I won't disappoint you. We'll find the bastard. I promise you."

Steve leans over and gives me a hug...and then kisses me on the cheek.

I look at Walter. Steam is coming out of his ears and his eyes are wide open. Not a good sign. Something triggers his anger...He stretches his torso as wide as he can and says to Steve, "Thanks for the vote of confidence, Steve, but watch the *Sweetheart* stuff. I may have a busted leg right now, but I took down Sylvan, one on one, and I can take you down..."

Walter puts his hands up and tries to rise from his place alongside me. His nostrils flare like those of a bull, as he balances himself on his one good leg.

Steve puts his arms up in the air, like a prisoner. "Easy buddy...I'm sorry," "I mean no disrespect to Tangie...or to you..."

"It sounded like a come-on..."

"No, Walter...It wasn't...it isn't...I'm sorry...I just have this loose tongue—It's a bad habit of mine—When I'm excited...I sometimes say the wrong thing...and...that was a friend's hug...and the kiss on the cheek---uh...I meant to show gratitude..."

I tug at the sleeve of Walter's pajama top, wanting to calm things down. "It's okay, Walter." *I'm exhausted from this interview...I can't deal with all this male posturing. I feel sorry for Steve. Walter never displays this kind of intense jealousy...He surprises me.*

I look at Steve...closer than I did before...Cute—definitely—but not my type. Handsome—in a rugged, in your face kind of way... *Kind of crass, I bet—when he is not in mixed company...I bet he's crass with some of his girlfriends, too. I can see him going on and on...He likes that kind of talk. I know he has a few babes he's stringing along. He likes to play up the tough cop image—which he developed when he worked the beat in New York—strong, assertive...and flirty. Hum...Sounds like the perfect match for Suzy.* I smile to myself—Suzy will be just desserts for Steve.

Interrupting my mind plotting, Steve looks from me to Walter and back again...and tries one more time. "Please...believe me...I meant no disrespect...Tangie...Walter."

Poor Steve...So ready to eat humble pie...again.

"Apology accepted." I hold up my hand and flash my engagement ring. "Just so you know..."

Steve eyes my rock. "Wow! Congratulations you two...I should have seen that one coming...but I'm not the psychic."

Walter backs down from his posturing and folds his arms. "Now you know..."

"Now I know." Steve stretches out his hand to Walter. "I'm very happy for the two of you...I'd offer to kiss the future bride, but I don't want to be socked."

I laugh out loud for the first time since Steve arrived. I feel refreshed and relieved, like a huge burden has been taken off my shoulders. "Come here you big lug." I lean towards Steve and plant a kiss on his cheek. I could swear he blushed.

Shortly after our exchange of pleasantries, Steve says he has to go, but that he'd be back ASAP with a safe phone so I could speak with Terese.

Before he leaves, I ask him if he knows a girl named Suzy Tripp. His eyes light up.

"No...but is she a friend of yours?"

"Of mine—Yes. Walter knows her also. It could be she's looking for the strong, silent type."

"Well, I'm strong, but not so silent."

"When you meet Suzy, you will be."

"Oh..." was all Steve could say.

Walter grins and pinches me on my rear.

I slap him and give him a silent stare with the warning, *"Watch it Buster...if you laugh, you're in trouble..."*

Unaware of our banter, Steve regains his composure. "I'd love to meet your friend, Tangie..."

Walter sensibly holds his tongue.

"But, maybe we should wait until this case is closed..."

"Yeah, Steve, good idea." I smile and my eyes light up. Meeting Suzy will give you something to look forward to—when all this is over."

Steve nods, gets up and bumps into my family as he rushes out the door. He excuses himself and races to the elevator, like a little kid let out of school early.

Chapter Forty-Four

My mother walked through the doorway. "So, Walter, that's your friend, Steve."

"Yes, Marianna."

"I thought he looked familiar—Yes...he was in your room when I visited you—and you were asleep—after your surgery...He was just sitting there with his head in his hands."

"That's my good ol' Steve."

"Walter...you never called us. They closed the cafeteria and requested we leave."

"Sorry, Marianna." Walter made an effort to sit up straight. "We just finished."

I decided to get Walter off the hot seat. "Yeah, Mom...we just got done. Thank goodness...I'm exhausted."

Walter gave me a squeeze around my waist. "Tangie, I'm sorry... Steve is not big on bedside manners."

"It's all right, Walter. I'm feeling more like myself...despite being tired. I hope Steve catches the bastard."

Bryan raised his eyebrows. "Which bastard?" I could see my brother's blood pressure cooking—His *I'm gonna take care of my big sister* mode consuming his mood.

"Well, Bryan," I answered, trying to sound cool and calm, "That *bastard* is one evil dude—name of Sargento. He's the guy that targeted Terese—the wife of my client—when I first took the case. I tried to find her... for my client, Fred Santigo. It's a little complicated..."

"I thought Walter disposed...of that bastard—that slime ball—*Sylvan Sargento...*"

"Well, he has a brother."

My mother let out a cry and collapsed onto my bed. I moved my foot just in time, so she'd have some room. The color in her face disappeared and she resembled a ghost. "No...it can't be..."

I became worried. My mother has an active imagination. I leaned over and reached for her hand and tried to comfort her. *Poor Marianna... she's been through so much already.* .

Walter noticed my concern for my mother and did his best to explain the present situation to my family. He hopped down off my bed and into his wheelchair. He cleared his throat. "Marianna... Bryan...after the explosion, we all thought Adolphus succumbed in the fire. Everyone, it seems...except Tangie. Just now, she told us the maniac got out before the blast. He's the one who plummeted Angelina on the head...and the one who attempted to poison her..."

"Then it's not over—my Angelina's still in danger...he's still out there!" My mother's voice took on a strange eerie tone—I never saw her acting so panic-stricken—Must be what a primitive mother sounds like when her babies are threatened. I thought of the mother bears out in the wild. That's what she sounded like to me.

"Yes and no." Walter tried to calm her down, by clarifying our involvement at this point in time. "We're not going after Adolphus this time—The police are. Our hunting days are over on this case."

"Well, that's a relief," Bryan said, as he continued to punch one fist into his other hand.

My mother needed convincing. *She knows me.* She stared at my face, searching my eyes for an answer. "I should feel better, but you worry me, Angelina."

"Mom, the police are going after him. I just give them information. That's my only role now."

"That's some comfort." She picked up my hand and patted it, then pushed the hair out of my face, like she did when I was a child.

I could see Bryan biting his tongue. When he got really upset he clammed up.

Walter spoke to them both in a soothing voice—in a tone that I have come to love—somber, yet reassuring. "The police have guns—high-powered weapons. They have sharpshooters, back-up policemen... and women...and the F.B.I. to run the entire operation. When Tangie and I first encountered the Sargento brothers—while trying to save Fred Santigo and his wife, Terese—we had nothing except our wits and our prayers...and a tracking device that went haywire."

"Hey, Walter..." My curiosity took over my patience. "How did you find me, without the tracking device? I could sense you looking for me...but I didn't know where you were..."

Walter looked at me, then Bryan, my mother...and Andee—who along with the twins—just entered my room. I didn't see her right away—as she and the twins kept themselves busy getting snacks in the hallway. Jason and Jeffrey love the vending machines...Right now, they amused each other playing traffic—taking turns pushing my food cart around the room.

Walter put his hands up in the air and surrendered to our waiting eyes. "You might as well all know the whole story."

Before my dear Watson began his R-rated tale of mystery and intrigue, he picked up a bag labeled *Techno-City* and pulled out a DVD player with two headphones. Then he called to the twins, "Hey, Jason... Jeffrey...Want to watch some cartoons? I've got *Space Kitty and Moon Dog* all loaded for you...all you have to do is camp by the window seat while we discuss grown up stuff..."

"Sure, Uncle Walter." Jeffrey and his brother ran to my honey.

"Gee...thanks." Jason embraced the DVD player Walter placed in his arms and smiled at his brother.

I studied Walter. He melted when he heard his name highlighted with *Uncle*.

Jeffrey grabbed the earphones from Walter's hand and raced his brother to the window seat. "We'll be right over here!"

"Don't forget to connect the headphones!" Bryan reminded them with a proud smile on his face. Along with Andee, they meant the world to him.

Jason returned his father's smile. "We won't, Daddy. We know how to do it." In less than two minutes he and his brother contented themselves on the miniscule window seat and tuned us out—lost in the wonderful world of cartoons.

Andee smiled at Walter. "Thanks…You're a thoughtful guy."

Walter gazed at the twins who resembled two baby robins who just found some worms for the first time. They devoured their catch. Walter nodded. "I thought that purchase would come in handy some day…I know you two don't want to leave and the twins don't need to hear all this stuff."

"Well, get on with it, Walter," Bryan said.

Men—so impatient—But to tell the truth, I almost said the same thing myself. I decided I needed to speed things up— and spoke with a calm I didn't feel. "Walter…I prayed the whole time I was with the Sargentos, that you would find me…"

"Well, Tangie…After we found Fred…and you refused to stay in the car…"

"My first mistake…"

"I was trying to revive Fred and told you to dial *911*…"

"Which I did…"

"I took my eyes off you for a moment while I was performing CPR…"

"And I disappeared."

"Yes…Without a sound…I think Sylvan waited for you on the side of the house, or behind the pyramidalis, near the corner of the front yard… Fred's body distracted you and me."

"Quite a distraction…"

"Sylvan snatched you and brought you to the house behind Fred's… The police found out Adolphus owns that place…and that he built a hidden gate between the two backyards…to pass back and forth at will…He parked the limo in the back of his house. The police determined that The Sargentos beat and poisoned Fred in Adolphus' home… and then carried Fred to his own home…and dumped him there…after they finished their dirty deed…"

"Convenient for Adolphus—*The Spider*—having his victims nearby…"

"That's how he finagled kidnapping Terese—when she snuck home to get her clothes—All he and Sylvan had to do was to walk through the back gate and grab her as she walked out Fred's back door…They drugged her and brought her to their lair...about the same time we met Fred Santigo at the funeral home...That's why they came kept us waiting at Price's funeral home. They needed to gag and tie up Terese...leaving her in their kitchen."

"You thought Sylvan carried me to that house also...but I don't remember being there...but then again, I think they drugged me."

"No doubt your were there...for a few minutes before they pushed you...and Terese into the limo. After that deed, the two of them simply drove away...diverting Steve and me along the way. They needed to return to Santigo's *Bath Boutique* to pick up their cache of money and drugs...They knew the police were getting close to finding them—or would be ...after Fred's death...they had to act fast...to get out of town..."

"I had my purse draped around my waist and shoulder."

"Yes...But they ripped it off you when you got to their home and used the tracking device against us."

"How?"

"Well...Tangie, you see...Steve showed up at Fred's house...a few minutes after you disappeared...Steve saw the panic on my face...and we immediately left the mansion. I turned on my tracking device...I picked up a signal that said you were headed to the freeway—southbound...we followed the signal to the Central District, and then the International District...where the signal stopped...before it began again.

"I hate to interrupt, Walter, but what happened to Fred...Did you just leave him there?"

"Well, not exactly. The medics arrived right after Steve...just as we were leaving and took over...They found a faint pulse and rushed Fred to the hospital...but I knew he wouldn't last...He turned blue, then white...The poison acted so fast...His heart stopped beating before you and I got to him...and we didn't know at the time, what happened to him...that he was poisoned..."

"Poor Fred..."

"I felt bad deserting him, but I needed to find you...I left him in good hands with the medics...I couldn't help him any more...and you... you were missing. Steve and I followed your signal. When we finally caught up with it, we found ourselves riding behind a Metro Bus, beyond the International District on route to Alkai. We pulled in front of it and stopped the bus. I got out of my car, and flashed my badge to the bus driver and told her to pull over. Then Steve and I boarded the bus…Steve called for back up.

"What about the bus?"

"A bust. Turns out some elderly lady, sitting in the back of the bus, with very thick glasses, disheveled mousey grey hair…shabbily dressed, found your…tattered and torn purse. She swore she found it that way. She said to Steve: *I was gonna turn it into the pol-leece. I was just lookin' inside for some ident-i-fi-cation when you came on da bus.*"

"So she found my purse, Walter. Anything missing?"

"Everything appeared intact…except the money. The purse no doubt answered the poor woman's prayers…She'll probably eat like a queen for a month on what she found. She didn't look healthy. Pale. Thin. I felt sorry for her. I knew she didn't have any involvement, but trying to convince Steve of that was a hopeless cause. He wanted to stay on the bus and grill her and the entire load of riders…you know…*who saw what and all that*…and all the time I kept seeing bidets and toilets…showers and sinks…and then a big fire. I started sweating…getting more and more freaked out…and I…so I…"

"So you ditched Steve?" I asked.

"Well, I told him I couldn't stay with him any longer…that I had to leave…I had a hunch. I took your purse, jumped off the bus, raced to my car and looked up the yellow pages on my Blackberry…Did you know there are a gazillion places selling toilets in King County—Did you know that?"

"Yeah, I believe you…and in the beginning…of our involvement with Santigo, I became side-tracked with Clancy's case…I never mentioned the name of Fred's business to you…"

"A detail that would have bought me…us…some valuable time…"

"So what did you do?"

"I called Fred's house. I found his name and phone number in your address book…from your purse…I called the number and the Black and Whites answered it. I knew they'd be securing the place…You know, scene of the crime and all that. I asked them to search the house for a business card. The search took them about ten minutes, but they called me back.

"Were they able to help you?"

"The cop on the phone says to me, *Is this Walter?* Like who else would be answering my phone? He continues, *Well, Pete here looked in the dead guy's coat lying on the ground.* I reply...*and what do you have for me?* He answers, *Bingo! You could have saved us a lotta trouble if you said to search his clothes.* Then I shout into the phone, *All right, already—Tell me!* And he says, *This here business card reads: Numero Uno Bath Boutique...151 Pike Street, Seattle, WA, 90911...Phone: 206-343-5555...Fred Santigo...Hey... that's the dead guy.*

So I reply, *No kidding*, thank them, disconnect and take off towards Pike Place Market."

"My love—you did it! Adolphus mocked me—bragged about putting my purse on a bus...said you'd never find me—You out-foxed him. I hoped and prayed you'd see through his scheme...and you did—*You* are my *Number One Detective*. I'm ecstatic you trusted your insight..."

"I'm ecstatic, too—that I found you, Sweetheart." Walter squeezed my hand. "Anyway...I went back on the bus and told Steve, *I'm outta here—I'm heading down towards Pike Street...Follow me, pronto.* He nodded, intent on questioning the bus passengers...Police procedure...told me he'd follow me later—a police car...was on route to meet us—I found out later the patrol car got stuck in a pile-up getting there...bad accident on Fifth Avenue..."

"*Police procedure,*" I reiterated. "So you headed out alone."

"Tangie...I had no choice." Walter looked at me with pain in his eyes. "I'm sorry—I thought Steve would be behind me—I wish I could have prevented Adolphus from hurting you...I never saw him coming... Sylvan knocked me out before Adolphus showed up..."

"Walter...you were shot! Twice! Give yourself a break. Remember... Never forget...you saved my life. If you didn't show up, when you did... and help me escape from Sylvan, I'd be dead, or stuck in some brothel in Columbia..."

I noticed my mother shuddering. Bryan sat down next to her on my bed and put his arm around her shoulder. Andee remained silent. Her eyes glazed over. *Andee's not used to the seedy side of life...Heck, I'm not used to the seedy side of life. I need to remind myself—the next time I get a creepy feeling—run the other way.*

My mother, who had calmed down considerably since her last outburst, stood up and hugged Walter. "Thank you, Walter. Thank you for my daughter..."

Bryan got up and reached out his hand to Walter. They shook each other's hand—Good solid handshake—I could see a bond forming between them. Better late than never. Then my mom let loose the tears she locked inside her for the past two weeks...I held out my good arm and motioned her to come back to me. We clung to each other for a long time. The whole time, the twins sat with their backs to us, watching their cartoons and chuckling, oblivious to the drama unfolding.

Andee came over to my bed and hugged me. "I'm glad you are all right." As an after thought, she hugged my mother. "Don't you worry, Marianna—Everything will be fine now." Then she went over to the window seat and sat down next to her boys.

I admire her...She's got her priorities right. Andee hugged her sons as they giggled and looked back at her, grateful for her presence. I could see tears streaming down her face as she ran her fingers through Jason's hair, then Jeffrey's. *At this moment, I know what it takes to be a mother...and what you receive in return. Happiness, joy, love, fear, anxiety and strength...all jumbled together—a sphere of many colors swirling around and around—I can see it in my head...going faster and faster and never stopping...not even for death.*

After Walter escorted my family to the elevator, I closed my eyes. For once I did not drift off to sleep as soon as I shut my eyes. Dr. Gibbs must be lowering my pain meds. *Good thing. I am tired of being dopey.* I heard the door shut and my fiancé returning. I opened my eyes.

Walter came up to me and smiled. "Do you mind if we have a sleepover?'

I pressed a button and lowered my nest for him. "Mi casa is your casa." I could feel Walter scooting himself into my bed and pulling up the covers. My eyes felt heavy and I could not open them, but I could feel everything...the best thing being Walter...kissing me goodnight.

I dozed off in Walter's arms...not waking until I heard footsteps in my room and a clink. I opened one eye. A midnight snack rested on my *bent* food cart. The twins are hard on their playthings. The snack rested on an angle. Good thing they serve milk in a sealed carton. The snack remained untouched. I closed my one eye. I could hear Walter shutting off the light that the tray bearer switched on. We lay there for another hour until Nurse Sheridan came in and whispered to Walter, "How about I help you back to your room?"

"Now is not a good time," Walter whispered back to her. "Doctor's orders...Therapy for Tangie."

"Oh..."

I heard the clunkity-clunk of her over-sized shoes as she turned around and walked out, without another word.

I pried my eyes open, leaned over and kissed Walter on the lips... remembering our life together, before the darkness took a hold of us. I smiled at him...grateful for his presence...Then I made a declaration. "Walter...I don't think I can do Whidbey at *The House of Charles.* I need you. My mother would put us in separate bedrooms. I'm sure of it."

"Me too...you know what, Tangie? I'm sure we can get along fine—just the two of us."

"I can be your feet."

"And I can be your arms."

"See, we've got it made—four working limbs. We can do take-out... and, Tangie...remember...I have a cleaning lady...she can help us."

I smiled at my fiancé. "Tell me her name."

"Patsy."

I giggled and the laughter made all my pain disappear.

"I love hearing you laugh, Angelina...and I guess for now we'll depend upon Patsy, my indispensible housekeeper...Pebbles will adapt to our temporary *handicaps*...He can use the doggie door...to visit nature in the backyard...and he can chase Hildie around the house for exercise...until we are able to go for walks again...together..."

"I love those walks."

"Me too."

"You hungry? I'll share my cookies with you."

"Just your cookies?"

"Well, you can have half my milk."

"Then what?"

"Then we sleep. We're in a hospital. I don't want to give anyone a heart attack."

Walter sighed. "Yes…I guess you're right…if you think about the dog Nazi—Mrs. Burns—Remember her? If Pebbles—the *Wonder Dog*—upset her, imagine how she'd respond to *Hanky-Panky* in the room next door. She's probably eavesdropping on us as we speak…"

"And so, my hero, let's go to sleep. We can dream."

"Yes…we can dream…" Walter sighed as he kissed my ear and whispered, "I love you, Angelina. I will forever. Never forget..."

I sighed, contented. Everything that happened the past two weeks evaporated into the mist that surrounded me—and I began to drift off into the wonderland of dreams. Tonight, I would sleep well—in Walter's arms...anticipating our nightmare would soon be over.

Chapter Forty-Five

The sun peeks through the closed blinds. Daylight calling. I sit up slowly, opening up my eyes to the light...and Walter...remembering how delicious it is to wake up in his arms...I gaze at him sleeping...so peaceful in his dreams...a smile on his face. Like me, he misses our nights together...

Nurse Sheridan clomped in pushing a tray cart from the hallway.

"Hi you two. Sleep well?"

For some reason, I was a little embarrassed to be found with a man in my bed; I felt like a teenager caught necking in the cemetery...

"Good morning...Nurse...er...Sheridan." I pulled my gown on over my shoulders. "Thank you...yes...best sleep I've had in weeks."

I recover well.

Walter opened his eyes. "Ah...Breakfast!"

"Yes." Shirley smiled at my prince and presented each of us with a rose. "Special delivery...Two breakfasts for the price of one...and I brought you a new cart. The other one is kind of bent."

"I wonder how that happened?" I faked any knowledge of the incident.

Walter smiled, turning on his ol' smooth charm. "Thank you, Shirley...you are too delicious for words."

And it seems he's on a first name basis with the medical staff. That's my Walter.

Shirley blushed upon receiving my sweetie's compliments. "Uh... Walter, there's a visitor to see you...I caught him peaking in your room. I didn't know what to tell him."

"It's okay, Shirley, you can send him in here..."

I frowned. Not dressed for visitors. Though I knew the visitor—the only one who comes in without a standing invitation.

Nurse Sheridan picked up on my distress. "How about you, Miss? Are you ready for company?"

"It's okay. I'll manage. But give us a few minutes if you can...and thank you for the roses..."

"Sure...I'll stall him at the nurses' station for about five. Then I have to get busy checking on the other patients."

"You're terrific, *Shirley*," I chirped, parroting Walter's term of address.

She winked at me as she clomped out. *Maybe some of Walter's charm is rubbing off on me. One could hope.*

"Hungry, Walter?"

"Yes, my love..." My honey moaned, as he started nibbling on my good arm.

It's a good thing we are physically challenged at the moment, otherwise it would have been embarrassing when Steve appeared in the doorway—with me wearing half a hospital gown. I managed to pull up the dang thing before he got near our bedside.

Needless to say, Steve has a way of screwing up. No way was I glad to see him...until I saw the two cappuccinos in his hands. Okay. Bribery will work on me. I can forgive his intrusion. Now I know why Walter squawked information to him. Steve knows his friends' weaknesses.

Steve placed a cell phone on our new cart and explained, "I'm sorry to disturb you so early, but I'm back with the *safe* phone...for you to call Terese."

I smiled at him and his face lit up.

Thanks, Steve. That's great." *I could be pleasant...sometimes.*

Walter shook Steve's hand. "Hey, buddy. Good to see you. Do you think you could help me get back into my wheelchair?"

Men. For them it is so easy to forgive and forget. Not so for those of us from Venus. I remember that Suzy took weeks to get over Walter and me. Suzy...Gosh it seems like months since I've seen her or Jean. They probably think I've dropped off the face of the earth. Maybe they'll forgive me if I ask them to be my brides-maids at our wedding—Sure thing—When this case is finally over, first thing I'll do is phone them...

"Hey, Steve," I asked. "When exactly did you arrive on the scene... you know...*Numero Uno Bath Boutique?*"

"After it was ablaze. Tangie...you know...I hate to admit...I screwed up. When I heard about the explosion on the dispatch, I gave up questioning the folks on the bus and followed the fire truck to the scene, in the patrol car, that finally arrived...As we cruised behind the fire truck to the burned-out building, Walter's warning sunk in my brain...I freaked out...I turned my head away from the sight of the burning building... and noticed Walter's body next to yours on the sidewalk...a block and a half up the street from the blaze...in the lamplight...

"Next time, trust Walter."

"I promise, Tangie. Walter knows best—My new motto. That's the last time I'm going by the book. Don't tell my boss I said that."

"Going by the book slows things down."

"You don't have to convince me of that a second time." Steve looked at his wristwatch. He reminded me of *Dick Tracy*.

"Expecting someone?" Walter asked.

"Ah, yes...*Barry*...Barry Cardoso will be joining us."

"Ah, yes...*The Boss*. Why?" I inquired.

Steve cleared his throat. "He has some news...and he wants to tell you about it—*In person*."

We heard a knock at the door. Steve shot us a sheepish grin. I grabbed my bathrobe from the foot of the bed and attempted to put it on. No luck. Walter noticed and assisted me in draping it over my injured shoulder, so I'd be ready for the *Daddy Fuzz*.

Barry Cardoso walked in, shook both our hands, nodded at Steve and shook his hand as an after thought.

He spoke to us in a barely audible voice—like he viewed hospitals the same way he does churches. "Tangie...Walter...the department would like to thank you for your actions...and when you are better, we have some certificates to present to you...at an upcoming ceremony. Your bravery under terrible circumstances is to be applauded...I'm honored that you helped us catch these criminals."

I interrupted his little speech. "Well, one of them, anyway."

Barry Cardoso's voice rose in volume as he addressed me. "Tangie, I know it's been a nightmare for you—this is not your usual line of work...I want you to know the department appreciates you...and Walter, of course.

"Thanks for your concern, Barry." I surprised myself by meaning what I verbalized.

"I have some good news for the two of you."

Walter and I did our best to act surprised.

"Yes?" I elevated my eyebrows and sat up straight.

"The F.B.I. is teaming up with us."

"About time." I cast a knowing look at Walter, then at Steve...and took a sip of my cappuccino. "Um...Thank you."

"You're welcome..." Barry nodded...

"I meant, *Steve*...for the espresso...But thank *you*, Barry...for coming to visit us."

"You're welcome...Tangie...Walter." Barry began pacing around my hospital room, like the surroundings made him nervous. "As you know, the department is grateful..."

I leaned over and smelled the roses on my bedside table. I could see the tables turning...*I don't have the sweaty palms anymore. Barry does. I guess I like to be difficult sometimes. Authority either makes me sweat or get mad. I could feel my anger getting the best of me. Eight days in a coma will do that to you. Seems I've lost my fear of authority figures.* I peaked under the cover of my morning breakfast plate, lifting the lid slowly to view to my gourmet meal. Peaches—canned. Oatmeal—decorated with raisins. Milk—lukewarm. Coffee—decaffeinated—on the lukewarm to cold side. Toast. Well, the toast looked promising. I spread some jam on it and took a bite. Not too bad once I dipped it in my creamy warm cappuccino. I saluted Steve.

Steve nodded and glanced at my breakfast. "Next time, I'll bring breakfast."

Feeling refreshed after my espresso, I disarmed him with a smile. "Great suggestion, Steve...I thank you in advance."

Barry interrupted our banter. "There's more to this..."

"I just see oatmeal."

"No...I mean, more to this than the F.B.I. being involved. Tangie, do you mind if I sit down?"

"Go for it." My mood changed like the wind, without warning to me—or my guests. I snarled, like a mean puppy dog not wanting to let go of his favorite possession. *My possession in this case is my peace of mind.* "Pull over that chair next to the window seat, Barry. It's comfy. My mom slept on it for over a week."

"Tangie…I..I'm sorry." Barry displayed a pained look on his face as he smoothed his thinning hair and took off his glasses. "I don't know what to say."

"Captain Cardoso…*Barry*…for Pete's sake, just tell me…why you came to see me…"

"Okay…Fair enough. We—the *S.P.D.* convinced the *F.B.I.* to do surveillance on this compound—*Adairwolf*—that you told Steve about. The F.B.I. located it—right where you said it would be—They were able to pinpoint the exact address…Just off I-90…and then off a feeder road that ends by a bridge…by the river. They are keeping the place under surveillance. Everything is in place for their agents—and a few chosen members of *The Seattle Police Department*—to pounce on the compound the moment that *Hummer* of yours enters the gates."

"Not my *Hummer*. It belongs to Adolphus."

"Yes…Of course—That's what I meant…Anyway, do you…and Walter…want to come along…and watch?"

Walter spoke up for the two of us. "What do you mean, *watch*?"

"From the air…I can secure a helicopter—We could fly over Sargento's hideout—after the F.B.I. take-down."

"You could arrange something like that?" My eyes lit up…*Closure…I need that.* I began to get excited about the job at hand—to feel the passion of the hunt. Adrenalin pumped through my body, blocking out all the pain that vibrated through it on a daily basis…*Yes. Work is good for my soul.*

Barry sensed my mood lightening and relaxed a bit. "Yes…it took some doing—convincing the F.B.I. to accept my idea—they don't like company on their assignments…but I worked on them." Barry smoothed down his hair and stood up, maintaining eye contact with me. "I informed our department we need you two as consultants. You deserve to be there…and who knows, you may be of some help in the end."

I leaned forward in my bed and looked at Walter. I could not read his reaction. *Poker face. No help. He's letting me call this one.* I swung my feet over the edge of the bed, *suddenly filled with a tremendous amount of energy... maybe a little too much energy. Ouch! It's a fine time to get a cramp in your foot. Seems my whole body's out of practice.*

Walter noticed my discomfort. He massaged my left ankle and shin until I felt relief. *Sometimes it's great to be in love with a psychic. He always knows what I need.*

I turned to Steve and stared at him. "Be honest, Steve. Will this be dangerous? I'm through with dangerous."

Steve started to speak, but thought better of it and just looked at me. Barry put his glasses back on and took control of our conversation. "Steve and I will personally keep you at a safe distance. We won't fly directly over the compound until the F.B.I. has neutralized Sargento's hideout."

"For real?"

"Yes."

I stared at Walter. Again, he gave me the poker face, and a look that read: *"It's up to you, kid."*

Smiling at my partner-in-crime, I turned to Barry, then Steve. Bobbing my head up and down, like the *Ichiro* doll I got at a *Mariners* game, I sighed.

"Don't tell my mother. She'll never understand."

Chapter Forty-Six

After our acquiescence to *The Plan*, Barry Cardoso excused himself, leaving Steve to finish up a few details. My stomach started growling, and then Walter's joined in harmony with mine.

"Why don't you guys finish your breakfast? I can wait." Steve sat down in the chair previously occupied by Barry. I smiled at him. Walter and I chomped down the breakfast chow. The meal tasted a lot better than it looked, except for the cold oatmeal—but what more can you expect from institutional food? *I thought of Walter's breakfasts...the ones he concocted for me with love...I am glad his arms still work. Can't wait to dig into his blueberry crepes.*

After Walter and I cleaned our plates, Steve winked at me, took out his *safe* phone, punched a button and handed me the cell.

I smiled at Steve, nodded, and answered the phone. "Terese?"

"Angelina! Is it really you? Are you all right?"

"I'm good. Mending."

"Me too...I'm sorry about the circumstances...upon which we met..."

"Horrendous, weren't they? But we survived...*Talk about a bonding experience*...Terese, I'm sorry about Fred...Sorry I couldn't attend the service...Seems my body lay comatose in the hospital at the time."

"I know...how terrible for you...Steve kept me posted...and now, I'm overjoyed you're recuperating..."

"Thanks, Terese...you're sweet..."

" But...I feel bad, still—responsible..."

"No...don't say that..."

"Tangie...about Fred's funeral—I would have liked you to be there—as you knew him—not too many people attended...but to be truthful...I think shock took over my being...I don't remember much...except that there was a priest there...and some ladies I didn't know..."

"Professional mourners."

"Who?"

"The ladies—My grandmother used to be one...*The Rosary Society*... They always pray for the deceased...Help the poor souls get to the pearly gates faster."

"Fred needs all the prayers he can get."

"In the end, Terese, Fred did the right thing. He showed courage. He fought for you."

"I know...but I can't help wishing...that he had the sense not to get involved with those evil men in the first place...He was such a fool...but I did love him...once..."

"You were a good wife to him, Terese...Leave it at that...don't beat yourself up...over Fred's mistakes...as my mom says, *Time heals all wounds.*"

"Thank you for reminding me...I need your words of wisdom. You know, you give me courage. Tangie...about what happened to you... when you tried to help me..."

"Don't worry about that anymore. I'm fine...I'll be back to normal faster than you realize."

Then I started to think...*Normal? What's normal? I've never been normal.*

I continued. "Terese...It's wonderful to hear your voice...and to know you are better—I was afraid you..."

"Thanks. That makes two of us...and Tangie...I can't thank you enough...for caring enough to find me...and saving me from Aldolphus... and Sylvan..."

"I didn't do much. You might say I just got myself kidnapped along with you."

"You *found* me...I know how hard you looked for me...Steve told me... and you didn't give up—You did help me get away from Adolphus—and you gave me hope...I'd say that's a lot..."

"You're sweet, Terese…Thanks…I have some wonderful news for you…Things are shaping up around here…you may be able to come out of hiding soon. Adolphus' days are numbered…and that's more than just a hunch…you see, the F.B.I. and the police are on his trail, as we speak."

"That's the best news I've heard all day."

"You must be lonely. Are the police treating you okay?"

"Yes. Only…Tangie…I can't reach Simone. Is there anyway you could contact her?"

"I can call the Sheriff in Kodiak…He's supposed to be keeping an eye out for her…He's got clout. I'll ask him to tell Simone you're safe. She'll be beside herself with happiness…She's been so worried about you."

I didn't go into the fact that Horst went back to Alaska to stalk Simone…

"Terese…any messages you want me to relay to your sister?"

"Yes—you…or the sheriff—Please tell Simone I'm much better now... that I love her…and I'll be up to see her the minute I am able."

"Will do."

"Hey, Angelina…I wanted to tell you something…about Fred's funeral. When I went to make arrangements with Mr. Price, the funeral director…Well…he almost had a heart attack. He collapsed in a chair. I brought him some water and yelled for help. He got up slowly and told me he was alright…but that I gave him a terrible fright."

"He probably thought you were the walking dead."

"I know I had a black eye and some cuts on my face, but I don't think I looked that bad. I had a lot of makeup and concealer on…"

I started to chuckle. I couldn't help it. I covered the phone speaker. I have such a wicked sense of humor. Can't wait to tell Walter. But I couldn't tell Terese about the body double—her look alike…and that Santigo was there…alive, the last time Price saw him…and that *Terese's Body Double* was not…"

"Are you there, Angelina?"

"Yes…" I clenched my teeth…stifling a hoot. "Go on, Terese..."

"And then…when the police brought in Fred's body, he collapsed again."

"Maybe the business is getting to be too much for Mr. Price."

"I guess so…Poor man."

"Yes...Poor man...Look Terese...I'll try to call you again, very soon. Get well...Stay safe...and I'm sure this nightmare will be over...for real...in a few days. Be strong."

"I will. Thank you, Angelina. God bless you."

"You too."

I barely hung up the phone before the comic floodgates consumed me. I started laughing, crying and hooting, all at the same time... loud—uncontrollably loud. Nurse Sheridan popped in to see what possessed me. Walter and Steve each asked me what happened...but all I could do was lay on my bed and shake with laughter.

Walter raised his eyebrows and shook his head.

Steve looked concerned. "What's so funny? Are you all right, Tangie?"

If I could have talked, I would have told them all, but I became engulfed with hysterics...until side pains came from laughing so hard.

I managed to sit up and get out the words, *"Laughter is the best medicine..."* so Nurse Sheridan would not call a red alert...Then I lay myself down on the bed and started giggling all over again. After about five minutes, I sat up, rubbed my shoulder and smiled at my two bewildered buddies. "You'll never guess who buried Fred."

Strange. Walter and Steve didn't think Terese's dilemma funny at all. They're not into dark comedy like me. I thought Steve would be...coming from New York City and all...but no. Not even a chuckle. For me, humor helps take the edge off all the gloom and doom floating around the universe. I continued laughing to myself and was wiping the tears off my cheeks when Mom and Bryan walked in my room.

"Hi dear." Marianna kissed my cheek. "It's good to see you so cheerful."

I'll spare her my funeral parlor humor. "Hi Mom...Yes, I just had a good laugh." Walter groaned. "Walter...and Steve think I'm a little crazy, but what is new?"

I hugged my brother. "Hi Bryan. Where's Andee...and how about my favorite nephews?"

Bryan came over and gave me a hug. "The twins...and Andee are taking a nap. All tired out from staying up late last night."

Bryan and Andee live in a cramped apartment in Fremont. Not far from my Ballard neighborhood. *At that moment a light bulb flashed in my mind.*

"Hey, Bryan…Since Walter and I are going to get married *this summer*…We don't need two houses in the city. How would you all like to move into my home in Ballard? You could turn the loft into a bedroom/ playroom for the boys—and you know how they love the park nearby."

I didn't mention that my home, until recently…had been under surveillance by three really bad dudes…But since two of them bit the dust—and the one remaining won't have long to join them—there or in prison, I felt sure it would be safe for my loved ones to reside in it.

"What are you saying, Tangie?" Bryan whispered, like his mouth was in need of lubrication. I handed him my water bottle. He drank the entire thing and set it done on my cart.

I could see his eyeballs popping out of their sockets. That image reminded me of Bryan as a little kid…when Mom and Dad promised to take him to his first *Seahawks* game. *I will never forget that look…I need to take him out of his misery*. "I'll be your landlady—*little brother*…until I can turn the deed over to you."

I looked at Walter. He gave me his best Cheshire Cat grin ever and nodded. I melted. *What a guy. Sweet. Understanding. That's why I love him.*

"I can't accept such an expensive gift." Bryan shook his head in protest.

"Sure you can—because it's not just for you…It's for Andee…and Jason and Jeffrey—your sons—my nephews…whom I love."

"I don't know what to say."

"Say, *Yes*. You know how Andee loves flowers. There's a big yard. You can plant a flower garden for her…even plant some vegetables…carrots for the boys, zucchini for Andee…With a little work, the yard and the house could look great. It's a classic."

"I know…I'm very handy…I love to work with my hands...and I could plant some raspberries…"

"See…it's the perfect house for you…"

"I am so grateful…"

"You can move in as soon as I get all my stuff out—That may take me awhile..."

"I could help..."

"Me too," piped in Walter.

"Me too," echoed Steve.

"And Bryan...the schools in Ballard are superb...the twins start kindergarten in the fall..."

"Of course...you don't have to convince me...*Tangie*...I am blown away by this gift...I'll have to talk to Andee first...but I know what her answer will be...She's been wanting a house for four years...since the twins joined us—We just couldn't afford to buy one in the city...or anywhere, for that matter...Gee...I'm sorry for all the rotten things I've done to you, over the years..."

"Well, Bryan, I forgive you for all of them, except one..."

"What's that?"

"For donning me with the name, *Tangerine*."

This time, Walter and Steve started hooting, along with my mother. Then Bryan joined in, with tears in his eyes. The warmth in the room intoxicated me. Who needs liquor? I've got my family. Things felt normal again. *Ah—That's what normal is. I like normal—'Tis a grand feeling.*

Chapter-Forty-Seven

Well, *normal* lasted about a day...the next morning, Steve waltzed into my room...with Walter wheeling himself in behind him, with a crutch in his lap, along with a shopping bag...just as I am sitting in my hospital bed eating breakfast—*a breakfast that has my taste buds on high alert.* Biscuits and gravy—still warm—*even smells good*...Hash browns—*one of my favorite foods*...Strawberries—*fresh from California...Washington's berries don't make an appearance until June, when all the strawberry festivals begin—Two more months before that bit of heaven.* But the coffee—*the hospital shouldn't even bother with coffee—They can't do coffee in this place.*

I looked up, hoping Steve smuggled a few espressos behind his back. He didn't disappoint me. But what he said put me on red alert.

"Here, Tangie...Drink up...fast...we gotta go quick. There's a helicopter on the roof."

"Steve...I can't leave this place...I'm wearing a hospital gown..."

Walter cast his smile my way and handed me a silver shopping bag with the logo *Nordstrom.*

"Let me guess, Walter...You called your personal shopper..."

"Last night. I had a hunch."

"Oh, so that's what you were up to while I lay sleeping."

"A guy's gotta get prepared. I used to be a boy scout."

"No you weren't. You're a musician."

"I know, but it sounds good."

"You're good, I'll give you that." I returned his smile and pushed my legs to the side the bed. "But I'm gonna need some help getting into these things."

"I had the shopper cut off all the tags. There are some boots, socks, jeans and a few tops for you to wear."

"No jewelry?"

Walter looked crushed.

"I'm only kidding, Walter. Look." I held up my hand and wiggled my fingers. "I have my ring...enough jewelry for anyone!"

Walter grinned and kissed my hand. Then he motioned to Steve. "Wait outside for a minute, good buddy...Watch the door—We'll be right out."

My stomach growled. "Oh Walter...can't I just eat a little breakfast? This is the best one they've ever served me. It could be my last breakfast."

"No time. Put these on, Tang, before the doctor comes on his rounds. We've got to get out of here before the nurse gets back. We haven't been discharged yet and we don't have time for paperwork."

"Could you at least leave my mom and the doctor a note...so they don't worry about us?"

Walter held up a piece of paper and placed it on my tray. "Already done!"

"Better tape it to the phone. Someone's liable to throw it away after they eat the leftovers."

"Gotcha."

I eased out of the bed as gingerly as I could with Walter's help. *He has such strong hands. I love his touch—strong but tender...Being injured has its rewards.* I sized up my *Wild West Lover*—dressed in hiking boots, jeans, a green and black plaid shirt, a fleece denim jacket. He leaned on his crutch—having ditched the wheel chair in the corner. He looked ready to round up a herd of cattle. I kissed him, tenderly, as he helped me take off my gown and put on my outfit. I could see the heat rising in his eyes and I could feel the heat rising in me as he put on my clothing.

"Soon," he whispered. "Soon this will all be over."

"Can't wait," I whispered back in his ear. I couldn't resist putting my tongue there as I leaned into his body. *What a tease I can be.*

Walter smiled as I tried to slip into my jeans. He didn't notice me wincing in pain from the movement. Then again, he wasn't looking at my face. "I'll get even with you, Tangie…you can count on it." He put his arm around my waist and leaned into me, taking my breath away…

"I am so ready for you…but…for now…all you can do now is pull up my jeans and zip them up…My arms and fingers aren't cooperating with my mind."

"Love to…*the better to see you my dear.*" Walter nuzzled my neck as he did so and patted my rear when he finished. "All done. You look great."

I kissed him on the cheek. "Thanks."

"Um…You taste so sweet, my love…but I'm getting side-tracked." Walter forced himself to pull away from me. He took my arm to lead me out the door. "Angelina…your mom is due in here any minute. She's even more on schedule than the medical staff. Hurry."

I grabbed the last of the strawberries, leaving one biscuit behind. Walter picked up the espresso for me. "You know, Walter…today, I almost feel like a healthy person…a visitor. Except for the sling around my arm. Thank goodness the patch came off my eye yesterday. I can see my way around. *No problem-o.*"

"I'm so glad, Tang…Let's go…"

"Just a minute…I want to conceal the black and blue marks with makeup." I looked in the mirror on my bedside table and did my magic act.

"Don't worry…you look beautiful just as you are…"

"All done!" I grabbed Walter's arm as he led the way—*The walking wounded.*

Steve poked his head in the room as Walter opened the door. "Come on, guys…let's go….Hurry…I pressed the button for the elevator…I hear Nurse Sheridan's footsteps…"

We ambled out of my room unnoticed. Running was not an option. We managed to get into the elevator without a hitch, but I could hear the clomping of Shirley's shoes as the elevator door closed. Steve pressed *Roof* on the control panel and we sailed to the top.

When the door opened, I could hear the deafening noise of the helicopter. We got out and approached the police aircraft. I spied Barry standing by its entrance. We shook hands and crawled in. Steve entered first, and then extended a hand to Walter, pulling him up...and then extended his hand to me. It took both Steve and Barry Cardoso to get me in, as I could only use one arm. Barry hopped in after me, fastened the door and in a few minutes the skies enveloped us.

I must admit...I never rode in a helicopter before. It felt comfortable...the views all around us thrilled me. The noise, however, would deliver to me one heck of a headache. Walter told me I'd get used to it. Then, seeing my distress, he handed me a set of earphones to block the constant roaring. When I put them on I just heard a dull hum. That I could take. I concentrated on the scenery—Breathtaking from our viewpoint. All of a sudden, I wasn't sorry I skipped most of my breakfast. Things might get bumpy. I never flew this low over the city. The chopper lifted us over the seven hills of Seattle—Capitol Hill, where we searched for Terese, Then Queen Anne—Walter's home, now my home... Queen Anne looked like a little village dwarfed by the city it kissed... We almost touched the *Space Needle* and passed the *Columbia Towers*...I wondered if the ladies in the restroom in the taller *Columbia Tower* could see us...I waved just in case—They have the best view of the entire top floor.

We zoomed over the other smaller skyscrapers and headed northwest over the *Ballard Bridge*...by my old neighborhood—now Bryan and Andee's home. Then, we flew south, heading towards 520— over the *Evergreen Floating Bridge*...and then due east over I-90. We would stay on this path until we got to Idaho. As we approached the peaks of the Cascades, I marveled at my favorite ice cream cone...Mount Rainier...I could reach out and taste it...almost...and then my morning pain meds kicked in and I could not keep my eyes open anymore. Walter told me to take a nap—That it would be awhile before we got there. I didn't need any coaxing. I leaned against his shoulder and he placed a pillow under my arm. I conked out...dead to the world.

I awoke to a gentle whispering in my ear.

"Tangie, wake up...We're almost there..."

"Walter... Where are we?"

"Idaho, my sweet."

"I slept through Eastern Washington."

"Just evergreen trees and thawing fields of brown."

"Oh... it's noon already, isn't it?"

"Yes. Are you warm enough?"

"Well, I love this furry camouflage jacket you provided... but I can't seem to get the chill out of my bones... Guess I've been in the hospital too long."

Then I did a whole body shiver, which startled Walter.

"Tangie... Are you sure you're all right?"

"*Adolphus is near.*"

"Yes, but we're safe. He will not get to us."

"Are you sure?"

Barry Cardoso turned around and leaned towards Walter and me. We sat in the rear of the helicopter and he perched near the pilot. "Tangie. Don't worry. There's no way Adolphus Sargento can get to you—or any of us. We've got you protected and the F.B.I. is all over the place. You will, however, see Adolphus apprehended. That I can assure you."

I smiled—wanting to believe him.

Steve looked at me and gave me a thumbs-up signal. "We're not going to disappoint you this time, Tangie."

Walter put his arm around my good shoulder. "I'll keep your warm, Angelina. You keep your eyes open and your spirits up."

"I am so ready for this to be over, Walter."

"Me too."

"I want my life back."

"Me too. It's going to happen. Believe me."

"I do, Walter... It's just that I can't stop shaking..."

"Look Sweetheart... Just think of you and me in Fiji... That will warm you up."

"You and me anywhere, except near Adolphus."

Walter hugged me. "It's almost over...You can do this, Tangie... I know you can. Think of our wedding..."

"*Wedding?*" Steve shouted like a crow...cawing. It was then that I realized all of us were yelling to be heard. .

"Yes, good buddy...that is what couples do after the engagement ring."

"Oh, yeah...but I was just getting used to the engagement."

"Well, Tangie and I move fast...Come to think of it, how about you be my best man?"

"*Best Man?*" Steve asked.

"Who's the best man?" Barry Cardoso barked, confused by all the noise.

"Steve is," I yelled.

"But I'm his boss." Barry's eyes widened. He looked bewildered.

"But this is our wedding."

"Oh, I thought you were talking about something else."

What can you expect from a helicopter. Not programmed for polite conversation. I looked at the pilot commandeering the aircraft. We left so lickety-split, I didn't get a chance to meet him. *Time for that later, I guess. He seems like an okay dude. Serious. Task oriented. Good thing. He has our lives in his hands. Right now, all our thoughts should be on catching Adolphus. No easy feat. He is one slippery madman.*

I decided to get back in work mode. "Okay, Barry...So what do we do now?" This time I shouted in my stage voice so he'd get all my words.

Barry returned my shout. "For now, Tangie, we circle."

Steve leaned closer to us so we could hear his words. "While the pilot is circling the aircraft, the ground crew will radio us a signal to let us know the compound's secure. That's when we'll do a fly-over, and land."

Walter nodded.

I smiled. "Sounds good to me." *I continued to shiver, despite my good mood.*

Barry reached under his seat, pulled out a canvas bag and like a magician, took some treasures out of the sack. He leaned back and handed two bags to Steve telling him to pass them around. Steve reached into one of the bags and pulled out a couple of submarine sandwiches and two bottles of vitamin water. He handed the picnic lunch to Walter and me.

He seemed so casual. *How could anyone eat at a time like this?*

Well, I couldn't, but Steve certainly could and so could Walter... and the guys up front—even the pilot. I sat in my seat, silently gazing out the window, until the scent of *Jersey Mike's Subs* drifted in my direction. *Um...oil, vinegar...peppers...onions...I detected my favorite—The Point Pleasant Special—I remember my grandmother telling me about these submarines—She used to eat them all the time...down the shore in New Jersey...And since Jersey Mike's opened in the Seattle area, I'm a devoted fan...*

My appetite alarm sounded—Time for serious eating...something I missed in the hospital—with the limited menu there. I opened my sandwich—Italian ham...cappacoli, provolone cheese, salami, lettuce, tomatoes and all the trimmings on a submarine roll—fresh and homemade—*Yum. I think I died and went to carb heaven.* I chomped, finishing the entire sub...and chugged the vitamin drink. Ham makes me desert thirsty. I think my blood sugar must have been really low, because suddenly, I felt great. No more shivers, no more fears. Just hope. I began to appreciate Steve...and Barry as well...Any one who brings me *Mike's Subs* in the afternoon—as well as cappuccinos in the morning— rates high with me—*Yes...Steve's a good choice for Best Man. May even invite Barry to our wedding...*

I feasted my eyes on Barry, Steve, Walter and the pilot. *Here we are—including me—just five cops on the beat...doing our job. Only...we're on air patrol. I could get used to this flying part—Much safer in the air. Out of harm's way—the helicopter is invincible...an eagle circling his prey.* Steve handed Walter and me a thermos of coffee. *What a guy—thinks of everything. Now if I had a cookie, everything would be perfect.* Barry passed another bag to Steve. Dessert. I moaned...Brownies—homemade—with macadamia nuts...even better than cookies. *Barry's wife must bake. Wonder how he stays so slim. Maybe he just passes the treats around. If he were my boss, I'd be grateful. I'd slave harder. Chocolate works wonders. Come to think of it, he is my boss...well, until this case is over. For today, I'm still the deputy. Still da Fuzz.*

As I finished off my second brownie, I could hear the pilot speaking. His voice carried to the back of the helicopter, as he was miked to a speaker, and we could hear his report on our earphones.

"I've got the signal. I'm going to lower the chopper. Take a good look. See if you notice anything out of order."

We flew over a forested area. We located the river...then the covered bridge appeared. It mirrored the one in my vision. Down the road to the compound, we saw the gates busted...and an olive green *Hummer* parked nearby. Near the gate sat four navy blue *Explorers*, blocking the entrance, so no one could leave or enter. Men, who looked like toy figures from the air, surrounded the compound. They wore blue jackets with what I assumed to be large FBI letters on the backs of the apparel. Bending in and out of the *Hummer*, two men surfaced, but I saw no sign of Adolphus. Lots of what appeared to be young men in brown shirts appeared to be lying on the ground. Some men, dressed the same way, stood up with their hands up in the air...Still no sign of Adolphus. I noticed a flagpole with a Nazi flag waving in the breeze—The dreaded Swastika still waved in these circles. One of the F.B.I. guys went over to the pole and pulled it down.

I tapped Steve's shoulder with my good arm. He lifted his earpiece so I wouldn't have to shout. "Steve...I don't see Adolphus. Something's wrong."

Walter's eyes penetrated the compound and then me. He caught Steve's bewildered stare and nodded. "Listen to Tangie. Tell the pilot to fly south. Looks like Senor Sargento escaped."

Steve relayed the message to Barry Cardoso who shouted to the pilot. They didn't question us. Just followed our orders. We flew south.

Nothing.

"Circle," I yelled.

Again—The relay...

We circled.

We searched like hawks with our bare eyes. Looking. I could feel tingling under my skin. *Close.*

Walter picked up a pair of binoculars and zeroed in on a target. "There's a figure down there...in the clearing...by that large boulder."

Well, the boulder looked small to me but heck, everything looked small to me from up here, just below the clouds.

Walter handed me the pair of high-powered binoculars. "Have a look, Tangie. See if you can identify him."

The helicopter jerks as I adjust the lenses. "Ouch!" *My shoulder bangs against the side of the aircraft—Even with a pillow resting against my arm, I feel*

the movement...It reminds me that I'm still injured—not a super woman...just human—with the usual weaknesses...I need to develop patience...I've said that before...but my mantra is not working. I focus the lenses again. Talk about power. I can see the dude's eyebrows—jagged. A backpack...No...a hunchback...His hands—Those long curved sharpened fingernails that crept into my skin. Their touch haunting me in my dreams—They come back again and again...to torture me—to...find me...I close my eyes and scream.

"Adolphus...He's here...Walter! Help me!"

"It's all right, Tangie...I'm here...you're not alone...we're together... here with Steve and Barry...you're safe..."

I sigh and relax, remembering where I am—in the clouds—safe. *I'm okay...I'm okay...*

Walter clarifies a detail to Barry and Steve as I come out of my stupor. He informs the rest of the crew and puts a rush on things. "These Neo-Nazis have a tunnel leading from the compound to here. Adophus thinks he's in the clear...Hurry!"

"Walter, honey, I think maybe he hears the helicopter." I fasten my eyes on the forest all around us.

Steve spots Adolphus creeping along the wooded path. He motions to the pilot. "I see him...I see him...He's gonna run for it—We've got to stop him before he disappears again..."

Barry instructs the pilot to put down the helicopter in the small clearing by the tunnel.

The pilot nods and expertly lowers the aircraft into the confined space. In minutes we bump into the ground. "Ouch!" *The shoulder again—my nightmare continues...*

The captain apologizes. "Sorry for the rough landing, guys...the ground is not level."

Steve puts a gun in his shoulder holster. "I gotta go after him. Tangie...Excuse me..."

Before I can open my mouth, Steve is climbing over his seat...then he scoots over Walter and me and jumps out of the helicopter like an overgrown jackrabbit. Before disappearing into the woods, he instructs his boss, "Stay with them, Barry. Protect them. I'll go after Adolphus. I owe Tangie this one."

With alarm written all over my face, I shout, "Be careful, Steve..."

I spy Walter squirming...he wants to jump out of his seat and join his Best Man. If he could jump at that moment, I believe he would have—busted leg and all. Steve catches on and signals us. "Stay put, you two. I mean it. No heroics! I can catch this guy. He's not that fast."

Barry nods. "I'll call for backup...be careful, Steve."

Steve gives a thumbs-up and starts towards the forest. He turns around one last time to remind Barry of a detail. "Tell the F.B.I. about the tunnel. They'll find it. They'll come."

I start thinking...*Remember to stay put...The last time I got out of a safe vehicle I ran into Sylvan...then Adolphus. Abraham Lincoln's words come to my mind, "I may be a slow walker, but I don't walk backwards."*

Walter, Barry, the pilot and I sit in the helicopter, with the blades whirling. We wait. Five minutes. The pilot turns off the blades. Ten minutes. Twenty minutes. The pilot turns off the engine. A gunshot blast startles us...shattering the momentary silence. The gunshot...not in the tunnel—but in the woods—beyond the clearing—where we last saw Steve running.

I close my eyes and start chanting. *"Let Steve be all right. Let Steve be all right..."*

Walter takes my hand and squeezes it. "He'll be okay. Steve's a pro."

And we sit. Playing the waiting game. It's murder to remain calm, closed in a safe environment... anticipating...hoping our friend will appear—alive and well...and not knowing what is going on...or if he will materialize...I grind my teeth and squeeze Walter's hand. He puts his other hand on my head and pulls me towards his shoulder...trying to ease my worrying. I hear Barry talking on his phone—communicating with the task force...I lean back in my seat, breathing in and out... slowly...trying to control my fear.

We hear voices outside the helicopter—at first a couple...then lots of them—buzzing—from the area of the tunnel. Twenty F.B.I. agents come running out like a swarm of bees looking for their honey—arriving just in the nick of time before the beekeeper takes off with their stash. Only this honey is not sweet...but how sweet it is...that they are here...so sweet! I feel like Christmas is coming twice this year. One agent comes to the chopper and knocks on the door. I try to open it, but my injured arm refuses to cooperate. Walter leans over and gives it a push...Voila!

I inform the F.B.I. agent about Adolphus Sargento escaping...and about Steve following him into the forest—and the path they took. Walter relates we heard a gunshot about five minutes ago. The agent motions to his ground crew—*Time for introductions later.* The head dude posts three agents in front of the helicopter and the rest follow him into the woods—after Adolphus...and Steve.

And so we wait...again...five minutes...ten minutes. After fifteen minutes, I speak to the pilot, who for the last few hours has remained nameless.

"Hi, er...Captain..." I shout out of habit. "I'm Angelina Seraphina... and this is..."

"Captain Stone at your service, Miss. I know Walter. Very pleased to meet the lovely and famous Angelina Seraphina."

I smile. "Call me, Tangie. That's my work name."

"Well, Tangie, you can call me Scott. I've heard a lot about you.

"Uh...Oh..."

No...All good—Your heroics speak for themselves. Great work spotting Sargento."

"Thanks." I nod and lean into my beloved. "But Walter spotted him first."

"You're a good team."

"We know." Walter grins at me and squeezes my hand.

Barry interrupts our chat. "Walter...Tangie...Look in the direction of the woods..."

We watch the drama unfold. First we see the leader of the F.B.I. group running out of the forest into the clearing. About ten men follow—jogging at a slower pace. Then, two men exit, walking...carrying...or should I say, dragging a crumpled body...I cannot identify it. I hold my breath. Walter places my hand to his lips and brushes the tears falling down my cheeks. "Steve will be okay, Tangie...you'll see...you'll see."

I look up at him, wanting to believe him. Barry shouts our names and points to the edge of the wooded path. I see a solitary figure staggering out of the brush—A man dragging his leg...limping slightly... having a hard time standing up. He comes closer...As he does, I squint to make out his face...*Steve!* Steve...stumbling out—all alone...gun in hand...*and alive.* I recite an ancient prayer and let out an audible sigh of relief, as I watch him shuffle up to the chief F.B.I. agent who spoke with us earlier. Another F.B.I. guy comes up to Steve and puts Steve's arm around his shoulder. Then another agent does the same. They help him hop the rest of the way back to the copter.

Walter pokes his head out of the aircraft. "Are you all right, good buddy?"

Steve gives us a thumbs-up. "I'm fine. Adolphus is the one with the gunshot wound. Me...I slipped in a hole. Those Neo-Nazis booby-trapped some foxholes with barbed wire...I think I busted my ankle... and Adolphus tried stabbing me with a knife he pulled out of his cane—he caught me by surprise...so I'm a bit cut up...but otherwise...I'm fine...Lucky to be back—in one piece." His grin spread from ear to ear.

I grin back at him—My weird sense of humor kicking in again. "Well, at least our next stop is the hospital—Welcome to our neighborhood—I'll introduce you to Dr. Gibbs...He'll take good care of you... but now, I don't know who's gonna bring all of us espresso."

Steve smiles at me...joining in my gallows humor, then winces in pain and collapses. The agents catch him before he falls to the ground. They lift our wounded warrior, place him alongside the helicopter door and tell him to stay put until the medics arrive.

As I reach out to give Steve a welcome back kiss...on the cheek, I notice the defeated, crumpled body kneeling on the ground, awaiting F.B.I. orders. Without warning, I lock eyes with Adolphus. His eyes—his ferret eyes—bloodshot and vacant bore into mine—and attempt to drag me into their hell.

"You! My little puta...you bitch." Adolphus snarls at me and spits on the ground. "You're alive..."

Steve forces himself up, with his arm, clenching his fists and staring at Adolphus. Walter does the same. I feel their anger—their willingness to beat Adolphus to a pulp...and I feel the warmth of their caring—they become my shield and my armor.

With a confidence I didn't realize I possessed—until now, I deflect the penetrating gaze of Adolphus— his insults—his aura of darkness. I am no longer afraid of my tormentor. No longer silent. No longer a victim. "I don't kill easy, Adolphus. And where you are going, you won't be killing anyone else...anymore."

"Wanna bet, my little bird? You think you're so smart, so clever—You're nothing...Nothing! I still have power over you...I'll follow you...you'll see me...in your nightmares. Sweet dreams...my little nightingale...try to get away..."

Adolphus cackles one last time as his licks his right index finger.

The thimble...his thimble of poison...gone...

My eyes widen as I hear that demented high-pitched laughter for the last time—on this earth—before convulsions take over the demon's body...Then silence...no movement...eyes wide open...like the girl in Fred's office—and the same tattoo on his arm...with a swastika glowing in red—like Horst's...

I see...Adolphus slumping to the ground, falling before one of the agents can catch and bind him.

Fearing a trap, two agents hold him down on the ground while another one ties his hands together. Another one checks his pulse and listens to his heartbeat.

"We're losing him!" shouts the agent, as he places his head on Adolphus' chest. "Call the medics..."

I grip Walter's hand. "He's taken one of his own pills..."

Walter leans out the door of the chopper and shouts to the agent standing closest to Adolphus. "CPR won't work—I've been there before—He's a goner."

"*Death comes quickly*," I whisper. I start to tremble...my knees shake...my lips are dry...my voice gives out...No sound left. I have no prayers for Adolphus—Just relief at his passing. I shudder and wince in pain. Bending over, I clasp my hands together and relive the hell I stumbled into a few weeks ago.

I remain in a trance, sensing what is going on around me, but not participating in the action, lost in the past. Barry hops out of the chopper to chat with the F.B.I. chief and crew. Walter exchanges information with the pilot and Steve. The medics arrive and administer first aid to Steve and confirm that Adolphus is dead. I remember thinking, "*Somehow I don't think Numero Uno Sargento of the Brotherhood is gonna rest in peace.*"

I feel a rush of wind on my face, followed by a feeling of peaceful warmth. This inner awareness grabs my attention and I focus on the present...I close my eyes and meditate on the day—chanting silently to myself—*I will take the joy in my life today...and leave the past...the trauma... behind...I will not look back." I breathe in. I breathe out. I breathe in...and sing a song of gratitude in my heart.*

Suddenly my girlie alarm sounds. Time to go to the little girls' room. I give Walter a glance that says, *"Help! I'm about to pee in my pants."* He knows that look. Panic. Must vacate the helicopter—Pronto! I don't think anyone will mind—The search concluded, area secure. Bad guys toast.

Walter motions to a female F.B.I. agent. With Walter's direction and Barry's help, she maneuvers me out of the aircraft. She smiles at me, nods and leads me down a wooded path to a private area behind the bushes.

"When in Rome..."

We approach the Seattle area just as the fairy lights began to twinkle. Twilight. I love this time. Between day and night—Things ending and beginning at the same time—like Walter and me. A new direction—a new adventure together. I can feel it, as we close this high-profile case together—This first chapter in our lives.

As we land on the helicopter pad on the roof of the hospital, a tall male nurse appears with a wheelchair for Steve and a smile for all of us.

He helps Steve into the chair and starts wheeling him at a fast pace towards the elevator. I shout for the last time, in a hoarse voice, " Steve... our hero!" As I wave to him, he turns around and smiles—displaying a look of contentment and peace on his face...before he disappears from sight.

Walter and I, with Barry's help, crawl out of the helicopter. We say our farewells to him and Scott—and thank each other for a good day's work. *Camaraderie. So this is what it is like to be a cop. Not bad...Band of brothers and sisters and all that. I could dig it. As long as I stay in the clouds, I can do this.*

Walter senses my satisfaction. I notice a smile plastered all over his face. "Ready?"

"Ready for what, Walter?"

"Time to face the music, Angelina."

"My mom."

"Your family...and our doctor."

"I have a feeling the medical staff will throw us out after our little caper."

"That wouldn't be such a bad thing, would it?"

I take my good hand and placed it on his cheek. "Kiss me, Walter."

"I thought you'd never ask."

Well, we didn't have to face my family. They faced us. After we broke up our prolonged kiss—Only because Walter couldn't stand upright any longer without falling down...and my shoulder started throbbing big time...

I heard little voices giggling. Jason...Jeffrey—their Care-Bear voices shouting as Scott lifted his aircraft to the sky. "Mommy, when can we go on a helicopter ride?"

Walter and I turned around and giggled along with them.

I threw out my good arm to the twins as they reached out to me. "Next time, Jason. I promise, Jeffrey!"

Bryan shook Walter's hand and turned to me. "We heard what happened, Sis. What you and Walter did...Steve told us."

"We didn't do anything, Bryan...We just went for a helicopter ride."

"Okay, Tangie...If you want to call it that way—That's fine with me. But we know. Mom knows. And now I know. You don't have to pretend with me anymore."

Tears came into my eyes. I stood up from hugging the boys and disappeared in my brother's arms. "Thank you, Bryan...Thank you, so much." I cried as I kissed him on the cheek. I looked at him and the tears in his eyes mirrored mine. Brother and sister. Past all hurts and arguments...Grown up at last.

Walter hugged my mom and Andee. My mom winked at Walter, then caught my glance and mouthed the words, "I love you, my dear Angelina." *I guess they forgive us for taking off on them. They understand. They are on our side. It's good to be home.*

Epilogue

What surprised me the most—The hospital staff didn't evict us...not right away—they gave us a day of rest. I remember clearly Dr. Gibbs saying, "Tangie Walter, despite your caper, you are still my patients and I...and only I...will discharge you."

We ate humble pie—the hospital dinner—that they served the night of our return, behaved ourselves and went to sleep. It didn't take much persuasion on anyone's part. Exhaustion took over from our day's journey.

The next morning, while Walter went to his final physical therapy appointment, I looked around the hospital room that sang *Home Sweet Home* to me these past few weeks. Would I miss it? Naw. Not a chance.

I leaned over on the table and there sat a diary. *My diary*. I hadn't written in it since...*Adolphus*...I thumbed through the pages. Read the part about calling Simone. Then I remembered...Simone...Terese... Sheriff Tokala—The missing piece...of my investigation. I dug Sheriff Tokala's card out of my stolen purse—the purse that Steve retrieved for me. The purse looked a little threadbare from its travels, but it contained all the necessary ingredients, except money. *Oh well, easy come, easy go. I'm here, alive—and so is Walter—And Steve—And Terese...That's what counts. And I can always get a new purse.*

I picked up the hospital phone and told the operator I needed to make a long distance phone call. I heard paper rattling and then, "No problem...Just give me the number and I'll connect you."

I must have clout.

On the fourth ring, Tokala picked up.

"Sheriff Tokala here."

"Hi! Remember me? Angelina Seraphina? Tangie?

"Tangie…Of course. You're a little hard to forget."

"So I've been told."

Great. So now I'm flirting with the Sheriff. What's gotten into me? Must be the coffee…or maybe it's Walter…maybe I'm getting better…maybe it's the clout. I've gotta stop making these lists…

"What can I do for you, Tangie?"

"Could you please get in touch with Simone Royale—Therese Santigo's sister—and let me know if everything is all right with Simone? And, please…tell her for me…*it's Springtime in Seattle…*"

"Some kind of code, huh?"

I'll give it to the sheriff. He's sharp.

"You're on to me. Just tell Simone I found her sister and that she is safe…and sound."

"That's wonderful—But I wish I could say the same thing about Simone."

Panic strikes.

"Oh no…"

"I tried to call you…"

"I've been tied up…"

"You didn't answer your phone…"

"I haven't been home…"

"Out on the town?"

"Not the way I wanted...You see, Horst's bosses…The Sargento brothers—They kidnapped me…and Terese…"

"Is this another one of your stories?"

"Well, sort of, but it's a true story."

Silence.

"Are you all right? How's *Terese?*"

"I'm recuperating. So is Terese. I think this is my last day in the hospital. I expect Terese to be coming out of protective custody today…"

Sheriff Tokala cleared his throat. "Simone will be discharged today… from the hospital."

"What? What happened? Did Horst…Did he…" *I couldn't finish my question…I wasn't so sure I wanted to know the answer.*

"Yes...Tangie. Seems your Horst attacked Simone...threw her around her cabin...he would have...I don't know what...if..."

"Look, Sheriff, he's not *my Horst...*"

James Tokala is beginning to tick me off.

"Tangie, listen to me...if Simone's friends weren't right next door and on the alert, I'd be looking for a murderer right now."

"Are you saying he got away?"

"Well, not exactly."

"What about Simone...is she all right? How about Pete and Michel? Were they with her?"

"Yeah, Pete—that's the caretaker, as you know...He came running... and Michel—Simone's friend... heard her screaming and rushed in... Simone sort of fell apart...you know...mentally, as well as physically... after Horst attacked her..."

"I kind of know the feeling, Sheriff..."

"Yes...she went into shock—Michel called me to help them...So I met him and Simone in Kodiak...along with Captain Turner...You remember him..."

I nodded, but of course, Tokala couldn't see me.

"From there, we flew Simone to Anchorage for treatment—and arranged for Captain Turner's wife to substitute teach in Simone's absence...Simone was all worried about her students, despite her condition."

"That was kind of you...to help out...Sheriff...Thanks...I know *Terese* will be appreciative."

"Yeah, well...Pete...her neighbor—stayed behind to watch over her place. He said he'd keep an eye on things and his hand on his rifle.

"Good plan."

"The doctor doesn't want Simone going home alone right away, so she'll stay at Michel's cabin on the west side of Akhiok—'til she's better."

"He'll take good care of her."

"My thoughts exactly."

Well...what do you know? Sheriff Tokala is a romantic—Now, who would've thought that? Not me, and I'm the psychic...He probably writes poetry on the side when not catching the bad guys...and no doubt has all the trimming for a candlelight dinner in his bachelor pad.

"So, Sheriff, what about Horst?"

"What do you suspect, Tangie?"

"I have a feeling the bears got him."

"Lady, you're good. But you're wrong. Singular. One bear—one very large, Kodiak bear—First killing of a human in seventy-five years."

"It seems to me he picked the right one."

"It's a she."

"How do you know these things? Did you have tea with the bear?"

"I have my ways."

Yeah—Psychic cop—I'm on to you...

"Sheriff, when did you find Horst?"

"After the storm high-tailed it out of here—The rangers headed out to spruce up the park for visitors—It's *springtime* in Kodiak also...you know—One of the lady rangers found his corpse after the snow melted... Half his face torn off...Looks like the Kodiak strangled him—then clawed him to death."

"He met his match," was all I could say. *Can't say that I felt any pity—except for Marlaine. After all, she's Horst's sister. She loved him—Probably the one person left in this world who cares what happened to Horst Blouzer. To Marlaine, he'll always be her baby brother—the little chap who chased her around the family's garden in Munich—her childhood companion... not the brute that went around torturing women*

What happens to people ...that turn them into sociopaths? Sometime in his life, Horst—perhaps as a little tyke— loved his family and they loved him in return—What happened?

I popped out of my mind-wandering daze when Sheriff Tokala grabbed my attention with an invitation—to visit him up in Kodiak. "Hey Tangie...the thing is, I need someone to make a positive ID on this Horst guy and you are the only one I can think of...and perhaps... maybe...Simone's sister—Terese. We could fly you both up here..."

"Sheriff...*Terese* saw Horst *up close and personal*...He got in her face. *Me*...I saw mostly his knuckles and his tattoo."

"Well, between the two of you, you could make a positive ID, Horst havin' only a half of face and all..."

Just what I want to gaze upon...I'm sure Terese will be just as thrilled as I am to view the deceased.

"What about Walter?"

"Walter?"

"My secretary...my bodyguard...my *fiancé*..."

"Oh...your *fiancé*...that's new—Congratulations. Well, bring him of course, I guess...if he could finger Horst."

"Thanks...he can and he will...and we have a sample of Horst's DNA for you."

"That's really great...but I'm stretching our budget with you and Terese."

"Walter can pay his own way."

"Thanks, Tangie. That would be generous of him...and a help to our department."

Yeah, and a help to me...I'll have someone to lean on when I faint.

Somehow I get the feeling Sheriff Tokala is only interested in seeing Terese—I'm positive he could do without both Walter and me. Probably just needs us for introductions...Hum...I wonder...I remember the way Tokala caressed Terese's photo—like it was a work of art that contained her spirit...There's something more going on here...Stranger things could happen...

"You know, Sheriff, coming up to Kodiak might be just the right medicine for Terese. She just buried her husband...you know. Her husband, Fred—a victim of homicide—and the poor girl's in pretty bad shape. I know she'd love to see her sister again—Also, she could use some moral support. She's rather fragile."

"You tell her we will take great care of her up here in Kodiak. I'll ring up her sister at Michel's. I'll tell her Terese is coming. It will be good medicine for each of them."

"Thank you, Sheriff. You won't regret your kindness, for helping Simone—and Terese."

Silence. Then I heard a sigh on the other end of the phone. *I could see Sheriff Tokala smiling as he answered me.*

"Call me, *James*."

"*James* it is. See you soon. We'll fill you in on everything when we get to Kodiak."

"Have a safe trip."

Somehow I figure James knew more about our adventure than I told him. Maybe he reads the Seattle newspapers. Maybe Walter communicates with him. Maybe I'm right on target about James being psychic—Maybe all of the above.

Anyway, now I know how Walter feels—to be on a first name basis with da Fuzz—Great.

After my conversation with James, I called James Benson, the porter from *Alaska Airlines*, and told him not to worry about Horst anymore—He would not be a bother to him or anyone, anymore.

"Great!" he replied. "Bernice and I are fixin' to pack for Las Vegas... and now we can travel without any distractions. You be good, Ms. Tangie."

I assured James Benson I would be.

Next, I contacted Clancy and confirmed arrangements for his entire family to travel *North to Alaska*—on the same flight I booked for Walter, Terese and myself. Might as well have the entire gang go at once, get everyone situated, and wrap up both cases.

"Clancy...I'm sorry I couldn't introduce you...I mean, re-introduce you to your mom in person...but...I..."

"Tangie...there is nothing to be sorry about...I cannot begin to tell you how much I appreciate what you have done."

In a voice that broke now and then, he related to me the details of his reunion with his mom...at *Our Lady of Peace Church*.

"A fitting place, Clancy...the beginning and end...*the alpha and the omega*." I smiled through my tears...imagining the embrace of mother and son—long awaited—an event that will never be forgotten...by either of them...

Walter appeared by my bed that evening, with fire in his eyes and leaned against my bed. I leaned into him and unfastened my robe, dropped it to the floor, and he took me in his arms.

And...we finally did get thrown out of the hospital—in a good way, however. The next morning, the staff presented us with a bouquet of yellow roses, tulips, daisies and carnations—and extended their congratulations on our recovery. Doctor Gibbs gave us his blessing and told us to stay out of trouble. He said he didn't want to see us anymore, except as visitors. The hospital food service made us a small cake and I managed to cut everyone a piece...and we toasted with sparkling cider served in plastic wine glasses.

As Walter and I stood up to leave, despite my resolve, tears formed in my eyes. All these wonderful people helped us heal. I tried to let them know how much they meant to Walter and me...but I couldn't put my feelings in words. Tongue-tied, I hugged each medical staff person, and sobbed when Shirley helped me into a wheel chair and pushed me out the door...on my way back to the real world outside—and my home with Walter.

The best-laid plans don't allow for time off. Our respite at our Queen Anne home lasted about one hour. *No rest for the weary*. Barry Cardoso drove us home from the hospital and carried our belongings into the house. At my insistence, my mother stayed home in Kirkland. She missed two weeks of sleep and Bryan missed mucho days of work..."I'll see you later, Mom...you don't need all this drama." I tried to reassure her...my mother gets more teary-eyed at these occasions than I do. I think Bryan appreciated the chance to sleep before going back to his job.

As we entered the living room, I thanked Barry. "Sorry I can't fix us something to eat, but our homecoming consists of a one-hour furlough—Business beckons us in Alaska...We have to catch an early flight to Anchorage...and then a connecting flight to Kodiak—before dark, as we don't want to crash into Barometer Mountain—I winked at Walter—It's necessary to land in the daylight."

Barry nodded, took off his glasses and cleaned them with his handkerchief. "No problem, Tangie. I'll wait for you two to pack for your trip. Then I'll do the honor of chauffeuring you to the airport. Let me know when your suitcases are loaded and I'll carry them down the stairs for you."

I leaned up and gave him a kiss on the cheek. "Thanks, Boss."

I think he blushed. *Barry is turning out to be as dependable a friend as Steve.* "Do me a favor, Barry? Please… Call my mom…Marianna… later…but don't tell her any details about our pending sojourn in Kodiak until the plane takes off. I don't want my mom trying to convince me to stay home. She's good at that and in weak moments, I cave under pressure. I don't want to miss this trip."

Every detective likes to tie up loose ends. After Alaska, my job is done. Kind of a happy/sad feeling—like graduating high school…saying goodbye and saying hello.

Barry nodded, picked up a newspaper from the coffee table and made himself at home, while Walter and I hobbled upstairs to get ready.

Our seats were booked for a twelve p.m. flight to Anchorage, with an afternoon connecting flight to Kodiak. Steve volunteered to drop Terese at Sea-Tac after he picked her up from the safe house. *How Steve planned to drive with that cast on his foot, I don't want to know.*

Clancy told me he rented a stretch limo for Mary Claire and her brood, his girlfriend, Jessica and himself…so they would arrive at *Sea-Tac* together. We all planned to meet at *Starbucks* by *Alaska Airlines* before eleven—give or take a half-hour.

At present, Terese, unlike Clancy, has no income—no savings and no trust fund. Any money Fred possessed is frozen— tied up in the criminal investigation. Maybe she'll see some money from the sale of Santigo's house—That would be enough for her to live on for a few years…but right now she's strapped. *Doesn't seem to bother her any…except she feels bad she cannot pay me. I think she sees the world through different lenses now—like*

me, happy to be alive. Anyway, my search for her, as a missing person, turned into a non-profit venture—or adventure, however scary.

As I keep telling myself..."Dead men don't pay." And Fred, unfortunately, is dead. Oh well...easy come, easy go. Like Terese, I've developed a new perspective on life—It's too short to sweat the small stuff. And thanks to Clancy, I'm out of the red. To my surprise, he turned out to be the kid with the big bucks. Good thing...being as I'm starting a new business-personal relationship with Walter—I've gotta bring something to the table—my work ethic kicking in. Not much of a dowry, but it'll work.

At my suggestion, Clancy booked all of us into the *Bear Pause Inn*. Upon our arrival in Kodiak, Nathan Sheldon arranged for Gus and a fellow driver to meet our entire gang at the airport. When Gus and his buddy deposited us at the inn, Nathan, his main squeeze—Terri... and Ceira—now house manager...and the rest of the staff—all four of them—greeted us with open arms...Handshakes and hugs all around. I felt like royalty—*Or maybe family—anyway 'tis a grand feeling...*

After we deposited our bags in our respective rooms, with much help from the staff, Clancy, his girlfriend—Jessica, his mom—Mary Claire and the rest of the family went out for a late lunch and a tour of the town. *I visualize Clancy coming to Kodiak a lot. Maybe even settling here someday... He possesses true pioneer spirit. He's willing to take chances...and now he's put his life together...and he and Jessica can move forward. Makes a difference, knowing your heritage.*

Walter and I opted for staying in our suite and ordering room service. Terese informed us she needed to take a nap. So The next few hours belonged to just the two of us...Ah...sweet thoughts crept into my brain...and then, I remembered—must call Sheriff Tokala...and I need to schedule a meeting with Father Joe...But how long could that take?

Clancy and Company loved the puddle jumper to Kodiak. They didn't even notice our close, nose-to-nose meeting with Barometer Mountain, as the fog began to settle in at the airport. Been there, done that, so I didn't echo the excitement they shared. They wanted to explore Kodiak. I just wanted to come to my room with Walter and relax a few hours.

Relax we did. Nathan Sheldon treated Walter and me to first class service, giving us his best suite, sending a mammoth lunch tray to our room. He even threw in a pitcher of Mai tai cocktails, compliments of the house. *I can see me passing out after lunch. Walter has other ideas.*

Ceira delivered our food. She didn't ask what happened to us after she gave us the once over—*I assume we still look like the walking dead to some folks*—I noticed her downcast eyes...as if trying not to pay attention to my sling or Walter's cast. *She remembers us before our injuries...well before our latest, more serious injuries. She should have seen us two weeks ago. Methinks she would have shuddered.*

She smiled at us and set our gourmet meal on the small table. "I am glad you have returned to the Bear Pause...Call me if you need anything else."

And in a flash, she was out the door. *That's what I like about her. Not nosy. Anyway, the whole town no doubt knows about us and why should she ask questions if she knows the answers? That's what a small town is—a news conductor. No one needs e-mail on this island. I'm sure, since Horst's body turned up in the state park, the local reporter did the usual research—No doubt Horst's demise turned out to be headline news in Kodiak. And I bet The Kodiak Newpaper, through Internet news service and Associated Press, discovered Horst's link to all the evil doings in Seattle.*

"Hey Walter," I slurred, after my second Mai tai. "I gotta call Sheriff Tokala—*James*..."

"*James*, huh—Can't he wait?"

"Yes, he can, as far as I'm concerned, but I have a feeling if I don't call him, he'll be over here on our doorstop."

Walter took my hand and kissed it. "Then we better get to work, pronto." He whispered sweet nothings in my ear and set my body whirling as he removed my blouse.

Abandoning my half-eaten lunch, and chugging my mind-altering Mai tai, I helped Walter over to our four-poster. Marvelous to lie down on a luxurious bed in an elegant bedroom, complete with romantic fireplace. No hospital distractions. Ah...if this is a preview of our honeymoon, I cannot wait any longer. In the heat of my passion, I struggled to pull Walter's jogging pants off him, as his cast was in the way. Walter smiled at me, bent down and tore them off like a male stripper.

"Velcro," he announced. "Comes in handy."

"You are such a tease." I laughed...I felt so ready for some really good...

"Knock, knock..."

"Ignore it." Walter, deep in heavy breathing, could not be bothered with a mere pounding on the door.

"Maybe it will go away..."

"My love..."

"Oh Walter...kiss me and block it out..."

Walter obliged. The pounding continued.

We ignored it.

Then the voice began. "Tangie...Walter...Are you all right? Should I call Sheldon? I know you're in there...Ciera just dropped off your lunch...Please answer me...Tell me you're all right."

Walter muttered some strange sounding words... "We're all right. Hang on...I'm coming."

I embellished Walter's sweaty speech as I felt my entire body tingle with excitement. "Yes, yes...I'm coming...it'll take me a while to get to...the door—I'm handicapped—We're handicapped...Hold your horses, hold your...Give us a few minutes...Do not open the door... Please...Oh...please..."

The last *please* I saved for Walter. *He always grants me my request. He likes to see me beg in the heat of passion.*

I sighed after Walter pulled away from me...so content...finally... but...no relaxation, no calm after the storm this time round. Back to work.

"Walter...One of these days, we're going to take a long, uninterrupted vacation and no one will be able to find us."

"I think we better get dressed." My love handed me my undergarments.

"Maybe I'll play sick. I'll put a bathrobe on. He won't stay long, that way."

"Don't count on it." Walter groaned as he jumped a bit on one leg and re-velcroed his trousers.

I took my own advice and opened the door in my yellow fleece robe, like a lady of leisure—or an invalid—*Take your pick, Sheriff.*

"Sorry, James—We're all tired out from the trip. I planned to call you in a couple of hours."

"Sorry to disturb you, but our morgue is minuscule. We need to get this Horst guy out of there, ASAP."

"You could bury him in Potter's Field."

"Very funny. We have to ID him first."

"How about tomorrow?"

"How about today?" James was not letting up on this one.

I looked at Walter. He shrugged his shoulders. *He caves so easily.*

"What happened to you two? You look a mess. Do I need to worry? You said you'd tell me when you got here."

"Well, we just got here…and Terese is taking a nap."

"She's staying here, also?"

Like he didn't know. What is his angle?

"Now, James, don't play cute with me. You know everything."

"Not really. I just know what I read and what the police in Seattle told me. They don't tell me everything." James eyed Walter with that remark… and continued his search for information. "Either because they don't know me—or they don't trust me."

"Oh…so you're in our room on a fishing expedition."

"No, I'm really concerned about you two."

"And Terese…"

"Well, of course, *Terese*…though I've never met her…She is Simone's sister after all, and I did keep watch over Simone for you…and for *Terese*."

The way he said *Terese* gave him away. *He's hooked.*

"Okay." I resigned myself to his request. Also, I sympathized with his plight. *What can I say—I'm a softie.* "Fair enough. I'll let Terese tell you the whole story…her way. Matter of fact, she's right next door, but you probably know that. I'll just get dressed." I exited with my suitcase—to the bathroom…No easy task with only one working arm… but a girl's gotta have privacy somewhere. I shut the door and looked at myself in the mirror. Oh boy—Someone needs to put on a turtleneck. Only thing, turtlenecks don't work with injured shoulders. I settled for my loose wrap-around silk blouse, a white cashmere scarf... and yoga pants, as I couldn't button my jeans by myself. I looked kinda tacky—a fancy silk blouse and yoga pants don't really go together, but at least I did it—Got dressed unassisted. Next time, Walter can help me. He loves to button and unbutton my jeans. Later on, he can untie my blouse...again.

Walter opted to stay in our suite and take a shower. *The coward.* Or maybe he knew I wouldn't be long, which happened to be the case.

I gave him an innocent kiss on the cheek and noticed a love bite on his neck. I whispered in his ear, "Put on a turtleneck." Then I smiled and walked out the door with the sheriff.

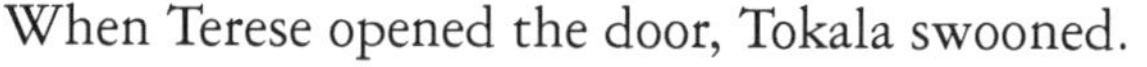

When Terese opened the door, Tokala swooned.

"He's gonna keel over on me," I thought.

I glanced at Terese. *She looks radiant. Showered, dressed, not a hair out of place. Rested and refreshed. How does she do it? It takes me hours to look just a smidgen as classy as she does right now. I look at Tokala. He takes her in with his eyes, his ears, his nostrils...and his mouth quivers. Love at first sight. No doubt about it. I could see the lightening bolts flashing. Tokala shuddering. Silent. Lips moving and no sound coming out. I figure I better do the talking. Good thing I came along. I never heard him stutter, let alone be speechless. Amazing.*

Terese isn't helping either—Standing there in the doorway looking magnificent in a tight-clinging ruby sheath that looked painted on her perfect body. Renoir would have fun with her—only he'd make her toss the dress aside before he painted her. Terese—All dressed up for her valentine—Sheriff James Tokala.

Okay, somebody has to do something and that somebody is—Yours truly. So I opened my mouth. "Terese, Let me introduce you to Sheriff James Tokala—He wants to ask you a few questions."

I nudged James. I could hear a slight sound coming from him and then full speech, however stilted.

"So...so...so...sorry to di...di...disturb you...mi...miss."

James got out a handkerchief and wiped his brow. The temperature surrounding him broke the thermometer, although outside it read fifty-five degrees. I never saw Sheriff Tokala sweat before—I chuckled inside myself—*Payback time for putting me on the carpet during my last visit.*

I decided it was my turn to talk. "Terese, along with Michel—Simone's friend and Pete—the caretaker of Simone's school, Sheriff Tokala helped your sister…Simone…He got a medical helicopter…He got her to a hospital."

"Thank you, Sheriff," Terese cooed, as she took his outstretched hand. "I'm sure my sister's been in exceptional hands."

"Tha…tha...thank…you. Call, call me…James."

"That's a lovely name…James."

Suddenly I became part of the scenery. I could have been a chair for all they cared…I stood in the hallway…not invited into Terese's room. How could I be? Terese didn't see me anymore—Just James. James entered Terese's room, without an invitation…or perhaps she invited him in with her smile and her handshake. I stayed outside, with the door open—separated from them by the doorway—but for all they knew, I slipped out of sight, light years away. Just as well. The sparks flew. I kept my distance.

James snapped out of his trance after three minutes of silence and his black eyes locked with Terese's green-blue irises. *My God—Her eyes change colors! She must be from another planet…I'm sure Tokala thinks so.*

He regained his voice. "I am so sorry, Terese…We…the police…I…need for you…to identify the body today…I know it's an ordeal for you…"

He didn't seem to think it was such an ordeal for me—or Walter.

Terese smiled. "That's okay…James…That is why you brought me to Kodiak, isn't it?"

"Yes, well, that and…I can take you to see Simone…after…"

"Whatever you say, James."

When I returned to our suite, Walter sat at the breakfast table, dressed and refreshed, reading the Kodiak equivalent of *The Seattle Times*.

"So how did everything go?" Walter yawned and put the paper down. I came over and dragged a chair next to him with my good arm.

"Like you didn't know what would happen, Walter."

"Not this time—This introduction is your baby. I don't have a clue."

"Well, they'll be back to pick us up...to go to the morgue...if they remember. Sheriff James Tokala is smitten."

"You don't say. You didn't have anything to do with that, did you?"

"I can't stop cosmic forces, Walter. I'd say they are both ripe for each other."

"She is a peach."

"He likes peaches."

"Not me. I like tangerines...and I've got the best one of all...Ultra-sweet, with a firm, soft, semi-tough exterior—that enhances all her inner beauty—that inner beauty she saves just for me...and those beautiful strawberry-blond locks that look somewhat tangerine in the sunlight... "

Walter picked up my hair and kissed the back of my neck. "Maybe Tangie is a perfect pet name for you after all—You are irresistible, Angelina...especially with your layers off." He licked my ear and started unbuttoning my blouse. *I knew it...*

I melted...but resisted temptation. "Walter...I love you, but I'm not getting entangled or undressed again—until there's no one lurking around our room.

"Where's your sense of danger, excitement?"

"I'm exhausted, trying to ward off intruders...I need some peace... I need some relaxation...We need some privacy...for a change...Let's wait...I know someone is going to make that door throb again...soon.

"*Knock, knock.*"

"See, what did I tell you?"

Walter smiled, picked up a cane, hobbled to the door and let Ceira in. She smiled, came in silently, took the tray and left without a peep. As she went out the door, Walter, with his cane for assistance, followed her out into the hallway, . I heard the sound of someone banging on Terese's door...*Seems like I'm not the only one into payback time.*

I heard Walter shouting to James Tokala through the door. "Hey, Sheriff, Tangie and I are ready to go identify the body, with you…and Terese."

The bear did a good job of mangling Horst. His face, practically unrecognizable, still possessed that smirk that I have trouble forgetting. Terese recognized his eyebrow and his ear and a mole on his right cheek. The whole experience reminded me of another horror show—like the ones I didn't want to go see in the cinema in my youth. Seeing that Nazi symbol and the Sargento initials branded into his arm didn't help either. *That's the only time I almost lost my lunch; I had to lean on Walter so I wouldn't fall down.*

Walter led me to a chair and sat me down. Then he took out the baggie filled with Horst's DNA out of his jacket pocket and gave it to Tokala…just in case the sheriff needed it. *However, with our positive ID, I have a feeling it just served as useful background information. Who needs to look for Horst Blouzer anymore?*

The way I see it, Horst taunted the bear. He would—that's how he operated with people…why should he act differently with animals? The hungry bear just wanted to sneak Horst's sauerbraten—just coming out of hibernation and all that—She needed nourishment…and Horst got in the way. Never get between a bear and her food supply. You never win—you wind up like Horst.

"What about the Kodiak?" I asked James Tokala.

"Well, Tangie, we found a gun near Horst's body, fully loaded, so Horst didn't get off a shot. Only blood around the campsite belonged to Horst. We don't have to worry about a wounded bear running around terrorizing people."

Walter squeezed my good shoulder. "Good for the bear."

I nodded as I leaned against Walter, feeling his warmth. "Gotta agree with you on that one, James."

"Ditto," said Terese.

James scratched his head. "You know, the way I see it…that bear saved the taxpayers a lot of money—Let the bear be…I'm not goin' huntin' for her. Case closed."

Exactly how Tokala knew the bear is a she...may be a mystery to some people, but not to me.

Tokala dropped Terese at her door and whispered to her that he'd be right back. He followed us into our suite and asked if he could have a word with us.

James looked at Walter, then me, and then around our room before he began his request. He spoke through a mouth half-open. "I don't know how to say this, but I didn't want to mention this in front of Terese. We need someone to take charge of the body...or ashes...when he gets cremated."

"Me?"

"You know his sister—Marlaine Blouzer."

"Yeah, I knew her...for about eight hours...after being kidnapped..."

"She may resurface and you could give them to her."

"What am I going to do with them until then?"

"I don't know...but I don't want Terese to know about this...It may upset her."

Yeah, like it won't upset me, carting a dead man's ashes around—a dead man named Horst who still gives me nightmares.

"We'll take them," Walter said. "Only disguise them so they don't look like ashes. Put them in something, like a metal box—meant for carrying jewelry."

"Walter..."

"You know, Tangie, we might be able to use Horst's ashes as a lure... *The Seattle P.D.* would love to talk to Marlaine...she knows stuff...about the Sargentos' operations..."

"Okay, but keep me out of it...*The Seattle P.D.* can hold on to Horst's ashes."

"You may have to meet with Marlaine...if she shows up—That's all—'cause you know her."

"Well, come to think of it, I never did thank her for saving my life—and Terese's...Okay. It's a deal—If and when she shows up, I'll meet with her...but that may not be for a while. She's probably hunkered in some far off place in British Columbia...on one of those remote islands—If she didn't already fly to Germany. You can tell Barry Cardoso to look for the car, look for the money. She just might come back...looking for Horst...Perhaps in six months...or a year...I give her twelve months of freedom, before her curiosity takes over."

Sheriff Tokala smiled at me as I gave my speech and sighed with relief. His job finished. He handed Walter a stainless steel container that looked like an over-sized thermos.

"Will this do?"

I groaned. *I'll never drink coffee on the run again.*

Walter grinned and shook Tokala's hand. "Just fine, Sheriff. We'll be sure to call you and let you know if the fish comes up for the bait."

After our summons to the morgue and Tokala's brief visit, Walter and I enjoyed a fancy dinner, courtesy of room service, compliments of James Tokala, with a thank you note attached. *At least the guy shows some class.*

Walter and I woofed down the food, as we never did finish lunch, and decided to go to bed early. Before I pulled the covers down, I called Clancy and left him a message—Explaining the details of our visit tomorrow to meet his uncle—Father Joe. Also I requested Clancy to not return my call until morning, as my injuries become painful at night. Pain—as in—*I can't take anymore visitors* pain—and—*I vant to be left alone with my honey* pain. I put the *Do Not Disturb* sign outside our door and then crawled under the covers to join my poor sick Walter.

The next morning I woke up early—refreshed, but annoyed—Another knock on the door. Who would ignore a *Do Not Disturb* sign*? Only one person that I know—James Tokala—Now what did he want—a cup of sugar? I know for a fact he didn't have to walk far. Last night when I tiptoed out of bed to get another bottle of wine for Walter and me, I heard giggling in the*

next room. Not loud, but I could hear a man and a woman laughing just before Walter popped the cork. The clock said midnight and at that time, Walter and I were deep into celebrating being alone...and our return to togetherness...so I didn't think much of it...but now, I surmise James and Terese were celebrating the beginning of their togetherness. Despite my annoyance, I chuckled.

So, this morning, I opened the door with a smile plastered all over my face. "Good morning, James."

"Uh...Tangie..."

"Yes?" I grinned...stifling a laugh...and then noticed my robe wasn't completely covering me. Well, I wasn't quite awake. I pulled my robe tightly around my torso...the best I could with one working arm.

James cleared his throat. "I just wanted to give you a heads up,"

I sighed. "You and Terese hit it off...Great!"

"Yes...but...well, I don't want to get into that right now, but... yes...and...I'll be taking Terese to see Simone today."

"I thought you would. Do you need me?" *What a silly question, but I had to ask. I couldn't help myself.*

"Oh no. You've been great. Really. A huge help—But no...Not this time—We'll be fine."

"Just the two of you?"

"Just the two of us."

"Well, I'm glad. Terese needs someone to lean on right now. Might as well be you. I know she'll be in safe hands."

"That she will...and Tangie..."

"Yes?"

"Thank you—for everything. Terese told me the risks you took...to help her...the entire story. You are one brave detective."

"Either brave or stupid. Either way, I don't see myself getting in over my head again. I'll leave the scary stuff to you guys."

"You're gonna be difficult to forget, Tangie." Tokala laughed and smoothed down his hair, which was sticking straight up. *I imagine he had a busy night.*

"Yeah, James, I'm sorry...I sometimes have that effect on people."

" Well, Tangie, for what it's worth, I'm sorry I came down so hard on you—It's my job, you know...I'm always on guard."

"Yeah. Sometimes we're just doing our jobs."

"You and Walter..." he nodded as he peeked at my sleeping prince.

I swear, Walter could sleep through anything...

"You and Walter are welcome anytime here in Kodiak. If you ever need anything, you know who to call."

"Thanks, James." I grasped his hand, which resembled a bear paw—strong, large...and warm. "Very kind of you—You never know when I might be pounding on your door. Say...before Walter and I leave Kodiak, we're taking Clancy and his family to visit Father Joe. Do you think the padre's up for company?"

"Most definitely. You know...of course, he's back at *St. Francis Mission*...and he's been anxiously waiting for you—ever since he got the news you'd be returning to Kodiak...with his family. That's another good thing you did—Finding Father Caine's family. I admire how you do...what you do."

"I work at it."

"It shows. You're an ace. But seriously, try to stay out of harm's way next time. Get well. Tell Walter *good-bye* for me...and good luck to both of you..."

"Thanks, James...I will..."

Then James smiled sheepishly at me and handed me a small wooden box. "My deputy just delivered these...Horst's ashes...Perhaps you can store them in the coffee thermos I gave you yesterday...if you wish to disguise them..."

I groaned, but returned his smile and watched him amble over to Terese's room. I closed the door and tossed the wooden box in Walter's suitcase, next to the coffee urn. Then I tiptoed over to the hearth, put a log on the fire, took off my robe and crawled back into bed with Walter.

"What time is it?" Walter murmured.

"It's still early, Adonis," I whispered..."Not meeting Father Joe until noon."

"Come here." He grinned, then closed his eyes and led me astray for the next three hours.

Around eleven a.m. I called Clancy's room and cemented the afternoon's agenda. Then I hung the phone up and paced around the suite, not wanting to disturb Walter. All the arrangements for the reunion... complete... We'd be driving over to Father Joe's in about an hour... Well, that is, Gus would be driving. Ol' dependable Gus...and Chuck, his assistant cabbie. No way the lot of us could fit in Gus' rig. So we'd have a caravan—more the merrier. Father Joe invited us all over for lunch and a long overdue celebration. I grinned. Sometimes life is worth all the trouble.

Walter opened his eyes. "Is it shower time?"

"Yes, my precious...fifteen minutes and counting."

"Piece of cake. We'll shower together to save time."

"I like the sound of that, Walter—Water...streaming down our faces, you scrubbing my back...me scrubbing yours...

Walter threw the covers off himself, exposing his naked body. "Let's do it."

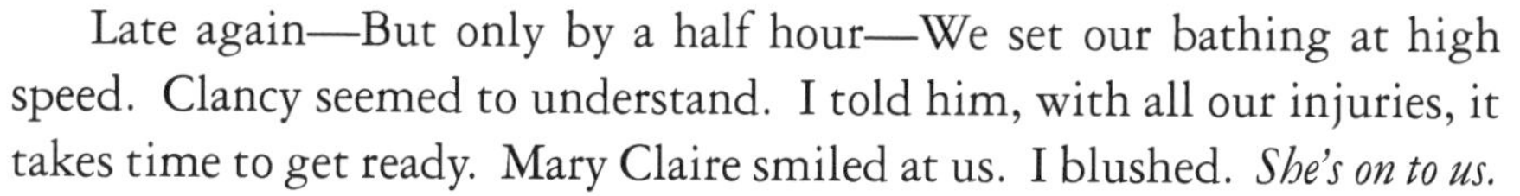

Late again—But only by a half hour—We set our bathing at high speed. Clancy seemed to understand. I told him, with all our injuries, it takes time to get ready. Mary Claire smiled at us. I blushed. *She's on to us.*

Gus, our *Number One Taxi Driver,* along with his buddy, met us at the Bear Pause Inn and helped me down the stairs. Clancy helped Walter. Mary Claire, her husband and children rode in Gus' *SUV.* Clancy, Jessica, Walter and I teamed with Chuck, in his dilapidated *Subaru* station wagon. One could say the car needed shock absorbers. My shoulder started pulsating.

When we pulled up to the mission, I noticed Father Joe standing in the doorway, next to the stained glass window, leaning on his crutches, with tears in his eyes. Gus helped Mary Claire and her family out of his rig and Mary Claire could not contain herself. She raced to her brother, like a filly let out of her stall, not waiting for anyone else. When she reached him, he locked her in an embrace that brought tears to my eyes. Clancy jumped out of the *Subaru*, leaving the door open and with Jessica alongside him, ran after his mother. Serenity and Peter ran after their older brother, followed by their father, Miguel. As Walter and I followed in the background, I heard Mary Claire reminding her children to be calm. "Serenity, Peter—Don't knock Father Joe down. He's been through a tough time."

Father Joe held onto his sister's hands. "So have you, Mary Claire." He stared at his sister for a few minutes...trying to take in her presence. He then smiled at Clancy and shook his hand. "So, Clancy... my nephew...Look at you! You remind me of my father—and you are his namesake. I'm delighted you've found your mother, after all these years...I'm elated...for you...for all of us. Perhaps we can be a family—a real family—If only we could make up for all the lost years..."

"I'd like that, Father Caine...Uncle Joe..."

Mary Claire started sobbing. Her husband, Miguel, put his arm around her and she leaned into him. Her younger children hugged her. Peter looked at her face. "Mommy, Mommy...are you all right?"

"Yes, my angels...I'm beside myself with happiness." She wiped the tears from her eyes with a handkerchief Miguel placed in her hand. "I'm grateful, my dear children...Do you know how fortunate our family is? We found your big brother...and your uncle...after sixteen years—It's a miracle! We're together! My tears are tears of joy."

Peter looked bewildered. "Gee, Mommy, I didn't know people cry when they're happy..."

Serenity explained things to her younger brother. "Peter, when you're older...like me, you'll understand. Grow ups do strange things."

Now that kid has sense.

"Hi Uncle Joe..." Serenity held out her hand to the priest. "Should I call you Father Joe?"

"Father Joe took her fragile hand in his and started to choke up. "No...for you, my dear...*Uncle* Joe is perfect...Come inside...I have lunch prepared for you. I hope you like it."

On the way into the gathering space, Father Joseph Caine shook hands with Miguel and young Peter. Then he kissed Serenity, Mary Claire, and Jessica each on the cheek and gave each of them a hug. Grinning, he leaned on his crutches and led them towards the feast awaiting them.

At that moment, I turned to Chuck and asked him to take us back to the *Bear Pause Inn*...but before Walter and I could depart from the *Mission of Saint Francis*, I noticed Father Joe—now an expert on his crutches—come charging out into the foyer to greet us—like a bronco let out of a holding pen. He raced to the doorway and grasped my hand. "Bless you child...Stay with us..."

I smiled. "Father...I'll see you again...but today is your special day with your family. Enjoy yourself—now...and the rest of the week. You've waited a long time for this reunion—Don't worry. I'll be back in Kodiak—You can count on it. I'll see you next time. Get well and take care of yourself...and your loved ones."

"You better be back!" Father Joe returned my smile and, doing his priestly duty, placed his hand on my head. "Go in peace...Have a safe trip...and God bless you, Angelina."

I shook his hand, and handed him the envelope he loaned me on my last visit. "Thank you, Father Joe. I think he already has...and now you have more than memories."

Father Joe smiled and tears formed in his eyes. He shook Walter's hand. "You take good care of Angelina. She needs some watching over."

Walter grinned at him. "You've got that right, Padre..."

I watched as the mission priest hobbled back to the church, a little slower on his feet this time, and noticed Clancy meeting him halfway—assisting his uncle, and taking the envelope to carry for him. Father Joseph Caine leaned on Clancy as he turned and waved one crutch at me. Then, with Clancy at his side, the padre rushed to join the rest of his family in their celebration—and I envisioned the promise of a future...filled with happiness and love.

Sometimes my job doesn't get any better than this. I took the handkerchief Walter handed me and blew my nose. Walter hugged me and wiped the tears painting my face.

"Are you okay, Angelina?"

"I'm wonderful." I leaned into him and kissed him, hard on the lips. "Let's go home."

On our return trip to *Sea-Tac Airport*, great tail winds carry us out of Kodiak and then Anchorage and we arrive in Washington State an hour early. Sometimes *time is on our side.* Steve picks us up in his black *Mustang* convertible. He puts the top down, Walter and I hop in the back seat and we cruise north on I-5.

As I lean against Walter's shoulder, holding his hand...feeling like his sweetheart on a first date, I hear a familiar tune on the radio...I look into Walter's eyes. We both smile and begin singing along with the band..."All silent in the moonlight...beside the crystal bay...the darkness doesn't hold me...for in your arms I lay..."

I could feel the night breeze blowing in my hair and the air...so clean and fresh...Ah...'tis wonderful to be in Seattle again...in Walter's embrace...

Steve stops his *Mustang* in front of our home, exits his car and comes to help us out. "I've missed you guys—It's not the same around here when you're gone."

"We've kinda missed you too, Steve." I plant a kiss on his cheek, almost knocking him and the luggage down as I do so. "Sorry, Steve. I'm such a klutz. Next week, I'll introduce you to Suzy. I owe you. Plus, It's been a long time since I saw her. I just have to call her...and explain where I've been for the last three months...Then Walter and I will arrange a dinner party. Gotta repay you for all those lattes."

Steve's smile turns to a grin as he straightens out the luggage. "Can't wait!"

I smile back. "How about the *Space Needle*? Good place to meet someone for the first time...unless you get dizzy from the restaurant spinning around..."

"No...that's great, Tangie, You're terrific."

Walter grins at Steve and winks at me. "Wait till you meet Suzy." "She's a handful."

I poke Walter in the ribs, signaling him to zip his lips. "Steve...I know you like the sultry, sexy type."

Walter takes the hint and dittoes my response. "Yes, good buddy... Suzy's a knock-out. Tangie will set the dinner thing up and we'll call you."

"I'll be waiting. When are you coming back to work?"

"I'm a consultant, remember?"

"Well, when will you...*and Tangie*, be available to consult?"

"Maybe after the wedding..."

"Maybe after the honeymoon," I interject. "Give us a few months..."

As we say our goodbyes, I notice a silly grin plastered all over Steve's face. I hope he can handle Suzy. Come to think of it, I'm sure he can. They will be good for each other. Steve is the strong silent type. Suzy loves to talk. She'll talk, he'll listen...and he'll probably adore her. He may wind up being her last number.

So here we are, home for good. I help Walter with my good arm. He helps me with his two good hands and good foot. *We are well matched—crazy for sure.* Walter's tough, though...He does most of the work getting us both up the stairs. He puts the key in the lock—As the door cracks open, a white flash of fur nearly blows us over.

"Pebbles! My long lost pooch...I didn't expect to see you until tomorrow." I bend over and pick up my furry friend with one arm and start to cry.

Walter wipes my tears with a gentle kiss. "I asked Bryan to bring Pebbles home—I gave him a key to the place...before we left...just in case."

"You think of everything, Walter. Thank you, Sweetheart." I lean up to return his kiss. Then I nuzzle my furry bundle with my nose. "I've missed you my little pooch. Or maybe I should say big pooch. You've gained weight. Eating Mom's food again—too many noodles for you... in Phad Thai. I hope you've been a good boy for Marianna. Where's Hildie?"

At the mention of her name, Hildie appears in the doorway leading to the kitchen. She looks at us as if to say, "Well, it's about time you got home." Then she turns and strolls back into the kitchen to munch on some cat nibbles. I could hear her crunching on them.

I've said it before and I'll say it again, animals live in the present. They enjoy you when you're here and don't waste time being jealous or angry. The swinging door to the kitchen creaks. Hildie saunters back from the kitchen, comes over to us and rubs her fur against both our legs and begins meowing non-stop. Walter bends down, picks her up and her purr motor turns on. Loud.

"She weighs a ton, Tangie. No doubt eating like a horse since we've been gone."

"And not much exercise since Pebbles wasn't here to chase her around the house for two weeks."

"Things are back to normal now."

"Normal...I like the sound of that. I can do normal."

"Tangie...I hate to say it, but you'll never be normal."

"I know. Frightful, isn't it?"

"Not at all. I like you...the way you are..."

"Handicapped?"

"You know what I mean...Alive...Vibrant...Cunning..."

"Dangerous..."

"Come here." Walter puts his hand in mine. "I want to show you something."

He leads me from the foyer into the living room. I see balloons... Lots of them... with messages on them—*Get Well Soon, Welcome Home... Thank You*...and bouquets of flowers—in vases, in pots—tulips, carnations, roses—yellow of course...and lilies...orchids...Ah...the orchids must be from Walter, as well as the yellow roses...I will check out all the notes and cards later...My eyes drift to the fireplace...and what's sitting on the rug in front of the hearth...

The Couch...from my old home in Ballard...mysteriously making an appearance—in its rightful place—in *our* Queen Anne Home...between the sofa table and the coffee table.

"How lovely—The puzzle is complete! Walter, my love...your old *bed* is here, in case you wind up in the dog house."

"Very funny." Walter frowns...then a wide grin appears on his face. "Maybe tomorrow you will want to contact the movers and have them bring over anything else you want moved from the Ballard house. Lots of space here...and the sooner we vacate our old home, the sooner Bryan, Andee and the boys can move in..."

"You haven't seen my garage."

"I have a garage...big enough for our two cars...It's empty. Fill it up—On second thought...Fill up half of it...Fifty-fifty..."

"Did anyone ever tell you you're adorable?"

"One or two people."

"Chicks?"

"Well, not spring chickens—My Aunt Hattie and my mother...a long time ago.

"Not Suzy?"

"I don't want to talk about Suzy—leave her to Steve. I want to discuss something with you...Come, sit down on our couch...I'll start the fire."

Walter goes over and strikes a match and lights the waiting bundle of kindling and logs, all set up to be torched. Then he picks up a waiting bottle of *Zardetto Prosecco Brut Treviso—my favorite sparkling wine...* and produces two glasses as if by magic. *It must be nice to be able to uncork a bottle of wine. At least as the one-armed detective, there's no chance of me drinking alone and becoming a drunk.*

"I see you planned our homecoming—When...how did you do all this?" I yawn and relax on the familiar sofa.

"I have my ways."

As I settle down on Walter's former bed—all of us home again, with Pebbles on one side and Hildie on the other side of me, Walter adjusts the pillow under my shoulder and arm and kisses my hand. Then he pulls an ottoman over to the couch so we can both stretch out our feet. As he does so, he takes off my shoes and massages my feet. I groan...and smile up at him. "You're a keeper, my love."

Walter lifts up his cat and sits next to me. Hildie doesn't seem to mind. She jumps to my other side, next to Pebbles and starts purring.

Walter gives me a nuzzle on my neck and whispers in my ear, "And you, my love, are a treasure...and these animals are getting in the way..."

"Oh…they're just glad to see us…Hey, Walter…I've been thinking…this piece of furniture brought us together. Fitting, isn't it, that your former bed joins us at our homecoming?"

"I thought so…But you know, Tangie, there's more to that story…"

"Pebbles?"

"Now you know, I love the beast, but, no…"

"Then, what?"

"I have to admit—The first time I saw you—You took my breath away."

"The first time I met you, you were dating Suzy…"

"I have a confession. After I saw you, I took her on that horrendous camping trip—That did the trick. Instant break up on her part."

"You devil…"

Walter starts nibbling on my ear. "I'm not wicked, Tangie. It's just that at that moment, I knew there could never be anyone else for me… but you…"

Now this is when Walter gets serious…When he does…I start to cry…He looks so somber…Humor I can take…Serious means taking chances…I try to stop the tears but the sobbing begins…Uncontrollable. I hate that…I can't turn the faucet off. Red eyes are such a turn off… except Walter doesn't seem to mind…

"Please…Angelina…" Walter says, as he wipes my eyes. "Please… don't be distressed…Honey…I don't ever want to make you sad."

"I'm not sad." I hiccup. "I like it when you call me *Honey*. I'm happy. Delirious. My head is spinning—The world is going faster and faster…I don't want to get off…"

"So…When are we getting married, Angelina?" Walter pulls me closer. I can hardly breathe. He begins kissing my neck and then my ear. Now that is one maneuver that pushes me totally out of control. I begin to moan.

"How about the *Fourth of July*?" I sigh…barely getting the words out. "We could set off fireworks."

"We don't need fireworks…"

"No…we just need each other…"

"Is a wedding in July enough time for you? We could wait till *Labor Day*…"

I can feel Walter's breathing intertwining with mine and I become dizzy…I feel myself being transported to another place, another time. "Any time is fine with me…just so I can slip into a slinky, sexy dress, for you…"

Where, when, how…Questions, questions…at least we don't have to find a place…Charles' home on Whidbey Island will be the ticket…a waterfront wedding…Yes…Don will officiate—What's to plan? We can do it…Walter will be off his crutches…He'll look fabulous in his tux…but you know… it doesn't really matter…all this stuff…doesn't matter…The really important thing is… we are committed to each other…and we love each other…

"Hey Walter," I whisper in my best sultry voice…"Our honeymoon—Remember…privacy…"

"Remember? Of course…I know that's already decided." He places his hand on my thigh.

"Fiji or bust…"

"Warm sunny days, gentle breezes…"

"Nights of passion…"

"Days of passion…"

"I gotta get a new bikini."

"Get one with ties—that unfasten in a hurry…" Walter croons as he unbuttons my blouse.

"Walter…" I start to breathe long slow breaths…feeling my lungs expanding with the beat of my heart pressed against Walter's chest and I feel his heart beating…My body temperature rises to match Walter's…He's on fire…and I want to mingle with his flames…*my cure…*

"Walter…This is the end of our adventure, isn't it?"

"No, Angelina. He moans and …extinguishes my last lingering tears. "It's just the beginning."

I nestle into Walter's waiting arms, safe, secure, loved…I can live this life…I love this life…

"Yes, Walter." I close my eyes and see things I have no right to see—*Our wedding on Whidbey…then…Fiji…calm, warm water, palm trees, swaying as we make love…a bungalow, charming…I smell flowers all around and then…a phone call…mysterious…and a laugh—sinister—and evil…* I open my eyes to shut out the conflicting visions…*Enough…*

I stare into my lover's eyes...I begin moaning. "Walter...please help me...take me away...I don't want to see anymore...I just want you... only you..."

Walter's eyes glow back into mine, and he protects me...He takes my pain away...and all I feel is warmth and excitement—electricity. It's more than a normal person can stand—but I'm not normal. And neither is Walter.

"You're right," I murmur, as Walter pulls me tighter to his chest, caressing me...as my whole being kindles...then lights up...on fire...I can hardly breathe. I am dizzy from flying through time and space...I surrender to our passion unfolding, as I whisper my last spoken words that evening.

"My love, you're right...it's just the beginning."

Made in the USA
Middletown, DE
03 August 2019